W. S. MERWIN, poet, playwright, and translator, was born in New York and educated at Princeton. He lived for a time in England where his plays, adaptations and translations of plays, and his poems were performed on the BBC, and his play *Darkling Child* was produced in the Arts Theatre in London. In 1962, Mr. Merwin became the poetry editor of *The Nation*. He has received many honors including a Rockefeller Playwriting Fellowship, administered by the Poet's Theatre in Cambridge, Massachusetts; a Ford Foundation grant; and in 1971, the Pulitzer Prize for his book of poems *Carrier of Letters*. A member of the National Institute of Arts and Letters, he is the author of numerous books of poems and plays, among them *Favorite Island, the Drunk in the Furnace, The Gilded West, The Moving Target* (poems), and *Life* (poems). He has also translated many French and Spanish works into English.

POEMA DEL CID

Texto Español de
Ramón Menéndez Pidal

POEM OF THE CID

English Verse Translation
and with an Introduction
by W. S. Merwin

A MERIDIAN BOOK
NEW AMERICAN LIBRARY
TIMES MIRROR

MERIDIAN TRADEMARK REG. U.S. PAT. OFF. AND FOREIGN COUNTRIES
REGISTERED TRADEMARK—MARCA REGISTRADA
HECHO EN CLINTON, MASS., U.S.A.

SIGNET, SIGNET CLASSICS, MENTOR, PLUME
and MERIDIAN BOOKS are published by
The New American Library, Inc.,
1301 Avenue of the Americas, New York, New York 10019

First Meridian Printing, October, 1975

1 2 3 4 5 6 7 8 9

PRINTED IN THE UNITED STATES OF AMERICA

CONTENTS

Introduction

The *Poem of The Cid* was written, as far as can be known, sometime around 1140. Its author, again as nearly as can be determined, was a native of the Castilian frontier which faced the Moorish kingdom of Valencia; quite possibly he was from somewhere around Medinaceli, or San Esteban de Gormaz, both of which figure in the poem. In the eleventh and early twelfth centuries Castilians and Moors fought back and forth over this bit of border country; Medinaceli was taken from the Moors in 1104, then lost again, then retaken definitively in 1120, only twenty years or so before the *Poema* was written. During the same period the border country was also a center of poetic activity. The *Poema del Cid* was not the only heroic poem of the period written in the vernacular, in a rough, spare, sinewy, rapid verse to be sung in marketplaces. But it is almost the only one which did not vanish, leaving only a reference in some chronicle, if that. The *Poema* itself has survived only in a single manuscript copy (and even from this three pages are missing) made by one Per Abbat in 1307.

In 1140, or more or less, when the poet set out to write his epic, there must have been men still alive who remembered Rodrigo Díaz of Bivar, who had been called "the Cid." He had died in Valencia, only forty-odd years before, on Sunday, the 10th of July, 1099, at the age of fifty-six. His relatives and his many vassals and their families had shown the signs of mourning that at the time were customary at the passing of a lord: the men beat their breasts, ripped their clothes, stripped their heads bald; the women lacerated their cheeks with their nails and covered

Rodrigo Diaz of Bivra ~The Cid~ 1043-1099

their faces with ashes; and both sexes wailed and shrieked their grief for days on end. But it was not only in Valencia, which he had taken from the Moors, that the Cid's death resounded. A contemporary French chronicle tells us that "his death caused grave sorrow in Christendom, and huge rejoicing among the Moorish enemies." To the two halves of the known world his passing was an event of great importance. Already in his lifetime he had been a legend.

Rodrigo Díaz had been born sometime around 1043—almost exactly a century before the poem was written—in Bivar, a village to the north of Burgos. His father's family was of highly honorable minor nobility; his father led a rather retired life in the ancestral home in Bivar. Rodrigo's mother's family was of a higher degree of nobility, with considerable influence at court. Rodrigo as a youth was brought up in the court of Prince Sancho, the eldest son of King Fernando, who at the time ruled León and Castile and held the title of Emperor, with hierarchical superiority over the Kings of Aragón and Navarre.

Feudal Spain of the mid-eleventh century was politically an extremely complicated place. By then the reconquest of the country from the Moors had made considerable progress. In the north of the peninsula were the Visigothic Christian kingdoms and states, most notably Castile, León, Aragón, Navarre, and the county of Barcelona. In the south were the Moorish kingdoms, chief among them Seville, Granada, Córdoba, and Valencia. To further complicate the division, the Christian states lived in rivalry with one another. Many of the Moorish states were dependencies of Christian kingdoms, paying them tribute in exchange for protection from other Moors or other Christians. These tributary kingdoms were a principal cause of the contentions and intermittent wars among the Christian states. Another was the Spanish kings' practice of dividing up their kingdoms among their heirs. Rodrigo, as a young man, was a witness to some of the tragic consequences of one of these partitions; they affected the whole course of his life.

By the spring of 1063, when Rodrigo was twenty, Prince Sancho had dubbed him a knight, and he accompanied the Prince on an expedition to lift the siege of Graus. This

[handwritten margin notes:]
VISIGOTHIC
CHRISTIAN
KINGDOMS

CASTILE
LEON
ARAGON
NAVARRE
BARCELONA

MOORISH
KINGDOMS

SEVILLE
GRANADA
CORDOBA
VALENCIA

PRINCE SANCHO / RODRIGO

place occupied a strategic position at an entrance to the Moorish kingdom of Zaragoza, which was a tributary of Castile and hence under the protection of Sancho's father, King Fernando. Zaragoza was unique among the Moorish kingdoms in being entirely surrounded by Christian states; it had to have the protection of one of them, and inevitably it would choose the strongest. Ramiro I of Aragón, Prince Sancho's uncle, had designs on Zaragoza, and had begun by besieging Graus. On Thursday, May 8, 1063, Sancho, with Rodrigo among his knights, attacked Ramiro's besieging force, and in the battle Ramiro I was killed.

In December of the same year, King Ferdinand divided his kingdom, including the Moorish tributary states, among his three sons, Sancho, Alfonso, and García. Sancho was given Castile and Zaragoza; Alfonso was given León and the dependency of Toledo. García received Galicia and a bit of what is now Portugal, with the Moorish kingdoms of Seville and Badajoz. To his daughters, Urraca and Elvira, the King gave only certain monasteries, and these only on the condition that they should never marry; this condition, presumably, was designed to prevent claims to the succession from becoming still more complicated. According to poems of the period, Sancho was opposed to the partition of the kingdom, as well he might have been. He was not the only member of the family who was displeased. Several medieval accounts agree that Urraca carried on an incestuous affair with her brother Alfonso, and used it to acquire the town of Zamora from him; her attempts to redistribute the patrimony did not stop there.

The heirs kept the peace, and honored Fernando's division while their parents were alive. Fernando died in 1065 and the Queen in 1067. Then five years of civil war broke out.

Prince Sancho had been crowned Sancho II of Castile and had appointed Rodrigo Díaz chief marshal, or *alférez*, of his army, a title which also gave Rodrigo the highest post at Sancho's court. In his capacity as *alférez*, Rodrigo, aged twenty-eight, was a principal in a bizarre form of feudal diplomacy: a trial by combat to settle a boundary dispute between Navarre and Castile, involving several fortified places. Rodrigo was spectacularly victorious over

chief marshal - alférez

the champion from Navarre, and the contest won him his first fame. Thereafter he was known as the "Campeador," meaning "the expert warrior."

There were other matters for Sancho to clear up. The Moorish King of Zaragoza, Moctádir, was not a prompt man with his tribute money. He had given the old King, Fernando, trouble on this account, and Fernando's final military campaign had been for the purpose of collecting from Zaragoza. Now Sancho was having the same difficulties. So in 1067, with Rodrigo Díaz (then twenty-four) as his general, he laid siege to Zaragoza. Moctádir capitulated. A contemporary Hebrew chronicle gives all the credit to "Cidi Ru Diaz"; Rodrigo must have been known already as "mio Cid"—"my lord."

Sancho wanted León. No doubt he felt that as the eldest son he had a good right to it. Furthermore there were family traditions and Christian traditions both behind him. León was the elder of the two kingdoms, the ancient imperial seat of Christian Spain, and it had formerly dominated the rest of the Christian states. But since the tenth century Castile had not been docile about this dominion, and by Sancho's time, Castile's political importance was greater than León's. Four generations of Sancho's ancestors had fought against León, including his father Fernando. In 1068—we do not know just how it happened—war broke out between Sancho's Castile and his brother Alfonso's León. The royal brothers arranged a time and place for a battle: on the border between the two kingdoms, on the plain of Llantada, on the banks of the Pisuerga, on July 19, 1068. There King Sancho, with the Cid at the head of his host, routed the army of León. The brothers had agreed that the victor should receive the kingdom of the vanquished without further fighting, but Alfonso fled to León and prepared to hold out there. The war decided nothing. In fact, the two brothers three years later found themselves on the same side, though only for a short time: Alfonso had fallen out with the third brother, García, and he and Sancho together, in 1071, attacked García, dethroned him, and split his kingdom between them.

A conscientious sensitivity about his rights and a respect

Campeador - expert warrior   mio Cid—my lord

for certain traditions may have been Sancho's guiding impulses; Alfonso, it is agreed, was plain covetous. In any case, in the beginning of January 1072, León and Castile were again at war, and a battle was fought on the plain of Golpejera. According to one account, Sancho was captured during the battle and rescued by the Cid. All accounts agree that Rodrigo was largely responsible for the Castilians' victory over León.

Sancho took his brother Alfonso, in chains, to a number of castles and cities in the kingdom of León and received their submission; then he had himself anointed and crowned in León on January 12, 1072. After that he imprisoned Alfonso in the castle of Burgos, where the third brother, García, had been a prisoner not a year before.

The Princess Urraca, bound by ties of more than sisterly tenderness to Alfonso, could not endure this treatment of him without some complaint. She went to Burgos and interceded for him, begging Sancho to set him free and exile him to the Moorish kingdoms in the south. Sancho complied with her request: Alfonso was sent to Toledo, to the court of King Mamún, who was a friend and former tributary of Alfonso's.

Urraca also arranged that Alfonso should be accompanied by his former tutor, Pedro Ansúrez, and by Pedro's two brothers, Gonzalo and Fernando. These brothers were the chief members of the Beni-Gómez clan, a family of importance to the Cid's subsequent career and of prime importance in the *Poema:* they were the "Heirs of Carrión." The Beni-Gómez were a family of great fame, position, and influence; they were counts—a much higher degree of nobility than the Cid's. They enjoyed, under King Alfonso, roughly the same favor which the Cid enjoyed under King Sancho. The battle of Golpejera had taken place within three leagues of their capital of Carrión, and the Cid, in contributing to the overthrow and disgrace of King Alfonso, had also helped to effect theirs.

León did not submit passively to the Castilian conquest; from the outset there were signs of rebellion. In Toledo, Alfonso spent nine months in exile—and not in idleness. Pedro Ansúrez slipped back and forth between Toledo and Doña Urraca in Zamora. And finally news reached Castile that many of Alfonso's vassals, including those of the Beni-Gómez clan, had gathered in Zamora to raise a rebellion. Whereupon Sancho and the Cid laid siege to Zamora.

The siege was effective; unable to throw off the Castilians, the knights and populace in Zamora began to grow hungry. A bold stroke was conceived. On Sunday, October 7, 1072, a knight named Vellido Adolfo managed to enter the Castilian camp, mounted and unsuspected. There he sought out King Sancho and ran him through the breast with his lance, mortally wounding him. He then spurred his horse and escaped to Zamora, where the gates opened to receive him. King Sancho had been thirty-four years old, at the height of his power. The author of his death had been his sister, Princess Urraca.

While King Sancho's funeral procession was on its way to Oña, Urraca sent messengers to Alfonso, in Toledo, to inform him of the assassination. The news reached him before they did. Alfonso had some fears that King Mamún, if he heard the news, might hold him for ransom; but he had been treated so hospitably in Toledo that he decided to act without duplicity, and when he told Mamún, the Moorish King sent him on his way with his blessing. Alfonso set out for Zamora and thence resumed his throne in León, giving Urraca the title of Queen. Shortly thereafter Alfonso, accompanied by Urraca and the Beni-Gómez clan, set out to receive the crown of Castile, in Burgos.

Naturally, a large number of Castilians, the Cid at their head, regarded Alfonso with anything but welcome. According to feudal law in Spain, in a case like this, where assassination was suspected, the vassals had a right to demand as a condition of vowing allegiance to their new lord that he swear that he had had nothing to do with the death of the person to whose position he had been elevated. The Cid and an assembly of Castilian knights demanded that Alfonso should swear this in the Church of Santa Gadea in Burgos. There the King laid hands on the statues of the apostles on the altar and with twelve others swore at the Cid's dictation. The Cid then replied, as was his right, with a wish that "if what Alfonso spoke was a lie, it might please God that Alfonso might be killed by a treacherous vassal, as

King Sancho had been by Vellido Adolfo." Alfonso and his co-swearers had to say "Amen," but the King turned pale. The Cid, still within his rights, repeated the oath and the wish and heard the replies three times. Then he kissed the King's hand, in token of vassalage. Whether to win him over, or for whatever reasons, the King began by favoring him highly at his court. Even so, the Cid was eclipsed by the Beni-Gómez clan (one of whom, García Ordóñez, assumed his post of *alférez*) and by many of Alfonso's other followers; his position in the Castilian court was far below what it had been under King Sancho, and far from secure at that.

The new *alférez* was not a great military success and was soon relieved of his post and given a county instead. Whether or not this had anything to do with the favor the King next bestowed on the Cid is not known. On July 19, 1074, when the Cid was thirty-one years old, the King married him to Doña Jimena Díaz, the King's own niece. It should be noted that her highly noble family was from León, not Castile. Children were born to the union, the first of them just a year later. And though he never regained the ascendancy he had enjoyed under King Sancho, the Cid continued to serve the King in important posts until toward the end of 1079, when he was sent to collect the tribute 36 from the Moorish King of Seville, Motámid.

The Cid arrived to find Motámid menaced by his old enemy Abdállah, the Moorish King of Granada, who was also a tributary of Alfonso's. The situation was further complicated by the fact that four important vassals of Alfonso's, including García Ordóñez, the Cid's most important rival in the Beni-Gómez clan, were in Abdállah's court to collect the tribute there. The Cid felt it his duty to protect the King of Seville, and sent a letter to Abdállah, asking him to keep the peace, in the name of Alfonso the Emperor. Abdállah, backed up by the knights who were with García Ordóñez, replied by invading the territory of Seville and sacking it as far as Cabra. This, of course, is the situation with which the *Poema* originally opened, before the first three pages were lost and reconstructed in prose.

The Cid, acting for Alfonso as the protector of Seville, fell upon the invaders, who far outnumbered him, and after a hard battle defeated them with heavy losses, taking prisoner García Ordóñez, among others. He held them for three days to emphasize the situation and then released them, keeping only the loot his men had taken. By May 1080, both the Cid and García Ordóñez were back in Castile. The King was not pleased at the affair: García Ordóñez was his favorite. Suddenly the Cid's enemies at court were more numerous, and they had fresh matter for their art. They accused the Cid of having kept for himself the greater part of the tribute money from Seville. The King said nothing, but he listened.

In the following year Rodrigo, because of sickness, stayed behind in Castile while the King and his chief vassals laid siege to the city of Toledo, which had been split by a rebellion. While the King was away, a host of Moors made a serious incursion into Castile, plundering heavily and attacking the castle of Gormaz. The Cid quickly assembled his vassals, attacked the Moors, plundered and razed their lands, and returned with nearly seven thousand prisoners and vast spoils. This action merely increased the jealousy which Alfonso's vassals felt toward the Cid. They accused him of having antagonized the friendly Moors, whose territory bordered that of the attackers. Alfonso took the occasion to banish the Cid from Castile.

With the Cid went his own vassals, as was customary. Rodrigo first went to the Count of Barcelona, Ramón Berenguer, and offered his services to the Count. He and his vassals established themselves there.

But the arrangement was not successful. The Cid received neither the welcome nor the position he expected; something said or done by a nephew of Berenguer's roused his anger, and he left Barcelona and proceeded to offer his services to the Moorish King of Zaragoza, who welcomed him. It was as an ally of the King of Zaragoza that he shortly found himself in the field against the Count of Barcelona, whom he defeated and held prisoner for five days.

Alfonso's ambition was to make all Spain his empire. In 1085, after triumphs in other parts of the peninsula, he marched against Zaragoza. The Cid had either to fight against his former lord or to go elsewhere. He camped for a while at Tudela. He was forty-two, and at the nadir of his fortunes.

Alfonso's fortunes, at the same time, were approaching their summit. In the same year (1085), after six years of fighting, Toledo fell to him; a diplomatic maneuver and a stroke of luck gave him control of Valencia; Zaragoza was on the point of surrendering; his knights were virtually laying siege to Granada, Murcia, and Almería, and he was pressing claims against Córdoba. Success followed success until his sway extended over all the Moorish kingdoms of the peninsula, from Castile south to the straits of Gibraltar; and his influence over the other Christian princes of Spain had grown enormously. For the first time since the Moors had invaded Spain, a Christian ruler could claim with some reason to be King of all Spain.

Meanwhile, across the straits in Africa a still more ambitious imperial scheme was unfolding. By the eleventh century, in many parts of Islam, the original ferocity of that faith had given place to a graceful and in some cases effete civilization. This was true of many of the Moorish kingdoms in Spain, as well as those in Africa. In 1039, a tribe on the edge of the Sudan began to convert the desert tribesmen to the way of Mohammed; they preached a reformation of Islam, a return to the unadorned, primitive faith, to conversion by the sword, to the Holy War. In 1055 the converts of the Sahara began their conquest of the older and more decadent Moorish civilization in North Africa, and by 1075 they had swept westward across the top of the continent as far as Ceuta and Tangier. They were led by an ascetic chieftain of extraordinary gifts, one Yúsuf ben Texufín.

In 1075 the King of Seville had begged Yúsuf to cross the straits and help him against Alfonso; Yúsuf had answered that he would not leave Africa until he had taken the Mediterranean coastal cities of Morocco. In 1084 the last of these, Ceuta, fell to him. And the following year (when Alfonso's dominion over the Spanish peninsula was nearly complete) the Moorish Kings of Seville and Badajoz again invited Yúsuf to cross to Spain and help throw off the yoke of the Christians. This was a grave decision on the part of the Moorish monarchs. The court of Seville in particular was a flourishing center of the arts, learning, and pleasure, and King Motámid was a lavish patron of all three. The Moorish kings of Spain could hardly expect the fierce, ignorant, fundamentalist zealots who had overrun the rich culture of North Africa to play a subservient or a gentle role in their kingdoms. Almost certainly they could expect worse treatment from Yúsuf than from Alfonso. Motámid's son opposed the invitation to Yúsuf. But Motámid, in the name of his religion, persisted.

Yúsuf sent a large force to occupy Algeciras and then crossed the straits himself with an enormous army. He had not reached Seville before the Kings of Granada, Málaga, and Almería were in league with him. Alfonso, hearing the news, raised the siege of Zaragoza and began to assemble an army to repel the new invasion. The King of Aragón and several other Christian princes sent him reinforcements; in his hosts there were even knights from Italy and France. But he did not choose to ask the Cid to accompany him.

The two armies came in sight of each other at a place called Sagrajas, near Badajoz. The Moors were encamped there, and Alfonso made camp, facing them across a small stream. For three days, while messengers came and went between the camps, both armies drank from the same waters. The battle took place on Friday, October 23, 1085.

The vanguard of the Christians, led by Alvar Fáñez, attacked the Moorish vanguard, composed of Spanish Moors, routed them, and set off in pursuit of them. The rest of the Castilians attacked, carried the field as far as the moat around Yúsuf's tents, only to find the Moors had circled around and attacked them from the rear and had entered the Christian camp, slaughtering and burning. The Castilians fell back to reorganize, whereupon Yúsuf, with his main force, charged them. As he did, there was a sound which had never before been heard in the armies of Europe: drums. The drummers of Africa built up a thunderous roar, and the sound was not without effect on the Christians; some of them thought the earth was shaking. At the same time they had to face other military phenomena which they had never encountered before: disciplined bodies of fighters, moving in formation and maneuvering to orders; parallel lines of Turkish archers firing on command. They were heavily outnumbered, besides. They were disastrously defeated, and King Alfonso himself barely escaped. That same night Yúsuf had all the Christian corpses beheaded and the heads piled up into hills, from whose tops at dawn his muezzins summoned the troop to prayer.

At once Yúsuf was recalled to Africa by the death of his son, so his Spanish campaign, for the moment, went no further. But he was securely established on the peninsula; and Alfonso, at one blow, had lost all hope of control of most of the Moorish states in what, only a short time before, had been his empire. He had also, of course, sustained great losses in men and in prestige, and if Yúsuf should return, his own kingdom was in danger. He effected a reconciliation with the Cid; apart from needing every knight he could muster, he no doubt remembered that nobody of knights ever led by the Cid had been defeated, though numbers and circumstances had often been heavily against them. In any case, the Cid returned to Castile and was showered with honors, lands, and castles.

It was as Alfonso's vassal that the Cid began to take an active part in the politics of the eastern coast of Spain. Chaos had resulted from Yúsuf's triumph and subsequent absence; loyalties were broken everywhere, alliances among the Moorish states shifted and dissolved; in some cases the Moors refused tribute and taxes not only to the Christians but to their own kings. The Moorish King of Valencia, Alcádir, threatened on all hands, sent out pleas for help to Alfonso and to the Moorish King of Zaragoza. The Cid, at the time, was in Zaragoza, and he arrived soon after in Valencia with three thousand knights.

In Valencia the Cid acted as Alfonso's lieutenant; he studied the country and sent back reports to Castile. Ramón Berenguer, of Barcelona, and Mostaín of Zaragoza combined against him; he conducted a skillful campaign that drove them from the region, and he subdued the country and restored order for the King of Valencia, all in the name of Alfonso. Alcádir, in Valencia, was enormously grateful; he became the Cid's tributary, offering him a large weekly sum; and the Cid forced tribute from a large number of lesser rulers throughout the territory. He had restored a large piece of Alfonso's empire.

From the castle of Aledo, in the Murcia region, García

Jiménez, one of the Cid's lieutenants, was carrying the campaign into the territories of Almería, to the grave discomfort of Motámid, the King of Seville. Motámid took a force against Aledo but was routed by a much smaller number of Christians. He decided that there was nothing to do but to call Yúsuf over again, and in June 1089 Yúsuf landed for the second time in Algeciras. He and the combined Kings of Seville, Granada, Málaga, Almería, and Murcia laid siege to the castle of Aledo.

By the end of four months the besieging armies were hungry, and the Kings had fallen to squabbling among themselves. They asked Yúsuf to arbitrate. His decision went against the King of Murcia, whereupon all the Murcians packed up and went home. At this point they learned that Alfonso was coming against them with a large army.

Alfonso had written to the Cid to join him, and the Cid had gone to meet him: but the armies missed each other by accident, and Alfonso arrived first at Aledo. Yúsuf, not trusting his allies, retired at once to Lorca, and the whole thing was not only over, but Alfonso and his army had started back, by the time the Cid arrived on the scene. The incident was a boon to the Cid's old enemies in Castile. Alfonso's latent jealousy, suspicion, and resentment of the Cid broke out afresh. He exiled him a second time; he took from him all the castles and privileges he had recently accorded him and all the gold and silver in the Cid's own house and lands, and he imprisoned Doña Jimena and her three children. The Cid was accused of having conspired against the King's life, and Alfonso would not entertain any messages from Rodrigo; but he did, after a short time, relent so far as to release Doña Jimena and the Cid's children and allow them to join him.

Yúsuf departed from Spain again, leaving behind him a large army to be used against the Cid. Alcádir of Valencia now refused tribute to the Cid (and all the other lords of the region were supposed to pay their tribute to the Cid through Alcádir). The Cid had no allies and many enemies. He conducted a raiding campaign, in the spring of 1089, in the Levant to the south of Valencia, and when the rulers there sued for peace, Alcádir in Valencia hastened to do the same.

Once again the Cid found himself ranged against the Count of Barcelona; Berenguer had raised a coalition to drive the Cid from the region and enjoy the tributes in his stead. The Cid met Berenguer's army, and though heavily outnumbered he managed to divide and defeat it, take enormous spoils and many prisoners, including Berenguer himself—for the second time. He released all the prisoners after exacting considerable ransoms, including, from the Count, the sword Colada. This is the battle with Berenguer that is described in the *Poema.*

Meanwhile the army which Yúsuf had left on the peninsula had not been winning hearts among the Spanish Moors. It was not long before the Moorish kings came to regard the Africans with a mixture of dislike and dread; and a number of Moorish kings, those of Granada and Seville among them, began secret negotiations with Alfonso.

But in 1090, Yúsuf landed in Spain for the third time. Without any help from the Spanish Moors, he laid siege to Toledo; and when this proved futile he visited his annoyance on the Moorish kings, sending the Kings of Granada and Málaga to Africa in chains. His next move was to attack the King of Seville. Again the peninsula's complex system of interreligious alliances shifted. The King of Seville called on Alfonso to help him against Yúsuf, and Alfonso, in March 1091, struck south and seized Granada. Here, through the efforts of his Queen, Constanza, he was met by the Cid, who had abandoned the seige of Liria to come and support him; once again the King and the Cid were reconciled, and once again the reconciliation did not last long. Only a slight and accidental pretext was necessary, the King's disfavor erupted once more, and the Cid and his vassals turned back toward Valencia.

Yúsuf's army took Córdoba, and Yúsuf's general decapitated the Moorish governor of that city. Then he marched on against Seville. Alfonso sent a force against him, under Alvar Fáñez, but this army was badly beaten and many of its knights taken prisoner. On September 7, 1091, Yúsuf's Africans took Seville. King Motámid was thrown into prison, and thence sent to a dungeon in Morocco. Almería and Murcia quickly went the way of Seville, and Alfonso seemed powerless to do anything against Yúsuf in the southern part of the peninsula. By the end of 1091, the only Christian outside Christian Spain who still opposed Yúsuf was the Cid.

The Cid drew back his line of outposts and fortified Peña Cadiella, which commanded the pass between the south, where Yúsuf's army was, and the plain of Valencia. At this point the King of Aragón, and Mostaín, the Moorish King of Zaragoza, offered him help. The Cid went to Zaragoza to sign a treaty of peace with Mostaín. While he was there, King Alfonso, with a large army, descended on Valencia. He had arranged to join forces with the fleets of Genoa and Pisa, to take the city. The Cid sent a letter to Alfonso expressing his astonishment, and at the same time his continued loyalty to the King. Alfonso's expedition proved a failure; the fleets arrived too late, the siege was ill-provided and had to be lifted.

The Cid, assuming with good reason that the Beni-Gómez clan were among the instigators of this expedition, decided at last to strike back: from Zaragoza he invaded their ancestral domains, sacking, burning, and leaving ruin everywhere behind him. García Ordóñez, in reply, sent a message to the Cid, challenging him to meet him for a battle. On the day appointed, the Cid arrived at the place that had been fixed, but there was no sign of García Ordóñez or his vassals. The Cid waited there for seven days, but the Beni-Gómez never appeared.

He remained in Zaragoza until the end of 1092. While he was there, a conspiracy led by one Ben Jehhaf had taken root within Valencia. The conspirators planned to turn the city to Ben Ayixa, Yúsuf's son, who was encamped in Murcia, to the south. Letters were sent to Ben Ayixa, who proceeded against Valencia and took possession of Alcira, a short distance from the city. Inside Valencia, open rebellion broke out. The old weak-hearted King, Alcádir, the Cid's ally and tributary, locked himself in the palace and was there besieged by the partisans, aided by a handful of Ben Ayixa's Africans. Alcádir dressed himself as a woman, filled a box with a collection of jewels which he prized as highly as his own life, and fastened around himself a jewel-studded girdle famous throughout the Arab

world, which had been worn by Zobeida, the wife of
Haroun Al-Raschid, and had brought disaster to owner
after owner. Then, surrounded by women, he fled the pal-
ace and hid in a little house in another part of the city.
The partisans stormed into the palace, killing and smash-
ing everywhere. Ben Jehhaf controlled Valencia. He knew
that Alcádir had not escaped from the city, and he wanted
the jewels and especially the famous girdle of Zobeida. A
hireling of his managed to locate Alcádir and at night
seized him, cut off his head, and returned to Ben Jehhaf
with the head and the jewels. The head was paraded around
the streets on a pike; the body, next day, was flung into a
manure heap where dead camels were buried. It was for-
bidden to mourn for him.

Too late, the Cid arrived in the territory of Valencia;
the city was already lost. He laid siege to the castle of Ju-
balla, on a hill in the neighborhood of Valencia, and from
his camp there he began at once to send out raiding parties
all around the city. He demanded provisions from all the
local Moorish chieftains. His depredations had their effect:
after a few months Ben Jehhaf sent to the Cid to try, with-
out success, to bargain with him. After eight months of
siege, in July 1093, the castle of Juballa fell to the Cid;
in a few weeks he built around the fortress an entire walled
city. In the same month he seized Villanueva and Alcudia,
the two suburbs to the north of Valencia, and Valencia
decided to yield. The conditions of the surrender were:
first, that Yúsuf's soldiers should leave the city; next, that
Ben Jehhaf should pay the Cid the same tribute that Al-
cádir had paid, and retroactively since the beginning of
the rebellion; and last, that the Cid and his host should
continue to occupy Juballa.

Yúsuf had already sent threatening letters to the Cid,
warning him not to remain in the territory of Valencia.
Rodrigo had answered with a scornful note, and at the
same time had sent letters to all the Moorish chieftains of
southern Spain, declaring that Yúsuf, then in Africa, did
not dare to cross the straits to attack him. Yúsuf, on hearing
that Valencia had fallen to the Cid, crossed to Spain and
prepared to attack the Campeador himself. The Cid sent a
new proposal to Valencia, a kind of ultimatum which was

customary in the wars of the period. He offered the Valencians thirty days in which to hope for succor from Yúsuf: if the African should arrive before that time, the Valencians then were to be released from their treaty with the Cid, and might side with Yúsuf; but if at the end of that time Yúsuf had not come to their aid, they were to side with the Cid against him. The Valencians accepted.

For a month the Cid prepared his fortifications. At the end of August 1093, when the term of the ultimatum was up, Yúsuf was nowhere in sight. The Cid had September and October, too, in which to continue his preparations for the defense. Then, with Yúsuf's army already in Lorca, to the south, the Cid camped in Villamediana, to the north of Valencia. Ben Jehhaf, he knew, was not to be trusted, and he had decided that it would be best to surround the city.

News came that Yúsuf's army, commanded by Abú Béker, was moving north from Lorca to Murcia. And news came from within Valencia that the pro-Yúsuf faction, led by the Beni-Uéjib clan, had seized power; that Ben Jehhaf had abdicated; and that the new rulers had abjured the July treaty with the Cid and planned to defend the city against him.

The Cid consolidated his position as well as he could, and waited for the Africans. They advanced closer; news of their approach came day after day, until they were within nine miles of Valencia. The Castilians, and the pro-Yúsuf Valencians who planned to despoil the Cid's camp, expected an encounter the next day. That night a cloudburst and thunderstorm of unprecedented violence struck the region, and in the middle of the night the Africans took panic and fled.

The Cid tightened the siege of the city. Inside Valencia, as conditions and morale grew worse, Ben Jehhaf regained power; in January 1094 he agreed to sign a treaty with the Cid, then changed his mind. The inhabitants began to suffer the extremes of hunger. In June the city surrendered unconditionally. The Cid was magnanimous and considerate to the inhabitants. But though he allowed Ben Jehhaf to remain the titular governor of the city, he required him to swear that he was not hiding the treasures of the Cid's old ally, Alcádir. Ben Jehhaf, in public, solemnly swore that he was not.

Two months later, news arrived that the Africans were assembling in Murcia for an attack on Valencia. Yúsuf's forces continued to grow; he landed more troops from Africa, and in September a vast army, commanded by Yúsuf's nephew, moved to the plain of Valencia and camped there. Certain of victory, for ten days their raiding parties pillaged the vicinity of the city and of the Cid's camp. The Campeador decided not to wait for reinforcements which were said to be coming to him; on the night of October 25, his force left camp. Parties of his knights managed to conceal themselves in the ravines around Yúsuf's camp. At daybreak the Cid's main host was drawn up facing the Africans. When Yúsuf's army charged, the Cid retreated, whereupon the rest of the Castilians, from the ravines, attacked the African camp. Yúsuf's army thought the Castilian reinforcements had arrived; they broke and fled, pursued by the Cid's knights, to be cut down or captured. The rout was complete, and immense quantities of booty were gathered up from the field.

King Alfonso was on his way to help the Cid when he heard of the victory. He changed his direction to take advantage of the situation, and attacked Guadix, further south, laying waste that part of the African empire.

In Valencia, new evidence indicated that Ben Jehhaf had been responsible for the death of Alcádir, the old King; the Cid had Ben Jehhaf seized and thrown into prison, where Ben Jehhaf shortly confessed and, upon some considerable prompting, told also where Alcádir's jewels were hidden. He was then tried before a court of Christians and Moors, and condemned, as a regicide, to be buried up to the waist and then burned alive. The sentence was carried out in May 1095.

The Cid spent the next year or so consolidating his position in Valencia. The new King of Aragón, Pedro, was now his firm ally and sent a force of knights to help him. The Cid, late in the year 1096, took an expedition to secure the outer fortresses of the territory, particularly Peña Cadiella, which he had fortified five years before. On this campaign he encountered an African army numbering thirty thousand knights, many times the Christian force. By brilliant maneuvering, the Cid caught them in a narrow place, and there was a repetition of his battle with the Africans before Valencia: a rout, great slaughter, and enormous spoils. In the same year, Alfonso was again defeated by Yúsuf at Consuegra (the Cid's son, serving with Alfonso, was killed in this battle) and another Christian army, under Alvar Fáñez, was routed by Ben Ayixa in the vicinity of Cuenca.

Ben Ayixa, on the heels of that victory, turned toward Valencia, met a detachment of the Cid's army at Alcira, and cut it to pieces. Notwithstanding intense grief at the death of his son, and at the disaster to his vassals at Alcira, the Cid laid siege to the two cities of Almenara and Murviedro, which were known to be sympathetic to the Africans. By the late summer of 1098 he had taken them both, Murviedro after a siege of some months. The capture of these two cities left the Cid in secure control of the whole province of Valencia.

A year later he died, aged fifty-six.

Two years after his death, Mazdalí, a new African general, laid siege to Valencia. Jimena successfully defended the city until King Alfonso arrived from Castile with his army, whereupon the Africans retired. Alfonso, after a reconnaissance of the territory and a few brushes with some of Mazdalí's forces, decided that it would be impossible for him to hold the city now that the Campeador was dead. He and his army, and Jimena and the Cid's army, taking with them Rodrigo's body, evacuated the city and set out for Toledo. Upon leaving, in order to prevent the Africans from taking it intact, they burned Valencia to the ground.

The *Poem of the Cid* is the best evidence we have of how far the legend of the Cid had developed forty years after Rodrigo's death. The author celebrates in the Cid not only the hero who defeated Yúsuf and stemmed the second African invasion of the peninsula; with considerable historical justification he presents the Campeador as the type of most of the virtues which in that era most impressed the people of feudal Spain. The Cid is seen not only as the unconquerable defender of Christendom, but as the champion of the Christian feudal order itself; proof of this is his loyalty to King Alfonso, even when according to feudal law all his obligations toward the King had been dissolved. His moderation, self-control, magnanimity, dignity, piety, and of course honor are emphasized by the poet. And it is important to notice that the Cid is presented as a hero of relatively humble origins, that the real villains of the piece are arrogant members of the upper courtly nobility, and that the Cid triumphs over them in the two ways that mattered to the Christians of feudal Spain: by force and by law. The same cast of sympathy is apparent in the account of the Cid's battle with Ramón Berenguer, where a band of "ill-shod outcasts" defeats and humiliates a highborn braggart.

A nation's character is projected more or less directly into the figure it idealizes as its national hero, and it was ultimately the Spanish character, at least of the period between the twelfth century and the Renaissance, that made the legend of the Campeador and continued to see Rodrigo as the national hero long after the order that he defended had changed.

The body of literature which, in the five hundred years after his death, grew around the figure of the Cid is unique in that it comprises a complete cycle. First, there are the historic facts—such as remain. Then the anonymous epics of the twelfth century; the *Poema* was not even the only poem of its period about the Cid. Then, for several hundred years, the ballads of the Cid. Even the verse form of the ballads is a direct continuation of the verse form of the popular epics. As an example, here is a translation of one of the most dramatic of the Cid ballads, describing a completely legendary episode. The ballad begins just after the death of the Cid; Valencia is threatened by a great army under the command of King Búcar.

The Cid's vassals, mounting his body
upon Babieca, defeat Búcar

Dead lies that good Cid
Rodrigo of Bivar.
Gil Díaz, his good servant,
Will do as he was bidden.

He will embalm his body,
And rigid and stiff it was left;
Its face is beautiful,
Of great beauty and well colored,
Its two eyes equally open,
Its beard dressed with great care;
It does not appear to be dead,
But seems to be still alive,
And to make it stay upright
Gil Díaz used this cunning:
He set it in a saddle
With a board between its shoulders
And at its breast another,
And at the sides these joined together;
They went under the arms
And covered the back of the head.
This was behind, and another
Came up as far as the beard,
Holding the body upright,
So that it leaned to no side.
Twelve days have passed
Since the Cid's life ended.
His followers armed themselves
To ride out to battle
Against that Moorish king Búcar
And the rabble he led.
When it was midnight
The body, thus as it was,
They placed upon Babieca
And onto the horse tied it.
Erect and upright it sits,
It looked as though it were living,
With breeches on its legs
Embroidered black and white,
Resembling the hose he had worn
When he was alive.
They dressed it in garments
Displaying needlework,
And his shield, at the neck,
Swung with its device.
A helmet on its head

xxvi

Of painted parchment
Looks as though it were iron,
So well it was fashioned.
In the right hand the sword Tizona
Was cunningly tied,
It as a wonder to watch it
Go forward in a raised hand.
On one side rode the bishop,
The famous Don Jerome,
On the other Gil Díaz,
Who guided Babieca.
Don Pedro Bermúdez rode forth
With the Cid's banner raised,
With four hundred nobles
In his company:
Then went forth the main file
With as many again for escort;
The Cid's corpse rode forth
With a brave company.
One hundred are the guardians
Who rode with the honored corpse,
Behind it goes Doña Jimena
With all her company,
With six hundred knights
There to be her guard:
They go in silence, and so softly
You would say they were less than twenty.
Now they have left Valencia,
The clear day has dawned;
Alvar Fáñez was the first
Who charged with fury
Upon the great force of the Moors
Assembled with Búcar.
He found before him
A beautiful Mooress,
Skilled at shooting
Arrows from a quiver
With a Turkish bow;
Star was what they called her
Because of her excellence
At striking with the javelin.

She was the first
Who took horse and rode forward
With a hundred others like her,
Valiant and daring.
With fury the Cid's vassals charged them
And left them dead on the ground,
King Búcar has seen them,
And the other kings who are with him.
They are filled with wonder
At the sight of the Christian host.
To them it looks as though
There are seventy thousand knights
All white as snow,
And one who fills them with dread,
Grown now more huge than ever,
Who rides on a white horse,
A crimson cross on his breast,
In his hand a white signal;
The sword looks like a flame
To torment the Moors;
Great slaughter it wields among them,
They flee, they do not wait.
King Búcar and his kings
Abandon the field;
They make straight for the sea
Where the ships were left;
The Cid's knights charge after them.
Not one of them escaped,
All gasped and sank in the sea;
More than ten thousand drowned,
All rushing there together,
Not one of them embarked.
Of the kings, twenty were killed;
Búcar escaped, fleeing;
The Cid's vassals seize the tents
And much gold and much silver.
The poorest was made rich
With what they took there.
They set out for Castile,
As the good Cid had commanded;
They have arrived at San Pedro,

San Pedro of Cerdeña;
There they left the body of the Cid
To whom all Spain has paid honor.

Finally, as the last phase of the cycle, in the great age of the Spanish drama there is Guillén de Castro's two-part play *Las Mocedades del Cid* (The Youth of the Cid). The connection between popular and cultivated poetry, which was one of the great strengths of Spanish literature in its great age, could scarcely be better exemplified: the basic verse form of Spanish classical drama grew directly out of the ballad form, and Guillén de Castro, like many other dramatists, based his story on incidents in the ballads. It was Guillén de Castro's plays which served as a model for Corneille's *Le Cid*.

In the whole cycle, the most magnificent single work is the oldest, the *Poema del Cid* itself. The author's governing design is simple: the *Poema* as a whole celebrates the rise of Rodrigo from his exile in disgrace from Castile to a position which represented, to twelfth-century feudal Spain, very nearly as complete a triumph as a human being not born to royalty could conceivably achieve this side of the grave. The poet simplifies history, but where he describes historical events he does so with considerable accuracy.

The poem is divided into three parts, or *cantares*. The first relates the cause of the Cid's disgrace and banishment, and his early triumphs in exile, culminating in his defeat of the Count of Barcelona. The second *cantar* describes his conquest of Valencia, his reconciliation with the King, and the marriage of his daughters to the two Heirs of Carrión, of the Beni-Gómez Clan. The third *cantar* tells how his two sons-in-law beat and abandoned the girls to insult the Campeador; how he was avenged on them, both in the royal court with the King sitting in judgment and in a trial-by-combat; and finally, how the Cid's daughters were remarried to the Princes of Navarre and Aragón.

Numerous incidents in the poem—such as the story of the coffers of sand in the first *cantar* and several episodes in the third *cantar*—are fictitious. On the other hand, most of the battles, sieges, and other military encounters in the poem actually took place, and a list of the characters who have been identified as historical personages would include very nearly all the names mentioned by the poet.

✠ ✠ ✠

The vocabulary of the *Poema* is small; the language is simple; there is little ornament of any kind. The versification relies on two things chiefly: rhythm and the use of assonance. I have felt that of these two, the rhythm was the more important, and I have tried to render the poem into an English line which would give some sense of the strength and sweep of the original.

Within the *cantares,* the poem is subdivided into groups of lines, known as *laisses,* all ending on the same vowel sound. I have not duplicated this scheme in the English version, since I was certain that too much would have to be sacrificed to the demands of making all the lines, in passages running in some cases to a hundred and twenty-five lines and more, end on the same assonance. Occasionally, where it seemed important, I have tried to indicate the effect of the assonance in the original; and in general I have tried to use a certain amount of assonance within the lines to suggest some of the effects which the original gets in other ways.

Apart from that, I have tried to put the poem into English that would be neither deathly archaic nor pointlessly and jarringly colloquial. In doing so I have kept close to the literal meaning of the original as I have known how to. In most places I have also kept the use of present and past tenses as they are in the original. It appears that the poet, following the traditions of the kind of poetry he was writing, used the historic present, in general, to bring details into the foreground, and the past tenses to hold them at a remove. (I am indebted to Professor Stephen Gilman of the Modern Languages Department of Harvard University for pointing this out to me.) I have not wanted to try to improve upon the poet's system of shading for the sake of a minor degree of clarity.

✠ ✠ ✠

I wish to thank Douglas Cleverdon, first, for commissioning this translation for the Third Programme of the British Broadcasting Corporation, on which it was broadcast. I cannot adequately express my gratitude to Professor Gilman, who found time and patience to go through the translation with me and to correct blunders which I would rather not remember—though I must say at once that he is not responsible for any that may still remain.

Anyone who has any pleasure or profit from the *Poema* is obligated to the great modern Spanish scholar, Ramón Menéndez Pidal; I should like just to indicate the extent of my debt. I have used his reconstructed text, in the Clásicos Castellanos edition, for my translation, and his reproduction of the original text (*Cantar de Mio Cid*) for reference. Without his notes to both texts, and his glossary, I would often have been at a loss. His *La España del Cid* is an indispensable guide to the background of the poem. Anyone familiar with his *El Cid Campeador* will realize how closely I have relied on that book for the biographical and historical matter in this preface. Finally, scattered essays of his on such subjects as the formation of the Spanish language and his book on the popular epics and the bards that sang them (*Poesía Juglaresca y Juglares*) have provided me, in the course of the work, not only with relevant information, but with excitement.

W. S. MERWIN

Boston, March 1958

Poema del Cid

CANTAR PRIMERO

DESTIERRO DEL CID

[*La falta de la primera hoja del códice del Cantar se suple con el relato de la Crónica de Veinte Reyes*]

El rey Alfonso envía al Cid para cobrar las parias del rey moro de Sevilla. Este es atacado por el conde castellano García Ordóñez. El Cid, amparando al moro vasallo del rey de Castilla, vence a García Ordóñez en Cabra y le prende afrentosamente. El Cid torna a Castilla con las parias, pero sus enemigos le indisponen con el rey. Este destierra al Cid.

Enbió el rey don Alfonso a Ruy Díaz mio Çid por las parias que le avían a dar los reyes de Córdova e de Sevilla cada año. Almutamiz rey de Sevilla e Almudafar rey de Granada eran a aquella sazón muy enemigos e queríansse mal de muerte. E eran entonçes con Almudafar rey de Granada estos ricos omnes que le ayudavan: el conde don García Ordóñez, e Fortún Sánchez el yerno del rey don García de Navarra, e Lope Sánchez ... e cada uno destos ricos omnes con su poder ayudavan a Almudafar, e fueron sobre Almutamiz rey de Sevilla.

Ruy Díaz Çid, quando sopo que assí venían sobre el rey de Sevilla que era vasallo e pechero del rey don Alfón su

32

Poem of the Cid

THE FIRST CANTAR

THE EXILE

[Since the opening pages of the poem are lost, the beginning of the story must be supplied from the *Chronicle of Twenty Kings;* the part of that chronicle relating to the Cid had, in the first place, been translated from the poem into Latin prose. The passage immediately preceding the beginning of Per Abbat's manuscript has been reconstructed in verse from the chronicle.]

King Alfonso sends the Cid to collect tribute from the Moorish King of Seville. The King of Seville is attacked by Count García Ordóñez of Castile. The Cid, defending the Castilian King's Moorish vassal, defeats García Ordóñez at Cabra and imprisons and humiliates him. The Cid returns to Castile with the tribute, but his enemies make mischief between him and the King. The King banishes the Cid.

King Alfonso sent Ruy Díaz, My Cid, to collect the annual tribute from the Kings of Córdoba and Seville. Almutamiz, King of Seville, and Almudafar, King of Granada, at that time were bitter enemies and wished each other's death. And there were then with Almudafar, King of Granada, these noblemen who supported him: the Count Don García Ordóñez, and Fortún Sánchez, the son-in-law of King García of Navarre, and Lope Sánchez; and each of these noblemen with all his power supported Almudafar, and went against Almutamiz, King of Seville.

Ruy Díaz Cid, when he heard that they were coming against the King of Seville, who was a vassal and tributary

33

señor, tóvolo por mal e pesóle mucho; e enbio a todos sus
cartas de ruego, que non quisiessen venir contra el rey de
Sevilla nin destruirle su tierra, por el debdo que avían con
el rey don Alfonso [ca si ende al quisiessen fazer, supiessen
que non podría estar el rey don Alfonso que non ayudasse
a su vasallo, pues su pechero era]. El rey de Granada e los
ricos omnes non presçiaron nada sus cartas del Çid e
fueron todos muchos esforçadamente e destruyeron al rey
de Sevilla toda la tierra, fasta el Castillo de Cabra.

Quando aquéllo vio Ruy Díaz Çid [tomó todo el poder
que pudo aver de cristianos e de moros, e fue contra el rey
de Granada, por le sacar de la tierra del rey de Sevilla. E el
rey de Granada e los ricos omnes que con él eran, quando
sopieron que en aquella guisa iva, enviáronle dezir que non
le saldrían de la tierra por él. Ruy Díaz Çid quando aquello
oyó, tovo que non le estaría bien si los non fuese cometer,
e] fue a ellos, e lidió con ellos en campo, e duróles la
batalla desde ora de terçia fasta ora de medio día, e fue
grande la mortandad que y ovo de moros e de cristianos
de la parte del rey de Granada, e venciólos el Çid e fízolos
fluir del campo. E priso el Çid en esta batalla al conde don
Garçía Ordóñez [e mesóle una pieça de la barba] . . . e a
otros cavalleros muchos, e tanta de la otra gente que non
avie cuenta; e tóvolos el Çid presos tres días, desí quitólos
a todos. Quando él los ovo presos, mandó a los suyos
coger los averes e las riquezas que fincaban en el canpo,
desí tornósse el Çid con toda su conpaña e con todas sus
riquezas para Almutamiz rey de Sevilla, [e dio a él a todos
sus moros quanto conosçieron que era suyo, e aun de lo
al quanto quisieron tomar. E de allí adelante llamaron
moros e cristianos a éste Ruy Díaz de Bivar el Cid
Campeador, que quiere dezir batallador].

Almutamiz dióles entonçes muchos buenos dones e las
parias por que fuera . . . E tornóse el Çid con todas sus
parias para el rey don Alfonso su señor. [El rey resçibióle
muy bien, e plógole mucho con él, e fue muy pagado de
quanto allá fiziera.] Por esto le ovieron muchos enbidia e

of his lord King Alfonso, took it ill and was much grieved; and he sent letters to all of them begging them not to come against the King of Seville nor destroy his land, because of the allegiance they owed to King Alfonso; for they might know if they continued to do so, King Alfonso could not do otherwise than to come to the aid of his vassal, who was his tributary. The King of Granada and the noblemen took no note of the Cid's letters, but using violence they destroyed all the land of the King of Seville as far as the castle of Cabra.

When Ruy Díaz Cid saw this, he took all the force of Christians and Moors that he could muster, and went against the King of Granada to expel him from the land of the King of Seville. And the King of Granada and the noblemen who were with him, when they knew that he was coming thus, sent to tell him that they would not leave the land on his account. Ruy Díaz Cid, when he heard this, could not rest until he had set upon them, and he went against them and fought with them in the field, and the battle lasted from nine o'clock until midday, and the Moors and Christians on the side of the King of Granada suffered great slaughter, and the Cid overcame them and forced them to flee from the field. And in this battle the Cid took prisoner the Count Don García Ordóñez and pulled out part of his beard, and took prisoner many other gentlemen and so many of the ordinaries that they lost count; and the Cid held them three days and then released them all. While he held them prisoner he sent his men to gather together the belongings and things of value which remained on the field; afterwards the Cid with all his company and all his gains returned to Almutamiz, King of Seville, and gave to him and to all his Moors whatever they knew to be theirs, and whatever they wished to take besides. And always after that, both Moors and Christians called this same Ruy Díaz of Bivar the Cid Campeador, which is to say, the warrior, the winner of battles.

Then Almutamiz gave him many fine presents and the tribute for which he had come, and the Cid with all the tribute went back to King Alfonso, his lord. The King received him very well and was highly pleased with him and most satisfied with all he had done there. Because of this,

buscáronle mucho mal e mezcláronle con el rey ...
El rey commo estava muy sañudo e mucho irado contra
él, creyólos luego ... [e enbio luego dezir al Çid por sus
cartas que le saliesse de todo el regno. El Çid después que
ovo leídas las cartas, como quier que ende oviesse grand
pesar, non quiso y al fazer, ca non avía de plazo más de
nueve días en que salliesse de todo el reyno].

I
El Cid convoca a sus vasallos; éstos se destierran con él.
Adiós del Cid a Bivar

[Enbió por sus parientes e sus vasallos, e díxoles cómmo
el rey le mandava sallir de toda su tierra, e que le non
dava de plazo más de nueve días, e que quería saber dellos
quáles querían ir con é o quáles fincar,]

   (aquí comienza el manuscrito de Per Abbati)

"e los que conmigo fuéredes de Dios ayades buen grado,
e los que acá fincáredes quiérome ir vuestro pagado."
 Estonçes fabló Alvar Fáñez su primo cormano:
"convusco iremos, Çid, por yermos e por poblados,
ca nunca vos fallesceremos en cuanto seamos sanos
convusco despenderemos las mulas e los cavallos
e los averes e los paños
siempre vos serviremos como leales vasallos."
Entonçe otorgaron todos quanto dixo don Alvaro;
mucho gradesçio mio Çid quanto allí fue razonado ...
 Mio Çid movió de Bivar pora Burgos adeliñado,
assí dexa sus palaçios yermos e desheredados.

De los sos ojos tan fuertemientre llorando,
tornava la cabeça i estávalos catando.
Vío puertas abiertas e uços sin cañados,
alcándaras vázias sin pielles e sin mantos
e sin falcones e sin adtores mudados.

many were envious and sought to do him evil, and spoke against him to the King.

The King, who already nursed an ancient rancor against him, came to believe them, and sent letters to the Cid telling him that he must leave the kingdom. The Cid, when he had read the letters, was much grieved, and yet he did not wish to disobey, although he was allowed only nine days' grace in which to leave the kingdom.

1

The Cid calls his vassals together. They will go with him into exile. The Cid's farewell to Bivar

[*He sent for his family and his vassals and told them of the King's ordering him to leave his lands, and that he was given no more than nine days in which to go, and that he wished to know from them which of them would go with him and which would stay.*]

[*Here Per Abbat's manuscript begins*]

"and those who come with me   God's good mercy sustain,
and those who remain here   I shall be content with them."
*   Then spoke Alvar Fáñez,   his first cousin:*
"We shall go with you, Cid,   through deserts, through towns,
and never fail you   while we are whole in limb;
with you we shall wear out   horses and beasts of burden
and our goods and our garments
and serve you always   as faithful liege men."
Then to what Don Alvaro had said   all gave their consent;
My Cid thanked them deeply   for all they had there spoken.

*   My Cid went out from Bivar,   toward Burgos riding,*
and left his palaces   disinherited and barren.
His eyes,   grievously weeping,
he turned his head   and looked back upon them.
He saw doors standing open   and gates without fastenings,
the porches empty   without cloaks or coverings
and without falcons   and without molted hawks.

37

Sospiró mio Çid,   ca mucho avié grandes cuidados.
Fabló mio Çid   bien e tan mesurado:
"grado a tí, señor padre,   que estás en alto!
"Esto me an buolto   mios enemigos malos."

2
Agüeros en el camino de Burgos

Allí pienssan de aguijar   allí sueltan las riendas.
A la exida de Bivar,   ovieron la corneja diestra,
e entrando a Burgos   oviéronla siniestra.
Meçió mio Çid los ombros   y engrameó la tiesta:
"albricia, Alvar Fáñez,   ca echados somos de tierra!
mas a grand ondra   tornaremos a Castiella."

↓opinión

3
El Cid entra en Burgos

Mio Çid Roy Díaz,   por Burgos entróve,
En sue conpaña   sessaenta pendones;
exien lo veer   mugieres e varones,
burgeses e burgesas,   por las finiestras sone,
plorando de los ojos,   tanto avien el dolore.
De las sus bocas   todos dizían una razóne:
"Dios, qué buen vassallo,   si oviesse buen señore!"

God what a good vassal, if only he had a good lord (the king)

4
Nadie hospeda al Cid. Sólo una niña le dirige
la palabra para mandarle alejarse. El Cid se ve obligado a
acampar fuera de la población, en la glera

Conbidar le ien de grado,   mas ninguno non osava:
el rey don Alfonso   tanto avie le grand saña.
Antes de la noche   en Burgos dél entró su carta,
con grand recabdo   e fuertemientre seellada:
que a mio Çid Roy Díaz   que nadi nol diessen posada,
e aquel que gela diesse   sopiesse vera palabra

38

He sighed, My Cid,   for he felt great affliction.
He spoke, My Cid,   well, and with great moderation.
"Thanks be to Thee, our Father   Who art in Heaven!
My evil enemies   have wrought this upon me."

2

Omens on the road to Burgos

There they set spur   there they released the reins.
At the gate of Bivar   on their right hand the crow flew;
as they rode into Burgos   it flew on their left.
My Cid raised his head   and shrugged his shoulders:
"Rejoice, Alvar Fáñez,   though this exile is ours!
We shall come back to Castile   laden with honor."

3

The Cid enters Burgos

My Cid Ruy Díaz   rode into Burgos,
in his company   sixty pennons.
They crowded to see him,   women and men;
townsmen and their wives   sat at the windows
weeping from their eyes,   so great was their sorrow.
And one sentence only   was on every tongue:
"Were his lord but worthy,   God, how fine a vassal!"

4

*No one gives lodging to the Cid. Only one little girl speaks
to him to tell him he must leave. The Cid finds he must
camp outside the town, on the shingle of the river bed*

They would have asked him in gladly,   but did not dare,
for King Alfonso   cherished such anger.
His letter had come   to Burgos the night before
with all formality   and sealed with a great seal:
that to My Cid Ruy Díaz   no one must give shelter,
that who should do so,   let him learn the truth of the
      matter,

que perderie los averes   e más los ojos de la cara,
e aun demás   los cuerpos e las almas.
Grande duelo avien   las yentes cristianas;
ascóndense de mio Çid,   ca nol osan dezir nada.

 El Campeador   adeliñó a su posada;
así como llegó a la puorta,   fallóla bien cerrada,
por miedo del rey Alfons,   que assí lo pararan:
que si non la quebrantás,   que non gela abriessen por
      nada.
Los de mio Çid   a altas vozes llaman
los de dentro   non les querién tornar palabra.
Aguijó mio Çid,   a la puerta se llegaua,
sacó el pie del estribera,   una ferídal dava;
non se abre la puerta,   ca bien era çerrada.

 Una niña de nuef años   a ojo se parava:
"Ya Campeador,   en buena çinxiestes espada!
El rey lo ha vedado,   anoch dél entró su carta,
con grant recabdo   e fuertemientre seellada.
Non vos osariemos   abrir nin coger por nada;
si non, perderiemos   los averes e las casas,
e aun demás   los ojos de las caras.
Çid, en el nuestro mal   vos non ganades nada;
mas el Criador vos vala   con todas sus vertudes santas."
Esto la niña dixo   e tornós pora su casa.
Ya lo vede el Çid   que del rey non avie graçia.
Partiós dela puerta,   por Burgos aguijaua,
llegó a Santa María,   luego descavalga;
finçó los inojos,   de coraçón rogava.
La oración fecha   luego cavalgava;
salió por la puerta   e Arlançon passava.
Cabo Burgos essa villa   en la glera posava,
fincava la tienda   e luego descavalgava.
Mio Çid Roy Díaz,   el que en buena çinxo espada,
posó en la glera   quando nol coge nadi en casa;
derredor dél   una buena conpaña.
Assí posó mio Çid   commo si fosse en montaña.
Vedada l'an conpra   dentro en Burgos la casa

he would lose all that he had   and the eyes out of his face
and, what is more, they would lose   their bodies and their
    souls.
Those Christian people,   great sorrow they had hiding from
My Cid,   for none dared say a word.
    The Campeador   rode up to the inn;
when he reached the portal   he found it closed against him.
For fear of King Alfonso   they had concluded thus:
unless he break the door   on no account admit him.
Those with My Cid   shouted out for them to open,
those within   would not answer them.
My Cid spurred forward,   to the door he came,
drew his foot from the stirrup,   kicked a gash in the wood;
the door was well secured   and did not open.
    A little girl of nine   appeared in sight:
"Ah, Campeador, in a good hour   you first girded on
    sword!
The King forbids us this;   last night his letter came here,
with all formality   and sealed with a great seal.
We dare not let you in   nor lodge you for any reason,
or we shall lose   our goods and our houses,
and besides these   the eyes out of our faces.
Cid, you will gain nothing   by our miseries;
but the Creator bless you   with all his holy virtues."
The child spoke this   and then turned back to her house.
Now the Cid can see that he finds   no grace in the King's
    eyes.
He went from the doorway   and spurred through Burgos;
at the Church of Santa María,   there he stepped from his
    horse;
there he knelt down,   from his heart he prayed.
The prayer ended,   once more he mounted,
rode out of the gate,   passed over the Arlanzón.
Outside the town of Burgos   at the river bed he stayed,
set his tent   and there dismounted.
My Cid Ruy Díaz,   who in good hour girded on sword,
when no house would have him   pitched camp on the
    shingle,
and a goodly company   encamped around him,
There he camped, My Cid   as in a wilderness.
In the town of Burgos   the law forbade

41

de todas cosas   quantas son de vianda;
nol osarien vender   al menos dinarada._

5

Martín Antolínez viene de Burgos a proveer de víveres al
    Cid

Martín Antolínez,   el Burgalés conplido,
a mio Çid e alos sos   abástales de pan e de vino;
non lo conpra,   ca él se lo avie consigo;
de todo conducho   bien los ovo bastidos.
Pagós mio Çid   el Campeador conplido
e todos los otros   que van a so çervicio.
Fabló Martín Antolínez,   odredes lo que a dicho:
"ya Campeador,   en buen ora fostes naçido!
esta noch yagamos   e vayámosnos al matino,
ca acusado seré   de lo que vos he seruido,
en ira del rey Alffons   yo seré metido.
Si con vusco   escapo sano o bivo,
aun çerca o tarde el rey   querer m'a por amigo;
si non, quanto dexo   no lo preçio un figo."

6

El Cid empobrecido acude a la astucia de Martín Antolínez.
Las arcas de arena

Fabló mio Çid,   el que en buen ora çinxo espada:
"Martín Antolínez,   sodes ardida lança!
si yo vibo,   doblar vos he la soldada.
Espeso e el oro   e toda la plata,
bien lo veedes   que yo no trayo nada,
huebos me serié   pora toda mi campaña;
fer lo he amidos,   de grado non avrié nada.
Con vuestro consejo   bastir quiero dos arcas;
inchámoslas d'arena,   ca bien serán pesadas,
cubiertas de guadalmeçi,   e bien enclaveadas.

42

that he should so much as buy   anything that was food;
no one dared sell him   a pennyworth of bread.

5

*Martín Antolínez comes from Burgos to bring food to the
    Cid*

Martín Antolínez,   the accomplished man of Burgos,
to My Cid and his men   brought bread and wine
which was not bought   because it was his own;
of all manner of food   they had ample provision.
He was pleased, My Cid   the accomplished Campeador,
and all the others   who were in his train.
Martín Antolínez spoke,   you will hear what he said:
"Ah, Campeador,   in a good hour you were born!
We stay here tonight,   we must be gone by morning,
for I shall be accused   of this service I have done;
in King Alfonso's anger   I shall be included.
If I escape with you   alive and sound of limb,
sooner or later the King   will love me as a friend;
if not, all that I leave,   I value at nothing."

6

*The Cid, impoverished, resorts to Martín Antolínez's cun-
ning. The coffers filled with sand*

My Cid spoke,   who in good hour girded on sword:
"Martín Antolínez,   you are a hardy lance!
If I live,   I will double your pay.
Gone is my gold   and all my silver;
you can see plainly   that I carry nothing
and I need money   for all my followers;
I am forced to this   since freely I can have nothing.
With your aid   I will build two coffers;
we shall stuff them with sand   to make them heavier,
stud them with nails   and cover them with worked leather,

43

7

Las arcas destinadas para obtener dinero de dos judíos burgaleses

Los guadameçis vermejos   e los clavos bien dorados.
Por Raquel e Vidas   vayádesme privado:
quando en Burgos me vedaron compra   y el rey me a
                                        [ayrado
non puedo traer el aver,   ca much es pesado,
enpeñar gelo he   por lo que fore guisado;
de noche lo lieven,   que non lo vean cristianos.
Véalo el Criador   con todos los sos santos,
yo más non puedo   e amidos lo fago."

8

Martín Antolínez vuelve a Burgos en busca de los judíos

*   Martín Antolínez   non lo detardava*
passó por Burgos,   al castiello entrava,
por Raquel e Vidas   apriessa demandava.

9

Trato de Martín Antolínez con los judíos. Estos van a la tienda del Cid. Cargan con las arcas de arena

*   Raquel e Vidas   en uno estavan amos,*
en cuenta de sus averes,   de los que avien ganados.
Llegó Martín Antolínez   a guisa de menbrado:
"¿O sodes, Raquel e Vidas,   los mios amigos caros?
En poridad   fablar querría con amos."
Non lo detardan,   todos tres se apartaron.
"Raquel e Vidas,   amos me dat las manos,
que non me descubrades   a moros nin a cristianos;
por siempre vos faré ricos,   que non seades menguados.
El Campeador   por las parias fo entrado,
grandes averes priso   e mucho sobejanos,
retovo dellos   quanto que fo algo;
por en vino a aquesto   por que fo acusado.

44

7

*The coffers destined to obtain money from the two Jews of
    Burgos*

the leather crimson   and the nails well gilded.
Go in haste and find me   Raquel and Vidas, and say:
'Since in Burgos I may not buy, and the King's disfavor
        pursues me,
I cannot carry this wealth   for it is too heavy.
I must put it in pawn   for whatever is reasonable.
So that no Christians may see it,   come and fetch it in by
        night.'
Let the Creator see it   and all His saints besides;
I cannot do otherwise   and for this have little heart."

8

Martín Antolínez goes back into Burgos

    Martín Antolínez   without delay
went into Burgos,   into the castle.
For Raquel and Vidas   he asked immediately.

9

*Martín Antolínez's negotiations with the Jews. They go to
the Cid's tent. They carry away the coffers of sand*

    Raquel and Vidas   were both in the same place
counting over the goods   that they had gained.
Martín Antolínez approached   with all shrewdness. ★ *defeated
    at their
    own game*
"Are you there, Raquel and Vidas,   my dear friends?
I would speak with you both   in secret confidence."
They did not keep him waiting;   all three withdrew
        together.
"Raquel and Vidas,   give me your hands,
swear you will not betray me   to Moors or Christians; — *to anyone*
I shall make you rich forever,   you will lack for nothing.
The Campeador   was sent for the tribute;
he seized much wealth   and great possessions.
He kept for himself   a considerable portion, —*to behoof that of Cid makes them
    attackable.*
whence he has come to this,   for he was accused.

45

Tiene dos arcas   llenas de oro esmerado.
Ya lo veedes   que el rey le a ayrado.
Dexado ha heredades   e casas e palaçios.
Aquellas non las puede levar,   sinon, serié ventado;
el Campeador   dexar las ha en vuestra mano,
e prestalde de aver,   lo que sea guisado.
Prended las arcas   e meterlas en vuestro salvo;
con grand jura   meted i las fedes amos,
que non las catedes   en todo aqueste año."
    Raquel e Vidas   seiense consejando:
"Nos huebos avemos   en todo de ganar algo.
Bien los sabemos   que él algo gañado,
quando duerme sin sospecha   qui aver trae monedado.
Estas arcas,   prendámoslas amos,
en logar las metamos   que non sea ventado.
    Mas dezidnos del Çid,   dé qué será pagado,
o qué ganançia nos dará   por todo aqueste año?"
Respuso Martín Antolínez   a guisa de menbrado:
"myo Çid querrá,   lo que ssea aguisado;
pedir vos a poco   por dexar so aver en salvo.
Acógensele omnes   de todas partes menguados,
a menester   seyçientos marcos."
Dixo Raquel e Vidas: "dar gelos hemos de grado."
—"Ya vedes que entra noch,   el Çid es pressurado,
huebos avemos   que nos dedes los marcos."
Dixo Raquel e Vidas: "non se faze assí el mercado,
siñon primero prendiendo   e después dando."
Dixo Martín Antolínez: "yo desso me pago.
Amos tred   al Campeador contado,
e nos vos ayudaremos,   que assí es aguisado,
por aducir las arcas   e meterlas en vuestro salvo,
que non lo sepan   moros nin cristianos."
Dixo Raquel e Vidas: "nos desto nos pagamos.
Las archas aduchas,   prendet seyesçientos marcos."
    Martín Antolínez   caualgó privado
con Raquel e Vidas,   de voluntad e de grado.

46

He has two coffers   full of pure gold.
You know full well   the King's disfavor pursues him.
He has left houses and palaces,   all his inheritance.
He cannot take these   for they would be discovered.
The Campeador   will leave the coffers in your hands;
lend him, in money,   whatever is reasonable.
Take the coffers   into your safekeeping,
but you must both pledge your faiths,   with a great oath,
for the rest of this year   not to look inside them."
    Raquel and Vidas   conferred together:
"In any business   we must gain something.
Of course we know   that he gained something;
in the lands of the Moors   he seized much booty.
His sleep is uneasy   who has money with him.
As for the coffers,   let us take both of them
and put them in a place   where no one will sniff them.
But tell us, concerning the Cid,   what sum will content
        him,
what interest will he give us   for the whole of this year?"
Martín Antolínez answered   with all shrewdness:
"My Cid desires   whatever is reasonable;
he asks little of you   for leaving his wealth in safety.
Needy men from all sides   are gathering around him;
he requires   six hundred marks."
Raquel and Vidas said,   "We will gladly give that many."
"You see, night is falling   the Cid has no time,
we have need   that you give us the marks."
Raquel and Vidas said,   "Business is not done that way,
but by first taking   and giving afterwards."
Martín Antolínez said,   "I am content with that.
Come, both of you,   to the famous Campeador,
and we will help you,   as is only just,
to carry away the coffers   to where you can keep them
        safely
so that neither Moors nor Christians   may know where
        they lie."
Raquel and Vidas said,   "That will content us.
When the coffers are here,   you may take the six hundred
        marks."
    Martín Antolínez   rode off at once
with Raquel and Vidas   willingly and gladly.

47

Non viene a la puent, ca por el agua a passado,
que gelo non ventassen de Burgos omne nado.
   Afévoslos a la tienda del Campeador contado;
assí commo entraron, al Çid besáronle las manos.
Sonrrisós mio Çid, estávalos fablando:
"¡ya don Raquel e Vidas, avédesme olbidado!
Ya me exco de tierra, ca del rey so ayrado.
A lo quem semeja, de lo mio avredes algo;
mientra que vivades non seredes menguados."
Raquel e Vidas a mio Çid besáronle las manos,
Martín Antolínez el pleyto a parado,
que sobre aquellas arcas dar le ien seysçientos marcos,
o bien gelas guardarien fasta cabo del año;
ca assil dieran la fed e gelo auien jurado,
que si antes las catassen que fossen perjurado,
non les diesse mio Çid de ganançia un dinero malo.
Dixo Martín Antolínez: "carguen las arcas privado.
Levaldas, Raquel e Vidas, ponedlas en vuestro salvo;
yo iré convusco, que adugamos los marcos,
ca a mover ha mio Çid ante que cante el gallo."
Al cargar de las arcas veriedes gozo tanto:
Non las podien poner en somo maguer eran esforçados.
Grádanse Raquel e Vidas con averes monedados,
ca mientra que visquiessen refechos eran amos.

10

Despedida de los judíos y el Cid. Martín Antolínez se va
con los judíos a Burgos

   Raquel a mio Çid la manol ha pesada:
"¡Ya Canpeador, en buena cinxiestes espada!
de Castiella vos ides pora las yentes estrañas.
Assí es vuestra ventura, grandes son vuestras ganancias;

He did not go by the bridge,   but through the water,
so that no man in Burgos   should get wind of it.
  They have come to the tent   of the famous Campeador;
they kiss the hands of the Cid   when they enter.
My Cid smiled   and spoke with them:
"Greetings, Don Raquel and Vidas,   had you forgotten
      me?
I must depart into exile   for the King's disfavor pursues
      me.
From the look of things   you will have something of mine;
as long as you live   you will not be paupers."
Raquel and Vidas   kissed My Cid's hands.
Martín Antolínez   sealed the bargain.
Six hundred marks   they would give for those coffers
and would guard them well   till the end of the year,
and to this they vowed their consent   and to this swore:
that should they break their promise   and open them
      before,
the Cid should not give so much   as one wretched farthing
      for their profit.
Martín Antolínez said,   "Carry them off at once.
Take them, Raquel and Vidas,   put them in your safe
      place;
I shall go with you   to bring back the money,
for My Cid must depart   before the cock sings."
When they went to load the coffers   you could see how
      great was their pleasure.
They could not lift them   although they were strong.
They rejoiced, Raquel and Vidas,   to have so much
      treasure;
they should be rich   as long as they lived.

10
*The Jews leave the Cid. Martín Antolínez goes back
to Burgos with the Jews*

  Raquel has kissed   the hand of My Cid:
"Ah, Campeador,   in good hour you girded on sword!
You go from Castile   forth among strangers.
Such is your fortune   and great are your gains;

una piel vermeja   morisca e ondrada,
Çid, beso vuestra mano   en don que la yo aya."
—"Plazme," diro el Çid,   "daquí sea mandada.
Si vos la aduxier dallá;   si non, contalda sobre las arcas."
    Raquel e Vidas   las arcas levavan,
con ellos Martín Antolínez   por Burgos entrava.
Con todo recabdo   llegan a la posada;
en medio del palaçio   tendieron un almoçalla,
sobrella una sávana   de rançal e muy blanca.
A tod el primer colpe   trezientos marcos de plata,
notólos don Martino,   sin peso los tomava;
los otros trezientos   en oro gelos pagavan.
Çinco escuderos tiene don Martino,   a todos los cargava.
Quando esto ovo fecho,   odredes lo que fablava:
"ya don Raquel e Vidas,   en vuestras manos son las arcas;
yo, que esto vos gané,   bien mereçía calças."

11

El Cid, provisto de dinero por Martín Antolínez, se dispone a marchar

    Entre Raquel e Vidas   aparte ixieron amos:
"démosle buen don,   ca él no' lo ha buscado.
Martín Antolínez,   un Burgalés contado,
vos lo mereçedes,   darvos queremos buen dado,
de que fagades calças   e rica piel e buen manto.
Dámosvo en don   a vos treínta marcos;
mereçer no'lo hedes,   ca esto es aguisado:
atorgar nos hedes   esto que avemos parado."
Gradeçiólo don Martino   e recibió los marcos;
gradó exir de la posada   e espidiós de amos.
Exido es de Burgos e Arlançón, a passado,
vino pora la tienda   del que en buen ora nasco.
    Reçibiólo el Çid   abiertos amos los braços:
"¡Venides, Martín Antolínez,   el mio fidel vassallo!

50

I kiss your hand,   begging you to bring me
a skin of crimson leather,   Moorish and highly prized."
My Cid said, "Gladly,   from this moment it is ordered.
I will send it to you from there.   If not, count it against
    the coffers."
    Raquel and Vidas   took up the coffers.
With Martín Antolínez   they went back to Burgos;
with all caution   they came to their house.
In the middle of the dwelling   a carpet was spread,
a sheet over it   pure white, of fine cloth.
At the first fling there fell   three hundred marks of silver.
Don Martino counted   and without weighing took them;
the other three hundred   in gold they paid him.
Don Martino has five squires.   He loaded them all.
You will hear what he said   when this was done:
"Raquel and Vidas,   in your hands are the coffers;
I who gained them for you   have well deserved my
    commission."

Martín demands a commission which the Jews grant

11

*The Cid, provided with money by Martín Antolínez,
makes ready to march*

    Raquel and Vidas   walked to one side:
"Let us make him a fine gift   since he found this for us.
Martín Antolínez,   renowned man of Burgos,
we will make you a fine gift.   You have deserved your
    commission;
we will give you enough to make trousers,   a good cloak
    and rich tunic.
We will make you a present   of thirty marks,
as is only proper   and what you have deserved,
since you shall testify   to this that we have agreed."
Don Martino thanked them   and took the money;
he was glad to go from the house   and leave them both.
    He has gone out of Burgos,   passed over the Arlanzón
and come to the tent of him   who in good hour was born.
    The Cid received him   with his arms open:
"Welcome, Martín Antolínez,   my faithful vassal!

51

Aun vea el día   que de mi ayades algo!"
—"Vengo, Campeador,   con todo buen recabdo:
vos seysçientos   e yo treynta he gañados.
Mandad coger la tienda   e vayamos privado,
en San Pero de Cardeña   i nos cante el gallo;
veremos vuestra mugier,   membrada fija dalgo.
Mesuraremos la posada   e quitaremos el reynado;
mucho es huebos,   ca çerca viene el plazdo."

12

El Cid monta a caballo y se despide de la catedral de
Burgos, prometiendo mil misas al altar de la Virgen

Estas palabras dichas,   la tienda es cogida.
Mio Çid e sus conpañas,   cavalgan tan aína.
La cara del cavallo   tornó a Santa María,
alçó su mano diestra,   la cara se santigua:
"A tí lo gradesco, Dios,   que çielo e tierra guías;
válanme tus vertudes,   gloriosa santa María!
D'aquí quito Castiella,   pues que el rey he en ira;
non sé si entraré y más   en todos los mios días.
Vuestra vertud me vala,   Gloriosa, en mi exida
e me ayude e me acorra   de noch e de día!
Si vos assí lo fiziéredes   e la ventura me fore complida
mando al vuestro altar   buenas donas e ricas;
esto he yo en debdo   que faga i cantar mill missas."

13

Martín Antolínez se vuelve a la cuidad

Spidiós el caboso   de cuer e de veluntad.
Sueltan las reindas—e pienssan de aguijar.
Dixo Martín Antolínez,   el Burgalés leal:
"veré a la mugier   a todo mio solaz,
castigar los he   commo abrán a far.

52

May I see the day   when you will receive something from
     me!"
"I come, Campeador,   with all care and prudence;
you have gained six hundred   and I thirty.
Bid them strike the tent   and let us leave at once;
in San Pedro of Cardeña   let the cock sing to us.
We shall see your wife   of gentle birth and good report,
rest for a little   then quit the kingdom,
as we must, for the term   of the sentence draws near."

12

*The Cid mounts and bids farewell to the Cathedral of
Burgos, promising a thousand Masses at the altar of the
Virgin*

These words said,   the tent is struck.
My Cid and his followers   mount at once.
He turned his horse   toward Santa María,
raised his right hand,   crossed himself:
"Praise be to Thee, O God,   Who guide earth and sky;
thy grace be with me,   glorious Santa María!
Now I depart Castile   since the King's wrath pursues me,
and know not if I shall return   in all my days.
Thy favor be with me,   thou Glorious, on my going;
aid and sustain me   by night and by day;
Grant thou as I beg,   and if fortune bear with me,
fine gifts on thy altar,   rich offerings I shall lay,
and a thousand Masses   have sung in thy chantry."

*Contradiction in character
makes him more human, unassuming
not completely sure of himself*

13
Martín Antolínez returns to the city

   He the excellent one   bade hearty farewell.
They release the reins   and set spur to their horses.
Martín Antolínez,   the loyal man of Burgos,
said, "I shall see my wife,   who is all my solace,
and leave instructions   as to what must be done.

Si el rey me lo quisiere tomar,   a mi non m'incal.
Antes seré convusco   que el sol quiera rayar."

14
El Cid va a Cardeña a despedirse de su familia

  Tornavas don *Martino a Burgos   e mio Çid aguijó*
pora San Pero de Cardeña   quanto pudo a espolón,
con estos cavalleros   quel sirven a so sabor.
  Apriessa cantan los gallos   a quieren crebar albores,
quando llegó a San Pero   el buen Campeador;
el abbat don Sancho,   cristiano del Criador;
rezaba los matines   abuelta de los albores.
Y estava doña Ximena   con çinco dueñas de pro,
rogando a San Pero   e al Criador:
  "Tú que a todos guías,   val a mio Çid el Campeador."

15
Los monjes de Cardeña reciben al Cid. Jimena y sus hijas
llegan ante el desterrado

  Llamavan a la puerta,   i sopieron el mandado;
Dios, qué alegre fo   el abbat don Sancho!
Con lumbres e con candelas   al corral dieron salto,
con tan grant gozo reçiben   al que en buen ora nasco.
"Gradéscolo a Dios, mio Çid,"   dixo el abbat don Sancho;
"pues que aquí vos veo,   prendet de mí ospedado."
Dixo el Çid,   el que en buen ora nasco:
"graçias don abbat,   e so vuestro pagado;
yo adobaré conducho   pora mí e pora mios vasallos:
mas por que me vo de tierra,   dovos çinquaenta marcos,
si yo algún día visquiero,   seervos han doblados.

I care not if the King   should seize my possessions.
I shall be with you   before the sun shines."

14
The Cid goes to Cardeña to say good-by to his family

Don Martino turned toward Burgos,   and My Cid
        spurred on
with all speed   toward San Pedro of Cardeña
with those knights   who do his pleasure.
    The cocks quicken their song   and dawn is breaking
when the good Campeador   rode up to San Pedro;
the abbot Don Sancho,   a servant of the Lord,
was saying his matins   in the gray morning.
And there Doña Jimena   with five gentlewomen
was praying to Saint Peter   and to the Creator praying:
"Thou Who guidest all creatures,   bless My Cid the
        Campeador."

15
*The monks of Cardeña receive the Cid. Jimena and her
daughters come to greet the outcast*

They called at the door,   the message was taken;
the abbot Don Sancho,   God, how great was his rejoicing!
There was running in the courtyard   with candles and
        torches
to receive with gladness   him who in good hour was born.
"Thanks be to God, My Cid,"   said the abbot Don Sancho,
"that I see you before me   to share my dwelling."
My Cid answered,   who in good hour was born:
"My thanks, abbot,   I am well pleased with you;
I would have a meal made ready   for myself and my
        followers,
and since I must leave this land   I give you fifty marks;
if I live,   you shall have two for each of these.

Non quiero far en el monesterio   un dinero de daño;
evades aquí pora doña Ximena   dovos çient marcos;
a ella e a sus fijas e a sus dueñas   sirvádeslas est año.
Dues fijas dexo niñas   e prendetlas en los braços;
aquí vos las acomiendo   a vos, abbat don Sancho;
dellas e de mi mugier   fagades todo recabdo.
Si essa despenssa vos falleçiere   o vos menguare algo,
bien las abastad,   yo assí vos lo mando;
por un marco que despendades   al monesterio daré yo
                                          quatro."
Otorgado gelo avie   el abbat de grado.
    Afevos doña Ximena   con sus fijas do va llegando;
señas dueñas las traen   e adúzenlas en los braços.
Ant el Campeador doña Ximena   fincó los inojos amos.
Llorava de los ojos,   quísol besar las manos:
"Merçed, Canpeador,   en ora buena fostes nado!
Por malos mestureros   de tierra sodes echado."

16
Jimena lamenta el desamparo en que queda la niñez
de sus hijas. El Cid espera llegar a casarlas
honradamente

"Merçed, ya Çid,   barba tan cumplida!
Fem ante vos   yo e vuestras ffijas
iffantes son   e de días chicas,
con aquestas mis dueñas   de quien so yo servida.
Yo lo veo   que estades vos en ida
e nos de vos   partir nos hemos en vida.
Dadnos consejo   por amor de santa María!"
    Enclinó las manos   la barba vellida,
a las sues fijas   en braço las prendía,
llególas al coraçón,   ca mucho las quería.
Llora de los ojos,   tan fuerte mientre sospira:
"Ya doña Ximena,   la mi mugier tan complida,
commo a la mie alma   yo tanto vos quería.
Ya lo veedes   que partir nos emos en vida,
yo iré y vos   fincaredes remanida.
Plega a Dios   e a santa María,

I would not occasion this abbey   a farthing of loss;
take these hundred marks   for Doña Jimena,
wait on her this full year   and on her daughters and ladies.
My two small daughters, clasp them safe in your arms;
they and my wife,   care for them closely.
I commend them to you,   to you, abbot Don Sancho.
If this money runs out   or you need anything,
yet provide for them well;   I shall pay accordingly,
for each mark you spend,   four to the abbey."
The abbot agreed   to all of this gladly.

   Behold where Doña Jimena   is coming with her
         daughters,
each carried and brought   in the arms of a nurse.
And Doña Jimena knelt down   on both knees before him.
She kissed his hands,   weeping from her eyes:
"Grace, Campeador,   who in good hour was born!
Because of evil meddlers   you are sent into exile."

16

Doña Jimena laments the helplessness in which her daughters will be left. The Cid hopes to be able to see them honorably married

   "Grace, Campeador   of the excellent beard!
Here before you   are your daughters and I,
and they in their infancy,   and their days are tender,
with these my ladies   who wait upon me.
I know well   that you pause here merely,
and in this life   must part from us.
In the name of Santa María,   give us counsel!"
   He stretched out his hands,   he of the splendid beard:
his two daughters   in his arms he took,
drew them to his heart   for he loved them dearly.
He weeps from his eyes   and sighs deeply:
"Ah, Doña Jimena,   my perfect wife,
I love you   as I do my own soul.
   You know well   we must part in this life;
I shall go from here   and you will stay behind.
May it please God   and Santa María

que aun con mis manos   case estas mis fijas,
e quede ventura   y algunos días vida,
e vos, mugier ondrada,   de mí seades servida!"

17

Un centenar de castellanos se juntan en Burgos para irse
    con el Cid

Grand yantar le fazen   al buen Canpeador.
Tañen las campanas   en San Pero a clamor.
Por Castiella   odienda van los pregones,
commo se va de tierra   mio Çid el Canpeador;
unos dexan casas   e otros onores.
En aqués día   a la puent de Arlançon
ciento quinze cavalleros   todos juntados son;
todos demandan   por mio Çid el Campeador;
Martín Antolínez con ellos' cojó.
Vansse pora San Pero   do está el que en buena nació.

18

Los cien castellanos llegan a Cardeña y se hacen vasallos
del Cid. Este dispone seguir su camino por la mañana.
Los matines en Cardeña. Oración de Jimena. Adiós del
Cid a su familia. Ultimos encargos al Abad de Cardeña.
El Cid camina al destierro; hace noche después de pasar
el Duero

Quando lo sopo   mio Çid el de Bivar,
quel creçe conpaña,   por que más valdrá
apriessa cavalga,   reçebir los sale;
dont a ojo los ovo, tornós a sonrisar;
lléganle todos,   la manol ban besar.
Fabló mio Çid   de toda voluntad:

*but he does not give with his own
hands at first*

one day with my own hands   I may give my daughters in
        marriage,

*The kings
gives
them
first.*

and may good fortune attend me   and few days be left me
that you, my honored wife,   may receive once more my
        homage!"

17

A hundred Castilians gather in Burgos to join the Cid

They laid a great banquet   for the good Campeador.
They clanged and pealed   the bells of San Pedro.
Through all Castile   the cry goes:
"He is leaving the land,   My Cid the Campeador."
Some leave houses   and others honors.
On that day   at the bridge on the Arlanzón
a hundred fifteen horsemen   are come together,
all of them asking   for My Cid the Campeador.
Martín Antolínez   rode up where they were.
They set off for San Pedro   to him who was born in good
        hour.

18

*The hundred Castilians arrive at Cardeña and make them-
selves vassals of the Cid. He makes ready to continue his
march in the morning. The matins at Cardeña. Jimena's
prayer. The Cid's farewell to his family. His last instruc-
tions to the abbot of Cardeña. The Cid sets out on his exile;
night falls after he has crossed the Duero*

When My Cid of Bivar   heard the news
that his band was growing,   that his strength was
        increasing,
he mounted in haste   and rode out to receive them;
he broke into smiles   as soon as he saw them.
Each of them came up   and kissed his hand.
My Cid spoke   with all his heart:

"yo ruego a Dios   e al Padre spiritual,
vos, que por mí dexades   casas e heredades,
enantes que yo muera,   algún bien vos pueda far:
lo que perdedes   doblado vos lo cobrar."
Plogo a mio Çid,   por que creçió en la yantar,
plogo a los otros omnes todos   quantos con él están.

   Los seys días de plazdo   passados los an,
tres an por troçir,   sepades que non más.
Mandó el rey   a mio Çid aguardar,
que, si después del plazo   en su tierral pudies tomar,
por oro nin por plata   non podríe escapar.
El día es exido,   la noch querié entrar,
a sos cavalleros   mandólos juntar:
"Oid, varones,   non vos caya en pesar;
poco aver trayo,   dar vos quiero vuestra part.
Seed membrados   commo lo devedes far:
a la mañana,   quando los gallos cantarán,
nos vos tardedes,   mandedes ensellar;
en San Pero a matines   tandrá el buen abbat,
la missa nos dirá,   de santa Trinidad;
la missa dicha,   penssemos de cavalgar,
ca el plazo viene açerca,   mucho avemos de andar."
Quomo lo mandó mio Çid,   assí lo an todos ha far.
Passando va la noch,   viniendo la man;
a los mediados gallos   pienssan de ensellar.

   Tañen a matines   a una priessa tan grande;
mio Çid e su mugier   a la eglesia vane.
Echós doña Ximena   en los grados delantel altare,
rogando al Criador   quanto ella mejor sabe,
que a mio Çid el Campeador   que Dios le curiás de male:
"Ya señor glorioso,   padre que en çielo estase,
fezist çielo e tierra,   el terçero el mare;
fezist estrellas e luna   y el sol pora escalentare;
prisist encarnaçión   en santa María madre,
en Belleem apareçist   commo fo tu veluntade;
pastores te glorifficaron,   ouieron te a laudare,
tres reyes de Arabia   te vinieron adorare.
Melchoir   e Caspar e Baltasare,
oro e tus e mirra   te offrecieron de veluntade;
60

"I pray to God   our Father in heaven
that you who for me have left   home and possessions,
before I die,   may receive from me some gain;
that all you lose now   twofold may be returned."
My Cid rejoiced   that his company had grown.
All rejoiced   who were there with him.
    Six days of the sentence   already have run;
three remain   and afterwards none.
The King has sent   to keep watch on My Cid,
so that if when the time was up   they could take him in
        the land,
not for silver nor gold   might he escape.
The day went   and night came in.
He called together   all his horsemen:
"Hear me, my knights,   let no heart be heavy.
I own little;   I would give you your portion.
Listen and learn   what must be done:
In the morning   when the cocks sing,
have the horses saddled   without delay;
in San Pedro   the good abbot will ring matins
and sing us the Mass   of the Holy Trinity.
We shall set out   when Mass has been sung,
for time runs out   and we have far to go."
All will do   as the Cid has commanded.
The night passes   and morning comes;
at the second cock   they saddle their horses.
    With all dispatch   the matins are rung;
My Cid and his wife   into the church have gone.
On the steps before the altar   Doña Jimena knelt down
praying to the Creator   with all her heart
that God might keep from harm   My Cid the Campeador:
"Glorious Lord, Father   Who art in heaven,
Who made heaven and earth   and the sea the third day,
Who made stars and moon   and the sun to warm us,
Who became incarnate   in Santa María Thy mother,
Who, as was Thy will,   appeared in Bethlehem;
shepherds praised Thee   and glorified Thee.
Three kings of Arabia   came to adore Thee,
Melchior   and Gaspar and Balthasar,
gold and frankincense and myrrh   with glad hearts they
        offered Thee;

61

salvest a Jonás,   quando cayó en la mare
salvest a Daniel   con sus leones en la mala cárçel,
salvest dentro en Roma   a señor san Sebastián,
salvest a santa Susanna   del falso criminal;
por tierra andidiste treynta y dos años,   Señor spirital,
mostrando los miraclos,   por en avemos qué fablar:
del agua fezist vino   e de la piedra pan,
resuçitest a Lázaro,   ca fo tu voluntad;
a los judios te dexeste prender;   do dizen monte Calvarie
pusiéronte en cruz   por nombre en Golgotá;
dos ladrones contigo,   estos de señas partes,
el uno es en paradiso,   ca el otro non entró allá;
estando en la cruz,   vertud fezist muy grant:
Longinos era çiego,   que nunqua vido alguandre,
diot con la lança en el costado,   dont yxió la sangre,
corrió por el astil ayuso,   las manos se ovo de untar,
alçolas arriva,   llególas a la faz,
abrió sos ojos,   cató a todas partes,
en ti crovo al ora,   por end es salvo de mal;
en el monumento   oviste a resuçitar,
fust a los infiernos,   commo fo tu voluntad;
crebanteste las puertas,   e saqueste los santos padres.
Tú eres rey de los reyes,   e de todel mundo padre,
a ti adoro e credo   de toda voluntad,
e ruego a san Peydro   que me ayude a rogar
por mio Çid el Campeador,   que Dios le curie de mal.
Quando oy nos partimos,   en vida nos faz juntar."
    La oración fecha,   la missa acabada la an,
salieron de la eglesia,   ya quieren cavalgar.
El Çid a doña Ximena   ívala abraçar;
doña Ximena al Çid   la manol va besar,
llorando de los ojos,   que non sabe qué se far.
E él a las niñas   tornólas a catar:
"a Dios vos acomiendo   e al Padre spirital;
agora nos partimos,   Dios sabe el ajuntar."
Llorando de los ojos,   que non vidiestes atal,
assis parten unos d'otros   commo la uña de la carne.
    Myo Çid con los sos vassallos   penssó de cavalgar,

Thou didst save Jonas   when he fell into the sea,
Thou savedst Daniel   from the evil den of lions,
Thou in Rome savedst   lord Saint Sebastian,
Thou didst save Saint Susannah   from the lying criminal;
Father in heaven, Thou didst walk   thirty-two years on
      earth
showing miracles   of which we must tell:
Thou didst from water make wine   and bread from stones,
Thou didst raise Lazarus   as was Thy intention,
Thou didst let the Jews take Thee;   on Mount Calvary
where it is called Golgotha   on a cross they hanged Thee
and, one on each side,   two thieves with Thee.
One is in paradise,   the other did not go there.
Much grace didst Thou work   on the cross hanging:
Longinus was blind   and had never seen anything;
he thrust his spear in Thy side,   from which blood came,
which down the shaft ran   and anointed his hands,
which covered his arm   and to his face came;
he opened his eyes   and looked in all directions
and believed in Thee then,   from whence came his
      salvation.
Thou from the sepulchre   didst rise again,
descended into hell,   as was Thy will,
burst open the doors   and saved the holy fathers.
Thou art King of Kings   and of the whole world Father.
I adore Thee and believe   with all my will,
and I pray to Saint Peter   that he may aid my prayer
that God may keep from harm   My Cid the Campeador,
Though we part now,   in this life may we come together."
    When the prayer was ended,   Mass was said.
They went out from the church   and made ready to ride.
My Cid went   and embraced Doña Jimena;
Doña Jimena   kissed My Cid's hand,
weeping;   she could not hold back the tears.
He turned and looked   upon his daughters.
"To God I commend you   and to the heavenly Father;
now we part./God knows   when we shall come together."
Weeping from his eyes,   you have never seen such grief,
thus parted the one from the others   as the nail from the
      Flesh.
    My Cid and his vassals   set off riding,

a todos esperando,   la cabeça tornando va,
A tan grand sabor   fabló Minaya Albar Fáñez:
"Çid, do son vuestros esfuerços?   en buena nasquiestes de
madre;

pensemos de ir nuestra via,   esto sea de vagar.
Aun todos estos duelos   en gozo se tornarán;
Dios que nos dió las almas,   consejo nos dará."

    Al abbat don Sancho   tornan de castigar,
commo sirva a doña Xiemena   e a las fijas que ha,
e a todas sus dueñas   que con ellas están;
bien sepa el abbat   que buen galardón dello prendrá.
Tornado es don Sancho,   e fabló Albar Fáñez:
"Si viéredes yentes venir   por connusco ir, abbat,
dezildes que prendan el rastro   e pienssen de andar,
ca en yermo o en poblado   poder nos han alcançar."

    Soltaron las riendas,   pienssan de andar;
çerca vien el plazdo   por el reyno quitar.
Vino mio Çid yazer   a Spinaz de Can;
grandes yentes sele acojen   essa noch de todas partes.
Otro día mañana   pienssa de cavalgar.
Ixiendos va de tierra   el Campeador leal,
de siniestro Sant Estevan,   una buena çipdad,
passó por Alcobiella   que de Castiella fin es ya;
la calçada de Quinea   ívala traspassar,
sobre Navas de Palos   el Duero va passar,
a la Figueruela   mio Çid iva posar.
Vánssele acogiendo   yentes de todas partes.

19
Ultima noche que el Cid duerme en Castilla.
Un ángel consuela al desterrado

    I se echava mio Çid   después que fo de noch,
un sueñol priso dulçe,   tan bien se adurmió.
El ángel Gabriel   a él vino en visión:
"Cavalgad, Çid,   el buen Campeador,
ca nunqua en tan buen punto   cavalgó varón;
mientra que visquiéredes   bien se fará lo to."
Quando despertó el Çid,   la cara se santigó.

he looking behind him   delaying them all.
Minaya Alvar Fáñez   spoke with great wisdom:
"Cid, who in good hour were born   of mother, where is
    your strength?
We must be on our way;   this is idleness.
All these sorrows   will yet turn to joy:
God who gave us souls   will give us guidance."
    They turned and bade   the abbot Don Sancho
to serve Doña Jimena   and her two daughters
and all the ladies   who were with them there;
the abbot knew well   that he would be recompensed.
Don Sancho has turned   and Alvar Fáñez spoke:
"Abbot, if you meet with any   who would come with us,
tell them to take up our trail   and ride after us,
so that in wasteland or town   they may overtake us."
    They slackened the reins   and rode forward;
the time draws near   when they must quit the kingdom.
The Cid pitched camp   by Espinazo de Can;
that night from all hands   men flocked to go with him.
Next day in the morning   they rode on again.
He is leaving the land,   the loyal Campeador.
By the left of San Esteban,   a goodly city;
he passed through Alcubilla   on the edge of Castile;
to the path of Quinea   they came, and passed over;
at Navapalos   crossed over the Duero;
at the Figueruela   My Cid paused for the night.
Still from all hands   men gathered to go with him.

19
The last night in which the Cid sleeps in Castile.
An angel consoles the exile

There lay down, My Cid,   after night had come;
he slept so deeply   a dream seized him sweetly.
The angel Gabriel   came to him in a vision:
"Ride forward, Cid,   good Campeador,
for no man ever rode forth   at so propitious a moment;
as long as you live   that which is yours will prosper."
He crossed himself, My Cid,   when he awoke.

20
El Cid acampa en la frontera de Castilla

Sinava la cara,   a Dios se fo acomendar,
mucho era pagado   del sueño que soñado a.
Otro día mañana   pienssan de cavalgar;
es día a de plazo,   sepades que non más.
A lā sierra de Miedes   ellos ivan posar,
de diestro Atiença las torres   que moros las han.

21
Recuento de las gentes del Cid

Aun era de día,   non puesto el sol,
mandó veer sus yentes   mio Çid el Campeador:
sin las peonadas   e omnes valientes que son,
notó trezientas lanças   que todas tienen pendones.

22
El Cid entra en el reino moro de Toledo,
tributario del rey Alfonso

"Temprano dat çevada,   sí el Criador vos salue!
El qui quisiere comer;   e qui no, cavalgue.
Passaremos la sierra   que fiera es e grand,
la tierra del rey Alfonso   está noch la podemos quitar.
Después qui nos buscare   fallar nos podrá."
De noch passan la sierra,   venida es la man,
e por la loma ayuso   pienssan de andar.
En medio d'una montaña   maravillosa e grand
fizo mio Çid posar   e çevada dar.

20

The Cid camps on the Castilian frontier

He made the sign of the cross,   and commended himself
   to God.
He was deeply glad   because of the dream he had
   dreamed.
Next day in the morning   they ride onward;
the last day of their time has come.   Know, after that there
   is no more.
By the mountains of Miedes   they were going to halt,
on the right the towers of Atienza,   which the Moors hold.

21

The tally of the Cid's followers

It was still day,   the sun not down,
When My Cid the Campeador   assembled his men.
Not counting the foot soldiers,   and brave men they were,
he counted three hundred lances,   each with its pennon.

22

The Cid enters the Moorish kingdom of Toledo,
a tributary of King Alfonso's

"Let the horses be fed early   and may the Creator keep
   you!
Let those who desire to, eat,   and those who do not,
   ride on.
We shall cross over that range,   high and forbidding;
this same night   we shall leave Alfonso's kingdom.
He who comes looking for us   may find us then."
They crossed the range in the night,   and morning came,
and on the downward ridge   they began riding.
Halfway down a mountain   which was marvelous and
   high,
My Cid halted   and fed the horses their barley.

Díxoles a todos   commo querié trasnochar;
vassallos tan buenos   por coraçón lo an,
mandado de so señor   todo lo han a far.
Ante que anochesca   pienssan de cavalgar;
por tal lo faze mio Çid   que no lo ventasse nadi.
Andidieron de noch,   que vagar non se dan.
O dizen Castejón,   el que es sobre Fenares,
mio Çid se echó en çelada   con aquellos que él trae.

23
Plan de campaña. Castejón cae en poder del Cid por
sorpresa. Algara contra Alcalá

Toda la noche   yace Mio Çid en çelada,
commo los consejava   Albar Fáñez Minaya:
"Ya Çid,   en buen ora çinxiestes espada!
Vos con çiento   de aquesta nuestra conpaña,
pues que a Castejón   sacaremos a çelada,
en él fincaredes   teniendo a la çaga;
a mí dedes dozientos   pora ir en algara;
con Dios e vuestra auze   feremos grand ganançia."
Dixo el Campeador: "bien fablastes, Minaya;
vos con los dozientos   id vos en algara;
allá vaya Albar Albarez   a Albar Salvadórez sin falla,
e Galín Garciaz,   una fardida lança,
cavalleros buenos   que acompañen a Minaya.
Aosadas corred,   que por miedo non dexedes nada.
Fita ayuso   e por Guadalfajara,
fata Alcalá   lleguen las algaras,
e bien acojan   todas las ganançias,
que por miedo de los moros   non dexen nada.
E yo con los çiento   aquí fincaré en la çaga,
terné yo Castejón   don abremos grand enpara.
Si cuenta vos fore   alguna al algara,
fazedme mandado   muy privado a la çaga;
D'aqueste acorro   fablará toda España."
Nombrados son   los que irán en el algara,
e los que con mio Çid   fincarán en la çaga.
Ya crieban los albores   e vinie la mañana,

He told them all that he wished   to ride on all that night;
all were stout hearted   and good liege men
who for their lord   would do anything.
Before night fell   they set off again;
My Cid pressed on   so that none might discover them.
They rode forward by night   without resting.
Where it is called Castejón,   on the bank of the Henares,
My Cid lay in ambush   with those who were with him.

23

The plan of the campaign. Castejón falls into the
Cid's power by surprise. The vanguard goes against Alcalá

All that night   My Cid lies in ambush.
Alvar Fáñez Minaya   thus advised them:
"Ah, Cid, in good hour   you girded on sword!
With one hundred   of our company,
after we have surprised   and taken Castejón,
do you remain there   and be our fixed base.
Give me two hundred   to go on a raid;
with God and good fortune   we shall take rich spoils."
The Campeador said,   "You speak well, Minaya.
You with two hundred   ride out raiding;
take Alvar Alvarez   and Alvar Salvadórez
and Galindo García,   who is a hardy lance,
all of them brave knights;   let them go with Minaya.
Ride forward boldly,   let no fear detain you.
Ride down along the Fita   and along the Guadalajara,
take your raiders   as far as Alcalá
and let them carry off   all that is of value,
leaving nothing behind   out of fear of the Moors.
I with the hundred   shall stay here behind
and hold Castejón,   where we will be secure.
If on your raiding foray   any trouble befalls you,
send word at once   to me here behind;
all Spain will talk   of the aid I shall bring."
   They have been named   who will ride out on the raid,
and they who will remain   with My Cid in the fixed base.
The dawn goes gray   and the morning comes.

ixie el sol,   Dios, qué fermoso apuntava!
En Castejón   todos se levantavan,
abren las puertas,   de fuera salto davan,
por ver sus lavores   e todas sus heredanças.
Todos son exidos,   las puertas abiertas an dexadas
con pocas de gentes   que en Castejón fincaran;
las yentes   de fuera todas son derramadas.
El Campeador   salió de la çelada,
en derredor corríe   a Castejón sin falla.
Moros e moras   avienlos de ganançia,
e essos gañados   quantos en derredor andan.
Mio Çid don Rodrigo   a la puerta adeliñava;
los que la tienen,   quando vidieron la rebata,
ovieron miedo   e fo desenparada.
Mio Çid Ruy Díaz   por las puertas entrava,
en mano trae   desnuda el espada,
quinze moros matava   de los que alcançava.
Gañó a Castejón   e el oro y ela plata,
Sos cavalleros   llegan con la ganançia,
déxanla a mio Çid,   todo esto non preçia' nada.

Afevos los dozientos   e tres en el algara,
e sin dubda corren,   toda la tierra preavan;
fasta Alcalá   llegó la seña de Minaya;
e desí arriba   tórnanse con la ganançia,
Fenares arriba   e por Guadalfajara.
Tanto traen   las grandes ganançias
muchos gañados   de ovejas e de vacas
e de ropas   e de otras riquizas largas.
Derecha viene   la seña de Minaya;
non osa ninguno   dar salto a la çaga.
Con aqueste aver   tornan se essa conpaña;
fellos en Castejón   o el Campeador estava.
El castiello dexó en so poder   el Campeador cavalga
Saliólos reçebir   con esta su mesnada,
los braços abierto   reçibe at Minaya:
"¿Venides, Albar Fáñez,   una fardida lança!
Do yo vos enbiás   bien abría tal esperança.
Esso con esto sea ajuntado,   e de toda la ganançia
dovos la quinta,   si la quisiéredes, Minaya."

the sun came forth.   God, how fair was the dawn!
All began to stir   in Castejón;
they opened the gates   and went out of the town
to see to their tasks   and all their property.
All have gone out   and left the gates open,
few there are   who remain in Castejón;
all who have gone out   are scattered abroad.
The Campeador   came out of hiding;
he rode around Castejón   all the way.
He had seized   the Moors and their women
and those cattle   that were about there.
My Cid Don Rodrigo   rode up to the gate;
those there to defend it,   when they saw the attack,
were taken with fear,   and the gate was unguarded.
My Cid Ruy Díaz   rode in at the gate;
in his hand he carried   a naked sword.
Fifteen Moors he killed   who came in his way,
took Castejón   and its gold and its silver.
His knights arrive   with the spoils:
they give it to My Cid;   all this, to them, is nothing.
    Behold now the two hundred and three   in the raiding
        party;
they ride on without pausing   and plunder all the land.
As far as Alcalá,   went the banner of Minaya,
and from there with the spoils   they return again,
up along the Henares   and along the Guadalajara.
Such great spoils   they bring back with them:
many flocks   of sheep and of cattle,
and clothing   and great quantities of other riches.
Forward comes   the banner of Minaya;
no one dares   attack the band of raiders.
That company returns   with its plunder;
see, they are in Castejón,   where the Campeador was.
Leaving the castle secure,   the Campeador rode out,
rode out to receive them   with his company.
He greeted Minaya   with his arms open:
"Have you returned, Alvar Fáñez,   hardy lance!
Wherever I send you   I may well be hopeful.
Your booty and mine together,   of all we have gained
a fifth is yours   if you will take it, Minaya."

71

24

Minaya no acepta parte alguna en el botín y hace un voto solemne

—*"Mucho vos lo gradesco,   Campeador contado.*
D'aqueste quinto   que me avedes mandado,
pagar se ya delle   Alfonso el Castellano.
Yo vos lo suelto   e avello quitado.
A Dios lo prometo,   a aquel que está en alto:
falta que yo me pague   sobre mío buen cavallo,
lidiando   con moros en el campo,
que enpleye la lança   e al espada meta mano,
e por el cobdo ayuso   la sangre destellando,
ante Roy Díaz   el lidiador contado,
non prendré de vos   quanto un dinero malo.
Pues que por mí ganaredes   quesquier que sea dalgo,
todo lo otro   afelo en vuestra mano."

25

El Cid vende su quinto a los moros. No quiere lidiar con el rey Alfonso

Estas ganançias   allí eran juntadas.
Comidiós mio Çid,   el que en buena çinxo espada,
el rey Alfonso   que llegarién sus compañas,
quel buscaríe mal   con todas sus mesnadas.
Mandó partir   tod aqueste aver sin falla,
sos quiñoneros   que gelos diessen por carta.
Sos cavalleros   i an arribança,
a cada uno dellos   caden çien marcos de plata,
e a los peones   la meatad sin falla;
todo el quinto   a mio Çid fincava.
Aqui non lo puede vender   nin dar en presentaja;
nin cativos nin cativas   non quiso traer en su conpaña.
Fabló con los de Castejón   y envió a Fita y a Guadalfajara
esta quinta   por quanto serié conprada,
aun de lo que diessen   oviessen grand ganançia.

24

*Minaya will take no part of the booty, and makes a
solemn vow*

"I thank you from my heart,   famous Campeador,
for this fifth part   which you offer me;
it would please   Alfonso the Castilian.
I give it up   and return it to you.
I make a vow   to God Who is in heaven:
Until I have satisfied myself   on my good horse
with joining battle   in the field with the Moors,
with handling the lance   and taking up the sword,
with the blood running   to above my elbow,
before Ruy Díaz   the famous warrior,
I shall not take from you   a wretched farthing.
Until by my hand you have won   something truly of value,
behold, I leave everything   in your hands."

25

*The Cid sells his fifth to the Moors. He does not wish
to fight with King Alfonso*

All they had taken   was gathered together.
My Cid, who girded on sword   in a good hour, considered
that King Alfonso   would send forces to follow him
and would seek to work him evil   with all his armies.
He bade them divide   all they had taken;
he bade his partitioners   parcel it out.
There good fortune   befell his knights:
a hundred marks of silver   went to each of them,
and to the foot soldiers   half as much without stint;
all the fifth part   remained to My Cid.
He could not sell it there   nor give it as a present,
nor did he wish to have men or women   as slaves in his
    train.
He spoke with those of Castejón,   he sent to Hita and
    Guadalajara,
to learn how much   they would give him for his fifth;
even with what they gave   their gain would be great.

Asmaron los moros   tres mill marcos de plata.
Plogo a mio Çid   d'aquesta presentaja.
A tercer día   dados foron sin falla.
   Asmó mio Çid   con toda su conpaña
que en el castiello   non i avrie morada,
e que serie retenedor,   más non i avrie agua.
"Moros en paz,   ca escripta es la carta,
buscar nos ie el rey Alfonsso,   con toda sue mesnada.
Quitar quiero Castejón,   oid, escuelas e Minaya!"

26
El Cid marcha a tierras de Zaragoza, dependientes
del rey moro de Valencia

   "Lo que yo dixiero   non lo tengades a mal:
en Castejón   non podriemos fincar;
cerca es el rey Alfonso   e buscar nos verná.
Mas el castiello   non lo quiero hermar;
çiento moros e çiento moras   quiero las i quitar,
por que lo pris dellos   que de mí non digan mal.
Todos sodes pagados   e ninguno por pagar.
Cras a la mañana   pensemos de cavalgar,
con Alfons mio señor   non querría lidiar."
Lo que dixo el Çid   a todos los otros plaz.
Del castiello que prisieron   todos ricos se parten;
los moros e las moras   bendiziéndol están.
   Vansse Fenares arriba   quanto pueden andar,
troçen las Alcarrias   e ivan adelant,
por las Cuevas d'Anquita   ellos passando van,
passaron las aguas,   entraron al campo de Taranz,
por essas tierras ayuso   quanto pueden andar.
Entre Fariza e Çetina   mio Çid iva albergar.
Grandes ganançias priso   por la tierra do va;

74

The Moors offered   three thousand marks of silver,
My Cid was content   with this offering.
On the third day   they paid it all.
  My Cid was of the opinion,   with all his company,
that in the castle   there would not be room for them
and that it might be held,   but there would be no water.
"Let us leave these Moors in peace   for their treaty is
    written;
King Alfonso will seek us out   with all his host.
Hear me, my men and Minaya,   I would quit Castejón!"

26

The Cid proceeds to the lands of Zaragoza, which are
dependencies of the Moorish King of Valencia

  "Let no one take amiss   what I have to say:
We cannot remain   in Castejón;
King Alfonso is near   and will come seeking us.
But as for the castle,   I would not lay it waste:
I wish to set free   a hundred Moors and a hundred
    Moorish women,
that they may speak no evil of me   since I took it from
    them.
You have full share, every one,   and no one is still
    unrewarded.
Tomorrow in the morning   we must ride on;
I do not wish to fight   with Alfonso my lord."
All are contented   with what My Cid spoke.
All went away rich   from the castle they had taken;
the Moors and their women   are giving them their
    blessings.
  They go up the Henares   as far as they can,
passed through Alcarria   and went on from there;
by the Caves of Anguita   they are going,
crossed over the waters   into the Plain of Taranz
and through those lands below there   as far as they extend.
Between Ariza and Cetina   My Cid pitched his tent.
Great spoils he takes   in the lands through which he goes;

75

non lo saben los moros   el ardiment que an.
Otro día moviós   mio Çid el de Bivar,
a passó a Alfama,   la Foz ayuso va,
passó a Bovierca   e a Teca que es adelant,
e sobre Alcoçer   mio Çid iva posar,
en un otero redondo,   fuerte e grand;
açerca corre Salón,   agua nol puedent vedar.
Mio Çid don Rodrigo   Alcoçer cueda ganar.

27
El Cid acampa sobre Alcocer

Bien puebla el otero,   firme prende las posadas,
los unos contra la sierra   e los otros contra la agua.
El buen Campeador   que en buena ora cinxo espada
derredor del otero,   bien cerca del agua,
a todos sos varones   mandó fazer una cárcava,
que de día nin de noch   non les diessen arrebata,
que sopiessen que mio Çid   allí avie fincança.

28
Temor de los moros

Por todas essas tierras   ivan los mandados,
que el Campeador mío Çid   allí avie poblado,
venido es a moros,   exido es de cristianos;
en la su vezindad   non se treven ganar tanto.
Alegrando se va mio Çid   con todos sos vassallos;
el castiello de Alcoçer   en paria va entrando.

the Moors do not know   what their intention is.
My Cid of Bivar   the next day moved on;
beyond Alhama,   beyond La Hoz he rode on,
beyond Bubierca   to Ateca farther on.
Close to Alcocer   My Cid came to camp
on a round hill   that stood high and strong.
The stream Jalón around them,   none could cut off their
        water.
My Cid Don Rodrigo   thinks to take Alcocer.

ALCOCER

27
The Cid encamps close to Alcocer

He mans the hill strongly,   makes strong the encamp-
        ments,
some along the hillside,   some near the water.
The good Campeador,   who in good hour girded on sword,
set all his men   to digging a moat
on all sides of the hill   down near the water,
so that by day or night   they might not be surprised
and that the Moors might know that My Cid   meant to
        remain there.

STRATEGY

28
The Moors' fear

    Through all those lands   the news had gone
that My Cid the Campeador   had built an encampment
        there.
He has gone out from the Christians   and come among
        the Moors;
all about their encampment   none dares work the land.
My Cid and all his vassals   begin to rejoice:
the castle of Alcocer   is beginning to pay tribute.

El Campeador toma a Alcocer mediante un ardid

Los de Alcoçer   a mio Çid yal dan parias
e los de Teca   e los de Terrer la casa;
a los de Calatauth,   sabet, ma'les pesava.
Allí yogo mio Çid   complidas quinze sedmanas.
    Quando vido mio Çid   que Alcoçer non se le dava,
elle fizo un art   e non lo detardava:
dexa una tienda fita   e las otras levava,
cojó' Salón ayuso,   la su seña alçada,
las lorigas vestidas   e çintas las espadas,
a guisa de menbrado,   por sacarlos a çelada.
Vidienlo los de Alcoçer,   Dios, cómmo se alabavan!
"Fallido ha a mio Çid   el pan e la çevada.
Las otras abés lieva,   una tienda a dexada.
De guisa va mio Çid   commo si escapasse de arrancada:
demos salto a él   e feremos grant ganançia,
antes quel prendan   los de Terrer la casa,
ca si ellos le prenden,   non nos darán dent nada;
la paria qu'él a presa   tornar nos la ha doblada."
Salieron de Alcoçer   a una priessa much estraña.
Mio Çid, quando los vio fuera,   cogiós commo de arran-
    Cojós Salón ayuso con los sos abuelta anda.   cada;
Dizen los de Alcoçer: "ya se nos va la ganançia!"
Los grandes e los chicos   fuera salto davan,
al sabor del prender   de lo al non pienssan nada,
abiertas dexan las puertas   que ninguno non las guarda.
El buen Campeador   la su cara tornava,
vió que entrellos y el castiello   mucho avié grant plaça;
mandó tornar la seña,   a priessa espoloneavan.
"¡Firidlos, cavalleros,   todos sines dubdança;
con la merçed del Criador   nuestra es la ganancia!"
Bueltos son con ellos   por medio de la llaña.
Dios, qué bueno es el gozo   por aquesta mañana!
Mio Çid e Albar Fáñez   adelant aguijavan;
tienen buenos cavallos,   sabet, a su guisa les andan;

The Campeador takes Alcocer by a stratagem

Those of Alcocer now send tribute to My Cid,
and those of Ateca and of the village of Terrer
and of Calatayud, you may know, though it weighed
    heavy on them.
Fully fifteen weeks My Cid remained there.
    When My Cid saw that Alcocer would not yield to him,
he thought of a stratagem and wasted no time: ←
He left one tent standing, he carried off the rest;
he went down the Jalón with his banner raised,
his men in their armor with their swords girded,
shrewdly to take them by ambush.
God, how those of Alcocer rejoiced to see it! ?
"My Cid has no more provisions of bread and barley.
He can hardly bear off the tents, he has left one standing.
He makes off, My Cid, like one fleeing from a rout.
Let us fall upon him and we shall seize great gains
before he is taken by those of the town of Terrer,
for if those of Terrer take him they will give us nothing.
He shall return twofold the tribute we sent him."
They went out from Alcocer, their haste was unseemly.
When My Cid saw them he rode on as from a rout.
    He went down the stream Jalón with his men.
Those of Alcocer said, "Our plunder is escaping!" ←
They ran out of the town, all, big and little,
thirsting to take him; beyond that, not thinking.
They left the gates open with none to guard them.
The Campeador turned his face round;
he judged the distance between the Moors and their
    castle,
bade them turn with the banner. With all speed they
    rode forward.
"Charge them, knights, let none lag behind.
With the Creator's blessing ours is the gain!"
Halfway across the meadow they came together.
God, their hearts were glad upon that morning!
My Cid and Alvar Fáñez rode on ahead;
they had good horses, you may know, that went at their
    pleasure;

entrellos y el castiello   en essora entravan.
Los vassallos de mio Çid   sin piedad les davan,
en un poco de logar   trezientos moros matan.
Dando grandes alaridos   los que están en la çelada,
dexando van los delant,   poral castiello se tornavan,
las espadas desnudas,   a la puerta se paravan.
Luego llegavan los sos,   ca fecha es el arrancada.
Mio Çid gañó a Alcoçer,   sabet, por esta maña.

30
La seña del Cid ondea sobre Alcocer

Vino Per Vermudoz,   que la seña tiene en mano,
metióla en somo   en todo lo más alto.
Fabló mio Çid Roy Diaz,   el que en buen ora fue nado:
"grado a Dios del çielo   e a todos los sos santos,
ya mejoraremos posadas   a dueños e a cauallos.

31
Clemencia del Cid con los moros

"Oíd a mí Albar Fáñez   e todos los cavalleros!
En este castiello   grand aver avemos preso;
los moros yacen muertos,   de bivos pocos veo.
Los moros e las moras   vender non los podremos,
que los descabeçemos   nada nos ganaremos;
cojámoslos de dentro,   ca el señorío tenemos;
posaremos en sus casas   e dellos nos serviremos."

32
El rey de Valencia quiere recobrar a Alcocer.
Envía un ejército contra el Cid

Mio Çid con esta ganançia   en Alcoçer está;
fizo enbiar por la tienda   que dexara allá.

they rode clear between   the Moors and the castle.
My Cid's vassals   attacked without mercy;
they kill three hundred Moors   in a short time.
Those who are in the ambush,   giving great shouts,
leaving those who are in the van,   charged upon the castle,
halted at the door   bare swords in their hands.
Then their own men rode up,   for they had routed them.
Know, in this manner   My Cid took Alcocer.

30
The Cid's banner floats over Alcocer

Pedro Bermúdez came   with the banner in his hand;
he flew it from the peak,   from the highest point of all.
My Cid spoke, Ruy Díaz,   who in good hour was born:
"Thanks be to God in heaven   and to all His saints,
both horses and riders   now shall have better lodging."

31
The Cid's mercy toward the Moors

"Hear me, Alvar Fáñez   and all my men!
In this castle   we have taken great gains;
the Moors lie dead,   I see few living.
We cannot sell   the Moors and their women;
it would gain us nothing   to cut off their heads.
Let us take them in   for we are the lords here;
we shall live in their houses   and they shall wait upon us."

32
The King of Valencia, wishing to recover Alcocer, sends an army against the Cid

My Cid is in Alcocer   with all he has taken;
he has sent back for the tent   which he left standing.

Mucho pesa a los de Teca   e a los de Terrer non plaze,
e a los de Calatayuth   sabet, pesando va.
Al rey de Valençia   enbiaron con mensaje,
que a uno que dizien   mio Çid Roy Díaz de Bivar
"ayrólo rey Alfonso,   de tierra echado lo ha,
vino posar sobre Alcoçer,   en un tan fuerte logar;
sacólos a çelada,   el castiello ganado a;
si non das consejo,   a Teca e a Terrer perderás,
perderás Calatayuth,   que non puede escapar,
ribera de Salón   todo irá a mal,
assí ferá lo de Siloca,   que es del otra part."
    Quando lo odió rey Tamín   por cuer le pesó mal:
"Tres reyes veo de moros,   derredor de mí estar,
non lo detardedes,   los dos id por allá,
tres mill moros levedes   con armas de lidiar;
con los de la frontera   que vos ayudarán,
prendétmelo a vida,   aduzídmelo delant;
por que se me entró en mi tierra   derecho me avrá a dar."
    Tres mil moros cavalgan   e pienssan de andar.
ellos vinieron a la noch   en Segorve posar.
Otro día mañana   pienssan de cavalgar,
vinieron a la noch   a Çelfa possar.
Por los de la frontera   pienssan de enviar;
non lo detienen,   vienen de todas partes.
Ixieron de Çelfa   la que dizen de Canal,
andidieron todo 'l día,   que vagar non se dan,
vinieron essa noche   en Calatayuth posar.
Por todas essas tierras   los pregones dan;
gentes se ajuntaron   sobejanas de grandes
con aquestos dos reyes   que dizen Fáriz e Galve;
al bueno de mio Çid   en Alcoçer le van çercar.

33
Fáriz y Galve cercan al Cid en Alcocer

    Fincaron las tiendas   e prendend las posadas,
creçen estos virtos,   ca yentes son sobejanas

They are grieved in Ateca,   and those of Terrer are not
     merry,
and those of Calatayud,   you may know, are heavy
     hearted.
They have sent a message   to the King of Valencia,
telling how one who is called   My Cid Ruy Díaz of Bivar,
"whom King Alfonso   has banished from his kingdom,
came to camp near Alcocer   in a strong place,
drew us out into ambush   and has taken the castle.
If you send us no help   you will lose Ateca, lose Terrer,
lose Calatayud,   which cannot escape;
all will go ill   here on the bank of the Jalón
as well as in Jiloca   on the other side."
     When King Tamín heard this   his heart was heavy.
"Three Kings of the Moors   are here with me;
let two without delay   proceed to the place,
take three thousand Moors   armed for battle.
Muster from the frontier   all who will come to your aid,
take him alive   and fetch him before me;
since he entered my lands   I will mete him his due."
     Three thousand Moors   mount and ride off;
they came at night   to camp in Segorbe.
Next day in the morning   they ride on again;
they came at night   to camp at Celfa.
From there to the frontier   they send letters ahead;
none lag behind,   from all sides they gather.
They went out from Celfa,   which is called the Canal.
All that day   without rest they went forward
and came that night   to camp in Calatayud.
Through all those lands   the cry goes
and many have come;   great crowds have assembled.
with those two Kings   called Fáriz and Galve
to surround My good Cid   in Alcocer.

33
Fáriz and Galve surround the Cid in Alcocer

     They set up their tents   and built an encampment;
their host is great already   and still it grows stronger.

Las arrobdas, que los moros sacan,
de día e de noche enbueltos andan en armas;
muchas son las arrobdas e grande es el almofalla.
A los de mio Çid ya les tuellen el agua.
Mesnadas de mio Çid exir querién a batalla,
el que en buen ora nasco firme gelo vedava.
Toviérongela en çerca complidas tres sedmanas.

34
Consejo del Cid con los suyos. Preparativos secretos. El Cid sale a batalla campal contra Fáriz y Galve. Pedro Vermúdez hiere los primeros golpes

A cabo de tres sedmanas, la quarta queríe entrar,
mio Çid con los sos tornós a acordar:
"el agua nos an vedada, exir nos ha el pan,
que nos queramos ir de noch no nos lo consintrán;
grandes son los podres por con ellos lidiar;
dezidme, cavalleros cómo vos plaze de far."
Primero fabló Minaya, un cavallero de prestar:
"de Castiella la gentil exidos sómos acá,
si con moros non lidiáremos, no nos darán del pan.
Bien somos nos seysçientos, algunos ay de más;
en el nombre del Criador, que non passe por al:
vayámoslos ferir en aquel día de cras."
Dixo el Campeador: "a mi guisa fablastes;
ondrástesvos, Minaya, ca aver vos los iedes de far."
Todos los moros e las moras de fuera los manda echar,
que non sopiesse ninguno esta su poridad.
El día e la noche piénssanse de adobar.
Otro día mañana, el sol querie apuntar,
armado es mio Çid con quantos que él ha;
fablava mio Çid, commo odredes contar:
"todos iscamos fuera, que nadi non raste,
sinon dos pedones solos por la puerta guardar;
si nos muriéremos en campo, en castiello nos entrarán,
si vençiéremos la batalla, creçremos en rictad.
E vos, Per Vermudoz, la mí seña tomad;

The sentinels   whom the Moors post
go armed   by day and by night;
many are the sentinels   and great is the host.
They cut off the water   from My Cid's men.
Those who were with My Cid   wished to give battle;
he who was born in good hour   strictly forbade it.
Fully three weeks   the Moors lay camped around them.

34

The Cid's council with his followers. Secret preparations.
The Cid rides out to pitched battle with Fáriz and Galve.
Pedro Bermúdez draws first blood

At the end of three weeks,   as the fourth was beginning,
My Cid called   his men to council.
"They have cut off our water,   our bread will soon be
        gone;
if we tried to leave by night   they would not let us;
if we should give battle   their strength is great;
tell me, my knights,   what you think were best done."
Minaya spoke first,   that worthy knight:
"From sweet Castile   we have come to this place;
unless we fight with the Moors   they will give us no bread.
We are six hundred   and something over;
in the name of the Creator   we can do no other
than attack them   when this next day dawns."
The Campeador said,   "You speak to my liking;
your speech does you honor, Minaya,   as will your action."
All the Moors and their women   he sent from the castle,
so that no one might know   what was planned in secret.
That day and that night   they made themselves ready.
Next day in the morning   as the sun rose
My Cid was armed,   and all his men.
He spoke, My Cid,   you will hear what he said:
"Let us all go out,   let no one remain behind
except two foot soldiers   who will guard the gate.
If we die in the field   they will possess the castle;
if we beat them in battle   we may add to our wealth.
And you, Pedro Bermúdez,   take my banner;

commo sodes muy bueno,   tener la edes sin arth;
mas non aguijedes con ella,   si yo non vos lo mandar."
Al Çid besó la mano,   la seña va tomar.

   Abrieron las puertas,   fuera un salto dan;
viéronlo las arrobdas de los moros,   al almofalla se van
      tornar.
¡Que priessa va en los moros!   e tornáronse a armar;
ante roído de atamores   la tierra querié quebrar;
veriedes armarse moros,   apriessa entrar en az.
De parte de los moros   dos señas ha cabdales,
e los pendones mezclados,   ¿quí los podrié contar?
Las azes de los moros   yas mueven adelant,
por a mio Çid e a los sos   a manos los tomar.

   "Quedas seed, mesnadas,   aquí en este logar,
non derranche ninguno   fata que yo lo mande."
Aquel Per Vermudoz   non lo pudo endurar,
la seña tiene en mano,   conpeçó de espolonar:
"El Criador vos vala,   Çid Campeador leal!
Vo meter la vuestra seña   aquella mayor az;
los que el debdo avedes   veré commo la acorrades."
Dixo el Campeador: "¡non sea, por caridad!"
Repuso Per Vermudoz: "non rastará por al."
Espolonó el cavallo,   e metiol en el mayor az.
Moros le reçiben   por la seña ganar,
danle grandes colpes,   mas nol pueden falssar.
Dixo el Campeador: "¡valelde, por caridad!"

35
Los del Cid acometen para socorrer a Pedro Vermúdez

   Enbraçan los ecudos   delante los coraçones,
abaxan las lanças   abueltas de los pendones,
enclinaron las caras   de suso de los arzones,
ívanlos ferir   de fuertes coraçones.
   A grandes vozes llama   el que en buen ora naçió:
"¡feridlos, cavalleros,   por amor del Criador!
Yo so Roy Díaz, el Çid   de Bivar Campeador!"
   Todos fieren en el az   do está Per Vermudoz.

you are a good vassal,   you will bear it faithfully;
but do not charge with it   until I send you word."
He kisses My Cid's hand   and goes to take the banner.
   They open the gates   and ride out onto the field;
the Moors' sentinels see them   and turn back to their
      army.
What haste among the Moors!   They set to arm;
it seemed the earth would split   with the noise of drums.
You could see the Moors arm   and rush into ranks.
On the side of the Moors   there were two kingly banners,
and as for the colored pennons,   who could number them?
The files of the Moors   are moving forward
to meet, hand to hand,   My Cid and his men.
   "Stay, knights, where you are,   here in this place;
let no one break ranks   till I give the word."
That same Pedro Bermúdez   could not abide it,
took the banner in hand   and spurred forward.
"The Creator bless you,   loyal Cid Campeador!
I shall set your standard   in the main rank there;
those who owe it allegiance,   let us see how they aid it."
The Campeador said,   "No, in charity's name!"
Pedro Bermúdez answered,   "Nothing can keep it here!"
He spurred his horse   into their main rank;
Moors rush upon him   to gain the banner,
give him great blows   but can break no armor.
The Campeador said,   "To his aid, for charity's sake!"

35
Those with My Cid attack to rescue Pedro Bermúdez

   They clasp their shields   over their hearts,
they lower the lances   swathed in their pennons,
they bowed their faces   over their saddletrees,
with strong hearts   they charged to attack them.
   He who in good hour was born   cried with a great
      voice:
"Attack them, knights,   for the love of the Creator!
I am Ruy Díaz, the Cid,   the Campeador of Bivar!"
   All rushed at the rank   where Pedro Bermúdez was.

Trezientas lanças son,   todas tienen pendones;
seños moros mataron,   todos de seños colpes;
a la tornada que fazen   otros tantos muertos son.

36
Destrozan las haces enemigas

   Veriedes tantas lanças   premer e alçar,

tanta adágara   foradar e passar,
tanta loriga   falssar e desmanchar,
tantos pendones blancos   salir vermejos en sangre,
tantos buenos cavallos   sin sos dueños andar.
Los moros llaman Mafómat   e los cristianos santi Yague.

Cadien por el campo   en un poco de logar
moros muertos   mil e trezientos ya.

37
Mención de los principales caballeros cristianos

   ¡Quál lidia bien exorado arzón
mio Çid Ruy Díaz   el buen lidiador;
Minaya Albar Fáñez,   que Çorita mandó,
Martín Antolínez,   el Burgalés de pro,
Muño Gustioz,   que so criado fo,
Martin Muñoz,   el que mandó a Mont Mayor,
Albar Albaroz   e Albar Salvadórez,
Galín Garciaz,   el bueno de Aragón,
Félez Muñoz   so sobrino del Campeador!
Desí adelante,   cuantos que y son,
acorren la seña   e a mio Çid el Campeador.

38
Minaya en peligro. El Cid hiere a Fáriz

They were three hundred spears,   each with its pennon;
all struck blows   and killed as many Moors;
on the second charge   they killed three hundred more.

36
They destroy the enemy ranks

You would have seen so many lances   rise and
    go under,
so many bucklers   pierced and split asunder,
so many coats of mail   break and darken,
so many white pennons   drawn out red with blood,
so many good horses   run without their riders.
The Moors call on Mohammed   and the Christians on
    Saint James
A thousand three hundred   of the Moors fell dead
upon the field   in a little space.

37
Mention of the principal Christian knights

How well they fight   above their gilded saddletrees:
My Cid Ruy Díaz,   the good warrior,
Minaya Alvar Fáñez,   who commanded at Zorita,
Martín Antolínez,   the excellent man of Burgos,
Muño Gustioz,   who was his vassal,
Martín Muñoz,   from Monte Mayor,
Alvar Alvarez   and Alvar Salvadórez,
Galindo García,   excellent knight from Aragón,
Félix Muñoz,   the nephew of the Campeador!
These and the rest,   as many as are there,
support the banner   and My Cid the Campeador.

38
Minaya in danger. The Cid wounds Fáriz

A Minaya Albar Fáñez,   matáronle el cavallo,
bien lo acorren   mesnadas de cristianos.
La lança a quebrada,   al espada metió mano,
maguer de pie   buenos colpes va dando.
Víolo mio Çid   Roy Díaz el Castellano,
acostós a un aguazil   que tenié buen cavallo,
diol tal espadada   con el so diestro braço.
cortól por la çintura,   el medio echó en campo.
A Minaya Albar Fáñez   ival dar el cavallo:
"Cavalgad, Minaya,   vos sodes el mio diestro braço!
Oy en este día   de vos abré grand bando;
firme' son los moros,   aun nos' van del campo,
a menester   que los cometamos de cabo."
Cavalgó Minaya,   el espada en la mano,
por estas fuerças   fuerte mientre lidiando,
a los que alcança   valos delibrando.
Mio Çid Roy Díaz,   el que en buena nasco,
al rey Fáriz   tres colpes le avié dado;
los dos le fallen,   y el únol ha tomado,
por la loriga ayuso   la sangre destellando;
bolvió la rienda   por írsele del campo.
Por aquel colpe   rancado es el fonssado.

39
Galve herido y los moros derrotados

Martín Antolínez   un colpe dio a Galve,
las carbonclas del yelmo   echógelas aparte,
cortól el yelmo,   que llegó a la carne;
sabet, el otro   non gel osó esperar.
Arrancado es   el rey Fáriz e Galve;
¡tan buen día   por la cristiandad,
ca fuyen los moros   della e della part!
los de mio Çid   firiendo en alcaz
el rey Fáriz   en Terrer se fo entrar,
e a Galve   nol cogieron allá;
para Calatayuth   quanto puede se va.

They have killed the horse from under   Minaya Alvar
      Fáñez;
hosts of Christians   charge to his aid.
His lance is broken,   his sword in his hand;
even afoot   he deals great blows.
Ruy Díaz the Castilian,   My Cid, saw him,
rode up to a Moorish lord   who had a good horse,
struck so with his sword,   with his right arm,
he cut him through at the belt;   half the body fell to the
      field.
He took the horse   to Minaya Alvar Fáñez.
"Mount, Minaya,   you who are my right arm!
This very day   I shall have need of you;
the Moors stand firm,   they have not yet fled the field.
We must fall upon them   relentlessly."
Minaya mounted,   his sword in his hand,
fighting bravely   through all that host,
delivering of their souls   all who came near him.
My Cid Ruy Díaz,   who in good hour was born,
has aimed three blows   at King Fáriz;
two of them missed   and the third struck home;
the blood ran down   over the tunic of chain mail;
he turned his horse   to flee from the field.
With that blow   the army was beaten. He does not kill King Fariz

39
Galve wounded and the Moors routed

   Martín Antolínez   struck Galve a blow.
He broke in pieces   the rubies of his helmet;
he split the helmet,   cut into the flesh;
the other dared not wait,   you may know, for another.
King Fáriz and King Galve   and their armies are routed.
It is a great day   for Christendom,
for the Moors flee   on either hand.
My Cid's vassals   ride in pursuit.
King Fáriz   has gone into Terrer;
as for Galve,   they would not receive him.
Toward Calatayud   he rode on at full speed.

El Campeador   íval en alcaz,
fata Calatayuth   duró el segudar.

40
Minaya ve cumplido su voto. Botín de la batalla.
El Cid dispone un presentè para el Rey

A Mynaya Albar Fáñez   bien l'anda el cavallo,
daquestos moros   mató treínta e quatro;
espada tajador,   sangriento trae el braço,
por el cobdo ayuso   la sangre destellando.
Dize Minaya: "agora so pagado,
que a Castiella   irán buenos mandados,
que mio Çid Roy Díaz   lid campal a arrancado."
Tantos moros yazen muertos   que pocos bivos a
  dexados.
Ca en alcaz   sin dubda les foron dando.
Yas tornan   los del que en buen ora nasco.
Andava mio Çid   sobre so buen cavallo,
la cofia fronzida.   ¡Dios, cómmo es bien barbado!
almófar a cuestas,   la espada en la mano.
Vio los sos   commos van allegando:
"Grado a Dios,   aquel que está en alto,
quando tal batalla   avemos arrancado."
Esta albergada   los de mio Çid luego la an robado
de escudos e de armas   e de otros averes largos;
de los moriscos,   quando son llegados,
ffallaron   quinientos e diez cavallos.
Grand alegreya va   entre essos cristianos,
más de quinze de los sos   menos non fallaron.
Traen oro e plata   que non saben recabdo;
refechos son   todos essos cristianos
con aquesta ganançia   que y avién fallado.
A so castiello a los moros   dentro los an tornados,
mandó mio Çid   aun que les diessen algo.

The Campeador   rode in pursuit;
they continued the chase   as far as Calatayud.

40

Minaya's vow is fulfilled. The loot from the battle.
The Cid puts aside a present for the King

The horse ran well   under Minaya Alvar Fáñez;
he killed thirty-four   of those Moors.
His sword cut deep,   his arm was crimson,
the blood ran   above his elbow.
Minaya said,   "My vow is fulfilled,
the news will travel   into Castile
that My Cid Ruy Díaz   has won in pitched battle."
So many Moors lie dead,   few are left living.
Pursuing without pause,   they struck them down.
Already his men turn back,   his who in good hour was
    born.
He rode, My Cid,   on his fine horse,
his skullcap pushed back—   God, how splendid his
    beard!—
his mailed hood on his shoulders,   his sword in his hand.
He saw his men   as they were returning:
"Thanks be to God   Who is in heaven
that we have triumphed   in such a battle."
My Cid's men   have sacked the Moors' encampment,
seized shields and arms   and much else of value;
when they had brought them in,   they found they had
    taken
five hundred and ten   Moorish horses.
There was great joy   among those Christians;
not more than fifteen   of their men were missing.
They took so much gold and silver,   none knew where to
    put it down;
all those Christians   were made rich
with the spoils   that had fallen to them.
They have called back the Moors   who lived in the castle;
My Cid ordered   that even they should be given some-
    thing.

93

Grant a el gozo mio Çid   con todos sos vassallos.
Dio a partir estos dineros   e estos averes largos;
en la su quinta   al Çid caen cient cavallos.
¡Dios, qué bien pagó   a todos sus vassallos,
a los peones   e a los encavalgados!
Bien lo aguisa   el que en buen ora nasco,
quantos él trae   todos son pagados.

   "Oíd, Minaya,   sodes mio diestro braço!
D'aquesta riqueza   que el Criador nos a dado
a vuestra guisa   prended con vuestra mano.
Enbiar vos quiero   a Castiella con mandado
desta batalla   que avemos arrancado;
al rey Alfons   que me a ayrado
quiérole enbiar   en don treínta cavallos,
todos con siellas   e muy bien enfrenados,
señas espadas   de los arzones colgando."
Dixo Minaya Albar Fáñez: "esto faré yo de grado."

41
El Cid cumple su oferta a la catedral de Burgos

   —*"Evades aquí   oro e plata fina,*
una uesa lleña,   que nada nol mingua;
en Santa María de Burgos   quitedes mill missas;
lo que romaneçiere   daldo a mi mugier e a mis fijas,
que rueguen por mí   las noches e los días;
si les yo visquiero,   serán dueñas ricas."

42
Minaya parte para Castilla

   Minaya Albar Fáñez   desto es pagado;
por ir con él   omnes son contados.
Agora davan çevada,   ya la noch avie entrado,
mio Çid Roy Díaz   con los sos se acordando:

My Cid rejoiced greatly,   and all his men.
He bade them divide the money   and those great spoils;
in the Cid's fifth   there were a hundred horses.
God, they were well content,   all his vassals,
both the foot soldiers   and they who rode horses!
He who in good hour was born   deals with them justly;
all who came with him   are well content.
    "Hear me, Minaya,   who are my right arm!
Take from this treasure,   which the Creator has given,
as much as may please you;   take it with your own hand.
I wish to send you   to Castile with the news
of this battle   which we have won.
I would send   a gift of thirty horses
to King Alfonso,   whose anger is turned against me,
each with its saddle   and lavishly bridled,
each with a sword   slung from the saddletree."
Minaya Alvar Fáñez   said, "I will do that gladly."

1st thing the Cid wants to do after the great battle

41

*The Cid pays what he had offered to the Cathedral of
    Burgos*

    "Here I have   gold and fine silver,
a bootful,   and the boot brimming over.
In Santa María of Burgos   pay for a thousand Masses;
give what is left over   to my wife and daughters,
ask them to pray for me   by night and by day;
they will command riches / if I live."

42

Minaya leaves for Castile

    Minaya Alvar Fáñez   is well pleased with this;
the men are named   who will go with him.
Now they give the beasts barley,   already the night has
        come;
My Cid Ruy Díaz   confers with his men.

43
Despedida

"¿Ides vos, Minaya,   a Castiella la gentil?
A nuestros amigos   bien les podedes dezir:
Dios nos valió   e vençiemos la lid.
A la tornada,   si nos falláredes aquí;
si non, do sopiéredes que somos,   indos conseguir.
Por lanças e por espadas   avemos de guarir,
si non, en esta tierra angosta   non podriemos bivir,
e commo yo cuedo   a ir nos avremos d'aquí."

44
El Cid vende Alcocer a los moros

Ya es aguisado,   mañánas ţo Minaya,
e el Campeador   fincó y con su mesnada.
La tierra es angosta   e sobejana de mala.
Todos los días   a mio Çid aguardavan
moros de las fronteras   e unas yentes extrañas;
sanó el rey Fáriz,   con él se consejavan.
Entre los de Teca   e los de Terrer la casa,
e los de Calatayut,   que es más ondrada,
así lo an asmado   e metudo en carta:
vendido les a Alcoçer   por tres mill marcos de plata.

45
Venta de Alcocer (Repetición)

Mio Çid Ruy Díaz   a Alcoçer ha vendido;
qué bien pago   a sos vassallos mismos!
A cavalleros e a peones   fechos los ha ricos,
en todos los sos   non fallariedes un mesquino.
Qui a buen señor sirve,   siempre bive en deliçio.

43
The Farewell

"Are you off, Minaya,   for Castile the noble?
When you meet our friends   you may say to them:
'God gave us aid   and we won the battle.'
When you come back,   if we are not here,
when you learn where we are   follow us there.
Lances and swords   must be our shelter
or else on this meager earth   we cannot live,
and for that same reason   I think we must move on."

44
The Cid sells Alcocer to the Moors

All is made ready;   Minaya will depart in the morning
and the Campeador   stayed there with his men.
The land is poor,   gaunt and barren.
Every day   Moors from the frontier
and some from beyond   kept watch on My Cid;
they plotted with King Fáriz,   whose wounds have healed. ←
Among those of Ateca   and those of the town of Terrer
and those of Calatayud,   which is a place of more note,
as the bargain was driven   and set down on paper,
My Cid sold them Alcocer   for three thousand marks of
      silver.

45
Sales of Alcocer (Repetition)

My Cid Ruy Díaz   has sold Alcocer;
how well he rewarded   each of his vassals!
He has made his knights rich   and his foot soldiers;
in all his company   you would not find a needy man.
Who serves a good lord   lives always in luxury.

Were his lord worthy, god what a good vassal

46

Abandono de Alcocer. Buenos agüeros. El Cid se asienta en el Poyo sobre Monreal

Quando mio Çid   el castiello quiso quitar,
moros e moras   tomáronse a quexar:
"¿vaste, mio Çid;   nuestras oraçiones váyante delante!
Nos pagados fincamos,   señor, de la tu part."
Quando quitó a Alcoçer   mio Çid el de Bivar,
moros e moras   compeçaron de llorar.
Alço su seña,   el Campeador se va,
passó Salón ayuso,   aguijó cabadelant,
al exir de Salón   mucho ovo buenas aves.
Plogo a los de Terrer   e a los de Calatayut más,
pesó a los de Alcoçer,   ca pro les fazié grant.
Aguijó mio Çid,   ivas cabadelant,
y ffincó en un poyo   que es sobre Mont Real;
alto es el poyo,   maravilloso e grant;
non teme guerra,   sabet, a nulla part.
Metió en paria   a Daroca enantes,
desí a Molina,   que es del otra part,
la terçera Teruel,   que estava delant;
en su mano tenié   a Çelfa la del Canal.

47

Minaya llega ante el Rey. Este perdona a Minaya, pero no al Cid

Mio Çid Roy Díaz   de Dios aya su graçia!
Ido es a Castiella   Albar Fáñez Minaya,
treynta cavallos   al rey los enpresentava;
vídolos el rey,   fermoso sonrrisava:
"¿quin los dio estos,   si vos vala Dios, Minaya!"
—"Mio Çid Roy Díaz,   que en buen ora cinxo espada.
Pues quel vos ayrastes,   Alcoçer gañó por maña;
al rey de Valençia   dello el mensaje llegava,

46

*They abandon Alcocer. Good omens. The Cid encamps on
the stone ledge at El Poyo near Monreal*

When My Cid came   to leave the castle,
the Moors and their women   fell to lamenting.
"Are you leaving us, My Cid?   Our prayers go before you,
We are well content, sire,   with what you have done."
When My Cid of Bivar   left Alcocer,
the Moors and their women   fell to weeping.
He raised the banner,   the Campeador departed,
rode down the Jalón,   spurred forward.
As they left the Jalón   there were many birds of good
    omen.
The departure pleased those of Terrer   and still more
    those of Calatayud;
it grieved those of Alcocer,   for he had done much for
    them.
My Cid spurred his horse   and rode on
and halted on a stone ledge   at El Poyo near Monreal;
high is that ledge   great and wonderful;
it fears no attack,   you may know, from any side.
From Daroca onwards   he forced them to pay tribute
as far as Molina,   on the other side,
and a third town, Teruel,   which is farther on;
he brought under his hand   Celfa of the Canal.

47

*Minaya arrives before the King. The King pardons Minaya,
but not the Cid*

My Cid Ruy Díaz,   God give him grace!
Alvar Fáñez Minaya   has gone to Castile.
Thirty horses   he gave to the King;
the King smiled with pleasure   when he saw them.
"Who gave you these,   as God may save you, Minaya?"
"My Cid Ruy Díaz,   who in good hour girded on sword.
When you had banished him,   he took Alcocer by a ruse;
the King of Valencia   sent a message

mandólo y çercar,   e tolléronle el agua.
Mio Çid salió del castiello,   en campo lidiava,
venció dos reyes de moros   en aquesta batalla,
sobejana es,   señor, la sue ganançia.
A vos, rey ondrado,   enbía esta presentaja;
bésavos los piedes   e las manos amas
quel ayades merçed,   si el Criador vos vala."
Dixo el rey: "mucho es mañana.
omne ayrado,   que de señor non ha graçia,
por acogello   a cabo de tres sedmanas.
Mas después que de moros fo,   prendo esta presentaja:
aun me plaze de mio Çid   que hizo tal ganancia.
Sobresto todo,   a vos quito Minaya,
honores e tierras   avellas condonadas,
id e venit,   d'aquí vos do mi graçia;
mas del Çid Campeador,   yo non vos digo nada.

48
El rey permite a los castellanos irse con el Cid

Sobre aquesto todo,   dezir vos quiero, Albar Fáñez:
de todo mio reyno   los que lo quisieren far,
buenos e valientes   pora mio Çid huyar,
suéltoles los cuerpos ·   e quítoles las heredades."
Besóle las manos   Minaya Albar Fáñez:
"Grado e graçias, rey,   commo a señor natural;
esto feches agora,   al feredes adelant;
con Dios nós guisaremos   commo vós lo fagades."
Dixo el rey: "Minaya, . . . esso sea de vagar.
Id por Castiella   e déxenvos andar,
si'nulla dubda   id a mio Çid buscar."

49
Correrías del Cid desde el Poyo. Minaya, con doscientos castellanos, se reúne al Cid

bidding them surround him,   and they cut off his water.
My Cid went out of the castle   and fought in the field
and overcame two Kings of the Moors   in that battle.
Enormous, sire,   are the spoils he has taken.
He sends this gift   to you, honored King;
he kisses your feet   and both your hands
and begs mercy of you   in the name of the Creator."
The King said,   "It is early in the day   only been
to receive into one's favor   at the end of three weeks   3 weeks
one who was banished   having lost his lord's love.
But I shall take this gift   since it comes from the Moors;
I am pleased that the Cid   has taken such spoils.
Above all,   I forgive you, Minaya.
I return to you freely   your lands and honors.
Come and go   henceforth in my favor;
but of the Cid Campeador   I will say nothing.

48

The King allows the Castilians to go with the Cid

   "And furthermore, Alvar Fáñez,   concerning this,
in all my kingdom   those good and valiant
who wish to go   to aid My Cid,
I shall not forbid them   nor seize their possessions."
Minaya Alvar Fáñez   kissed his hands.
"Thanks, thanks, my King   and natural lord; [?]
you concede this now,   later you will grant more;
with God's aid we shall do   such things as will persuade
      you."
The King said, "Minaya,   enough has been said.
Go through Castile   unmolested,
return at your liberty   to My Cid."

49

*The Cid's raids from El Poyo. Minaya, with two hundred
Castilians, returns to the Cid*

Quiérovos dezir   del que en buena çinxo espada:
aquel poyo   en él priso posada;
mientra que sea el pueblo de moros   e de la yente cristiana,
el Poyo de mio Çid   asil dirán por carta.
Estando allí   mucha tierra preava,
el val de río Martín   todo lo metió en paria.
A Saragoça   sus nuevas legavan,
non plaze a los moros,   firme mientre les pesava.
Allí sovo mio Çid   conplidas quinze sedmanas;
quando vío el caboso   que se tardava Minaya,
con todas sus yentes   fizo una trasnochada;
dexó el Poyo,   todo lo desenparava,
allén de Teruel   don Rodrigo passava,
en el pinar de Tévar   Roy Díaz posava;
todas essas tierras   todas las preava,
a Saragoça   metuda lâ en paria.
   Quando esto fecho ovo,   a cabo de tres sedmanas
de Castiella   venido es Minaya,
dozientos con él,   que todos çiñen espadas;
non son en cuenta,   sabet, las peonadas.
Quando vido mio Çid   asomar a Minaya,
el cavallo corriendo,   valo abraçar sin falla,
besóle la boca   e los ojos de la cara.
Todo gelo dize,   que nol encubre nada.
El Campeador   fermoso sonrrisava:
"grado a Dios   e a las vertudes santas;
mientra vos visquiéredes,   bien me irá a mí, Minaya!"

50
Alegría de los desterrados al recibir noticias de Castilla

   ¡Dios, cómmo fo alegre   todo aquel fonssado,
que Minaya Alvar Fáñez   assi era llegado,
diziéndoles saludes   de primos e de hermanos,
e de sus compañas,   aquellas que avien dexado!

I would tell you of him   who in good hour girded on
    sword:
By the stone ledge of El Poyo   he set up his camp;
as long as there are Moors   and Christian people
it will be called: The Chair of My Cid.
While he was there   he pillaged much of the country.
All the Martín valley   he forced to pay tribute.
The news of him went   to Zaragoza
and did not please the Moors   but weighed heavy on them.
Fully fifteen weeks   My Cid stayed there.
When it was clear to My Cid   that Minaya delayed,
he took all his men   and marched by night;
he left El Poyo,   abandoned the place.
Beyond Teruel   Don Rodrigo passed;
in the pine grove of Tévar   Ruy Díaz pitched his camp.
He overran   all the country around there
and made them pay tribute   as far as Zaragoza.
   At the end of three weeks   when this was done,
Minaya came   out of Castile
and two hundred with him,   all with swords girded,
and of foot soldiers, you may know,   there were great
    numbers.
When My Cid   sets eyes on Minaya
he spurs his horse,   rides forward to embrace him;
he kissed his mouth, and the eyes in his face.
All was told to him,   nothing left hidden.
The Campeador   smiled with pleasure.
"Thanks be to God   and His holy virtues,
as long as you live   I shall prosper, Minaya!"

[handwritten margin note: JOYOUS REUNION]

50
The joy of the exiles at receiving news from Castile

   God, how they rejoiced,   all that company,
that Minaya Alvar Fáñez   had returned thus,
bringing them greetings   from cousins and brothers
and from the families   they had left behind!

51

Alegría del Cid (Serie gemela)

Dios, cómmo es alegre   la barba vellida,
que Albar Fáñez   pagó las mill missas,
e quel dixo saludes   de su mugier e de sus fijas!
Dios, cómmo fo el Çid pagado   e fizo grant alegría!
"Ya Alvar Fáñez,   bivades muchos días!
más valedes que nos,   ¡tan buena mandadería!"

52

El Cid corre tierras de Alcañiz

Non lo tardó   el que en buen ora nasco,
priso dozientos cavalleros   escollechos a mano,
fizo una corrida   la noch trasnochando;
tierras d' Alcañiz   negras las va parando,
e a derredor   todo lo va preando.
Al terçer día,   don ixo i es tornado.

53

Escarmiento de los moros

Hya va el mandado   por las tierras todas,
pesando va   a los de Monçon e a los de Huosca;
por que dan parias   plaze a los de Saragoça,
de mio, Çid Roy Díaz   que non temién ninguna fonta.

54

El Cid abandona el Poyo. Corre tierras amparadas
por el conde de Barcelona

51

The joy of the Cid. (*Parallel passage*)

God, how he rejoices,   he, bearded handsomely,
because Alvar Fáñez   had paid the thousand Masses
and had given greetings   to his wife and his daughters!
God, the Cid was pleased   and rejoiced!
"Ah, Alvar Fáñez,   may you live many days!
You are worth more than us all,   you have done your
      mission so well!"

52

The Cid raids the countryside of Alcañiz

He who in good hour was born   did not delay;
he took two hundred knights,   chose them with his own
      hand;
he went on a raid,   riding all night.
He leaves black behind him   the lands of Alcañiz;
he goes pillaging   the lands round about.
One the third day   he has come back again.

53

The chastisement of the Moors

The news has gone   through all the country around
      there;
it grieves the people of Monzón   and of Huesca;
it pleases those of Zaragoza   to give tribute
that they may fear no affront   from My Cid Ruy Díaz.

54

*The Cid abandons El Poyo. He raids lands which are
under the protection of the Count of Barcelona*

Con estas gananças   a la posada tornando se van,
todos son alegres,   gananças traen grandes;
plogo a mio Çid,   e mucho a Albar Fáñez.
Sonrrisós el caboso,   que non lo pudo endurar:
"ya cavalleros,   dezir vos he la verdad:
qui en un logar mora siempre,   lo so puede menguar;
cras a la mañana   penssemos de cavalgar,
dexat estas posadas   e iremos adelant."
    Estonçes se mudó el Çid,   al puerto de Alucat;
dent corre mio Çid   a Huesa e a Mont Alván;
en aquessa corrida   diez dias ovieron a morar.
Foron los mandados   a todas partes,
que el salido de Castiella   así los trae tan mal.

55
Amenazas del conde de Barcelona

    Los mandados son idos   a las partes todas;
llegaron las nuevas   al comde de Barçilona,
que mio Çid Roy Díaz   quel corrié la tierra toda!
ovo grand pesar   e tóvoslo a gran fonta.

56
El Cid trata en vano de calmar al conde

    El conde es muy follón   e dixo una vanidat:
"Grandes tuertos me tiene   mio Çid el de Bivar.
Dentro de mi cort   tuerto me tovo grand:
firióm el sobrino   e non lo enmendó más;
agora córrem las tierras   que en mi enpara están;
non lo desafié   nil torné el amiztad,
mas quando él me lo busca,   ir gelo he yo demandar."
    Grandes son los poderes   e a priessa llegandos van,
entre moros e cristianos   gentes se le allegan grandes

With what he had taken   he came back to the
        encampment.
All rejoice,   they bear with them great spoils;
My Cid was pleased,   and Alvar Fáñez also.
My Cid, the perfect one,   could not help smiling.
"Ah, knights,   I must tell you the truth:
One would grow poor   staying in one place always;
tomorrow in the morning   let us move on,
let us leave the encampment   and go forward."
My Cid moved next   to the Pass of Olocau;
from there he overran   as far as Huesa and Montalbán;
he was away ten days   on that foray.
The news went out   in all directions
that the exile from Castile   was using them ill.

55
Threats from the Count of Barcelona

The tidings have gone out   in all directions;
the news has come   to the Count of Barcelona
that My Cid Ruy Díaz   overruns all his land!
It weighed on him heavily,   he took it as an affront.

56
The Cid tries in vain to calm the Count

The Count is a great braggart   and spoke foolishly:
"My Cid of Bivar   inflicts great losses on me.
He offended me once   in my own court:
he struck my nephew   and gave no reparation;
now he sacks the lands   under my protection.
I have never affronted him   nor withdrawn my
        friendship,
but since he seeks me out   I shall force him to a
        reckoning."
Great are his armies,   they assemble with speed.
Moors and Christians   all gather about him

adeliñan tras mio Çid   el bueno de Bivar,
tres días e dos noches   penssaron de andar,
alcançaron a mio Çid   en Tévar e el pinar;
así vienen esforçados   que a manos se le cuydan tomar.
    Mio Çid don Rodrigo   trae ganançia grand,
diçe de una sierra   e llegava a un val.
Del conde don Remont   venido lês mensaje;
mio Çid quando lo oyó,   enbió pora allá:
"digades al conde   non lo tenga a mal,
de lo so non lievo nada,   déxem ir en paz."
Respuso el comde: "esto non será verdad!
Lo de antes e de agora   tódom lo pechará;
sabrá el salido   a quien vino desondrar."
Tornós el mandadero   quanta pudo más.
Essora lo connosçe   mio Çid el de Bivar
que a menos de batalla   non pueden den quitar.

57
Arenga del Cid a los suyos

    "Ya cavalleros,   apart fazed la ganançia;
apriessa vos guarnid   e metedos en las armas;
el comde don Remont   dar nos ha grant batalla,
de moros e de cristianos   gentes trae sobejanas,
a menos de batalla   non nos dexarié por nada.
Pues adelant irán tras nos,   aquí sea la batalla;
apretad los cavallos,   e bistades las armas.
Ellos vienen cuesta yuso,   e todos trahen calças;
elas siellas coçeras   e las cinchas amojadas;
nos cavalgaremos siellas gallegas,   e huesas sobre calças;
çiento cavalleros   devemos vençer aquellas mesnadas.
Antes que ellos lleguen a llaño,   presentémosles las
        lanças
por uno que firgades,   tres siellas irán vázias.
Verá Remont Verenguel   tras quien vino en alcança
oy en este pinar de Tévar   por tollerme la ganançia."

and ride forward toward My good Cid of Bivar;
three days and two nights, still they rode on
and came to My Cid in the pine grove of Tévar;
they came in such numbers they think to take him in
     their hands.
   My Cid Don Rodrigo, bringing great spoils,
came down from a mountain into a valley.
The message arrives from Count Ramón;
when my Cid heard it he sent back an answer:
"Tell the Count not to take it amiss.
I have nothing of his. Tell him to let me alone."
The Count answered, "That is not true!
Now he shall pay me all from now and from before;
he shall learn, this outcast, whom he has dishonored."
The messenger returned at full speed.
Thereupon My Cid of Bivar understood
that he could not leave that place without a battle.

57
The Cid's speech to his men

   "Now, knights, set the spoils to one side.
Arm yourselves quickly, put on your armor;
Count Ramón seeks a great battle;
he has with him multitudes of Moors and Christians,
Without a battle, on no account will he let us go.
If we go on, they will follow us; let the battle be here.
Cinch tight the saddles and arm yourselves.
They are coming downhill, all of them in breeches;
their saddles are flat and the girths loose.
We shall ride with Galician saddles, with boots over our
     hose;
with a hundred knights we should overcome their host.
Before they reach the plain let us greet them with lances;
for every one that you strike, three saddles will be
     emptied.
Ramón Berenguer will see whom he has come seeking
in the pine grove of Tévar, to take back the spoils from
     me."

Count Don Ramón Berenguer
          de Barcelona

58
El Cid vence la batalla. Gana la espada Colada

Todos son adobados   quando mio Çid esto ovo
                                                    fablado;
las armas avién presas   e sedién sobre los cavallos.
Vidieron la cuesta yuso   la fuerça de los francos;
al fondón de la cuesta,   çerca es de'llano,
mandólos ferir mio Çid,   el que en buen ora nasco:
esto fazen los sos   de voluntad e de grado;
los pendones e las lanças   tan bien las van enpleando,
a los unos firiendo   e a los otros derrocando.
Vençido a esta batalla   el que en buena nasco;
al comde don Remont   a preson le a tomado;
hi gañó a Colada   que más vale de mill marcos.

59
El conde de Barcelona, prisionero. Quiere dejarse morir de hambre

I venció esta batalla   por o ondró su barba,
prísole al comde,   pora su tienda lo levava;
a sos creenderos   guardar lo mandava.
De fuera de la tienda   un salto dava,
de todas partes   los soso se ajuntavan;
plogo a mio Çid,   ca grandes son las ganancias.
A mio Çid don Rodrigo   grant cozínal adobavan;
el conde don Remont   non gelo preçia nada;
adúzenle los comeres,   delant gelos paravan,
él non lo quiere comer,   a todos los sosoñava:
"Non combré un bocado   por quanto ha en toda España,
antes perderé el cuerpo   e dexaré el alma,
pues que tales malcalçados   me vençieron de batalla."

58

The Cid wins the battle and the sword Colada

When My Cid had spoken, all made ready;
they have taken up their arms   and mounted their
    horses.
They saw the Catalans   descending the slope;
when they came near the foot of the hill,   where it joins
    the plain,
My Cid, who in good hour was born,   called to his men
    to attack.
His knights charged forward   with a will,   *NOT A SLAUGHTER AS BEFORE.* (handwritten)
skillfully handling   their pennons and lances,
wounding some   and unhorsing the rest.   *not bloody like battles with the moors* (handwritten)
He who was born in good hour   has won the battle.
He has taken prisoner   the Count Ramón;
he has taken the sword Colada,   worth more than a
    thousand marks.

59

The Count of Barcelona prisoner. He would rather die of hunger

Thus he won the battle,   honor to his beard,   *?* (handwritten)
took the Count prisoner   and brought him to his tent
and ordered his servants   to mount guard upon him.
He went at once   out of the tent again;
from all sides   his men came together.
My Cid was pleased   with the great spoils they had taken.
For My Cid Don Rodrigo   they prepared a great banquet.
The Count Don Ramón   takes no interest in this;
they bear him food, -- they bring it before him.
He will not eat it.   He rebuffed them all:
"I will not eat a mouthful   for all the wealth in Spain;   *If My Cid had been someone else-- if Count Don Ramón had been taken by someone* (handwritten)
I will not abandon my body first   and give up the ghost,
since such ill-shod outcasts / have beaten me in battle."   *[к 1067?] other than My Cid. would this question have the ring of truth?* (handwritten)

111

60
El Cid promete al conde la libertad

Mio Çid Roy Díaz   odredes lo que dixo:
"comed, comde, deste pan   e beved deste vino.
Si lo que digo fiziéredes,   saldredes de cativo;
si non, en todos vuestros días   non veredes cristianismo."

61
Negativa del conde

—"Comede, don Rodrigo,   e penssedes de folgar,
que yo dexar mê morir,   que non quiero comer al."
Fasta terçer día   nol pueden acordar;
ellos partiendo   estas gananças grandes,
nol pueden fazer   comer un muesso de pan.

62
El Cid reitera al conde su promesa. Pone en libertad al conde y le despide

Dixo mio Çid: "comed, comde, algo,
ca si non comedes,   non veredes cristianos;
e si vos comiéredes   don yo sea pagado,
a vos, el comde,   e dos fijos dalgo
quitarvos e los cuerpos   e darvos e de mano."
Quando esto oyó el comde,   ya iva alegrando:
"Si lo fiziéredes, Çid,   lo que avedes fablado,
tanto quanto yo biva,   seré dent maravillado."
—"Pues comed, comde,   e quando fóredes yantado,
a vos e a otros dos   dar vos he de mano.
Mas quanto avedes perdido   e yo gané en canpo,
sabet, non daré a vos   de ello un dinero malo;

60
The Cid promises the Count his freedom

As for My Cid Ruy Díaz,   you will hear what he said:
"Count, eat this bread   and drink this wine.
If you do as I say,   I shall set you free;
if not, for the rest of your days   you will never see
      Christendom."

61
The Count refuses

"Eat if you please, Don Rodrigo,   and lie down and
      rest.
I would rather die;   I will eat nothing."
They could not persuade him   until the third day.
They continued to make division   of the great spoils they
      had taken,
but they could not make him eat   a morsel of bread.

62
The Cid repeats his promise to the Count. He sets the Count free and bids him farewell

My Cid said,   "Count, eat something,
for unless you eat   you will see no Christian soul;
if you eat   to satisfy me,
I shall set free,   out of my hand,
You, Count,   and two of your knights."
When the Count heard this   he felt more joyful.
"Cid, if you do   as you have promised,   honor — ?
as long as I live   I will marvel at it."
"Then eat, Count,   and when you have eaten
I shall set you at liberty,   and the two knights besides.
But of all that which you lost   and I won on the field,
you may know, I will not give you   so much as one
      wretched farthing.

113

ca huebos me lo he pora estos   que comigo andan
    lazrados.
Prendiendo de vos e de otros   ir nos hemos pagando:
abremos esta vida   mientras ploguiere al Padre santo,
commo que ira a de rey   e de tierra es echado."

    Alegre es el conde   e pidió agua a las manos
e tiénengelo delant   e diérongelo privado.
Con los cavalleros   que el Çid le avie dados
comiendo va el comde.   ¡Dios, qué de buen grado!
Sobreél sedie   el que en buen ora nasco:
"Si bien non comedes, comde,   don yo sea pagado,
aquí feremos la morada,   no nos partiremos amos."
Aquí dixo el comde: "de voluntad e de grado."
Con estos dos cavalleros   apriessa va yantando:
pagado es mio Çid,   que lo está aguardando,
por que el comde don Remont   tan bien bolvie las manos.

    "Si vos ploguiere, mio Çid,   de ir somos guisados;
mandadnos dar las bestias   e cavalgaremos privado:
del día que fue comde   non yanté tan de buen grado,
el sabor que dend   e non será olbidado."

    Danles tres palafrés   muy bien ensellados
e buenas vestiduras   de pelliçones e de mantos.
El comde don Remont   entre los dos es entrado.
Fata cabo del albergada   escurriólos el Castellano:
"Ya vos ides comde,   a guisa de muy franco,
en grado vos lo tengo   lo que me avedes dexado.
Si vos viniere emiente   que quisiéredes vengallo,
si me viniéredes buscar,   fazedme antes mandado;
o me dexaredes de lo vuestro   o de lo mio levaredes algo."
—"Folguedes, ya mio Çid,   sodes en vuestro salvo.
Pagado vos he   por todo aqueste año;
de venirvos buscar   sol non será penssado."

I need it for my men,   who share my pauperdom.
We keep alive   by taking from you and from others.   *Pleasing God To steal?*
And while it pleases our heavenly Father,   we shall
       continue thus,
as one must who is out of favor   and exiled from his
       country."
   The Count was joyful;   he asked for water for his hands
and they brought it before him   at once, and gave it to
       him.
And with the two knights   whom the Cid had promised   *The Cid as Jewish mother*
       him,
the Count began to eat.   God, he ate with a will!
He who was born in good hour   sat beside him.
"Unless you eat well, Count,   and to my full satisfaction,
you will remain here;   we shall not part from each other."
The Count said,   "I will eat,   I will eat with a will."
With those two knights   he eats quickly.
My Cid, sitting there watching,   is well pleased
because the Count Don Ramón   moved his hands so
       expertly.
   "If it please you, My Cid,   we are ready to go;
tell them to give us our beasts   and we shall ride at once.
I have not eaten so heartily   since I was made a Count;
the pleasure of that meal   will not be forgotten."
   They were given three palfreys,   all with fine saddles,   *? palfreys*
and rich garments,   fur tunics and cloaks.
The Count Don Ramón   entered between his two knights;
the Castilian rode with them   to the end of the
       encampment.
"Now depart from us, Count,   a free Catalan.
I extend you my thanks   for what you have left me.
If it should occur to you   to wish vengeance   *?*
and come seeking me,   let me know beforehand, →
and either you will leave something of yours   or bear off
       something of mine."
"Be at peace, My Cid,   on that account.
I have paid you tribute   for all this year;
I have no intention   of coming to seek you."

63
El conde se ausenta receloso. Riqueza de los desterrados

Aguijaba el comde   e penssava de andar,
tornando va la cabeça   e catándos atrás;
miedo iva aviendo   que mio Çid se repintrá,
lo que non ferié el caboso   por quanto en el mundo ha,
una deslealtança   ca non la fizo alguandre.
   Ido es el comde,   tornós el de Bivar,
juntós con sus mesnadas,   conpeçós de alegrar
de la ganançia que han fecha   maravillosa e grand;
tan ricos son los sos   que non saben qué se an.

The Count mistrustfully departs. The wealth of the exiles

    The Count spurred his horse   and rode forward,
turning his head   and looking behind him
for fear that the Cid   might change his mind,
which that perfect one would not have done   for the
    world's wealth,
for in all his life he had done no treachery.
    The Count is gone;   he of Bivar turned back,
returned to his vassals.   God, how great was their
    rejoicing,
for great and wonderful   was the booty they had won.
His men are so rich   they cannot count all they have.

CANTAR SEGUNDO

64
El Cid se dirige contra tierras de Valencia

Aquis conpieça la gesta   de mio Çid el de Bivar.
Poblado ha mio Çid   el puerto de Alucat,
dexado ha Saragoça   e a las tierras ducá,
e dexado ha Huesa   e tierras de Mont Alván.
Contra la mar salada   conpeçó de guerrear;
a orient exe el sol,   e tornós a essa part.
Myo Çid gañó a Xérica   e a Onda e Almenar,
tierras de Borriana   todas conquistas las ha.

65
Toma de Murviedro

Ayudól el Criador,   el Señor que es en çielo.
El con todo esto   priso a Murviedro;
ya vidie mio Çid   que Dios le iva valiendo.
Dentro en Valençia   non es poco el miedo.

66
Los moros valencianos cercan al Cid. Este reúne
sus gentes. Arenga

Pesa a los de Valençia,   sabet, non les plaze;
prisieron so consejo   quel viniessen çercar.
Trasnocharon de noch,   al alva de la man
açerca de Murviedro   tornan tiendas a fincar.

118

THE SECOND CANTAR

THE WEDDING

64
The Cid proceeds against the domain of Valencia

Here begins the story   of My Cid of Bivar.
My Cid has made his camp   by the Pass of Olocau;
he has left Zaragoza   and the country there;
he has left Huesa   and the lands of Montalbán.
He has carried his war   toward the salt sea;
the sun comes from the east,   he turned to that direction.
My Cid took Jérica   and Onda and Almenara,
and he has overrun   all the lands of Burriana.

65
The taking of Murviedro

The Creator aided him,   the Lord in heaven,
and by that means,   he took Murviedro;
My Cid knew well   that God was his strength.
There was great fear   in the city of Valencia.

66
*The Moors of Valencia surround the Cid. He assembles
his men. His speech*

It grieves those of Valencia.   Know, they are not
      pleased
They took counsel   and came to besiege him.
They rode all night;   next day at dawn
around Murviedro   they set up their tents.

Viólo mio Çid,   tomós a maravillar:
"Grado a tí,   Padre spirital!
En sus tierras somos   e femosles tod mal,
bevemos so vino   e comemos el so pan;
si nos çercar vienen,   con derecho lo fazen.
A menos de lid   aquesto nos partirá;
vayan los mandados   por los que nos deven ayudar
los unos a Xérica   e los otros a Alucad,
desí a Onda   e los otros a Almenar,
los de Borriana   luego vengan acá;
conpeçaremos   aquesta lid campal,
yo fío por Dios   que en nuestro pro eñadrán."
    Al terçer día   todos juntados s'an,
el que en buen ora nasco   compeçó de fablar:
"Oíd, mesnadas,   sí el Criador vos salve!
Después que nos partiemos   de la linpia cristiandad,
—non fo a nuestro grado   ni nos non pudiemos mas,—
grado a Dios,   lo nuestro fo adelant.
Los de Valençia,   çercados nos han;
si en estas tierras   quisiéremos durar,
firme mientre   son estos a escarmentar.

67
Fin de la arenga del Cid

    Passe la noche   e venga la mañana,
aparejados me seed   a cavallos e armas;
iremos veer   aquella su almofalla.
Commo omnes exidos   de tierra estraña
allí pareçra   el que mereçe la soldada."

68
Minaya da el plan de batalla. El Cid vence otra lid campal.
Toma de Cebolla

    Oíd qué dixo   Minaya Albar Fáñez:
"Campeador,   fagamos lo que a vos plaze.

120

My Cid saw them   and exclaimed:
"Thanks be to Thee,   Father Who art in heaven!
We ride through their lands   and do them mischief,
we drink their wine   and eat their bread;
if they come to besiege us   they are within their rights.←
We shall not leave here   without a battle;
send out the messages   to those who should aid us,
some in Jérica   and others in Olocau,
from there to Onda   and to Almenara,
and to those of Burriana,   bid them come here.
We shall begin   this pitched battle;
I trust in God   Who will favor us,"
    On the third day   all have come together.
He who was born in good hour   began to address them:
"Hear me, my vassals,   as the Creator may save you!
Ever since we came   out of clean Christendom —
not at our own choice,   for we could not do otherwise —
God be thanked,   we have met no reverses.
Now those of Valencia   have encircled us;
if we are to remain   in these lands,
we must defeat them   most severely.

67
End of the Cid's speech

    "When the night has passed   and morning has come,
I would have the horses saddled   and the arms ready;
we shall go and see   that army of theirs.
We are exiles   from a foreign country;
there we shall see   who is worth his wages."

68
*Minaya gives the plan of battle. The Cid wins another
pitched battle. The taking of Cebolla*

    Hear Minaya Alvar Fáñez,   what he had to say:
"Campeador,   let us do as you will.

121

A mí dedes çien cavalleros,   que non vos pido más;
vos con los otros   firádeslos delant.
Bien los ferredes,   que dubda non i avrá,
yo con los çiento   entraré del otra part,
commo fío por Dios,   el campo nuestro será."
Commo gelo a dicho   al Campeador mucho plo~~.
Mañana era   e piénssanse de armár,
quis cada uno dellos   bien sabe a que ha de far.
   Con los alvores   mio Çid ferirlos va:
"¡En el nombre del Criador   e d'apostol santi Yague,
feridlos, cavalleros,   d'amor e de voluntad,
ca yo so Roy Díaz,   mio Çid el de Bivar!"
   Tanta cuerda de tienda   i veriedes crebar,
arrancarse las estacas   e acostarse a todas partes los
                                                        tendales
Moros son muchos,   ya quieren reconbrar.
Del otra part   entróles Albar Fáñez;
maguer les pesa   oviéronse a dar e a arrancar:
de piedes de cavallo   los ques pudieron escapar.
Dos reyes de moros   mataron en es alcaz,
fata Valençia   duró el segudar.
Grandes son las gananças   que mio Çid fechas ha;
robavan el campo   e piénssanse de tornar.
Entravan a Murviedro   con estas gananças que traen;
grand es el gozo   que va por es logar.
"Prisieron Çebolla   e quanto que es i adelant;
miedo an en Valençia   que no saben qué se far;
las nuevas de mío Çid,   sabet, sonondo van."

69
Correrías del Cid al sur de Valencia

   Sonando van sus nuevas,   alent parte del mar andan;
alegre era el Çid   e todas sus compañas,
que Dios le ayudara   e fiziera esta arrancada.
Davan sus corredores   e fazien las trasnochadas.

122

Give me a hundred knights,   I ask for no more.   MINAYA
You with the rest   ride to the attack.   100 KNIGHTS.
You will strike them hard,   I have no doubt.
I with the hundred   will charge from another side.
As I trust in God,   the field will be ours."
The Campeador was much pleased   with what he had
    said.
It was morning   and they set to arm;
each of them knows well   what he must do.
    When the dawn came,   My Cid rode to attack them.
"In the name of the Creator   and of Saint James the
    apostle,
attack them, knights,   heartily, with a will.
I am Ruy Díaz,   My Cid of Bivar!"
    You would have seen   so many tent cords snapped,
the poles wrenched out,   the canvas collapsing.
The Moors are many   and begin to recover.
Alvar Fáñez   rode in from another side;
hard against their wills   they were forced to flee
on foot or on horse,   those who could escape.
In that chase they killed   two Kings of the Moors;
they continued the pursuit   as far as Valencia.
My Cid   has taken great spoils;
they despoil the camp   and start to return;
they enter Murviedro   with those spoils they bear;
great is the rejoicing   in that town.
"They have taken Cebolla   and all that lies beyond it;
they are frightened in Valencia,   they do not know what
    to do.
Know, the fame of My Cid   has gone everywhere."

69
The Cid's raids to the south of Valencia

    His fame goes re-echoing   even beyond the sea;
My Cid rejoiced,   and all his company,
because God had given him aid   and he had routed them
    there.
He sent out raiders,   all night they rode;

123

llegan a Gujera   e llegan a Xátiva,
aun mas ayusso,   a Denia la casa;
cabo del mar tierra de moros   firme la quebranta.
Ganaron Peña Cadiella,   las exidas e las entradas.

70
El Cid en Peña Cadiella

   Quando el Çid Campeador   ovo Peña Cadiella,
ma'les pesa en Xátiva   e dentro en Gujera,
non es con recabdo   el dolor de Valençia.

71
Conquista de toda la región de Valencia

   En tierra de moros   prendiendo e ganando,
e durmiendo los días   e las noches tranochando,
en ganar aquellas villas   mio Çid duró tres años.

72
El Cid asedia a Valencia. Pregona a los cristianos
la guerra

   A los de Valençia   escarmentados los han,
non osan fueras exir   nin con él se ajuntar;
tajávales las huertas   e fazíales grand mal,
en cada uno destos años   mio Çid les tollió el pan.
Mal se aquexan los de Valençia   que non sabent ques far.
De ninguna part que sea   non les viníe pan;
nin da conssejo padre a fijo,   nin fijo a padre,
nin amigo a amigo   nos pueden consolar.
Mala cueta es, señores,   aver mingua de pan,

they came to Cullera   and to Játiva
and below there   to the town of Denia.
They destroyed the lands of the Moors /as far as the
      seashore. /
They took Benicadell,   its exits and entrances.

70
The Cid in Benicadell

   When the Cid Campeador   had taken Benicadell,
they are grieved in Játiva,   and in Cullera.
As for Valencia,   its dismay is boundless. ⇐

71
The conquest of the entire region of Valencia

   Seizing and despoiling, /riding at night./
/sleeping in the daytime, / taking those towns,
My Cid spent three years   in the lands of the Moors.

3 YEARS

72
*The Cid lays siege to Valencia. He sends heralds
among the Christians announcing the war*

   And he has chastised severely   those of Valencia.
They do not dare leave the city   or meet him in battle;
he has laid waste their farmlands   and brought havoc
      among them;
every year of those three,   My Cid deprived them of
      bread.
They grieve in Valencia,   not knowing what to do.
They cannot obtain   bread from anywhere;
the father cannot help his son   nor the son his father,
friend and friend   cannot console each other.
Great hardship it is, sirs,   to be without bread,

125

fijos e mugieres   veer los morir de fanbre.
Delante veyen so duelo,   non se pueden huviar,
por el rey de Marruecos   ovieron a enbiar;
con el de los Montes Claros,   avíe guerra tan grand,
non les dixo consejo,   nin los vino huviar.

  Sópolo mio Çid,   de coraçón le plaz;
salió de Murviedro   una noch a trasnochar
amaneció a mio Çid   en tierras de Mon Real.
Por Aragón e por Navarra   pregón mandó echar,
a tierras de Castiella   enbió sos menssajes:
Quien quiere perder   cueta e venir a rritad,
viniesse a mio Çid   que a sabor de cavalgar;
çercar quiere a Valençia   pora cristianos la dar:

73
Repítese el pregón (Serie gemela)

"quien quiere ir comigo   çercar a Valençia,
—todos vengan de grado,   ninguno non ha premia,—
tres días le speraré   en Canal de Çelfa."

74
Gentes que acuden al pregón. Cerco
y entrada de Valencia

  Esto dixo mio Çid   el Campeador leal.
Tornávas a Murviedro,   ca él ganada se la a.
Andidieron los pregones,   sabet, a todas partes,
al sabor de la ganançia,   non lo quieren detardar,
grandes yentes se le acojen   de la buena cristiandad.
Sonando van sus nuevas   todas a todas partes;
mas le vienen a mio Çid,   sabet, que nos le van;
creçiendo va riqueza   a mio Çid el de Bivar:

to see children and women   dying of hunger.
And they see their affliction growing,   that there is no
     remedy,
and they have sent word   to the King of Morocco;
he was so deep in war   with the King of the Atlas,
that he neither sent to advise them   nor came to their
     rescue.
  My Cid learned of this;   it gladdened his heart.
He went out from Murviedro   one night, and rode all
     night;
he appeared at daybreak   in the lands of Monreal.
He sent forth a herald   to Aragón and Navarre;
he sent his messages   to the lands of Castile:
"Whoever would leave   his toil and grow rich,
let him come to My Cid,   whose taste is for battle.
He would now lay siege to Valencia   to give it to the
     Christians."

73

Repetition of the announcement (*Parallel passage*)

"Whoever will come with me   to besiege Valencia—
let all come freely   and no one against his will—
I shall wait three days for him   by the Canal of Celfa."

74

*Those who reported to the herald. The siege and
entry of Valencia*

This he spoke, My Cid,   the loyal Campeador.
He returned to Murviedro,   which he had already taken.
The cries went out,   you may know, in all directions;
at the odor of riches   they do not wish to delay;
great numbers gather to him   from good Christendom.
The fame of him resounds   in every direction;
more flock to My Cid,   you may know, than go from him
and his wealth increases,   My Cid's of Bivar.

quando vido las gentes juntadas,   compeços de pagar.
Mio Çid don Rodrigo   non lo quiso detardar,
adeliñó pora Valençia   e sobrellas va echar,
bien la çerca mio Çid,   que non i avía hart;
viédales exir   e viédales entrar.
Metióla en plazdo,   si les viniessen huviar.
Nueve meses complidos,   sabet, sobrella yaz,
quando vino el dezeno   oviérongela a dar.

   Grandes son los gozos   que van por es logar
quando mio Çid gañó a Valençia   e entró en la çibdad.
Los que foron de pie   cavalleros se fazen;
el oro e la plata   ¿quien vos lo podrie contar?
Todos eran ricos   quantos que allí ha.
Mio Çid don Rodrigo   la quinta mandó tomar,
en el aver monedado   treynta mill marcos le caen,
e los otros averes   ¿quien los podrié contar?

   Alegre era el Campeador   con todos los que ha,
quando su seña cabdal   sedié en somo del alcáçer.

75
El rey de Sevilla quiere recobrar Valencia

   Ya folgava mio Çid   con todas sus conpañas:
âquel rey de Sevilla   el mandado llegava,
que presa es Valençia,   que non gela enparan,
vino los veer   con treynta mill de armas.
Aprés de la uerta   ovieron la batalla,
arrancólos mio Çid   el de la luenga barba.
Fata dentro en Xátiva   duró el arrancada,
en el passar de Xúcar   i veriédes barata,
moros en arruenço   amidos bever agua.
Aquel rey de Sevilla   con tres colpes escapa.
Tornado es mio Çid   con toda esta ganançia.
Buena fo la de Valençia   quando ganaron la casa,
mas mucho fue provechosa,   sabet, esta arrancada;
a todos los menores   cayeron çient marcos de plata.

When he saw so many assembled   he rejoiced.
My Cid Don Rodrigo   did not wish to delay;
he set out for Valencia   and will attack them.
My Cid besieges it closely;   there was no escape.
He permits no one   to enter or depart.
He gave them a term of grace   if any would come and
   save them.
Nine full months   his tents surrounded them;
when the tenth began   they were forced to surrender.
Great is the rejoicing   in that place
when My Cid took Valencia   and entered the city.
Those who had gone on foot   became knights on horses,
and who could count   the gold and the silver?
All were rich,   as many as were there.
My Cid Don Rodrigo   sent for his fifth of the spoils;
in coined money alone   thirty thousand marks fell to him;
and the other riches,   who could count them?
   My Cid rejoiced,   and all who were with him,
when his flag flew from the top   of the Moorish palace.

75
The King of Seville tries to retake Valencia

   Then my Cid rested,   and all his men.
The news came   to the King of Seville
that Valencia was taken,   there had been no help for it;
he set out to attack it   with thirty thousand armed men.
Beyond the farmlands   they joined battle.
My Cid of the long beard   routed them there;
as far as Játiva   the pursuit went on.
Crossing the Júcar,   you would have seen them struck
   down;
Moors caught in the current,   forced to drink water.
That King of Seville   escaped with three wounds.
My Cid returned   with all his gains.
Great were the spoils of Valencia   when they took that
   city;
those from this victory,   you may know, were still richer;
to the least among them   fell a hundred marks of silver.

76
El Cid deja su barba intonsa. Riqueza de los del Cid

Grand alegría es   entre todos essos cristianos
con mio Çid Roy Díaz,   el que en buen ora nasco.
Yal creçe la barba   e vale allongando;
ca dixera mio Çid   de la su boca atanto:
"por amor de rey Alffonsso,   que de tierra me a echado"
nin entrarié en ella tigera,   ni un pelo non avrié tajado,
e que fablassen desto   moros e cristianos.
Mio Çid don Rodrigo   en Valençia está folgando,
con él Minaya Albar Fáñez   que nos le parte de so braço.
Los que exieron de tierra   de ritad son abondados,
a todos les die en Valençia   el Campeador contado
casas y heredades   de que son pagados;
el amor de mio Çid   ya lo ivan provando.
Los que foron después   todos son pagados;
veelo mio Çid   que con los averes que avién tomados,
que sis pudiessen ir,   fer lo ien de grado.
Esto mandó mio Çid,   Minaya lo ovo conssejado:
que ningún omne de los sos   que con él ganaron algo
ques le non spidiés   o nol besás la mano,
sil pudiessen prender   o fosse alcançado,
tomássenle el aver   e pusiéssenle en un palo.
Afevos todo aquesto   puesto en buen recabdo;
con Minaya Albar Fáñez   él se va consejando:
"si vos quisiéredes, Minaya,   quiero saber recabdo
de los que son aquí   e comigo ganaron algo;
meterlos he en escripto,   e todos sean contados,
que si algunos furtare   o menos le fallaro,
el aver me avrá a tornar,   âquestos myos vassallos

You can see how the fame   of this warrior has grown.

76

The Cid leaves his beard untrimmed. The wealth of the Cid's men

There is great rejoicing   among all those Christians
with My Cid Ruy Díaz,   who in good hour was born.
His beard grows on him,   it grows longer upon him;
these words My Cid   spoke of it with his mouth:
"For love of King Alfonso,   who sent me into exile."
No scissors would touch it   nor one hair be cut,
and let Moors and Christians   all tell of this.
   My Cid Don Rodrigo   is resting in Valencia;
Minaya Alvar Fáñez   does not leave his side.
Those who came with him into exile   have all grown rich.
The renowned Campeador   gave them all, in Valencia,
houses and fiefs   with which they are satisfied;
they all have tasted   of the Cid's generosity.
Those who joined him later   are content also;
My Cid knows   that with the gains they have taken,
if they might depart now,   they would go gladly.
My Cid commanded,   as Minaya had advised him,
that no man among them   who with him had gained
      anything
should leave without bidding farewell   and kissing his
      hand,
or else he would seize him again   wherever he might be
      hidden
and take from him everything   and hang him on a gallows.
Behold, all this   was put in good order;
he is talking things over   with Minaya Alvar Fáñez:
"If you please, Minaya,   I should like to know
how many are with me here   and have received of the
      spoils.
I would have them all counted   and set down in writing
so that if anyone hide,   or anyone is missing,
his possessions may be returned to me   by those vassals
      of mine

que curian a Valençia   e andan arrobdando."
Allí dixo Minaya: "consejo es aguisado."

77
Recuento de la gente del Cid. Este dispone nuevo
presente para el rey

Mandólos venir a la corth   e a todos los juntar,
quando los falló,   por cuenta fízolos nonbrar:
tres mill e seys çientos   avie mio Çid el de Bivar;
alégrasle el coraçón,   e tornós a sonrrisar:
"Grado a Dios, Minaya,   e a santa María madre!
Con más pocos ixiemos   de la casa de Bivar.
Agora avemos riquiza,   más avremos adelant.
Si a vos ploguiere, Minaya,   e non vos caya en pesar,
enbiar vos quiero a Castiella,   do avemos heredades,
al rey Alfonsso   mio señor natural;
destas mis ganançias,   que avemos fechas acá,
dar le quiero çient cavallos,   e vos ídgelos levar;
desí por mí besalde la mano   e firme gelo rogad
por mi mugier doña Ximena   e mis fijas naturales,
si fore su merçed   quenlas dexe sacar.
Enbiaré por ellas,   e vos sabed el mensage:
la mugier de mio Çid   e sus fijas las iffantes
de guisa irán por ellas   que a grand ondra vernán
a estas tierras estrañas   que nos pudiemos ganar."
Essora dixo Minaya: "de buena voluntad."
Pues esto an fablado,   piénssanse de adobar.
Ciento omnes le dio   mio Çid a Albar Fáñez
por servirle en las carrera   a toda su voluntad,
e mandó mil marcos de plata   a San Pero levar
e que los quinientos diesse   a don Sancho el abbat.

who guard Valencia,   keeping watch around it."
Then Minaya said,   "That is well advised."   *MINAYA HIMSELF ADVISED IT*

77
*The numbering of the Cid's followers. He arranges to
send a new present to the King*

He bade them all come to the court   and gather
      together.
When they had come   he numbered them all: *3600 MEN W/ EL CID*
three thousand six hundred   were under My Cid of Bivar;
his heart was pleased   and he began to smile.
"God be praised, Minaya,   and Santa María His mother!
With less than these we rode out   from the gate at Bivar,
and now riches are ours   and more shall be ours hereafter.
"If you please, Minaya,   and it would not burden you,
I would send you to Castile,   where our lands are,
to King Alfonso,   my natural lord.
Out of these my gains   which we have taken here
I would give him a hundred horses,   I would have you
      take them,
kiss his hand for me   and urgently beg him
that he, of his grace, may allow me   to bring from there
Doña Jimena, my wife,   and my daughters.
I shall send for them;   know, this is the message: *SENDING FOR WIFE + DAUGHTERS.*
'My Cid's wife   and his daughters
in such wise will be sent for   that with great honor they
      will come
to these foreign lands   which we have taken.'"
Then Minaya said,   "I will do it gladly."
When they had spoken this   they began to make ready.
My Cid gave a hundred men   to Alvar Fáñez
to serve him on his way   and do his will,
and he sent a thousand marks   of silver to San Pedro,
five hundred of them to be given   to the abbot Don
      Sancho.

*women in a monastary
guarded by abbot
Don Sancho*

133

78
Don Jerónimo llega a Valençia

En estas nuevas   todos se alegrando,
de parte de orient   vino un coronado;
el obispo don Jerome   so nombre es llamado.
Bien entendido es de letras   e mucho acordado,
de pie e de cavallo   mucho era arreziado.
Las provezas de mio Çid   andávalas demandando,
sospirando ques viesse   con moros en el campo:
que sis fartás lidiando   e firiendo con sus manos,
a los días del sieglo   non le llorassen cristianos.
Quando lo oyó mio Çid   de aquesto fo pagado:
"Oíd, Minaya Albar Fáñez,   por aquel que está en alto,
quando Dios prestar nos quiere,   nos bien gelo
        gradescamos:
en tierras de Valençia   fer quiero obispado,
e dárgelo a este   buen cristiano;
vos; quando ides a Castiella,   levaredes buenos
        mandados."

79
Don Jerónimo hecho obispo

Plogo a Albar Fáñez   de lo que dixo don Rodrigo.
A este don Jerome   yal otorgan por obispo;
diéronle en Valencia   o bien puede estar rico.
¡Dios, qué alegre era   tod cristianismo,
que en tierras de Valençia   señor avie obispo!
Alegre fo Minaya   e spidiós e vinos.

80
Minaya se dirige a Carrión

Tierras de Valençia   remanidas en paz,
adeliñó pora Castiella   Minaya Albar Fáñez.
Dexarévos las posadas,   non las quiero contar.
Demandó por Alfonsso,   do lo podrie fallar.

78
Don Jerome arrives in Valencia

While they were rejoicing   at this news,
out of the east   came a cleric,
the Bishop Don Jerome   is his name.
Learned in letters   and with much wisdom
and a ready warrior   on foot or on horse,
he came inquiring   of the Cid's brave deeds,
sighing to see himself   with the Moors in the field,
saying if he should weary   of fighting them with his hands,
let no Christian mourn him   all the days of this world.
When My Cid heard this   he was well pleased.
"Hear, Minaya Alvar Fáñez,   by Him Who is in heaven,
when God would give us aid   let us heartily thank Him
        for it:
I would ordain a bishopric   in the lands of Valencia;
I would give it   to this good Christian.
Take the good news   when you go to Castile."

79
Don Jerome ordained Bishop

Alvar Fáñez was pleased   with what Don Rodrigo said.
That same Don Jerome   they ordained Bishop;
they arranged that he might live   richly in Valencia.
God, how great was the rejoicing   of all those Christians
for in the lands of Valencia   there was a lord Bishop!
Minaya was joyful   and bade farewell and set out.

80
Minaya goes to Carrión

Leaving the lands of Valencia   lying in peace,
Minaya Alvar Fáñez   rode toward Castile.
I do not wish to recount   all the places where he paused.
He asked for King Alfonso,   asked where he might find
        him.

Fora el rey a San Fagunt   aun poco ha,
tornós a Carrión,   i lo podrie fallar.
    Alegre fo de aquesto   Minaya Albar Fáñez,
con esta presentaja   adeliñó pora allá.

81
Minaya saluda al rey

    De missa era exido   essora el rey Alfonsso,
afe Minaya Albar Fáñez   do llega tan apuosto:
fincó sos inojos   ante tod el puoblo,
a los piedes del rey Alfons   cayó con gran duolo,
besávale las manos   e fabló tan apuosto:

82
Discurso de Minaya al rey. Envidia de Garci Ordóñez.
El rey perdona a la familia del Cid. Los infantes de
Carrión codician las riquezas del Cid

    "Merced, señor Alfonsso,   por amor del Criador!
Besávavos las manos   mio Çid lidiador,
los piedes e las manos,   commo a tan buen señor,
quel ayades merçed,   si vos vala el Criador!
Echástesle de tierra,   non ha la vuestra amor;
maguer en tierra agena,   él bien faze lo so:
ganada a Xérica   e a Onda por nombre,
priso a Almenar   e a Murviedro que es miyor,
assí fizo Çebolla   e adelant Castejón,
e Peña Cadiella,   que es una peña fuort;
con aquestas todas   de Valençia es señor,
obispo fizo de su mano   el buen Campeador,
a fizo çinco campales   e todas las arrancó.
Grandes son las gananças   quel dio el Criador,

136

The King had gone to Sahagún   only shortly before
and thence to Carrión,   and there he might find him.
   Minaya Alvar Fáñez   was pleased to hear this;
he rode toward that place   with the gifts he had brought.

81
Minaya greets the King

   Just as King Alfonso   had come out from Mass,
behold where Minaya Alvar Fáñez   arrives most
      opportunely.
He knelt down on his knees   before all the people;
he fell down in great sorrow   at the feet of King Alfonso;
he kissed the King's hands   and spoke with all eloquence.

82
Minaya's speech to the King. The envy of García Ordóñez.
The King pardons the Cid's family. The Heirs of
Carrión covet the Cid's riches

   "Grace, lord Alfonso,   for the love of the Creator!
My Cid the warrior   kisses your hands,
kisses your feet and your hands   as his duty to so good
      a lord,
and may you grant him grace   as the Creator may bless
      you!
You sent him from your lands,   he is without your favor;
nevertheless, in foreign lands   he manages well:
he has taken Jérica   and the place called Onda
and seized Almenara,   and Murviedro, which is larger;
likewise he took Cebolla   and Castejón farther on,
and Benicadell,   which is a strong hill,
and besides all these   he is lord of Valencia.
The good Campeador   a Bishop has ordained with his
      own hands,
fought five pitched battles   and triumphed in them all.
Great are the gains   the Creator has given him.

137

fevos aquí las señas, verdad vos digo yo:
çient cavallos gruessos e corredores,
de siellas e de frenos todos guarnidos son,
bésavos las manos que los prendades vos;
razones por vuestro vassallo e a vos tiene por señor."

   Alçó la mano diestra, el rey se santigó:
"De tan fieras ganançias commo a fechas el Campeador
¡sí me vala sant Esidre! plázme de coraçón.
e plázem de las nuevas que faze el Campeador;
reçibo estos cavallos quem enbía de don."

   Maguer plogo al rey, mucho pesó a Garci Ordóñez:
"Semeja que en tierra de moros non a bivo omne,
quando assí faze a su guisa el Çid Campeador!"
Dixo el rey al comde: "dexad essa razón,
que en todas guisas mijor me sirve que vos."

   Fabalba Minaya i a guisa de varón:
"merçed vos pide el Çid, si vos cadiesse en sabor,
por su mugier doña Ximena e sus fijas amas a dos
saldríen del monasterio do elle las dexó,
e iríen pora Valençia al buen Campeador."
Essora dixo el rey: "Plazme de coraçone;
yo les mandaré dar conducho mientra que por mi tierra
                                                        foren,

de fonta e de mal curiallas e de desonore;
quando en cabo de mi tierra aquestas dueñas foren,
catad cómmo las sirvades vos e el Campeadore.
Oídme, escuelas, e toda la mi cort!
non quiero que nada pierda el Campeador;
a todas las escuelas que a él dizen señor
por que los deseredé, todo gelo suelto yo;
sírvanle' sus heredades do fore el Campeador,
antrégoles los cuerpos de mal e de ocasíon,
por tal fago aquesto que sirven a so señor."
Minaya Albar Fáñez las manos le besó.
Sonrrisós el rey, tan vellido fabló:
"Los que quisieren ir servir al Campeador

Here are the proofs   that it is the truth I tell you:
a hundred horses,   strong-limbed and swift,
each one provided   with saddle and bridle.
He kisses your hands   and begs you to accept them;
he calls himself your vassal   and regards you as his lord.
   The King raised his right hand   and crossed himself.
"Saint Isidore bless me,   my heart is pleased
with the vast spoils   the Cid has taken!
And I am pleased with the deeds   the Campeador has
      done;
I accept these horses   which he sends as a gift."
   Though it pleased the King,   it grieved García
      Ordóñez:
"It seems that in the lands of the Moors   there is no
      man living
since the Cid Campeador   thus does as he pleases."
The King said to the Count,   "Leave off such talk;
in whatever he does   he serves me better than you do."
   Then manfully   Minaya spoke:
"The Cid begs of your grace,   if it meet your pleasure,
that his wife Doña Jimena   and both his daughters
may leave the monastery   where he left them
and go to Valencia   to the good Campeador."
Then the King said,   "It pleases my heart;
I shall provide them with escort   while they go through
      my lands
and keep them from harm and grievance   and from
      dishonor,
and when these ladies have come   to the end of my lands,
then you and the Campeador   take care to guard them.
Hear me, my vassals   and all my court!
I would not have the Campeador   lose anything,
and as for all those vassals   who call him lord,
whom I disinherited,   I return to them all that they had;
let them keep their inheritances   while they serve the
      Campeador,
and I free their bodies   from threat of injury;
all this I do   that they may serve their lord."
Minaya Alvar Fáñez   kissed him on the hands.
The King smiled   and spoke thus sweetly:
"Those who wish to go   to serve the Campeador

de mí sean quitos   e vayan a la graçia del Criador.
Más ganaremos en esto   que en otra desamor."
    Aquí entraron en fabla   iffantes de Carrión:
"Mucho creçen las nuevas   de mio Çid el Campeador,
bien casariemos con sus fijas   pora huebos de pro.
Non la osariemos   acometer nos esta razón.
Mio Çid es de Bivar   e nos de comdes de Carrión."
Non lo dizen a nadi,   e finçó esta razón.
    Minaya Albar Fáñez   al buen rey se espidió.
"¿Hya vos ides, Minaya?   id a la graçia del Criador!
Levedes un portero,   tengo que vos avrá pro;
si leváredes las dueñas,   sírvanlas a su sabor,
fata dentro en Medina   denles quanto huebos les for,
desí adelant   piensse dellas el Campeador."
Espidiós Minaya   e vasse de la cort.

83

Minaya va a Cardeña por doña Jimena. Más castellanos se
prestan a ir a Valencia. Minaya en Burgos. Promete a
los judíos buen pago de la deuda del Cid. Minaya vuelve
a Cardeña y parte con Jimena. Pedro Bermúdez parte de
Valencia para recibir a Jimena. En Molina se le une
Avengalvón. Encuentran a Minaya en Medinaceli

Iffantes de Carrión   so consejo preso ane,
dando ivan conpaña   a Minaya Albar Fáñez:
"En todo sodes pro,   en esto assí lo fagades:
saludadnos   a mio Çid el de Bivare,
somos en so pro   quanto lo podemos fare;
el Çid que bien nos quiera   nada non perderave."
Respuso Minaya: "esto non me a por qué pesare."
    Ido es Minaya,   tórnansse los iffantes.
Adeliñó pora San Pero,   o las dueñas están,
tan grand fue el gozo   quandol vieron assomar.

140

have my leave,   and may the Creator bless them.
We shall gain more by this   than by disaffection."
   Then the Heirs of Carrión   spoke between themselves:
"Great grows the fame   of My Cid the Campeador;
it would serve our advantage   to marry his daughters.
Yet we would not dare   propose such a plan.
My Cid is from Bivar   and we, of the Counts of Carrión."
They spoke of it to no one   and there the scheme rested.
   Minaya Alvar Fáñez   bade the good King farewell.
"Are you leaving us now, Minaya? May the Creator bless
      you.
Take with you a royal herald,   who will serve your needs;
if you go with the ladies,   care for their comfort
as far as Medinaceli;   in my name demand all they
      require.
From that point forward   they concern the Campeador."
Minaya bade farewell   and went from the court.

plot of the Heirs of CARRIÓN

83

*Minaya goes to Cardeña for Doña Jimena. More Castilians
offer to go to Valencia. Minaya in Burgos. He promises
the Jews full payment for the Cid's debt. Minaya returns
to Cardeña and leaves with Jimena. Pedro Bermúdez sets
out from Valencia to receive Jimena. In Molina they are
met by Abengalbón. They meet Minaya in Medinaceli*

   The Heirs of Carrión   have made their decision;
they went out a little way   with Minaya Alvar Fáñez.
"We have been your friends in all things,   now be friend
      to us:
give our greetings   to My Cid of Bivar,
we shall serve him in all things   as well as we may;
we wish the Cid to lose nothing   by the friendship he
      bears us."
Minaya answered, "Your message   will not overburden
      me."
   Minaya had ridden on   and the Heirs turn back.
He rode toward San Pedro,   where the ladies are;
great was their joy   when he appeared.

Deçido es Minaya,   a ssan Pero va rogar.
Quando acabó la oraçion,   a las dueñas se fo tornar.
"Omíllom,   doña Ximena,   Dios vos curie de mal,
assí ffaga a vuestras fijas,   amas a dos las iffantes.
Salúdavos mio Çid   allá onde elle está;
sano lo dexé   e con tan gran rictad.
El rey por su merçed,   sueltas me vos ha,
por levaros a Valençia   que avemos por heredad.
Si vos viesse el Çid   sanas e sin mal,
todo serié alegre,   que non avrié ningún pesar."
Dixo doña Ximena: "el Criador lo mande!"
Dio tres cavalleros   Minaya Albar Fáñez,
enviólos a mio Çid,   a Valençia do está:
"Dezid al Canpeador   —que Dios le curie de mal—
que su mugier e sus fijas   el rey sueltas me las ha,
mientra que fóremos por sus tierras   conducho nos mandó

dar.

De aquestos quinze días,   si Dios nos curiare de mal,
sermos i yo e su mugier   e sus fijas él a
y todas las dueñas con ellas   quantas buenas ellas han."
Idos son los cavalleros   e dellos penssarán,
remaneçió en San Pero   Minaya Albar Fáñez.

Veriedes cavalleros   venir de todas partes,
irse quieren a Valençia   a mio Çid el de Bivar.
Que les toviesse pro   rogavan a Albar Fáñez;
diziendo Minaya: "esto feré de veluntad."
Sessaenta e çinco cavalleros   acreçídol han,
e él se tenié çiento   que aduxiera d'allá;
por ir con estas dueñas   buena conpaña se faze.

Los quinientos marcos   dió Minaya al abbat;
de los otros quinientos   dezir vos he que faze:
Minaya a doña Ximena   e a sus fijas que ha,
e a las otras dueñas   que las sirven delant,
el bueno de Minaya   pensólas de adobar
de los mejores guarnimientos   que en Burgos pudo fallar,
palafrés e mulas,   que non parescan mal.
Quando estas dueñas   adobadas las ha,

Minaya has dismounted   and prays to San Pedro.
When the prayer ended   he turned to the ladies.
"I humble myself before you,   Doña Jimena;
may God keep you   and both your daughters from evil.
My Cid sends you greetings   from where he is;
I left him in health   and with great riches.
The King, in his grace,   has set you free
so that you may come to Valencia   which is ours for
      inheritance.
If the Cid might see you   well and without harm,
all would be joy   and he would grieve no longer."
Doña Jimena said,   "May the Creator will it so!"
Minaya Alvar Fáñez   chose three knights
and sent them to My Cid   in Valencia where he was:
"Say to the Campeador   —whom may God keep from
      harm—
that the King has set free   his wife and daughters;
while we are in his lands   he will provide us with escort.
Within fifteen days   if God keep us from harm
we shall be with him,   I and his wife and his daughters
and all their good ladies with them,   as many as are here."
The knights have set out   and will take care to do this.
Minaya Alvar Fáñez   remained in San Pedro.

   You would have seen knights   ride in from all directions
wishing to go to Valencia   to My Cid of Bivar,
asking Alvar Fáñez   to aid them in this,
Minaya saying,   "I shall do so gladly."
Sixty-five warriors   have assembled with him there
besides the hundred   whom he had brought with him;
they made a fine escort   to go with those ladies.
   Minaya gave the abbot   the five hundred marks;
I must tell what he did   with the other five hundred.
The good Minaya   took thought to provide
Doña Jimena   and her daughters there,
and the other ladies   who served them and went before
      them,
with the finest garments   to be found in Burgos
and with palfreys and mules,   that their appearance might
      be seemly.
When he had thus   decked out these ladies

el bueno de Minaya   pienssa de cavalgar;
afevos Raquel e Vidas   a los piedes le caen;
"Merçed, Minaya,   cavallero de prestar!
Desfechos nos ha el Çid,   sabet, si no nos val;
soltariemos la ganançia,   que no diesse el cabdal."
—"Yo lo veré con el Çid,   si Dios me lieva allá.
Por lo que avedes fecho   buen cosiment y avrá."
Dixo Raquel e Vidas: "el Criador lo mande!
Si non, dexaremos Burgos,   ir lo hemos buscar."

   Ido es pora San Pero   Minaya Albar Fáñez,
muchas yentes se le acogen,   penssó de cavalgar,
grand duelo es   al partir del abbat:
"¡Sí vos vala el Criador,   Minaya Alvar Fáñez!
por mí al Campeador   las manos le besad
aqueste monesterio   no lo quiera olbidar;
todos los días del sieglo   en levarlo adelant
el Çid Campeador   siempre valdrá más."
Respuso Minaya: "fer lo he de veluntad."

   Yas espiden   e pienssan de cavalgar,
el portero con ellos   que los ha de aguardar;
por la tierra del rey   mucho conducho les dan.
De San Pero fasta Medina   en çinco días van;
felos en Medina   las dueñas e Albar Fáñez.

   Direvos de los cavalleros   que levaron el menssaje;
al ora que lo sopo   mio Çid el de Bivar,
plógol de coraçon   e tornós a alegrar;
de la su boca   conpeço de fablar:
"Qui buen mandadero enbía,   tal deve sperar.
Tú, Muño Gustioz   e Per Vermudoz delant,
e Martín Antolínez,   un Burgalés leal,
el obispo don Jerome,   coronado de prestar,
cavalguedes con çiento   guisados pora huebos de lidiar;
por Santa María   vos vayades passar,
vayades a Molina,   que iaze más adelant,
tiénela Avengalvón,   mio amigo es de paz,
con otros çiento cavalleros   bien vos conssigrá;
id pora Medina   quanto lo pudiéredes far,
mi mugier e mis fijas   con Minaya Albar Fáñez,
así commo a mí dixieron,   hi los podredes fallar;

the good Minaya   made ready to ride,
when behold Raquel and Vidas   fall at his feet.
"Grace, Minaya,   worthy knight!
The Cid has undone us,   you may know, if he will not
     aid us;
we shall ignore the interest   if he give back the capital."
"I shall speak of it with the Cid   if God will take me there.
You will be well rewarded   for all you have done."
Raquel and Vidas said,   "May the Creator will it so!
If not, we shall leave Burgos   and go to seek him in
     Valencia."

PROMISE OF REPAYMENT TO THE JEWS

    Minaya Alvar Fáñez   has gone to San Pedro;
many gathered about him,   he made ready to ride.
Their sorrow is great   at the parting from the abbot.
"The Creator keep you,   Minaya Alvar Fáñez!
In my name kiss the hands   of the Campeador,
let him not forget   this monastery;
all the days of the world   as he may give it aid,
the Cid Campeador   will increase in honor."
Minaya answered,   "I shall tell him gladly."

REMEMBER THE MONASTERY!

    They bid farewell   and ride forward,
the King's herald with them   to be at their service;
through the lands of the King   they were well escorted.
They go in five days   from San Pedro to Medinaceli;
behold them in Medinaceli,   the ladies and Alvar Fáñez.
    I shall tell you of the knights   who took the message.
When My Cid of Bivar   heard the news
it pleased his heart   and he rejoiced,
and in these words   he began to speak:
"He who sends a good messenger   may expect good news.
You, Muño Gustioz   and Pedro Bermúdez
and Martín Antolínez,   loyal man of Burgos,
and you, Bishop Don Jerome,   honored cleric,
ride with a hundred   armed as though for battle,
ride forward   through Santa María
to Molina,   which is farther on:
Abengalbón is lord there,   my friend, at peace with me.
He is certain to join you   with another hundred knights;
ride toward Medinaceli   at your best speed;
my wife and my daughters   with Minaya Alvar Fáñez
you will find there,   as I have been told;

con grand ondra   aduzídmelas delant.
E yo fincaré en Valençia,   que mucho costadom ha;
grand locura seríe   si la desenparás;
yo ffincaré en Valençia,   ca la tengo por heredad."
    Esto era dicho,   pienssan de cavalgar,
e quanto que pueden   non fincan de andar.
Troçieron a Santa María   e vinieron albergar a
                                Fronchales,
e el otro día vinieron   a Molina posar.
El moro Avengalvón,   quando sopo el menssaje,
saliólos reçibír   con grant gozo que faze:
"¿Venides, los vassallos   de myo amigo natural?
A mí non me pesa,   sabet, mucho me plaze!"
Fabló Muño Gustioz,   non speró a nadi:
mío Çid vos saludava,   e mandólo recabdar,
"con ciento cavalleros   que privádol acorrades;
su mugier e sus fijas   en Medina están;
que vayades por ellas,   adugades gelas acá,
e ffata en Valençia   dellas non vos partades."
Dixo Avengalvón: "fer lo he de veluntad."
Essa noch   conducho les dió grand.
a la mañana   pienssan de cavalgar;
çientol pidieron,   más él con dozientos va.
Passan las montañas,   que son fieras e grandes,
passaron desí Mata de Taranz
de tal guisa   que ningún miedo non han,
por el val de Arbuxuelo   pienssan a deprunar.
    E en Medina   todo el recabdo está;
vídolos venir armados   temiós Minaya Albar Fáñez.
envió dos cavalleros   que sopiessen la verdad;
esto non detardan,   ca de coraçón lo han;
el uno fincó con ellos   y el otro tornó a Albar Fáñez:
"Virtos del Campeador   a nos vienen buscar;
afevos aquí   Per Vermudoz delant
e Muño Gustioz   que vos quieren sin hart
e Martín Antolínez,   el Burgalés natural,
e obispo don Jerome,   coranado leal,
"e alcáyaz Avengalvón   con sus fuerças que trahe,
por sabor de mio Çid   de grand óndral dar;

conduct them here before me   with great honor.
And I shall stay in Valencia,   whose conquest was costly.
It would be great folly   to abandon it now;
I shall stay in Valencia,   which is my inheritance."
    When this was said   they make ready to ride,
and as far as they can   they ride on without resting.
They passed Santa María   and lodged at Bronchales,
then another day's riding   and they slept in Molina.
When the Moor Abengalbón   knew of the message
he rode out to receive them   with great rejoicing:
"Have you come, vassals   of my dear friend?
It does not sadden me,   believe me, it fills me with joy!"
Muño Gustioz spoke,   he waited for no one:
"My Cid sent you greetings   and asked you to provide us
with a hundred knights   to ride with us at once;
his wife and his daughters   are in Medinaceli;
he would have you go   and escort them here
and not go from them   as far as Valencia."
Abengalbón said,   "I will do it gladly."
That night he served them   a great banquet.
In the morning   they made ready to ride.
They had asked for a hundred,   but he came with two
        hundred.
They ride into the mountains   which are wild there and
        high,
and they pass   the Plain of Taranz
riding in such manner   that none feels fear;
by the Valley of Arbujelo   they begin to descend.
    Close guard is mounted   in Medinaceli;
Minaya Alvar Fáñez,   seeing them come armed,
was alarmed, and sent two knights   to find out the truth;
at this they did not take long   for they were eager to know;
the one stayed and the other   turned back to Alvar Fáñez:
"Forces of the Campeador   have come to find us;
behold, there at their head   is Pedro Bermúdez,
and Muño Gustioz,   your unfailing friend,
and Martín Antolínez,   who was born in Burgos,
and the Bishop Don Jerome,   the loyal cleric,
and the chief Abengalbón,   and his warriors with him;
for the love of My Cid   and to do him honor

todos vienen en uno,   agora llegarán."
Essora dixo Minaya: "vayamos cavalgar."
Esso ffo apriessa fecho,   que nos quieren detardar.
Bien salieron den ciento   que non pareçen mal,
en buenos cavallos   a cuberturas de çendales
e peytrales a cascaviellos,   e escudos a los cuellos traen,
e en las manos lanças   que pendones traen,
que sopiessen los otros   de qué seso era Albar Fáñez
o quomo saliera de Castiella con estas dueñas que trahe.

    Los que ivan mesurando   e llegando delant
luego toman armas   e tómanse a deportar;
por çerca de Salón   tan grandes gozos van.
Don llegan los otros,   a Minaya se van homillar.
Quando llegó Avengalvón,   dont a ojo ha,
sonrrisándose de la boca,   hívalo abraçar,
en el ombro lo saluda,   ca tal es so husaje:
"Tan buen día convusco,   Minaya Albar Fáñez!
Traedes estas dueñas   por o valdremos más,
mugier del Çid lidiador   e sus ffijas naturales
ondrar vos hemos todos,   ca tal es la su auze,
maguer que mal le queramos,   non gelo podremos far,
en paz o en guerra   de lo nuestro abrá;
muchol tengo por torpe   qui non conosçe la verdad."

84
Los viajeros descansan en Medina. Parten de Medina
a Molina. Llegan cerca de Valencia

    Sorrisós de la boca   Albar Fáñez Minaya:
"Ya Avengalvón,   amígol sodes sin falla!
Si Dios me llegare al Çid   e lo vea con el alma,
desto que avedes fecho   vos non perderedes nada.

they are all riding together;   now they are about to arrive."
Then Minaya said,   "Let us mount and ride."
They did so at once   without delay.
All the hundred rode out;   the sight of them was splendid,
mounted on good horses   caparisoned with sendal,
bells on their breast leathers,   shields from their necks
        hanging,
the knights bearing lances,   from each its pennon hanging,
that all might know   with what prudence came Alvar
        Fáñez
and how he would leave Castile   with these ladies he was
        bringing.
    Those who rode as scouts   and arrived first
grasped their weapons   and jousted for the sport;
not far from Jalón   there was great rejoicing.
When the others came up   they made obeisance to Minaya.
When Abengalbón came up   and set eyes on him,
smiling with his mouth   he went to embrace him;
he kisses him on the shoulder   as is the Moors' custom.
"It is a glad day in which I meet you,   Minaya Alvar
        Fáñez!
You bring with you these ladies   whose presence does us
        honor,
the wife and the daughters   of the Cid, the warrior;
we must all do them honor   for such is his fortune
that though we should wish him evil   we could not
        perform it;
in peace or in war   he will have what is ours;   ⁊
who does not know the truth   I hold stupid."   .

84
*The travelers rest in Medinaceli. They leave Medinaceli
for Molina. They arrive near Valencia*

    Alvar Fáñez Minaya   smiles at these words.
"Greetings, Abengalbón,   unfailing friend!
If God allow me to reach the Cid   and this soul may see
        him,
you will lose nothing   for this that you have done.
149

Vayamos posar,   ca la çena es adobada."
Dixo Avengalvón: "plazme desta presentaja;
antes deste terçer día   a vos la daré doblada."
Entraron en Medina,   sirvíalos Minaya,
todos fueron alegres   del çerviçio que tomaron,
el portero del rey   quitar lo mandava;
ondrado es mio Çid   en Valençia do estava
de tan grand conducho   commo en Medínal sacaran;
el rey lo pagó todo,   e quito se va Minaya.

   Passada es la noche,   venida es la mañana,
oída es la missa,   e luego cavalgavan.
Salieron de Medina   e Salón passavan,
Arbuxuelo arriba   privado aguijavan,
el campo de Taranz   luego atravessavan,
vinieron a Molina,   la que Avengalvón mandava.
El obispo don Jerome   buen cristiano sin falla,
las noches e los días   las dueñas aguardava;
e buen cavallo en diestro   que va ante sues armas.
Entre él e Albar Fáñez   hivan a una compaña.
Entrados son a Molina,   buena e rica casa;
el moro Avengalvón   bien los sirvié sin falla,
de quanto que quisieron   non ovieron falla,
aun las ferraduras   quitar gelas mandava;
a Minaya e a las dueñas.   ¡Dios cómmo las ondrava!
Otro día mañana   luego cavalgavan,
fata en Valençia   sirviálos sin falla;
lo so despendié el moro,   que dellos non tomava nada.
Con estas alegrías   e neuvas tan ondradas
aprés son de Valençia   a tres leguas contadas.
A mio Çid,   el que en buena çinxo espada,
dentro a Valençia   el mandádol levavan.

85
El Cid envía gentes al encuentro de los viajeros

   Alegre fo mio Çid,   que nunqua más nin tanto,

Come rest for the night with us   for a banquet is spread."
Abengalbón said,   "This courtesy delights me;
before three days have passed   I shall return it to you
    twofold."
They entered Medinaceli;   Minaya saw to their comfort.
All were well pleased   with the care that was shown them.
The King's herald   bade farewell and left them;
far off in Valencia   the Cid was honored
by such pomp and celebration   as were seen in Medinaceli;
the King paid for it all   and Minaya owed no one.

    The night has passed   and morning come
and Mass heard   and then they mounted.
They rode out of Medinaceli   and passed Jalón;
up the river by Arbujuelo   they spurred without pausing,
then they passed by   the Plain of Taranz;
they came to Molina   where Abengalbón was lord.
The Bishop Don Jerome,   a good Christian without fault,
guarded the ladies   day and night
with a good war horse on his right   which rode ahead of
    his weapons.
He and Alvar Fáñez   rode together (MINAYA)
They have entered Molina,   a rich and goodly town.
The Moor Abengalbón   without fail serves them well;
there was no lack   of all they might desire.
Even their horses   he shod newly.
And Minaya and the ladies,   God, how he honored them!
Another day in the morning   they mounted again;
as far as Valencia   without fail he served them.
The Moor spent his own   and would take nothing from
    them.
Amid such rejoicings   and tidings of honor
they came within three leagues   of Valencia.
The news came   into Valencia
to My Cid,   who in good hour girded sword.

85
The Cid sends people to meet the travelers

Never greater joy,   nor as great, as My Cid's then,

ca de lo que más amava   yál viene el mandado.
Dozientos cavalleros   mandó exir privado,
que reçiban a Minaya   e a las dueñas fijas dalgo;
él sedié en Valençia   curiando e guardando,
ca bien sabe que Albar Fáñez   trahe todo recabdo;

86
Don Jerónimo se adelanta a Valencia para preparar una
procesión. El Cid cabalga al encuentro de Jimena.
Entran todos en la ciudad
afevos todos aquestos   reçiben a Minaya
e a las dueñas e a las niñas   e a las otras conpañas.
    Mandó mio Çid   a los que ha en sue casa
que guardassen el alcáçer   e las otras torres altas
e todas las purtas   e las exidas e las entradas,
e aduxiéssenle a Bavieca;   poco avié quel ganara
d'aquel rey de Sevilla   e de la sue arrancada,
aun non sabié mio Çid,   el que en buen ora çinxo espada,
si serié corredor   o ssi abrié buena parada;
a la puerta de Valençia,   do en so salvo estava,
delante su mugier e de sus fijas   querié tener las armas.
    Reçebidas las dueñas   a una gran ondrança,
obispo don Jerome   adelant se entrava,
y dexava el cavallo,   pora la capiella adeliñava;
con quantos que él puede,   que con oras se acordaran,
sobrepelliças vestidas   e con cruzes de plata,
reçibir salién las dueñas   e al bueno de Minaya
    El que en buen ora nasco   non lo detardava:
vistiós el sobregonel;   luenga trahe la barba;
ensiellanle a Bavieca,   cuberturas le echavan,
mio Çid salió sobrél,   e armas de fuste tomava.
Por nombre el cavallo   Bavieca cavalga,

for the news had come   from that which he most loved.
He sent two hundred knights   to ride with all speed
to receive Minaya   and the noble ladies;
he himself remained in Valencia   keeping watch and
    guard
for he trusts Alvar Fáñez   to take every care.

86
Don Jerome rides ahead to Valencia to prepare a
procession. The Cid rides out to meet Jimena. All enter
the city

Behold, how all these   receive Minaya
and the ladies and the girls   and the rest of their
    companions.
My Cid ordered   those who were with him
to guard the castle   and the other high towers
and all the gates   and the exits and entrances,
and to lead him his horse Babieca,   which he had taken
    lately
from that King of Seville   when he had defeated him.
My Cid, who in good hour girded sword,   had not yet
    ridden him
nor learned whether he were swift   and answered the
    reins well;
at the gate of Valencia,   where it was safe,
he wished to bear arms   before his wife and daughters.
The ladies were received   with great honor;
the Bishop Don Jerome   entered ahead of them
and dismounted   and went to the chapel;
with as many as he might muster   who were ready in time,
dressed in surplices   and with crosses of silver,
he went out to receive the ladies   and the good Minaya.
He who was born in good hour   did not delay:
he put on his silk tunic,   his long beard hung down;
they saddled for him Babieca   and fastened the caparisons.
My Cid rode out upon him   bearing wooden arms.
On the horse they called   Babieca he rode,

hizo una corrida,   ésta fo tan estraña,
quando ovo corrido,   todos se maravillavan;
des día se preçió Bavieca   en quant grant fo España.
En cabo del cosso   mio Çid descavalgava,
adeliñó a su mugier   e a sues fijas amas;
quando lo vio doña Ximena,   a piedes se le echava:
"Merced, Campeador,   en buen ora cinxiestes espada!
Sacada me avedes   de muchas vergüenças malas;
afeme aquí, señor,   yo e vuestras fijas amas,
con Dios e convusco   buenas son e criadas."
A la madre e a las fijas   bien las abraçava,
del gozo que avíen   de los sos ojos lloravan.
Todas las sus mesnadas   en grant deleyt estavan,
armas tenién   e tablados crebantavan.
Oíd lo que dixo   el que en buena çinxo espada:
"vos doña Ximena,   querida mugier e ondrada,
e mas mis fijas   mio coraçón e mi alma,
entrad comigo   en Valençia la casa,
en esta heredad   que vos yo he ganada."
Madre e fijas   las manos le besavan.
A tan grand ondra   ellas a Valençia entravan.

87
Las dueñas contemplan a Valencia desde el Alcázar

    Adeliñó mio Çid,   con ellas al alcáçer,
allá las subie   en el más alto logar.
Ojos vellidos   catan a todas partes,
miran Valençia   cómmo yaze la çibdad,
e del otra parte   a ojo han el mar,
miran la huerta,   espessa es e grand,
e todas las otras cosas   que eran de solaz;
alçan las manos   pora Dios rogar,
desta ganançia   cómmo es buena e grand.
    Mio Çid e sus compañas   tan a grand sabor están.
El ivierno es exido,   que el março quiere entrar.
Dezir vos quiero nuevas   de allent partes del mar,
de aquel rey Yúcef   que en Marruecos está.

rode at a gallop; it was a wonder to watch.
When he had ridden one round everyone marveled;
from that day Babieca was famous through all Spain.
When he had ridden, My Cid dismounted.
He went up to his wife and his two daughters; *at the gate of Valencia*
when Doña Jimena saw him she fell at his feet:
"Grace, Campeador, who in good hour girded sword!
You have delivered me from much vile shame.
Here am I, sire, I and both your daughters;
with God's help and yours they are good and well
      brought up."
He took his wife in his arms and then his daughters;
such was his joy the tears flowed from his eyes.
All his vassals were filled with jubilation;
they jousted with arms and rode at targets.
Hear what he said, who in good hour girded sword:
"You, Doña Jimena, my honored and dear wife,
and both my daughters, my heart and my soul,
enter with me the town of Valencia,
the inheritance which I have won for you."
Mother and daughters kissed his hands.
They entered Valencia with great celebration.

87

The ladies see Valencia from the castle

  My Cid and they went to the castle;
there he led them up to the highest place. → *compared to limited rows of the monastery*
Then fair eyes gaze out on every side;
they see Valencia, the city, as it lies,
and turning the other way their eyes behold the sea.
They look on the farmlands, wide and thick with green,
and all the other things which gave delight;
they raised their hands to give thanks to God
for all that bounty so vast and so splendid.
  My Cid and his vassals lived in great content.
The winter has gone and March begun.
I would tell you news from across the sea,
from that King Yúsuf, who is in Morocco.

88
El rey de Marruecos viene a cercar a Valencia

Pesól al rey de Marruecos   de mio Çid don Rodrigo:
"que en mis heredades   fuertemientre es metido,
e él non gelo gradeçe   sinon a Jesu Cristo."
Aquel rey de Marruecos   ajuntava sus virtos;
con çinquaenta vezes mill de armas   todos foron
        conplidos,
entraron sobre mar,   en las barcas son metidos,
van buscar a Valençia   a mio Çid don Rodrigo.
Arribado en las naves,   fuera eran exidos.

89

Llegaron a Valençia,   la que mio Çid a conquista,
fincaron las tiendas,   e posan las yentes descriedas.
Estas nuevas   a mio Çid eran venidas.

90
Alegría del Cid al ver las huestes de Marruecos. Temor de Jimena

"¡Grado al Criador   e al Padre espirital!
Todo el bien que yo he,   todo lo tengo delant:
con afán gané a Valençia,   e ela por heredad,
a menos de muert   no la puodo dexar;
grado al Criador   e a santa María madre,
mis fijas e mi mugier   que las tengo acá.
Venídom es deliçio   de tierras d'allent mar,
entraré en las armas,   non lo podré dexar;
mis fijas e mi mugier   veerme an lidiar;
en estas tierras agenas   verán las moradas cómmo se
        fazen,
afarto verán por los ojos   cómmo se gana el pan."
Su mugier e sus fijas   subiólas al alcáçer,

The King of Morocco comes to lay siege to Valencia

The King of Morocco was troubled   because of My Cid
    Don Rodrigo:
"For in lands that are mine   he has trespassed gravely
and gives thanks for it to no one   save Jesus Christ."   *not Mohammad*
That King of Morocco   assembled his nobles.
Fifty times a thousand armed men   gathered under him;
they have embarked on the sea,   they have entered into
    the ships,
they leave for Valencia   to find My Cid Don Rodrigo.
The ships have entered harbor,   the men have come
    forth on land.

89

They arrived at Valencia,   which My Cid conquered.
The unbelievers have made camp,   they have pitched
    their tents.
The news of this   has come to My Cid.

90

The Cid's joy at seeing the Moroccan hosts.
Jimena's fear

"Thanks be to the Creator   and to the heavenly Father!
All that I own   is here before me;
with toil I took Valencia   for my inheritance;
as long as I live   I will not leave it.
Thanks be to the Creator   and Santa María Mother,
that I have here with me   my wife and my daughters.
Delight has come to me   from the lands beyond the sea;
I shall arm myself,   I cannot evade it;
my wife and my daughters   will see me in battle,
in these foreign lands they will see   how houses are made,
they will see clearly   how we earn our bread."
He led his wife and daughters   up into the castle;

alçavan los ojos,   tiendas vidieron fincar:
"¿Quês esto, Çid,   sí el Criador vos salve!"
—*"Ya mugier ondrada,   non ayades pesar!*
Riqueza es que nos acreçe   maravillosa e grand:
a poco que viniestes,   presend vos quieren dar:
por casar son vuestras fijas,   adúzenvos axuvar."
—*"A vos grado, Çid,   e al Padre spirital."*
—*"Mugier, seed en este   palaçio, en el alcáçer;*
non ayades pavor   por que me veades lidiar,
con la merced de Dios   e de santa María madre,
créçeme el coraçón   por que estades delant;
con Dios aquesta lid   yo la he de arrancar."

91
El Cid esfuerza a su mujer y a sus hijas. Los moros
invaden la huerta de Valencia

Fincadas son las tiendas   e pareçen los alvores,
a una grand priessa   tañién los atamores;
alegravas mio Çid e dixo: "tan buen día es oy!"
Miedo a su mugier   e quiérel crebar el coraçón,
assí ffazie a las dueñas   e a sus fijas amas a dos:
del día que nasquieran   non vidieron tal tremor.
Prisos a la barba   el buen Çid Campeador:
"Non ayades miedo,   ca todo es vuestra pro;
antes destos quinze días,   si ploguiere al Criador,
abremos a ganar   aquellos atamores;
a vos los pondrán delant   e veredes quáles son,
desí an a sseer   del obispo don Jerome,
colgar los han en Santa María   madre del Criador."
Vocaçión es que fizo   el Çid Campeador.
Alegre' son las dueñas,   perdiendo van el pavor.
Los moros de Marruecos   cavalgan a vigor,
por las huertas adentro   entran sines pavor.

they raised their eyes   and saw the tents pitched.
"What is this, Cid,   in the name of the Creator?"
"My honored wife,   let it not trouble you!
This is great and marvelous wealth   to be added unto us;
you have barely arrived here   and they send you gifts,
they bring the marriage portion   for the wedding of your
      daughters."
"I give thanks to you, Cid,   and to our heavenly Father."
"Wife, stay here in the palace,   here in the castle;
have no fear   when you see me fighting;
by the grace of God   and Santa María Mother,
my heart grows within me   because you will be watching;
with God's help I shall triumph   in this battle."

91
The Cid reassures his wife and daughters. The Moors
invade the farmlands of Valencia

The tents are pitched   and the dawn comes;
with a quickening stroke   the Moors beat on the drums.
My Cid rejoiced and said,   "A day of delight is this!"
His wife is frightened,   thinks her heart must shatter;
the ladies are frightened also   and both the daughters;
they had not known such terror   since the day they were
      born.
He stroked his beard,   the good Cid Campeador.
"Have no fear, for all this   is to your favor;
before these two weeks have gone,   if it please the
      Creator,
we will have wrenched from them   those same drums;
they shall be fetched before you   and you shall see what
      they are,
then they shall be given   to the Bishop Don Jerome
and hung in the Church   of Santa María, mother of God."
This is the vow   the Cid Campeador made.
   The ladies are reassured   and their fear goes from them.
The Moors of Morocco   ride out boldly;
without fear   they have entered the farmlands.

159

92
Espolonada de los cristianos

Vídolo el atalaya   e tanxo el esquila;
prestas son las mesnadas   de las yentes de Roy Díaz,
adóbanse de coraçón   e dan salto de la villa.
Dos fallan con los moros   cometiénlos tan aína,
sácanlos de las huertas   mucho a fea guisa;
quinientos mataron dellos   conplidos er ese día.

93
Plan de batalla

Bien fata las tiendas   dura aqueste alcaz,
mucho avién fecho,   pienssanse de tornar.
Albar Salvadórez   preso fincó allá.
Tornados son a mio Çid   los que comién so pan;
él se lo vió con los ojos,   cuéntangelo delant;
alegre es mio Çid   por quanto fecho han:
"Oídme, cavalleros,   non rastará por al;
oy es día bueno   e mejor será cras:
por la mañana prieta   todos armados seades,
el obispo de Jerome   soltura nos dará,
dezir nos ha la missa,   e penssad de cavalgar;
ir los hemos fferir,   non passará por al,
en el nombre del Criador   e d' apóstol santi Yague.
Más vale que noslos vezcamos,   que ellos cojan el pan."
Essora dixieron todos: "damor e de voluntad."
Fablaya Minaya,   non lo quiso detardar:
"pues esso queredes,   Çid, a mí mandedes al;
dadme çiento e treínta cavalleros   pora huebos de lidiar;
quando vos los fóredes ferir,   entraré yo del otra part;
o de amas o del una   Dios nos valdrá."
Essora dixo el Çid: "de buena voluntad."

92
The Christians attack

The sentinel saw them   and rang the bell;
the vassals are ready,   the men of Ruy Díaz;
they arm themselves with a will   and ride from the city.
Where they met the Moors   they charged them at once,
drove them from the farmlands   with much harsh
        treatment.
They killed five hundred of them   on that day.

93
The plan of battle

As far as the tents   they pursued them;
they have accomplished much   and they turn back.
Alvar Salvadórez   remained captive there.
Those who eat the Cid's bread   have returned to his side;
he saw it with his own eyes   yet they retell it;
My Cid is pleased   with what they have done.
"Hear me, knights, it must be   thus, and not otherwise;
today has been a good day, / tomorrow will be better./
Be armed all of you   by the time day breaks;
the Bishop Don Jerome   will give us absolution;
he will sing us Mass   and then we shall ride.
In the name of the Creator   and of Saint James the
        apostle
we shall attack them;   thus it must be.
It is better that we should beat them   than that they
        should take our bread."
Then all said, "Willingly   and with all our hearts."
Minaya spoke,   he waited no longer:
"Since you wish it so, Cid,   send me another way;
give me for the battle   a hundred and thirty knights;
when you fall upon them, I shall attack from the other side.
On both sides, or one only,   God will aid us."
Then the Cid answered,   "I will do it gladly."

94

El Cid concede al obispo las primeras heridas

Es día es salido   e la noch es entrada,
nos detardan de adobasse   essas yentes cristianas.
A los mediados gallos,   antes de la mañana,
el obispo don Jerome   la missa les cantava;
la missa dicha   gran sultura les dava:
"El que aquí muriere   lidiando de cara,
préndol yo los pecados,   e Dios le abrá el alma.

A vos Çid don Rodrigo   en buena çinxiestes espada,
yo vos canté la missa   por aquesta mañana;
pídovos una dona   e seam presentada:
las feridas primeras   que las aya yo otorgadas."
Dixo el Campeador: "desaquí vos sean mandadas."

95

Los cristianos salen a batalla. Derrota de Yúcef. Botín extraordinario. El Cid saluda a su mujer y sus hijas. Dota a las dueñas de Jimena. Reparto del botín

Salidos son todos armados   por las torres de Quarto,
mio Çid a los sos vassallos   tan bien los acordando.
Dexan a las puertas   omnes de grant recabdo.
Dios salto mio Çid   en Bavieca el so cavallo;
de todas guarnizones   muy bien es adobado.
La seña sacan fuera   de Valençia dieron salto,
quatro mill menos treínta   con mio Çid van a cabo
a los çinquaenta mill   vanlos ferir de grado;
Alvar Fáñez e Minaya   entráronles del otro cabo.
Plogo al Criador   e ovieron de arrancarlos.

Mio Çid empleó la lança,   al espada metió mano,
atantos mata de moros   que non fueron contados;
por el cobdo ayuso   la sangre destellando.

94

*The Cid grants the Bishop the right of striking the first
blows*

The day has gone   and the night come.
That Christian host   was not slow in making ready.
By the second cock crow,   before morning came,
the Bishop Don Jerome   sang them the Mass.
When the Mass was said   he gave them full absolution:
"He who may die here   fighting face to face
I absolve of his sins,   and God will receive his soul.
    "Cid Don Rodrigo,   who in good hour girded sword,
I sang Mass   for you this morning;
I crave a boon of you,   I beg you to grant it;
I would have you let me strike   the first blows in the fight."
The Campeador said,   "From this moment it is granted."

95

*The Christians sally to battle. The rout of Yúsuf. The
enormous spoils. The Cid greets his wife and daughters.
He settles dowries on Jimena's ladies. The division of the
    spoils*

All have ridden out armed   from the towers of Cuarto,
My Cid giving full instructions   to his vassals.
They leave at the gates   men they can count on.
My Cid sprang   onto his horse, Babieca,
that is splendidly caparisoned   with all manner of
    ornaments.
They ride out with the banner,   they ride out from
    Valencia;
four thousand less thirty   ride with My Cid;
gladly they go   to attack the fifty thousand.
Alvar Fáñez and Minaya   rode in from the other side.
As pleased the Creator,   they overcame them.
    My Cid used his lance   and then drew his sword;
he killed so many Moors   that the count was lost;
above his elbow   the blood ran.

163

Al rey Yúcef   tres colpes le ovo dados,
salióse del sol espada,   ca muchol andido el cavallo,
metiósle en Gujera,   un castiello palaçiano;
mio Çid el de Bivar   fasta allí llegó en alcanço
con otros quel consiguen   de sos buenos vassallos.
Desd' allí se tornó   el que en buen ora nasco,
mucho era alegre   de lo que an caçado;
allí preçió a Bavieca   de la cabeça fasta a cabo.
Toda esta ganançia   en su mano a rastado.
Los çincuenta mill   por cuenta fuero' notados:
non escaparon   más de çiento e quatro.
Mesnadas de mio Çid   robado an el campo;
entre oro e plata   fallaron tres mil marcos,
de las otras ganançias   non avía recabdo.
Alegre era mio Çid   e todos sos vassallos,
que Dios les ovo merçed   que vençieron el campo:
quando al rey de Marruecos   assí lo an arrancado,
dexó Albar Fáñez   por saber todo recabdo;
con çient cavalleros   a Valençia es entrado,
fronzida trahe la cara,   que era desarmado,
assí entró sobre Bavieca,   el espada en la mano.
   Reçibiendo las dueñas   que lo están esperando;
mio Çid fincó antellas,   tovo la rienda al cavallo:
"A vos me omillo, dueñas,   grant prez vos he gañado:
vos teniendo Valençia,   e yo vençí el campo;
esto Dios se lo quiso   con todos los sos santos,
quando en vuestra venida   tal ganançia nos ha dado.
Veedes el espada sangrienta   e sudiento el cavallo:
con tal cum esto   se vençen moros del campo.
Rogad al Criador   que vos viba algunt año,
entraredes en prez,   e besarán vuestras manos."
Esto dixo mio Çid,   diciendo del cavallo.
Quandol vieron de pie   que era descavalgado,
las dueñas e las fijas,   e la mugier que vale algo
delante el Campeador   los inojos fincaron:
"Somos en vuestra merced   e bivades muchos años!"
   En buelta con él   entraron al palaçio,
e ivan posar con él   en unos preçiosos escaños.

He has struck King Yúsuf   three blows;
Yúsuf escaped from his sword   for hard he rode his horse
and sheltered in Cullera,   a noble castle;
My Cid of Bivar   arrived there in pursuit
with those of his good vassals   who stay by his side.
And there he turned back,   he who in good hour was born.
Great was his joy   at what they had taken,
and there he knew the worth of Babieca   from head to tail.
All those spoils   remain in his hands.
A count was made: of the fifty thousand Moors,
only a hundred and four   had escaped.
My Cid's vassals   have despoiled the field;
they found three thousand marks   of mixed gold and
       silver;
the other spoils   were beyond numbering.
My Cid was joyful,   and all his vassals,
because God of His grace   had given them triumph.
When they had thus routed   the King of Morocco
My Cid left Alvar Fáñez   to attend to the rest;
with a hundred knights   he returned to Valencia.
He had his helmet off   and his hood drawn back;
thus he rode in on Babieca,   his sword in his hand.
    There he received the ladies,   who were waiting for
       him;
My Cid reined in his horse   and stopped before them.
"I bow before you, ladies,   great spoils I have won for you;
you kept Valencia for me   and I have won in the field;
this was the will of God   and of all His saints;
upon your arrival   they have sent us great treasure.
You see the sword bloody   and the horse sweating:
thus it is   that one conquers Moors in the field.
Pray to the Creator   to grant me a few years' life;
you will grow in honor   and vassals will kiss your hands."
This My Cid spoke,   dismounting from his horse.
When they saw him on foot   when he had dismounted,
the ladies and the daughters   and the noble wife
all kneeled   before the Campeador.
"By your grace we are all that we are;   may you live
       long!"
    Then with him   they entered the palace
and sat with him   on the elaborate benches.

"Ya mugier doña Ximena,   nom lo aviedes rogado:
Estas dueñas que aduxiestes,   que vos sirven tanto,
quiérolas casar   con de aquestos mios vassallos;
a cada una dellas   doles dozientos marcos,
que lo sepan en Castiella,   a quién sirvieron tanto.
Lo de vuestras fijas   venir se a más por espacio."
Levantáronse todas   e besáronle las manos,
grant fo el alegría   que fo por el palaçio.
Commo lo dixo el Çid,   asší lo han acabado.

    Minaya Albar Fáñez   fuera era en el campo,
con todas estas yentes   escriviendo e contando;
entre tiendas e armas   e vestidos preçiados
tanto fallan ellos desto   que mucho es sobejano.
Quiérovos dezir   lo que es más granado:
non pudieron saber la cuenta   de todos los cavallos
que andan arriados   e non ha qui tomallos;
los moros de las tierras   ganado se an y algo;
maguer de todo esto,   el Campeador contado
de los buenos e otorgados   cayéronle mill cavallos;
quando a mio Çid   cayeron tantos;
los otros bien pueden   fincar pagados.
Tanta tienda preciada   e tanto tendal obrado
que a ganado mio Çid   con todos sos vassallos!
La tienda del rey de Marruecos,   que de las otras es cabo,
dos tendales la sufren,   con oro son labrados;
mandó mio Çid   el Campeador contado,
que fita sovisse la tienda,   e non la tolliesse dent cristiano:
"Tal tienda commo esta,   que de Marruecos ha passado,
enbiar la quiero   a Alfonso el Castellano,
que croviesse sus nuevas   de mio Çid que avié algo."

    Con aquestas riquezas tantas   a Valençia son entrados.
El obispo don Jerome,   caboso coronado,
quando es farto de lidiar   con amas las sus manos,
non tiene en cuenta   los moros que ha matado;
lo que cadié a él   mucho era sobejano;
mio Çid don Rodrigo,   el que en buen ora nasco,

"'My wife, Doña Jimena, have you not begged this of
  me?
These ladies you bring with you who so well serve you,
I wish to marry them with those vassals of mine;
to each of them I give two hundred marks.
Let it be known in Castile who it is they have served so
  well.
For your daughters, we shall come to decide that more
  slowly."
All rose and kissed his hands;
great was the rejoicing in the palace.
And the Cid had spoken, so it was done.

   Minaya Alvar Fáñez was abroad in the field
with all those men counting and writing down;
as for tents and arms and garments of value,
it passed belief what they found.
I will tell you what was most important:
there was no counting all the horses
who went without riders and none to take them.
Even the Moors in the farmlands captured some,
and despite this there fell to the famous Campeador
a thousand horses of the best and best broken,
and when My Cid received so many,
surely the others were well requited.
So many precious tents and jeweled tent poles
My Cid has taken with all his vassals!
The tent of the King of Morocco, which surpassed all the
  others,
hangs on two tent poles wrought with gold;
My Cid commanded, the famous Campeador,
that no Christian touch it, that it be left standing.
"Such a tent as this, which has come from Morocco,
I wish to send to Alfonso the Castilian
that he may believe the news that My Cid has
  possessions."
With all these riches they have returned to Valencia.
The Bishop Don Jerome, the mitered man of great merit,
when he has finished fighting with both his hands
has lost count of the Moors he has killed.
The spoils that fell to him also were enormous;
My Cid Don Rodrigo, who was born in good hour,

de toda la su quinta   el diezmo l'a mandado.

96
Gozo de los cristianos. El Cid envía nuevo presente al rey

Alegres son por Valençia   las yentes cristianas,
tantos avien de averes,   de cavallos e de armas;
alegre es doña Ximena   e sus fijas amas,
e todas las otras dueñas   ques tienen por casadas.
El bueno de mio Çid   non lo tardó por nada:
"¿Do sodes, caboso?   venid acá, Minaya;
de lo que a vos cadió   vos non gradeçedes nada;
desta mi quinta,   dígovos sin falla,
prended lo que quisiéredes,   lo otro remanga.
E cras ha la mañana   ir vos hedes sin falla
con cavallos desta quinta   que yo he ganada,
con siellas e con frenos   e con señas espadas;
por amor de mi mugier   e de mis fijas amas,
por que assí las enbió   dond ellas son pagadas,
estos dozientos cavallos   irán en presentajas,
que non diga mal el rey Alfons   del que Valençia
        manda."
Mandó a Per Vermudoz   que fosse con Minaya.
Otro día mañana   privado cavalgavan,
e dozientos omnes   lievan en su conpaña,
con saludes del Çid   que las manos le besava:
desta lid   que mío Çid ha arrancada
dozientos cavallos   le enbiava en presentaja,
"e servir lo he siempre   mientra que oviesse el alma."

97
Minaya lleva el presente a Castilla

Salidos son de Valençia   e pienssan de andar,
tales ganancias traen   que son a aguardar.

has sent him a tithe out of his own fifth.

96
The rejoicing of the Christians. The Cid sends a new present to the King

These Christian people in Valencia rejoice
at their great wealth, at so many horses and weapons;
Doña Jimena is pleased, and her daughters,
and all the other ladies, who count themselves already
    married.
My good Cid delayed for nothing.
"Where are you, worthy knight? Come here, Minaya.
For that which has fallen to you you owe me no thanks;
I mean what I say; out of this fifth that is mine
take what you wish and leave the rest for me.
And when tomorrow dawns you must go without fail
with horses from this fifth which I have taken,
with saddles and bridles and each with its sword;
for my wife's sake and that of my daughters,
since he sent them here where they are content,
these two hundred horses will go to him as a gift,
that King Alfonso may speak no ill of him who rules in
    Valencia."
He commanded Pedro Bermúdez to go with Minaya.
The next day in the morning they rode off early
to kiss the King's hands with the Cid's greetings,
and two hundred men rode as their retinue.
My Cid sent as a gift two hundred horses
from this battle in which he had triumphed.
"And I shall serve him always while my soul is with me."

97
Minaya takes the gift to Castile

They have left Valencia and begin their journey;
they bear such riches with them they must guard them
    closely.

Andan los días e las noches,   que vagar non se dan
e passada han la sierra,   que las otras tierras parte.
Por el rey don Alfons   tómanse a preguntar.

98
Minaya llega a Valladolid

Pasando van las sierras   e los montes e las aguas,
llegan a Valladolid   do el rey Alfons estava;
enviávale mandado   Per Vermudoz e Minaya,
que mandasse reçebir   a esta conpaña
mio Çid el de Valençia   enbía sue presentaja.

99
El rey sale a recibir a los del Cid. Envidia
de Garci Ordóñez

Alegre fo el rey,   non vidiestes atanto,
mandó calvalgar apriessa   todos sos fijos dalgo
i en los primeros   el rey fuera dió salto,
a veer estos mensajes   del que en buena ora nasco.
Ifantes de Carrion,   sabet, is açertaron,
e comde don García   del Çid so enemigo malo.
A los unos plaze   e a los otros va pesando.
A ojo los avien   los del que en buen ora nasco,
cuédanse que es almofalla,   ca non vienen con mandado;
el rey don Alfonso   seíse santiguando.
Minaya e Per Vermudoz   adelante son llegados,
firiéronse a tierra,   diçiendo de los cavallos;
antel rey Alfons   los inoios fincados,
besan la tierra   e los piedes amos:
"Merced, rey Alfonsso,   sodes tan ondrado!

They ride two days and nights   without pausing to rest,
and they have passed the mountains   that cut off the other
      country.
They begin to inquire   for King Alfonso.

98
Minaya arrives in Valladolid

They have passed the ranges,   the mountains and the
      waters;
they arrive in Valladolid   where King Alfonso is.
Pedro Bermúdez and Minaya   sent a message
requesting him to prepare   to receive this company,
for My Cid of Valencia   was sending him a gift.

99
*The King rides out to receive the Cid's men. The envy
of García Ordóñez*

The King rejoiced;   you have not seen him so pleased.
He commanded all his nobles   to mount at once,
and the King rode out   among the first
to see those messengers   from him who was born in good
      hour.
The Heirs of Carrión,   you may know, murmured at this,
and the Count Don García,   the Cid's sworn enemy.
What pleases some   weighs heavy upon others.
Those sent by My Cid   came into sight;
one would have thought them an army,   not mere
      messengers;
King Alfonso   crosses himself.
Minaya and Pedro Bermúdez   have arrived before him;
they set foot on the earth,   they get down from their
      horses,
they kneel down   before King Alfonso,
they kiss the ground   and both his feet.
"Grace, King Alfonso,   greatly honored!

171

por mio Çid el Campeador   todo esto vos besamos;
a vos llama por señor,   e tienes por vuestro vassallo
mucho preçia la ondra   el Çid quel avedes dado.
Pocos días ha, rey,   que una lid a arrancado:
a aquel rey de Marruecos,   Yúcef por nombrado,
con çincuaenta mill   arrancólos del campo.
Los ganados que fizo   mucho son sobejanos,
ricos son venidos   todos los son vassallos,
e embíavos dozientos cavallos,   e bésavos las manos."
Dixo rey don Alfons: "Reçíbolos de grado.
"Gradéscolo a mio Çid   que tal don me ha enbiado;
aun vea ora   que de mí sea pagado."
Esto plogo a muchos   e besáronle las manos.

    Pesó al comde don García,   e mal era irado;
con diez de sos parientes   aparte davan salto;
"¡Maravilla es del Çid,   que su ondra creçe tanto.
En la ondra que él ha   nos seremos abiltados;
por tan biltadamientre   vençer reyes del campo,
commo si los fallasse muertos   aduzirse los cavallos
por esto que él faze   nos abremos enbargo."

100
El rey muéstrase benévolo hacia el Cid

    Fabló el rey don Alfons   odredes lo que diz:
"Grado al Criador   e a señor sant Esidre
estos dozientos cavallos   quem enbía mio Çid.
Mio reyno adelant   mejor me podrá servir.
A vos Minaya Albar Fáñez   e a Per Vermudoz aquí
mándovos los cuorpos   ondradamientre vestir
e guarnirvos de todas armas   commo vos dixiéredes aquí,
que bien parescades   ante Roy Díaz mio Çid;
dovos tres cavallos   e prendedlos aquí.
Assí commo semeja   e la veluntad me lo diz,
todas estas nuevas   a bien abrán de venir."

We kiss your feet   for My Cid the Campeador;
he calls you his lord   and remains your vassal
and prizes greatly   the honor you have given him.
A few days since, King,   he triumphed in a battle
over that King of Morocco   whose name is Yúsuf
and fifty thousand besides;   he beat them from the field.
The spoils that he took   are very great;
all of his vassals   have become rich men,
and he sends you two hundred horses   and kisses your
     hands."
King Alfonso said, "I receive them with pleasure.
I send thanks to My Cid   for this gift he has sent me;
he will yet see the hour   I shall do as much for him."
This pleased many   and they kissed his hands.
   It weighed heavy on Count Don García;   it enraged
     him deeply.
With ten of his kinsmen   he rode to one side.
"What a marvel, this Cid,   how his honor grows.
And in his honor   we are dishonored.
For killing Kings in the field   as casually
as though he had found them dead   and seized their
     horses,
for his deeds of this sort   we shall suffer."

100

The King shows himself benevolent toward the Cid

   King Alfonso spoke,   hear what he said:
"I thank the Creator   and lord Saint Isidore
for these two hundred horses   which My Cid has sent me.
In the coming days of my kingdom   I shall expect still
     greater things.
You, Minaya Alvar Fáñez,   and Pedro Bermúdez there,
I command   that you be given rich garments,
and choose arms for yourselves   at your pleasure
so that you may appear well   before Ruy Díaz, My Cid.
I give you three horses;   take them now.
Thus it seems to me,   and I am convinced
that from these new things   good must follow."

173

101

Los infantes de Carrión piensan casar con las hijas del Cid

Besáronle las manos   y entraron a posar;
bien los mandó servir   de cuanto huebos han.
   D'iffantes de Carrión   yo vos quiero contar,
fablando en so conssejo,   aviendo su poridad:
"Las nuevas del Çid   mucho van adelant,
demandemos sus fijas   pora con ellas casar;
creçremos en nuestra ondra   e iremos adelant."
Vienen al rey Alfons   con esta poridad:

102

Los infantes logran que el rey les trate el casamiento. El rey pide vistas con el Cid. Minaya vuelve a Valencia y entera al Cid de todo. El Cid fija el lugar de las vistas

   "Merced vos pedimos   commo a rey e a señor;
con vuestro conssejo   lo queremos fer nos,
que nos demandedes   fijas del Campeador;
casar queremos con ellas   a su ondra y a nuestra pro."
Una grant ora   el rey penssó e comidió:
"Yo eché de tierra   al buen Campeador,
e faciendo yo a él mal,   e él a mí grand pro,
del casamiento   non sé sis abrá sabor;
mas pues bos lo queredes,   entremos en la razón."
   A Minaya Albar Fáñez   e a Per Vermudoz
el rey don Alfonsso   essora los llamó
a una quadra   elle los apartó:
"Oídme Minaya   e vos, Per Vermudoz:
sírvem mio Çid   Roi Díaz Campeador
elle lo mereçe   e de mí abrá perdón;
viniéssem a vistas   si oviesse dent sabor.

101

The Heirs of Carrión think of marrying the
Cid's daughters

They kissed his hands   and went in to rest;
he commanded that they should be served   with whatever
    they needed.
   I would tell you   of the Heirs of Carrión
taking counsel together,   plotting in secret:
"The Cid's affairs   prosper greatly;
let us ask   for his daughters in marriage;
our honor will grow   and we shall prosper."
They come to King Alfonso   with this secret.

102

The Heirs persuade the King to arrange the marriage
for them. The King asks to see the Cid.
Minaya returns to Valencia and informs the Cid of
    everything.
The Cid fixes the place of meeting

   "We beg your grace   as our King and lord,
by your leave   we would have you ask for us
for the hands of the daughters   of the Campeador;
we would marry them,   to his honor and our advantage." CHANGED BEHAVIOR
A long while   the King thought and meditated:
"I sent the good Campeador   into exile
and wrought him harm,   and he has returned me much
    good.
I cannot tell   if he will favor this marriage,
but since you wish it   I shall discuss it with him." measured behavior
   Then King Alfonso   called to himself
Minaya Alvar Fáñez   and Pedro Bermúdez
and took them aside   into another room.
"Hear me, Minaya,   and you, Pedro Bermúdez.
Ruy Díaz, Campeador,   My Cid, serves me well.
He shall receive my pardon   as he deserves; Cid pardoned
let him come and appear before me   if it meet his pleasure.

175

Otros mandados ha   en esta mi cort:
Dídago e Ferrando,   los iffantes de Carrión,
sabor han de casar   con sus fijas amas a dos.
Seed buenos mensageros,   e ruégovoslo yo
que gelo digades   al buen Campeador:
abrá y ondra   e creçrá en onor,
por conssagrar   con iffantes de Carrión."
Fabló Minaya   e plogo a Per Vermudoz:
"Rogar gelo emos   lo que dezides vos;
después faga el Çid   lo que oviere sabor."
—"Dezid a Roy Díaz,   el que en buen ora naçió,
quel iré a vistas   do aguisado fore;
do elle dixiere,   y sea el mojón.
Andar le quiero   a mio Çid en toda pro."
Espidiensse al rey,   con esto tornados son,
van pora Valençia   ellos e todos los sos.
    Quando lo sopo   el buen Campeador,
apriessa cavalga,   a reçebirlos salió;
sonrrisós mio Çid   e bien los abraçó:
"¿Venides, Minaya,   e vos, Per Vermudoz!
En pocas tierras a   tales dos varones.
¿Commo son las saludes   de Alfons miọ señor?
¿si es pagado   o reçibió el don?"
Dixo Minaya: "d'alma e de coraçón
es pagado,   e davos su amor."
Dixo mio Çid: "grado al Criador!"
Esto diziendo,   conpieçan la razón,
lo quel rogava   Alfons el de León
de dar sues fijas   a ifantes de Carrión,
quel connosçie i ondra   e creçrié en onor,
que gelo conssejava   d'alma e de coraçón.
Quando lo oyó mio Çid   el buen Campeador,
una grand ora   penssó e comidío:
"Esto gradesco a Cristus   el mio señor
echado fu de tierra,   he tollida la onor,
con grand afán gané   lo que he yo;
a Dios lo gradesco   que del rey he su amor,
e pídenme mis fijas   pora ifantes de Carrión.
¿Dezid, Minaya   e vos Per Vermudoz,

There are further tidings   from here in my court:
Diego and Fernando,   the Heirs of Carrión,
wish to marry   his two daughters.
Be good messengers,   I beg of you,
and tell all this   to the good Campeador:
his name will be ennobled   and his honor increase   *wrong*
by thus contracting marriage   with the Heirs of Carrión."
Minaya spoke,   in agreement with Pedro Bermúdez:
"We shall ask him   as you have told it to us,
then the Cid may do   what meets his pleasure."
"Say to Ruy Díaz,   who in good hour was born,
that I shall come to meet him   wherever he prefers;
wherever he says,   let us meet each other.
I wish to help My Cid   however I may."
They said farewell to the King   and turned away;
they depart for Valencia   with all who are with them.

      When the good Campeador   heard they were coming
he mounted in haste   and rode out to receive them.
He smiled, My Cid,   and warmly embraced them:
"Have you come, Minaya,   and you, Pedro Bermúdez!
In few lands   are there two such knights.
What greeting   from Alfonso my lord?
Is he satisfied?   Did he receive the gift?"
Minaya said,   "With heart and soul
he is satisfied   and returns you to his favor."
My Cid replied,   "The Creator be thanked!"
And when this was said   they began to tell
what Alfonso of León   had asked of them,
of giving the Cid's daughters   to the Heirs of Carrión
that his name might be ennobled   and he increase in
      honor,
that the King approved this   with heart and soul.
When he heard this, My Cid,   the good Campeador,
a long while   he thought and meditated:
"I give thanks   to Christ, to my lord.
I was sent into exile,   my honors were taken away;
with toil and pain I have taken   what is now mine.
I give thanks to God   that I have regained the King's love
and that he asks for my daughters   for the Heirs of
      Carrión.
Tell me, Minaya,   and you, Pedro Bermúdez,

177

d' aqueste casamiento   que semeja a vos?"
—"Lo que a vos ploguiere   esso dezimos nos."
    Dixo el Çid: "de grand natura   son infantes de
        Carrión,
ellos son mucho urgullosos   e an part en la cort,
deste casamiento   non avría sabor;
mas pues lo conseja   el que más vale que nos,
fablemos en ello,   en la poridad seamos nos.
Afé Dios del çielo   que nos acuerde en lo mijor."
—*"Con todo esto,   a vos dixo Alfons*
que vos vernié a vistas   do oviéssedes sabor;
querer vos ye veer   e darvos su amor,
acordar vos yedes después   a todo lo mejor."
Essora dixo el Çid: "plazme de coraçón."
—*"Estas vistas   o las ayades vos,"*
dixo Minaya,   "vos seed sabidor."
—*"Non era maravilla   si quisiesse el rey Alfons,*
fasta do lo fallássemos   buscar lo iriemos nos,
por darle grand ondra   commo a rey e señor.
Mas lo que él quisiere,   esso queramos nos.
Sobre Tajo,   que es una agua mayor,
ayamos vistas   quando lo quiere mio señor."
    Escrivien cartas,   bien las seelló,
con dos cavalleros   luego las enbió:
lo que el rey quisiere,   esso ferá el Campeador.

103
El rey fija plazo para las vistas. Dispónese con los
suyos para ir a ellas

    Al rey ondrado   delante le echaron las cartas;
quando las vió,   de coraçón se paga:
"Saludadme a mio Çid,   el que en buena çinxo espada;
sean las vistas   destas tres sedmanas;
s' yo bivo so,   allí iré sin falla."
Non lo detardan,   a mio Çid se tornavan.
    Della part e della   pora las vistas se adobavan;
¿quién vido por Castiella   tanta mula preçiada,

what do you think   of this marriage?"
"Whatever would please you   seems best to us."
   The Cid spoke: "They have a great name,   these Heirs
      of Carrión;
they are swollen with pride   and have a place in the court,
and this marriage   would not be to my liking.
But since he wishes it   who is worth more than we,
let us talk of the matter   but do it in secret,
and may God in heaven   turn it to the best."
   "And besides this,   Alfonso sends to tell you
that he will meet you   wherever you please;
he wishes to see you   and make manifest his favor,
after which you may decide   what you think best."
Then the Cid said,   "It pleases my heart."
   And Minaya said,   "As for this meeting,
you are to decide   where it is to be."
   "It would be no marvel   if King Alfonso had bid me
come where he was,   and we should have gone
to do him honor   as befits a King and lord.
But what he wishes   we must wish also.
By the Tagus,   the great river,
let us meet   when my lord pleases."
   They wrote letters   and sealed them straitly,
and they sent them   in the hands of two horsemen;
the Campeador will do   what the King desires.

103

*The King fixes the time of the meeting. He prepares his
retinue to go there*

   The letters have come   to the honored King;
he rejoiced   when he saw them.
"My greetings to My Cid,   who in good hour girded on
      sword,
let the meeting be   three weeks from now;
if I live   I shall be there without fail."
They returned to My Cid   without delay.
   On this side and that   they made ready for the meeting;
who had ever seen   so many fine mules in Castile,

179

e tanto palafré   que bien anda,
cavallos gruessos   e corredores sin falla,
tanto buen pendón   meter en buenas astas,
escudos boclados   con oro e con plata,
mantos e pielles   e buenos çendales d' Andriá?
Conduchos largos   el rey enbiar mandava
a las aguas de Tajo,   o las vistas son aparejadas.
Con el rey   atantas buenas conpañas.
Iffantes de Carrión   mucho alegres andan,
lo uno adebdan   e lo otro pagavan;
commo ellos tenien,   creçer les ya la ganançia,
quantos quisiessen   averes d' oro o de plata.
El rey don Alfonso   a priessa cavalgava,
cuemdes e podestades   e muy grandes mesnadas.
Ifantes de Carrión   lievan grandes conpañas.
Con el rey van leoneses   e mesnadas gallizianas,
non son en cuenta,   sabet, las castellanas;
sueltan las riendas,   a las vistas se van adeliñadas.

104

El Cid y los suyos se disponen para ir a las vistas. Parten
de Valencia. El rey y el Cid se avistan a orillas del
Tajo. Perdón solemne dado por el rey al Cid. Convites.
El rey pide al Cid sus hijas para los infantes.
El Cid confía sus hijas al rey y éste las casa. Las
vistas acaban. Regalos del Cid a los que se despiden.
El rey entrega los infantes al Cid

Dentro en Valençia   mio Çid el Campeador
non lo detarda,   pora las vistas se adobó.
Tanta gruessa mula   e tanto palafré de sazón,
tanta buena arma,   e tanto buen cavallo corredor,
tanta buena capa   e mantos e pelliçones;

and so many palfreys   of graceful gait,
heavy chargers   and swift horses,
so many fair pennons   flown from good lances,
shields braced at the center   with gold and with silver,
cloaks and furs,   fine cloth from Alexandria?
The King has them send   ample provisions
to the banks of the Tagus   where the meeting will be.
A splendid company   goes with the King.
In high spirits   go the Heirs of Carrión;
here they make new debts   and there pay the old,
as though their fortunes   had so much increased already
and they had gold and silver   as much as they could wish
    for.
The King Don Alfonso   mounts without delay;
counts and nobles ride with him   and a host of vassals.
And a goodly company goes   with the Heirs of Carrión.
With the King go men of León   and of Galicia,
and Castilians,   you may know, without number;
they release the reins,   they ride to the meeting.

104

*The Cid and his men make ready to go to the meeting. The
departure from Valencia. The King and the Cid meet on
the banks of the Tagus. The King solemnly pardons the
Cid. Invitations. The King asks the Cid for the hands of his
daughters for the Heirs of Carrión. The Cid gives his
daughters to the King, who marries them. The end of the
meeting. The Cid's gifts to those who depart. The King
commends the Heirs to the Cid*

   In Valencia   My Cid the Campeador
does not delay,   but makes ready for the meeting.
So many fat mules   and fine palfreys,
so many splendid weapons   and so many swift horses,
so many fine capes   and cloaks and furs;

chicos e grandes   vestidos son de colores.
Minaya Albar Fáñez   e aquel Per Vermudoz.
Martín Muñoz   el que mandó a Mont Mayor,
e Martín Antolínez,   el Burgalés de pro,
el obispo don Jerome,   coronado mejor,
Albar Alvaroz,   e Alvar Salvadórez,
Muño Gustioz,   el cavallero de pro
Galind Garçiaz,   el que fo de Aragón:
estos se adoban   por ir con el Campeador,
e todos los otros   quantos que i son.
    Alvar Salvadórez   e Galind Garciaz el de Aragón,
a aquestos dos   mandó el Campeador
que curien a Valençia   d' alma e de coraçón,
e todos los otros   que en poder dessos fossen.
Las puertas del alcáçer,   mio Çid lo mandó
que non se abriessen   de día nin de noch;
dentro es su mugier   e sus fijas amas a dos,
en que tiene su alma   e so coraçon,
e otras dueñas   que las sirven a su sabor;
recabdado ha,   commo tan buen varón,
que del alcáçer   una salir non puode,
fata ques torne,   el que en buen ora nació.
    Salien de Valençia   aguíjan a espolón.
Tantas cavallos en diestro,   gruessos e corredores,
mio Çid se los gañara,   que non ge los dieran en don.
Hyas va pora las vistas   que con el rey paró.
    De un día es llegado antes   el rey don Alfons.
Quando vieron que vinie   el buen Campeador,
reçebir lo salen   con tan gran onor.
Don lo ovo a ojo   el que buen ora nació,
a todos los sos   estar los mandó,
si non a estos cavalleros   que querie de coraçón.
Can unos quinze   a tierras firió,
como le comidía   el que en buen ora nació;
los inojos e las manos   en tierra los fincó,
las yerbas del campo   a dientes las tomó,

everyone, young and old,   all dressed in colors.
Minaya Alvar Fáñez   and that same Pedro Bermúdez,
Martín Muñoz,   lord of Monte Mayor,
and Martín Antolínez,   the loyal citizen of Burgos,
the Bishop Don Jerome,   the worthy cleric,
Alvar Alvarez   and Alvar Salvadórez,
Muño Gustioz, that excellent knight,
Galindo García   who came from Aragón,
these make ready   to go with the Campeador,
and all the others,   as many as there were.
   Alvar Salvadórez   and Galindo García of Aragón,
the Campeador commanded these two
to guard Valencia   with heart and soul,
and he commanded all who should remain there   to obey
      these two.
My Cid ordered   that they should not open
the gates of the palace   by day or by night;
his wife and both his daughters   are within,
in whom his heart is   and his soul,
and there also are the other ladies   who wait upon their
      pleasure.
My Cid in his prudence   has commanded
that none may come forth   out of the castle
until he himself returns   who in good hour was born.
   They went out from Valencia and spurred forward,
so many fine horses,   sleek, and swift runners;
My Cid had won them,   they had not been given as gifts.
And they rode on toward the meeting   arranged with the
      King.
   The King arrived   one day before him,
and when he saw   the Campeador coming
he rode out to meet him   to do him honor.
When he who was born in good hour   saw the King
      coming
he commanded those who were with him   to come to a
      halt,
all except a few knights   nearest to his heart,
Then as he had thought to do   who in good hour was born,
he and fifteen knights   got down from their horses
and on his knees and hands   he knelt down on the ground;
he took the grass of the field   between his teeth

llorando de los ojos,   tanto avié el gozo mayor;
assí sabe dar omildança   a Alfons so señor.
De aquesta guisa   a los piedes le cayó;
tan grand pesar ovo   el rey don Alfons:
"Levantados en pie,   ya Çid Campeador,
besad las manos,   cado piedes no;
si esto non feches,   non avredes mi amor."
Hinojos fitos   sedie el Campeador,
"¡Merced vos pido a vos,   mio natural señor,
assí estando,   dédesme vuestra amor,
que los oyan todos   quantos aquí son."
Dixo el rey: "esto feré   d'alma e de coraçón."
aquí vos perdono   e dovos mi amor,
ên todo mio reyno   parte desde oy."
Fabló mio Çid   e dixo esta razón:
"merced; yo lo reçibo,   Alfons mio señor;
gradéscolo a Dios del çieló   e después a vos.
e a estas mesnadas   que están a derredor."
Hinojos fitos   los manos le besó.
Levós en pie   e en la bócal saludó.
Todos los demás   desto avien sabor;
pesó a Albar Diaz   e a Garci Ordóñez.
    Fabló mio Çid   e dixo esta razón:
"Esta gradesco   al padre Criador,
quando he la graçia   de Alfons mio señor;
valer me a Dios   de dia e de nocb.
Fossedes mio huesped,   si vos ploguiesse, señor."
Dixo el rey: "non es aguisado oy:
vos agora llegastes,   e nos viniemos anoch;
mio huesped seredes,   Çid Campeador,
e cras feremos   lo que ploguiere a vos."
Besóle la mano   mio Çid, le otorgó.
Essora se le omillan   iffantes de Carrión:
"Omillámósnos, Çid,   en buena nasquiestes vos!
En quanto podemos   andamos en uestro pro."
Respuso mio Çid: "assí lo mande el Criador!"
Mio Çid Roy Diaz,   que en ora buena nació,
en aquel día   del rey so huesped fo;
non se puede fartar dél,   tántol querie de coraçón;

and wept from his eyes   so great was his joy,
and thus he rendered homage   to Alfonso his lord
and in this manner   fell at his feet.
The King Alfonso   was grieved at this sight:
"Rise, rise,   Cid Campeador,
kiss my hands   but not my feet;
if you humble yourself further   you will lose my love."
The Campeador   remained on his knees:
"I beg grace of you,   my natural lord,
thus on my knees I beg you   to extend to me your favor
so that all may hear it,   as many as are here."
The King said, "I will do it   with all my heart and soul;
I hereby pardon you   and grant you my favor;
be welcome from this hour   in all my kingdom."
My Cid spoke,   here is what he said:
"My thanks, I accept the pardon,   Alfonso, my lord;
I thank God in heaven   and afterwards you
and these vassals   here about us."
Still on his knees   he kissed the King's hand
then rose to his feet   and kissed him on the mouth.
And all who were there   rejoiced to see it,
but it grieved Alvar Díaz   and García Ordóñez.
    My Cid spoke.   Here is what he said:
"I give thanks   to our Father the Creator
for this grace I have received   from Alfonso my lord;
now God will be with me   by day and by night.
If it please you, my lord,   be my guest."
The King said,   "That would not be right.
You arrive only now   and we came here last night;
you must be my guest,   Cid Campeador,
and tomorrow we shall do   what meets your pleasure."
My Cid kissed his hand   and agreed to this.
Then the Heirs of Carrión   came and made him
        obeisance.
"We bow before you,   Cid, who in good hour were born!
We shall serve your fortune   as far as we are able."
The Cid answered,   "God grant that it may be so."
My Cid Ruy Díaz,   who in good hour was born,
on that same day   was the guest of the King,
who so loved him   he could not have enough of his
        company

185

catándol sedie la barba, que tan aínal creçió.
Maravíllanse de mio Çid quantos que y son.
  El día es pasado, e entrada es la noch.
Otro día mañana, claro salie el sol,
el Campeador a los sos lo mando
que adobassen cozina pora quantos que i son;
de tal guisa los paga mio Çid el Campeador,
todos eran alegres e acuerdan en una razón:
passado avie tres años no comieran mejor.
  Al otro día mañana, assí commo salió el sol,
el obispo don Jerome la missa cantó.
Al salir de la missa todos juntados son;
non lo tardó el rey, la razón conpeço:
"Oidme, las escuelas, cuemdes e ifançones!
cometer quiero un ruego a mio Çid el Campeador;
assí lo mande Cristus que sea a so pro.
Vuestras fijas vos pido, don Elvira e doña Sol,
que las dedes por mugieres, a ifantes de Carrión.
Semejan el casamiento ondrado e con grant pro,
ellos vos las piden e mándovoslo yo.
Della e della parte, quantos que aquí son,
los mios e los vuestros que sean rogadores;
dándoslas, mio Çid, si vos vala el Criador!"
—"Non abría fijas de casar," repuso el Campeador,
"ca non han grant hedad e de días pequeñas son.
De grandes nuevas son ifantes de Carrión,
perteneçen pora mis fijas e aun pora mejores.
Hyo las engendré amas e criásteslas vos,
entre yo y ellas en vuestra merçed somos nos;
afellas en vuestra mano don Elvira e doña Sol,
dadlas a qui quisiéredes vos, ca yo pagado so."
—"Graçias," dixo el rey, "a vos e a tod esta cort."
Luego se levantaron iffantes de Carrión,
ban besar las manos al que en ora buena naçió;

186

and looking a long while at his beard,   which had grown
      so long.
All who beheld the Cid   marveled at the sight of him.
   The day has passed   and the night has come.
Next day in the morning   the sun rose bright;
the Campeador   called together his men,
bade them prepare a meal   for all who were there.
My Cid the Campeador   so well contented them,
all were merry   and of one mind;
they had not eaten better,   not for three years.
   The next day in the morning   as the sun was rising
the Bishop Don Jerome   sang Mass for them.
When they came from Mass,   all assembled together;
the King did not delay,   but began to speak.
"Hear me, my vassals,   counts and barons:
I would express a wish   to My Cid the Campeador,
and may Christ grant   that it be for the best.
I ask you for your daughters,   Doña Elvira and Doña Sol;
I ask you to give them as wives   to the Heirs of Carrión.
The marriage, to my eyes,   is honorable and to your
      advantage;
the Heirs request it   and I commend it to you.
And on this and on that side   as many as are here,
your vassals and mine,   may they second what I ask for;
give us your daughters, My Cid,   and may the Creator
      bless you."
"I have no daughters ready for marriage,"   the
      Campeador answered,
"for their age is slight   and their days are few.
I fathered them both   and you brought them up;
they and I   wait upon your mercy.
The fame is great   of the Heirs of Carrión,
enough for my daughters   and for others of higher station.
Doña Elvira and Doña Sol   I give into your charge;
give them to whom you think best   and I shall be
      content."
"My thanks," said the King,   "to you and to all this
      court."
The Heirs of Carrión   then got to their feet,
went and kissed the hands   of him who was born in
      good hour,

camearon las espadas   antel rey don Alfons.

Fabló rey don Alfons   commo tan buen señor:
"Graçias, Cid, commo tan bueno,   e primero al Criador,
quem dades vuestras fijas   pora ifantes de Carrión.
Daquí las prendo por mis manos   don Elvira e doña Sol,
e dólas por veladas   a ifantes de Carrión.
Yo las caso vuestras fijas   con vuestro amor,
al Criador plega   que ayades ende sabor.
Afellos en vuestras manos   ifantes de Carrión,
ellos vayan convusco,   ca d' aquén me torno yo.
Trezientos marcos de plata   en ayuda les do yo,
que metan en sus bodas   o do quisiéredes vos;
pues fueren en vuestro poder   en Valençia la mayor,
los yernos e las fijas   todos vuestros fijos son:
lo que vos ploguiere,   dellos fet, Campeador."
Mio Çid gelos reçibe,   las manos le besó:
"Mucho vos lo gradesco,   commo a rey e a señor!
Vos casades mis fijas,   ca non gelas do yo."

Las palabras son puestas,   los omenajes dados son,
que otro día mañana   quando saliesse el sol,
ques tornasse cada uno   don salidos son.
Aquís metió en nuevas   mio Çid el Campeador;
tanta gruessa mula   e tanto palafré de sazón,
tantas buenas vestiduras   que d' alfaya son,
conpeçó mio Çid a dar   a quien quiere prender so don;
cada uno de lo que pide,   nadi nol dize de no.
Mio Çid de los cavallos   sessaenta dio en don.
Todos son pagados de la vistas   quantos que y son;
partir se quieren,   que entrada era la noch.

El rey a los ifantes   a las manos les tomó,
metiólos en poder   de mio Çid el Campeador:
"Evad aquí vuestros fijos,   quando vuestros yernos son;
de oy mas, sabed   qué fer dellos, Campeador;
sírvanvos commo a padre   e guárdenvos cum a señor."

and they exchanged swords   before Alfonso the King.
    The King Don Alfonso spoke   as a worthy lord:
"My thanks, Cid, for your goodness,   you, favored of the
        Creator,
who have given me your daughters   for the Heirs of
        Carrión.
Here I take into my charge   Doña Elvira and Doña Sol
and give them as wives   to the Heirs of Carrión.
By your leave   I marry your daughters;
may it please the Creator   that good may come of it.
Here I give into your hands   the Heirs of Carrión;
they will go with you now   for I must return.
Three hundred marks of silver   I give to help them,
to be spent on the wedding   or whatever you please;
let them remain under you   in Valencia, that great city.
Sons-in-law and daughters,   all four are your children:
do with them   as seems best to you, Campeador."
My Cid kissed his hands   and received the Heirs.
"My deep thanks,   my King and lord.
It is you, not I,   who have married my daughters."
    The words are said,   the promises given
The next day in the morning   when the sun rose
each one would return   to the place from which he had
        come.
Then My Cid the Campeador   did a thing they would tell
        about:
So many fat mules   and so many fine palfreys,
so many precious garments   of great value
My Cid gave   to whomever would receive gifts,
and he denied no one   whatever he asked for.
My Cid gave as gifts   sixty of his horses.
All went from the meeting contented,   as many as there
        were;
it was time to part   for the night had come.
    The King took   the Heirs' hands.
and put them in the hands   of My Cid the Campeador.
"These now are your sons,   since they are your
        sons-in-law.
Know, from today forward   they are yours, Campeador;
let them serve you as their father   and honor you as their
        lord."

189

—"Gradéscolo, rey,   a prendo vuestro don;
Dios que está en çielo   devos dent buen galardon.

105
El Cid no quiere entregar las hijas por sí mismo.
Minaya será representante del rey

Yo vos pido merçed   a vos, rey natural:
pues que casades mis fijas,   así commo a vos plaz,
dad manero a qui las dé,   quando vos las tomades;
non gelas daré yo con mi mano,   nin dend non se
alabarán."
Respondió el rey: "afé aquí Albar Fáñez;
prendellas con vuestras manos   e daldas a los ifantes,
assí commo yo las prendo daquent,   commo si fosse
delant,
sed padrino dellas   a tod el velar;
quando vos juntáredes comigo   quem digades la verdat."
Dixo Albar Fáñez: "señor, afé que me plaz."

106
El Cid se despide del rey. Regalos

Tod esto es puesto,   sabed, en grand recabdo.
"Ya rey don Alfons,   señor tan ondrado,
destas vistas que oviemos,   de mí tomedes algo.
Tráyovos treínta palafrés,   estos bien adobados,
e treínta cavallos corredores,   estos bien enssellados;
tomad aquesto,   e beso vuestras manos."
Dixo el rey don Alfons: "mucho me avedes enbargado.
"Reçibo este don   que me avedes mandado;
plega al Criador,   con todos los son santos,
este plazer quem feches   que bien sea galardonado.
Mio Çid Roy Díaz,   mucho me avedes ondrado,
de vos bien so servido,   e tengon por pagado;
aun bivo sediendo,   de mí ayades algo!

"My thanks, King,   and I accept your gift.
May God Who is in heaven   give you reward.

105
The Cid refuses to give his daughters in marriage himself.
Minaya will be the King's representative

"I beg grace of you,   my natural King:
Since you marry my daughters   as suits your will,
name someone to give them in marriage   in your name.
I will not give them with my hand;   none shall boast of
    that."
The King answered,   "Here is Alvar Fáñez;   MINAYA
let him take them by the hand   and give them to the
    Heirs.
Let him act at the wedding   as though he were myself;   ACTS FOR
                                                          ALFONSO.
at the ceremony   let him be as the godfather
and let him tell me of it   when next we come together."
Alvar Fáñez said,   "With all my heart, sire."

106
The Cid bids farewell to the King. Gifts

You may know, all this was done   with great care.
"Ah, King Alfonso,   my honored lord,
take something of mine   to commemorate our meeting;
I have brought you thirty palfreys   with all their trappings
and thirty swift horses   with their saddles;
take these   and I kiss your hands."
King Alfonso said,   "You fill me with confusion.
I accept this gift   which you have brought me;
may it please the Creator   and all His saints besides
that this pleasure you give me   may be well rewarded.
My Cid Ruy Díaz,   you have done me great honor;
you have served me well   and I am contented;
if I live   I shall reward you somehow.

A Dios vos acomiendo,   destas vistas me parto.
Afé Dios del çielo,   que lo ponga en buen recabdo!"

107
Muchos del rey se van con el Cid a Valencia.
Los infantes acompañados por Pedro Vermúdez

Sobre so cavallo Babieca   mio Çid salto dio:
"Aqui lo digo,   ante mio señor el rey Alfons:
qui quiere ir a las bodas,   o reçibir mio don,
daquend vaya comigo;   cuedo quel avrá pro."
Yas espidió mio Çid   de so señor Alfons,
non quiere quel escurra,   dessí luégol quitó.
Veriedes cavalleros,   que bien andantes son,
besar las manos,   espedirse de rey Alfons:
"Merçed vos sea   e fazednos este perdón:
hiremos en poder de mio Çid   a Valençia la mayor;
seremos a las bodas   d' ifantes de Carrión
he de fijas de mio Çid,   de don Elvira e doña Sol."
Esto plogo al rey,   e a todos los soltó;
la conpaña del Çid creçe,   e la del rey mengó,
grandes son las yentes   que van con el Canpeador.
Adeliñan pora Valençia   la que en buen punto ganó.
A Fernando e a Díago   aguardar los mandó
a Per Vermudoz   e Muño Gustioz,
—en casa de mio Çid   non a dos mejores,—
que sopiessen sus mañas   d' ifantes de Carrión.
E va i Ansuor Gonçálvez,   que era bullidor,
que es largo de lengua,   mas en lo al non es tan pro.
Grant ondra les dan   a ifantes de Carrión.
Afelos en Valençia,   la que mio Çid ganó;
quando a ella assomaron,   los gozos son mayores.
Dixo mio Çid a don Pero   e a Muño Gustioz:

I commend you to God;   now I must leave.
May God Who is in heaven   turn all to the best."

107
Many of the King's men go with the Cid to Valencia.
The Heirs accompanied by Pedro Bermúdez

    My Cid mounted   his horse Babieca.
"Here I say   before Alfonso my lord:
Whoever will come to the wedding   and receive gifts
        from me,
let him come with me   and he shall not regret it."
    The Cid has said good-by   to Alfonso his lord;
he would not have the King escort him   on his way, but
        parted there.
You would have seen knights   of excellent bearing
saying farewell to King Alfonso,   kissing his hands:
"Grant us your grace   and give us your pardon;
we go as the Cid's vassals   to Valencia, that great city;
we shall be at the wedding   of the Heirs of Carrión
and the daughters of My Cid,   Doña Elvira and
        Doña Sol."
This pleased the King,   he gave them all his consent;
the Cid's company grows   and that of the King dwindles.
There are many   who go with the Campeador.
    They ride for Valencia,   which in a blessed hour he had
        taken.
He sent Pedro Bermúdez   and Muño Gustioz—
there were not two better knights   among all the Cid's
        vassals—
to ride as companions   with Fernando and Diego
that they might learn the ways   of the Heirs of Carrión.
And with them went Asur González,   who was a noisy
        person,
more ready of tongue   than of other things.
They paid much honor   to the Heirs of Carrión.
They have arrived in Valencia,   which My Cid had taken;
the closer they come   the greater is their rejoicing.
My Cid said to Don Pedro   and to Muño Gustioz:

"Dad les un reyal   a ifantes de Carrión,
e vos con ellos seed,   que assí vos lo mando yo.
Quando viniere la mañana,   que apuntare el sol,
verán a sus esposas,   a don Elvira e a doña Sol."

108
El Cid anuncia a Jimena el casamiento

Todos essa noch   foron a sus posadas,
mio Çid el Campeador   al alcáçer entrava;
reçibiólo doña Ximena   e sus fijas amas:
"¿Venides, Campeador,   buena çinxiestes espada!
muchos días vos veamos   con los ojos de las caras!"
—"Grado al Criador,   vengo, mugier ondrada!
yermos vos adugo   de que avremos ondraça;
gradídmelo, mis fijas,   ca bien vos he casadas!"

109
Doña Jimena y las hijas se muestran satisfechas

Besáronle las manos   la mugier e las fijas
e todas las dueñas   de quien son servidas:
"Grado al Criador   e a vos, Çid, barba vellida!
todo lo que vos feches   es de buena guisa.
Non serán menguadas   en todos vuestros días!"
—"Quando vos nos casáredes   bien seremos ricas."

110
El Cid recela del casamiento

"See to the lodging   of the Heirs of Carrión
and stay with them   for I command it.
When the morning comes   and the sun rises
they will see their wives,   Doña Elvira and Doña Sol."

108
The Cid announces the marriage to Doña Jimena

That night everyone   went to his lodging.
My Cid the Campeador   entered the palace;
Doña Jimena received him   and both his daughters.
"Have you returned, Campeador,   who girded sword in
      good hour?
Many days may we look upon you   with these eyes of
      ours."
"The Creator be thanked,   honored wife, that I have
      returned;
I bring you two sons-in-law   in whom we have much
      honor;
give me thanks, my daughters,   for I have married you
      well."

109
Doña Jimena and the daughters are pleased

His wife and his daughters   kissed his hand,
as did all the ladies   who wait upon them.
"The Creator be thanked,   and you, Cid of the splendid
      beard.
All you have done   has been done well.
They will lack for nothing   as long as you live."
"When you give us in marriage,   father, we shall be rich."

110
The Cid's misgivings concerning the marriage

—"*Mugier doña Ximena,   grado al Criador.*
A vos digo, mis fijas,   don Elvira e doña Sol:
deste vuestro casamiento   creçemos en onor;
mas bien sabet verdad   que non lo levanté yo:
pedidas vos ha e rogadas   el mio señor Alfons,
atan firme mientre   e de todo coraçón
que yo nulla cosa   nol sope dezir de no.
Metivos en sus manos,   fijas, amas ados;
bien me lo creades,   que él vos casa, ca non yo."

111
Preparativos de las bodas. Presentación de los infantes.
Minaya entrega las esposas a los infantes. Bendiciones
y misas.
Fiestas durante quince días. Las bodas acaban; regalos
a los convidados. El juglar se despide de sus oyentes

Penssaron de adobar   essora el palaçio,
por el suelo e suso   tan bien encortinado,
tanta pórpola e tanto xámed   e tanto paño preciado.
Sabor abriedes de seer   e de comer en palaçio.
Todos sos cavalleros   apriessa son juntados.
    Por iffantes de Carrión   essora enbiaron,
cavalgan los iffantes,   adelant adeliñavan al palaçio,
con buenas vestiduras   e fuertemientre adobados;
de pie e a sabor,   Dios, qué quedos entraron!
Reçibiólos mio Çid   con todos sos vasallos;
a elle e a ssu mugier   delant se le omillaron,
e ivan posar   en un preçioso escaño.
Todos los de mío Çid   tan bien son acordados,
están parando mientes   al que en buen ora nasco.
    El Campeador   en pie es levantado:
"Pues que a fazer lo avemos,   por qué lo imos tardando?
Venit acá, Albar Fáñez,   el que yo quiero e amo!

196

"Doña Jimena, my wife,   I give thanks to the Creator.
And I say to you, my daughters,   Doña Elvira and
    Doña Sol,
that by your marriage   we shall increase in honor.
But you may know   that none of this was my doing:
my lord Alfonso   asked me for your hands,
and that so urgently   with all his heart,
that I in no way   could have denied him.
I gave you into his hands,   both of you, my daughters;
believe this that I say: he will marry you, not I,"

*Reassure them,
reassure
himself*

111

*Preparations for the wedding. The presentation of the
    Heirs.
Minaya gives the wives to the Heirs. Benedictions and
    Masses.
The two-week festivities. The end of the wedding
    festivities;
the gifts given to the guests. The poet bids his audience
    farewell*

   Then they began   to get the palace ready:
they covered the floor   and the walls with carpets,
with bolts of silk and purple   and many precious fabrics.
You would have been well pleased   to sit and eat in the
    palace.
All the Cid's knights   have gathered together.
   Then they sent   for the Heirs of Carrión,
and the Heirs took horse   and rode to the palace
covered in finery   and splendid garments;
on foot and in seemly fashion   God, how meekly they
    entered!
My Cid received them   with all his vassals;
they humbled themselves   before him and his wife
then went and sat down   on a bench of precious work.
All My Cid's vassals,   quiet and prudent,
sit watching his face   who in good hour was born.
   The Campeador   rose to his feet:
"Since it must be done,   why should we delay?
Come here, Alvar Fáñez,   beloved knight.

affé amas mis fijas, métolas en vuestra mano;
sabedes que al rey assí gelo he mandado,
no lo quiero fallir por nada de quanto ay parado:
a ifantes de Carrión dadlas con vuestra mano,
e prendan bendiçiones e vayamos recabdando."
—Estoz dixo Minaya: "esto faré yo de grado."
Levántanse derechas e metiógelas en mano.
A ifantes de Carrión Minaya va fablando:
"Afevos delant Minaya, amos sedes hermanos.
Por mano del rey Alfons, que a mí lo ovo mandado,
dovos estas dueñas, —amas son fijas dalgo,—
que las tomassedes por mugieres a ondra e a recabdo."
Amos las reçiben d'amor e de grado,
mio Çid e a su mugier van besar la mano.

    Quando ovieron aquesto fecho, salieron del palacio,
pora Santa María a priessa adelinnando;
el obispo don Jerome vistiós tan privado,
a la puerta de la eclegia sediellos sperando;
dióles bendictiones, la missa a cantado.

    Al salir de la ecclegia cavalgaron tan privado,
a la glera de Valençia fuera dieron salto;
Dios, qué bien tovieron armas el Çid e sos vasallos!
Tres cavallos cameó el que en buen ora nasco.
Mio Çid de lo que vidie mucho era pagado:
ifantes de Carrión bien an cavalgado.
Tórnanse con las dueñas, a Valençia an entrado;
ricas fueron las bodas en el alcaçer ondrado,
e al otro día fizo mio Çid fincar siete tablados:
antes que entrassen a yantar todos los crebantaron.

    Quinze días conplidos en las bodas duraron,
çerca de los quinze días yas van los fijos dalgo.
Mio Çid don Rodrigo, el que en buen ora nasco,
entre palafrés e mulas e corredores cavallos,
en bestias sines al çiento ha mandados;
mantos e pelliçones e otros vestidos largos;
non foron en cuenta los averes monedados.

Both my daughters   I hereby give into your hands;
you know that the King   has commanded that it be so
and I would in every way   satisfy the agreement.
With your hand give them   to the Heirs of Carrión,
let them receive the benediction   and let it be properly
        done."
Then Minaya said,   "I will do it gladly."
The girls stood up   and he took them by the hands.
Minaya speaks   to the Heirs of Carrión:
"Now both you brothers   stand before Minaya.
By the hand of King Alfonso,   who has commanded me
        thus,
I give you these ladies,   both of gentle birth;
take them for wives   for the honor and good of all."
Both received them   with love and joy
and went to kiss the hands   of My Cid and his wife.
    When they had done this   they went out from the
        palace
and without delay   rode to Santa María;
the Bishop Don Jerome   put on his vestments;
at the door of the church   he waited for them,
gave them his benedictions   and sang them Mass.
    When they came from the church   all mounted in haste
and rode out   to the arena of Valencia.
God, how well they jousted,   My Cid and his vassals!
Three times he changed horses   he who was born in good
        hour.
My Cid was well content   with what he saw there:
the Heirs of Carrión   proved themselves good horsemen.
They returned to the ladies   and re-entered Valencia;
there were rich wedding feasts   in the gorgeous palace,
and the next day   My Cid set up seven tablets:
all must be ridden at and broken   before they went in
        to eat.
    Two full weeks   the wedding feasts went on;
at the end of that time   the noble guests went home.
My Cid Don Rodrigo,   who in good hour was born,
gave at least a hundred   of all sorts of beasts,
palfreys and mules   and swift running horses,
besides cloaks and furs   and many other garments,
and there was no counting   the gifts of money.

199

'Los vassallos de mio Çid   assí son acordados,
cada uno por sí   sos dones avien dados.
Qui aver quiere prender   bien era abastado;
ricos tornan a Castiella   los que a las bodas llegaron.
Yas ivan partiendo   aquestos ospedados,
espidiéndos de Roy Díaz,   el que en buen ora nasco,
e a todas las dueñas   e a los fijos dalgo;
por pagados se parten   de mio Çid e de sos vasallos.
Grant bien dizen dellos   ca será aguisado.
Mucho eran alegres   Dídago e Ferrando;
estos foron fijos   del comde don Gonçalvo.

   Venidos son a Castiella   aquestos hospedados,
el Çid e sos yernos   en Valençia son rastados.
Y moran los ifantes   bien cerca de dos años,
los amores que les fazen   mucho eran sobejanos.
Alegre era el Çid   e todos sos vasallos.
¡Plega a Santa María   e al Padre santo
ques pague des casamiento   mio Çid a el que lo ovo âlgo.

   Las coplas deste cantar   aquis van acabando.
El Criador vos vala   con todos los sos santos.

My Cid's vassals   also gave presents;
each one gave something   to the guests who were there.
Whatever the guests might wish for   their hands were
      filled;
all who had come to the wedding   returned rich to Castile.
Then those guests   made ready to leave,
took leave of Ruy Díaz,   who in good hour was born,
and of all those ladies   and the knights who were there;
they parted contented   from My Cid and his vassals.
They spoke well   of the way they had been treated.
And Diego and Fernando   were highly pleased,
they, the sons   of the Count Don Gonzalo.
   The guests have departed   for Castile;
My Cid and his sons-in-law   remain in Valencia.
And there the Heirs dwell   nearly two years,
and all in Valencia   showered them with their favor.
My Cid was joyful,   and all his vassals.
May it please Santa María   and the heavenly Father
to bless My Cid   and him who proposed this marriage.
   Herewith are ended   the verses of this cantar.
The Creator be with you   and all His saints besides.

maintains tension

CANTAR TERCERO

LA AFRENTA DE CORPES

112

Suéltase el león del Cid. Miedo de los infantes de Carrión.
El Cid amansa al león. Vergüenza de los infantes

En Valençia sedí   mio Çid con todos los sos,
con ello amos sos yernos   ifantes de Carrión.
Yazies en un escaño,   durmie el Campeador,
mala sobrevienta,   sabed, que les cuntió:
saliós de la red   e desatós el león.
En grant miedo se vieron   por medio de la cort;
enbraçan los mantos   los del Campeador,
e çercan el escaño,   e fincan sobre so señor.
Fernant Gonçalvez,   ifant de Carrión,
non vido allí dos alçasse,   nin cámara abierta nin torre;
metiós sol escaño,   tanto ovo el pavor.
Díag Gonçalvez   por la puerta salió,
diziendo de la boca: "non veré Carrión!"
Tras una viga lagar   metiós con grant pavor;
el manto trae al cuello,   e adeliñó pora' león;
    En esto despertó   el que en buen ora naçió;
vido çercado el escaño   de sos buenos varones:
"Qués esto, mesnadas,   o qué queredes vos?"
—"Ya señor ondrado,   rebata nos dió el león."
Mio Çid fincó el cobdo,   en pie se levantó,
el manto trae al cuello,   e adeliñó pora' león;
el león quando lo vío,   assí envergonçó,
ante mio Çid la cabeça   premió e el rostro fincó.

THE THIRD CANTAR

THE OUTRAGE AT CORPES

112

*The Cid's lion gets loose. The fear of the Heirs of
Carrión. The Cid tames the lion. The shame of the Heirs*

My Cid is in Valencia   with all his vassals,
and with him his sons-in-law,   the Heirs of Carrión.
The Campeador was asleep,   lying on a bench,
when, you may know, there occurred   an unlooked-for
    misfortune:
the lion broke from his cage   and stalked abroad.
Great terror ran   through the court;
the Campeador's men   seize their cloaks
and stand over the bench   to protect their lord.
Fernando González,   Heir of Carrión,
could find nowhere to hide,   no room nor tower was open;
he hid under the bench,   so great was his terror.
Diego González   went out the door
crying, "I shall never   see Carrión again."
Behind a beam of the wine press   he hid in his fear;
there his cloak and his tunic   were covered with filth.
    At this point he wakened   who in good hour was born;
he saw the bench surrounded   by his brave vassals.
"What is this, knights,   what do you wish?"
"Ah, honored lord,   we are frightened of the lion."
My Cid rose to his elbow,   got to his feet,
with his cloak on his shoulders   walked toward the lion;
the lion, when he saw him,   was so filled with shame,
before My Cid he bowed his head   and put his face down.

Mio Çid don Rodrigo   al cuello lo tomó,
e liévalo adestrando,   en la red le metió.
A maravilla lo han   quantos que i son,
e tornáronse al palaçio   pora la cort.

  Mio Çid por sos yernos   demandó e no los falló;
maguer los están llamando,   ninguno non responde.
Quando los fallaron,   assí vinieron sin color;
non vidiestes tal juego   commo iva por la cort;
mandólo vedar mio Çid   el Campeador.
Muchos tovieron por enbaídos   ifantes de Carrión,
fiera cosa les pesa   desto que les cuntió.

113
El rey Búcar de Marruecos ataca a Valencia

  Ellos en esto estando,   don avien grant pesar,
fuerças de Marruecos   Valençia vienen çercar;
en el campo de Quatro   ellos fueron posar,
cinquaenta mill tiendas   fincadas ha de las cabdales;
aqueste era el rey Búcar,   sil oviestes contar.

114
Los infantes temen la batalla. El Cid les reprende

  Alegravas el Çid   e todos sos varones,
que les creçe la ganaçia   grado al Criador.
Mas, sabed, de cuer les pesa   a ifantes de Carrión;
ca veyen tantas tiendas de moros   de que non avien sabor.
Amos hermanos   a part salidos son:
"Catamos le ganançia   e la pérdida no;
ya en esta batalla   a entrar abremos nos;
esto es aquisado   por non veer Carrión,
bibdas remandrán   fijas del Campeador."

My Cid Don Rodrigo   took him by the neck,
led him as with a halter   and put him in his cage.
And all marveled,   as many as were there,
and the knights returned   from the palace to the court.
   My Cid asked for his sons-in-law   and could not find
      them;
though he calls out   no one answers.
When at last they were found,   their faces were without
      color;
you have not seen such mockery   as rippled through the
      court;
My Cid the Campeador   commanded silence.
And the Heirs of Carrión   were covered with shame
and bitterly mortified   at this occurrence.

113
King Búcar of Morocco attacks Valencia

   While they were still sore   with the smart of this,
hosts from Morocco   came to surround Valencia;
they pitched their camp   in the field of Cuarto;
they set up their tents,   fifty thousand of the largest:
this was King Búcar,   of whom you have heard tell.

114
The Heirs are afraid of battle. The Cid reprimands them

   The Cid rejoiced   and all his knights;
they thanked the Creator,   for the spoils would enrich
      them.
But, you may know, it grieved   the Heirs of Carrión;
so many Moorish tents   were not to their taste.
Both brothers   walked to one side:
"We thought only of the wealth   and not of the dangers;
for we have no choice   but to go into this battle.
This could keep us from ever again   seeing Carrión,
and the daughters of the Campeador   will be left widows."

Oyó la poridad   aquel Muño Gustioz,
vino con estas nuevas   a mio Çid el Campeador:
"Evades vuestros yernos   tan osados son,
por entrar en batalla   desean Carrión.
Idlos conortar,   sí vos vala el Criador,
que sean en paz   e non ayan i ración.
Nos con vusco la vençremos,   e valer nos ha el Criador."
Mio Çid don Rodrigo   sonrrisando salió:
"Dios vos salve, yernos,   ifantes de Carrión,
en braços tendes mis fijas   tan blancas commo el sol!
Yo desseo lides,   e vos a Carrión,
en Valençia folgad   a todo vuestra sabor,
ca d' aquellos moros   yo so sabidor;
arrancar me los trevo   con la merçed del Criador."

115

Mensaje de Búcar. Espolonada de los cristianos. Cobardía
del infante Fernando. (*Laguna del manuscrito, 50 versos
que se*
suplen con el texto de la Crónica de Veinte Reyes.)
Generosidad de Pedro Vermúdez

Ellos en esto fablando, enbió el rey Búcar dezir al Cid
que le dexase Valençia e se fuesse en paz; sinón, que le
pecharie quanto y avie fecho. El Çid dixo a aquel que
troxiera el mensaje: "id dezir a Búcar, a aquel fi de
enemigo, que ante destos tres días le daré yo lo que él
demanda."

Otro día mandó el Çid armar todos los suyos e sallió a
los moros. Los infantes de Carrión pidiéronle entonces la
delantera; e después que el Çid ovo paradas sus azes, don
Ferrando, el uno de los infantes, adelantóse por ir ferir a
un moro a que dizian Aladraf. El moro quando lo vio, fue
contra él otrossí; e el infante, con el grand miedo que ovo
dél, bolvió la rienda e fuxó, que solamente non lo osó
esperar.

Pero Vermúdez que iva açerca dél, quando aquéllo vio,

Muño Gustioz   overheard them talking in secret
and brought what he had heard   to My Cid the
     Campeador.
"These sons-in-law of yours   are so filled with daring
that now at the hour of battle   they yearn for Carrión.
Go and console them,   as God is your grace,
let them sit in peace   and not enter the battle;
with you we shall conquer   and the Creator will give us
     aid."
My Cid Don Rodrigo   went up to them smiling:
"God save you, sons-in-law,   Heirs of Carrión,
you have in your arms my daughters   white as the sun.
I look forward to battle   and you to Carrión;
remain in Valencia   at your pleasure,
for I am seasoned   at managing the Moors
and shall make bold to rout them   with the help of the
     Creator."

115

*Búcar's message. The charge of the Christians. The
cowardice of the Heir Fernando.* (Lacuna in the
manuscript; fifty verses supplied out of the *Chronicle of
Twenty Kings.*) *The generosity of Pedro Bermúdez*

As they were speaking of this, King Búcar sent to tell
the Cid to leave Valencia, and he, Búcar, would let him
go in peace; but if he would not go, then Búcar would
make the Cid pay for everything he had done. The Cid
said to the messenger: "Go and tell Búcar, that son of my
enemies, that within three days I shall give him what he
asks for." The next day My Cid bade them all arm, and
they rode out against the Moors. The Heirs of Carrión then
begged of him the honor of striking the first blows; and
when the Cid had formed his ranks, Don Fernando, one
of the Heirs, rode forward to attack a Moor named Ala-
draf. When the Moor saw him he spurred toward him, and
the Heir, overcome with terror, turned his horse and fled,
not daring to wait.
    Pedro Bermúdez, who was near him, when he saw this,

fue ferir en el moro, e lidió con él e matólo. Desí tomó el
cavallo del moro, e fue en pos el infante que iva fuyendo e
díxole: "don Ferrando, tomad este cavallo e dezid a todos
que vos matastes al moro cúyo era, e yo otorgarlo e con
vusco."

El infante le dixo: "don Pero Vermúdez, mucho vos
gradezco lo que dezides;
aun vea el ora que   vos meresca dos tanto."
En una conpaña   tornados son amos.
Assí lo otorga don Pero   quomo se alaba Ferrando.
Plogo a mio Çid   e a todos sos vasallos;
"Aun si Dios quisiere   e el Padre que está en alto,
amos los mios yernos   buenos serán en canpo."

Esto van diziendo   e las yentes se allegando,
en la ueste de los moros   los atamores sonando;
a maravilla lo avien   muchos dessos cristianos,
ca nunca lo vieran,   ca nuevos son llegados.
Mas se maravillan   entre Díago e Ferrando
por la su voluntad   non serien allí llegados.
Oíd lo que fabló   el que en buen ora nasco:
"¡Ala, Per Vermudoz,   el mio sobrino caro!
cúriesme a Dídago   e cúriesme a Fernando
mios yernos amos a dos,   la cosa que mucho amo,
ca los moros, con Dios,   non fincarán en canpo."

116
**Pedro Vermúdez se desentiende de los infantes. Minaya
y don Jerónimo piden el primer puesto en la batalla**

—*"Yo vos digo, Çid,   por toda caridad,*
que oy los ifantes   a mí por amo non abrán;
cúrielos qui quier,   ca dellos poco m'incal.
Yo con los mios   ferir los quiero delant,

attacked the Moor and fought with him and killed him.
Then he took the Moor's horse and went after the Heir,
where he was still fleeing, and said: "Don Fernando, take
this horse and tell everyone that you killed the Moor who
was its master, and I will affirm it."

The Heir said to him: "Don Pedro Bermúdez,   I thank
you deeply,
and may the hour come   when I can doubly repay you."
Then they returned   riding together.
And Don Pedro affirmed the deed   of which Don
    Fernando boasted.
It pleased My Cid   and all his vassals.
"It if please God,   our Father Who is in heaven,
both my sons-in-law   will prove brave in the battle."
    As they speak thus,   the armies draw together.
The drums are sounding   through the ranks of the Moors,
and many of these Christians   marveled much at the
    sound,
for they had come lately to the war   and never heard
    drums.
Don Diego and Don Fernando   marveled more than any;
they would not have been there   if the choice had been
    theirs.
Hear what he said,   he who was born in good hour:
"Ho, Pedro Bermúdez,   my dear nephew,
watch over Don Diego   and watch over Don Fernando,
my sons-in-law,   for whom I have much love,
and with God's help   the Moors will not keep the field."

116
*Pedro Bermúdez declines to guard the Heirs. Minaya and
the Bishop Don Jerome ask for the foremost position in
the battle*

"I say to you, Cid,   in the name of charity,
that today the Heirs   will not have me for protector;
let who likes watch over them   for I care little for them.
I wish to attack in the van   with my men,

vos con los vuestros   firme mientre a la çaga tengades;
si cuenta fuere,   bien me podredes huviar."
  Aqué llegó   Mynaya Albar Fáñez:
"Oíd, ya Çid,   Canpeador leale!
Esta batalla   el Criador la ferave,
e vos tan dinno   que con él avedes parte.
Mandádno'los   ferir de qual part vos semejare,
el debdo que ha cada uno   a conplir serave.
Verlo hemos con Dios   e con la vuestra auze."
Dixo mio Çid: "ayamos más vagare."
  Afevos el obispo don Jerome   muy bien armado estave.
Parávas delant al Campeador   siempre con la buen auze:
"Oy vos dix la missa   de santa Trinidade.
Por esso salí de mi tierra   e vin vos buscare,
por sabor que avía   de algún moro matare;
mi orden e mis manos   querría las ondrar,
e a estas feridas   yo quiero ir delant.
Pendón trayo a corças   e armas de señal,
si plogiesse a Dios   querríalas ensayar,
mio coraçón   que pudiesse folgar,
e vos, mio Çid,   de mí más vos pagar.
Si este amor non feches,   de vos me quiero quitar."
Essora dixo mio Çid: "Lo que vos queredes plazme.
Afé los moros a ojo,   idlos ensayar.
Nos d' aquent veremos   cómmo lidia el abbat."

117
El obispo rompe la batalla. El Cid acomete.
Invade el campamento de los moros.

  El obispo don Jerome   priso a espolonada
e ívalos ferir   a cabo del albergada.
Por la su ventura   e Dios quel amava
a los primeros colpes   dos moros matava.
El astil a crebado   e metió mano al espada.
Ensayavas el obispo,   Dios, qué bien lidiava!
Dos mató con lança   e çinco con el espada.

210

and you with yours   might guard the rear;
and if I have need,   you can come to my aid."
   Minaya Alvar Fáñez   then rode up.
"Hear me, Cid,   loyal Campeador.
This battle   the Creator will decide
and you, of so great worth,   who have His favor.
Send us to attack   where you think best,
let each one of us   look to his obligation.
With God and your good fortune   we shall attack them."
My Cid said,   "Let us proceed calmly."
   Then came Don Jerome   the Bishop, heavily armed.
He stopped before the Campeador   of unfailing fortune.
"Today I have said you the Mass   of the Holy Trinity;
I left my own country   and came to find you
because of the hunger I had   for killing Moors;
I wish to gain honor   for my hands and for my order,
and I wish to go in the van   and strike the first blows.
I bear pennon and arms   blazoned with crosiers;
if it please God   I wish to display them,
and thus my heart   will be at peace,
and you, My Cid,   will be further pleased with me.
Unless you do me this favor   I shall leave you."
Then My Cid answered,   "I am pleased with your request.
Now the Moors are in sight;   go try yourself against them.
Now we shall see   how the monk does battle."

117
The Bishop begins the battle. The Cid attacks.
He invades the Moorish camp

   The Bishop Don Jerome   began
and charged against them   at the end of the camp.
By his good fortune   and the grace of God Who loved
   him,
with the first blows   he killed two Moors.
His lance splintered   and he drew his sword.
God, how hard he fought,   the Bishop, how well he did
   battle!
He killed two with his lance   and five with the sword.

211

Moros son muchos,   derredor le çercavan,
dávanle grandes colpes,   mas nol falssan las armas.
   El que en buen ora nasco   los ojos le fincava,
enbraçó el escudo   e abaxó el asta,
aguijó a Bavieca,   el cavallo que bien anda,
ívalos ferir   de coraçón e de alma.
En las azes primeras   el Campeador entrava,
abatió a siete   e a quatro matava.
Plogo a Dios,   aquesta fo el arrancada.
Mio Çid con los sos   cade en alcança;
veries crebar tantas cuerdas   e arrancarse las estacas
e acotarse los tendales,   con huebras eran tantas.
Los de mio Çid a los de Búcar   de las tiendas los sacan.

118
Los cristianos persiguen al enemigo. El Cid alcanza
y mata a Búcar. Gana la espada Tizón

   Sácanlos de las tiendas,   cáenlos en alcaz;
tanto braço con loriga   veriedes caer a part,
tantas cabeças con yelmos   que por el campo caden,
cavallos sin dueños   salir a todas partes.
Siete migeros complidos   duró el segundar.
   Mio Çid al rey Búcar   cadiól en alcaz:
"Acá torna, Búcar!   venist dalent mar.
Veerte as con el Çid,   el de la barba grant,
saludar nos hemos amos,   e tajaremos amiztat."
Respuso Búcar al Çid: "cofonda Dios tal amiztad!
Espada tienes en mano   e veot aguijar;
así commo semeja,   en mí la quieres ensayar.
Mas si el cavallo non estropieça   o comigo non cade,
non te juntarás comigo   fata dentro en la mar."

And many Moors came   and surrounded him
and dealt him great blows   but could not break through
    his armor.
   He who was born in good hour   kept his eyes upon him,
clasped his shield   and lowered his lance,
set spur to Babieca,   his swift horse,
and rode to attack them   with heart and soul.
In the first ranks   which he entered, the Campeador
unhorsed seven   and killed four.
There the rout began,   as it pleased God.
My Cid and his knights   rode in pursuit;
you would have seen so many tent cords   snapped, and
    the poles down,
and so many embroidered tents   lying on the ground;
My Cid's vassals   drove Búcar's men from their camp.

118

*The Christians pursue the enemy. The Cid overtakes and
kills Búcar. The capture of the sword Tizón*

   They drove them from the camp   and pursued them
    closely;
you would have seen fall   so many arms with their
    bucklers,
and so many heads in their helmets   fall in the field,
and horses without riders   running in all directions.
Seven full miles   the pursuit went on.
   My Cid overtook   Búcar the King:
"Turn, Búcar,   who have come from beyond the sea!
Now you must face the Cid,   he of the long beard;
we must greet each other   and swear friendship."
Búcar answered the Cid,   "God confound such
    friendship:
you have a sword in your hand,   you ride at full speed,
and it would seem that you wish   to prove your sword
    upon me.
But if my horse does not stumble   or fall under me,
you will not overtake me   though you follow me into the
    sea."

Aquí respuso mio Çid: "esto non será verdad."
Buen cavallo tiene Búcar   e grandes saltos faz,
mas Bavieca el de mio Çid   alcançándolo va.
Alcançólo el Çid a Búcar   a tres braças del mar,
arriba alçó Colada   un grant colpe dádol ha,
las carbonclas del yelmo   tollidas gelas ha,
cortól el yelmo   e, librado todo lo al,
fata la çintura   el espada llegado há.
Mató a Búcar,   al rey de allén mar,
e ganó a Tizón   que mill marcos d' oro val.
Vençió la batalla   maravillosa e grant,
Aquís ondró mio Çid   e quantos con elle están.

119
Los del Cid vuelven del alcance. El Cid satisfecho de sus
yernos; éstos, avergonzados. Ganancias de la victoria

    Con estas gananças   yas ivan tornando;
sabet, todos de firme   robavan el campo.
A las tiendas eran llegados   con el que en buena nasco,
mio Çid Roy Diaz,   el Campeador contado.
Con dos espadas   que él preçiava algo
por la matança   vinía tan privado,
la cara fronzida   e almófar soltado,
cofia sobre los pelos   fronzida della yaquanto.
De todas partes   sos vassallos van llegando;
algo vidie mio Çid   de lo que era pagado,
alçó sos ojos,   estava adelant catando,
e vido venir a Díago   e a Fernando;
amos son fijos   del comde don Gonçalvo.
Alegrós mio Çid   fermoso sonrrisando:
"¿Venides, mios yernos,   mios fijos sodes amos!
Sé que de lidiar   bien sodes pagados;
a Carrión de vos   irán buenos mandados,
cómmo al rey Búcar   avemos arrancado.

214

Then My Cid answered,   "That cannot be true."
Búcar had a good horse,   he rode in great bounds,
but the Cid's Babieca   gained steadily on him.
The Cid overtook Búcar   three fathoms from the sea,
raised Colada   and struck him a great blow,
and there he cut away   the jewels of his helmet,
split the helmet   and, driving through all below,
as far as the waist   his sword sank.
He killed Búcar,   the King from beyond the sea,
and captured the sword Tizón,   worth a thousands marks
    of gold.
My Cid has won   that marvelous great battle;
here all who are with him   have gained honor.

119

The Cid's men return from the pursuit. The Cid is content
with his sons-in-law; their shame. The spoils of the victory

They turned back from the chase   with the spoils they
    had taken;
you may know, before they went   they stripped the field.
They have come to the tents   with him who was born in
    good hour,
My Cid Ruy Díaz,   the famous Campeador;
he came with two swords   which were worth much to him,
at full speed came riding   over the field of slaughter,
his face bare,   hood and helmet off,
and the cowl loose   over his hair.
From all directions   his knights regather;
My Cid saw a thing   which pleased him greatly;
he lifted his eyes   and looked before him
and saw approaching him   Diego and Fernando,
both the sons   of the Count Don Gonzalo.
My Cid rejoiced,   fair was his smiling:
"Greetings, my sons-in-law,   both of you are my sons!
I know you are well contented   with the fighting you have
    done;
the good news of your deeds   will go to Carrión,
and the tidings of our conquest   of Búcar the King.

Commo yo fío Dios   y en todos los sos santos,
destra arrancada   nos iremos pagados."
Minaya Albar Fáñez   essora es llegado,
el escudo trae al cuello   e todo espadado;
de los colpes de las lanças   non avie recabdo;
aquellos que gelos dieran   non gelo avien logrado.
Por el cobdo ayuso   la sangre destellando;
de véinte arriba   ha moros matado:
"Grado a Dios   e al padre que está en alto,
e a vos, Çid,   que en buen ora fostes nado!
Matastes a Búcar   e arrancamos el canpo.
Todos estos bienes   de vos son e de vuestros vasallos.
E vuestros yernos   aquí son ensayados,
fartos de lidiar   con moros en el campo."
Dixo mio Çid: "yo desto so pagado;
quando agora son buenos,   adelant serán preçiados."
Por bien lo dixo el Çid,   mas ellos lo touieron a escarnio.

      Todos los ganados   a Valencia son llegados;
alegre es mio Çid   con todos sos vassallos,
que a la ración cadie   de plata seys çientos marcos.

      Los yernos de mio Çid   quando este aver tomaron
desta arrancada,   que lo tenien en so salvo,
cuydaron que en sos días   nunqua serien minguados.
Foron en Valençia   muy bien arreados,
conduchos a sazones,   buenas pieles e buenos mantos.
Mucho son alegres   mio Çid e sos vassallos.

120
El Cid satisfecho de su victoria y de sus yernos
      (Repetición)

      Grant fo el día   por la cort del Campeador,
después que esta batalla vencieron   e al rey Búcar mató,
alçó la mano,   a la barba se tomó:

I trust in God   and in all His saints
that we shall be satisfied   with the results of this victory."
Minaya Alvar Fáñez   rode up at this moment,
his shield at his neck   marked with sword dents
and with blows of lances   beyond number;
and those who had aimed them   had not profited by it.
Down from his elbow   the blood is dripping;
he had killed more than twenty   of the Moors.
"Thanks be to God   and to our heavenly Father
and to you, Cid,   who in good hour were born!
You have killed Búcar   and we have won the field.
All these spoils   are for you and your vassals.
And your sons-in-law   here have proved themselves
and sated themselves with fighting   with Moors in the
    field."
My Cid said,   "I am pleased with this;
they have been brave today,   and in time to come they
    will be braver."
My Cid intended it kindly   but they took it as a jeer.
  All the spoils   have been brought to Valencia;
My Cid rejoices,   and all his vassals;
to each one there falls   six hundred marks of silver.
  My Cid's sons-in-law,   when they had taken this portion
which was theirs from the victory   and had put it safely
    away,
were sure that in all their days   they should not lack for
    money.
Those in Valencia   were lavishly provided
with excellent food,   fine furs and rich cloaks.
And My Cid and his vassals   all rejoiced.

·

120
The Cid pleased with the victory and with his sons-in-law
    (Repetition)

  It was a great day   in the court of the Campeador
after they had won that battle   and King Búcar had been
    killed;
the Cid raised his hand   and grasped his beard.

"Grado a Cristus,   que del mundo es señor,
quando veo   lo que avía sabor,
que lidiaran comigo en campo   mios yernos amos a dos:
mandados buenos irán   dellos a Carrión,
commo son ondrados   e aver nos han grant pro."

121
Reparto del botín

Sobejanas son las gananças   que todos an ganado
lo uno es dellos,   lo otro han en salvo.

Mandó mio Çid,   el que en buen ora nasco,
desta batalla   que han arrancado
que todos prisiessen   so derecho contado,
e el so quinto de mio Çid   non fosse olbidado.
Assí lo fazen todos,   ca eran acordados.
Cadierónle en quinta al Çid   seys çientos cavallos,
e otras azémilas   e camellos largos
tantos son de muchos   que non serién contados.

122
El Cid, en el colmo de su gloria, medita dominar a Marruecos.
Los infantes ricos y honrados en la corte del Cid

    Todas estas gananças   fizo el Canpeador.
"Grado ha Dios   que del mundo es señor!
Antes fu minguado,   agora rico so,
que he aver e tierra   e oro e onor,
e son mios yernos   ifantes de Carrión;
arranco las lides   commo plaze al Criador,
moros e cristianos   de mi han grant pavor.
Allá dentro en Marruecos,   o las mezquitas son,
que abrán de mi salto   quiçab alguna noch
ellos lo temen,   ca non lo piensso yo:
no los iré buscar,   en Valençia seré yo,
ellos me darán parias   con ayuda del Criador,
que paguen a mí   o a qui yo ovier sabor."

"I give thanks to Christ   Who is lord of the world,
that now I have seen   what I have wished to see:
both my sons-in-law   have fought beside me in the field;
good news concerning them   will go to Carrión;
they have been much help to us   and won themselves
     honor."

121
The division of the spoils

   All have received   enormous spoils;
much was theirs already,   now these new gains are stored
     away.
My Cid, who was born   in a good hour, commanded
that from this battle   which they had won
each one should take   what fell by rights to him,
and the fifth which went to My Cid   was not forgotten.
This they all do   without disagreements.
In the fifth which fell to My Cid   were six hundred horses,
and other beasts of burden   and large camels;
there were so many   they could not be counted.

122
The Cid at the height of his glory meditates the capture of Morocco.
The Heirs live rich and honored in the Cid's court

   All these spoils   the Campeador has taken.
"Thanks be to God   Who is lord of the world!
In the old days I was poor,   now I am rich,
for I have wealth and domains   and gold and honor,
and my sons-in-law   are the Heirs of Carrión;
I win battles,   as pleases the Creator;
Moors and Christians   go in fear of me.
There in Morocco,   where the mosques are,
they tremble   lest perhaps some night
I should take them by surprise,   but I plan no such thing.
I shall not go seeking them,   but stay in Valencia,
and they will send me tribute,   as the Creator aids me;
they will send money to me   or to whomever I please."

Grandes son los gozos   en Valençia la mayor
de todas sus conpañas   de mio Çid el Campeador,
d' aquesta arrancada   que lidiaron de coraçón;
grandes son los gozos   de sos yernos amos a dos:
valía de çinco mill marcos   ganaron amos a dos;
muchos tienen por ricos   ifantes de Carrión.

    Ellos con los otros   vinieron a la cort;
aquí está con mio Çid   el obispo de Jerome,
el bueno de Albar Fáñez,   cavallero lidiador,
e otros muchos   que crió el Campeador;
quando entraron   ifantes de Carrión,
recibiólos Minaya   por mio Çid el Campeador:
"Acá, venid, cuñados,   que mas valemos por vos."
Assí commo llegaron,   pagós el Campeador:
"Evades aquí, yernos,   la mie mugier de pro,
e amas las mis fijas,   don Elvira e doña Sol;
bien vos abraçen   e sírvanos de coraçón.
Grado a santa María,   madre del nuestro señor Dios!
destos vuestros casamientos   vos abredes honor.
Buenos mandados irán   a tierras de Carrión."

123
Vanidad de los infantes. Burlas de que ellos son objeto

    A estas palabras   fabló ifant Ferrando:
"Grado al Criador   e a vos, Çid ondrado,
tantos avemos de averes   que no son contados;
por vos avemos ondra   e avemos lidiado,
vençiemos moros   en campo e matamos
a aquel rey Búcar,   traydor provado.
Pensad de lo otro,   que lo nuestro tenésmoslo en saluo."
    Vassallos de mio Çid   sediense sonrrisando:
quien lidiara mejor   o quien fora en alcanço;
mas non fallavan i   a Dídago ni a Ferrando.
Por aquestos juegos   que ivan levantando,
elas noches e los días   tan mal los escarmentando,
tan mal se conssejaron   estos iffantes amos.
Amos salieron a part,   veramientre son hermanos;

Great were the rejoicings   in Valencia, that great city,
among all the company   of My Cid the Campeador
at this rout   in which heartily they had fought;
and great was the joy   of both the sons-in-law;
five thousand marks   was the portion which fell to them.
These Heirs of Carrión   considered themselves rich.

   They with the others   came to the court;
there with My Cid   was the Bishop Don Jerome,
the good Alvar Fáñez,   knight and warrior,
and many others   whom the Campeador had reared.
When the Heirs of Carrión   entered there
Minaya received them,   for My Cid the Campeador:
"Come here, my kinsmen,   we profit by your company."
As they approached,   the Campeador grew more pleased:
"Here, my sons-in-law,   are my excellent wife
and both my daughters,   Doña Elvira and Doña Sol,
to embrace you closely   and serve you with all their hearts.
I thank Santa María,   mother of the lord our God,
that from this marriage   you shall have gained honor.
Good news will go   to the lands of Carrión."

123
The Heirs' vanity. The jibes of which they are the butt

   At these words   the Heir Fernando spoke:
"I thank the Creator   and you, honored Cid,
that so much wealth,   that riches beyond measure are
      ours.
From you we receive our honor   and for you we fought;
we conquered the Moors   in the field and killed
that King Búcar,   a proved traitor.
Think of other things,   for our affairs are in good order."
   The vassals of My Cid   smiled to hear this;
some had battled bravely   and some ridden in pursuit,
but they had not seen   Diego nor Fernando there.
Because the mockeries   made at their expense,
day and night, always,   so tormented them,
both the Heirs   conceived of an evil plan.
They walked aside.   Indeed, they were brothers;

desto que ellos fablaron   nos parte non ayamos;
—"*Vayamos pora Carrión,   aquí mucho detardamos.*
Los averes que tenemos   grandes son e sobejanos,
despender no los podremos   mientras que bivas seamos."

124
Los infantes deciden afrentar a las hijas del Cid. Piden al Cid sus mujeres para llevarlas a Carrión. El Cid accede. Ajuar que da a sus hijas. Los infantes dispónense a marchar. Las hijas despídense del padre

—"*Pidamos nuestras mugieres   al Çid Campeador,*
digamos que las llevaremos   a tierras de Carrión,
enseñar las hemos   do ellas heredadas son.
Sacar las hemos de Valençia,   de poder del Campeador;
después en la carrera   feremos nuestro sabor,
ante que nos retrayan   lo que cuntió del león.
Nos de natura somos   de comdes de Carrión!
Averes levaremos grandes   que valen grant valor;
escarniremos   las fijas del Canpeador."
—"*D' aquestros averes   sienpre seremos ricos omnes,*
podremos casar con fijas   de reyes o de enperadores
ca de natura somos   de comdes de Carrión.
Assí las escarniremos   a fijas del Campeador,
antes que nos retrayan   lo que fo del león."
    Con aqueste conssejo   amos tornados son,
fabló Ferrant Gonçálvez   e fizo callar la cort:
"*Sí vos vala el Criador,   Çid Campeador!*

let us have no part   in what they said:
"Let us go to Carrión;   we have stayed here too long.
The wealth we have   is great and immeasurable;
we could not spend it all   in the rest of our lives.

124

The Heirs decide to do injury to the Cid's daughters. They
    ask
the Cid for permission to take their wives to Carrión.
    The Cid consents.
The bridal clothing he gives to his daughters. The
    Heirs make
ready to travel. The daughters say good-by to their father

"Let us ask for our wives   from the Cid Campeador;
let us say we will take them   to the lands of Carrión,
for we must show them   the lands that are theirs.
We shall take them from Valencia,   from the power of the
    Campeador;
afterwards, on the journey,   we shall do as we please with
    them
before they reproach us   with the story of the lion.
For we are descended   from the Counts of Carrión!
We shall take much wealth with us,   riches of great value;
we shall work our punishment   on the daughters of the
    Campeador."
"With the wealth we have now,   we shall be rich
    forever;
we can marry the daughters   of kings or emperors,
for we are descended   from the Counts of Carrión.
Therefore we shall punish   the daughters of the
    Campeador
before they throw in our faces   what happened with the
    lion."
    When they had made up their minds   they turned back
    again.
Fernando González spoke,   requesting silence in the
    court:
"As the Creator may bless you,   Cid Campeador,

223

que plega a doña Ximena   e primero a vos
e a Minaya Albar Fáñez   e a quantos aquí son:
dadnos nuestras mugieres   que avemos a bendiçiones
levar las hemos   a nuestras tierras de Carrión,
meter las hemos en arras   que les diemos por onores;
veran vuestras fijas   lo que avemos nos,
los fijos que oviéremos   en qué avrán partiçión."
    Nos curiava de fonta   mio Çid el Campeador:
"Darvos he mis fijas   e algo de lo mio;
vos les diestes villas por arras   en tierras de Carrión,
yo quiéroles dar axuvar   tres mill marcos de valor;
darvos e mulas e palafrés,   muy gruessos de sazón,
cavallos pora en diestro   fuertes e corredores,
e muchas vestiduras   de paños e de çiclatones;
darvos he dos espadas,   a Colada e a Tizón,
bien lo sabedes vos que las gané   a guisa de varón;
mios fijos sodes amos,   quando mis fijas vos do;
allá me levades   las telas del coraçón.
Que lo sepan en Gallizia   e en Castiella e en León,
con que riqueza enbio   mios yernos amos a dos.
A mis fijas sirvades,   que vuestras mugieres son;
si bien las servides,   yo vos rendré buen galardón."
Atorgado lo han esto   iffantes de Carrión.
Aquí reçiben   fijas del Campeador;
conpieçan a reçibir   lo que el Çid mandó.
    Quando son pagados   a todo so sabor,
ya mandavan cargar   iffantes de Carrión.
Grandes son las nuevas   por Valençia la mayor,
todos prenden armas   e cavalgan a vigor,
por que escurren fijas del Çid   a tierras de Carrión.
    Ya quieren cavalgar,   en espidimiento son.
Amas hermanas,   don Elvira e doña Sol,
fincaron los inojos   antel Çid Campeador:
"Merçed vos pedimos, padre,   sí vos vala el Criador?
vos nos engendrastes,   nuestras madre nos parió;

224

may it please Doña Jimena   and before all others, you,
and Minaya Alvar Fáñez   and as many as are here,
to give us our wives,   who have been blessed to us;
we would take them with us   to our lands of Carrión
so that they may possess the lands   we have given them
     for their honor;
your daughters will see   what belongs to us,
in which our children   will have a share."
My Cid the Campeador   suspected no harm:
"I will give you my daughters   and more things that are
     mine;
you have given them as wedding gifts   villages in Carrión;
I would give them for their betrothal   three thousand
     marks,
and I give you mules and palfreys   sleek and fine limbed,
and war horses   strong, and swift runners,
and many garments of cloth   and of cloth-of-gold,
and I will give you two swords,   Colada and Tizón;
you know well that I gained them   as befits a man.
Both of you are my sons   since I give you my daughters;
you bear away with you   the threads of my heart.
Let them know in Galicia   and in Castile and in León
how richly I send from me   my two sons-in-law.
Cherish my daughters,   who are your wives;
if you treat them well   I shall reward you handsomely."
The Heirs of Carrión   have agreed to everything.
They receive the daughters   of the Campeador,
and now they take   the Cid's gifts.
    When they are sated   with receiving presents
the Heirs of Carrión bade them   load up the beasts of
     burden.
There is much bustle   in Valencia, that great city;
all seize their arms   and mount in haste;
they are sending off the Cid's daughters   to the lands of
     Carrión.
    They are ready to ride,   they are saying good-by.
Both the sisters,   Doña Elvira and Doña Sol,
knelt down   before the Cid Campeador:
"We beg your blessing, father,   and may the Creator be
     with you;
you sired us,   our mother brought us forth;

225

delant sodes amos,   señora e señor.
Agora nos enviades   a tierras de Carrión,
debdo nos es a cunmplir   lo que mandáredes vos.
Assí vos pedimos merçed   nos amas a dos,
que ayades vuestros menssajes   en tierras de Carrión."
Abraçólas mio Çid   e saludólas amas a dos.

125

Jimena despide a sus hijas. El Cid cabalga para despedir
a los viajeros. Agüeros malos

Elle fizo aquesto,   la madre lo doblava:
"Andad, fijas; d' aqui   el Criador vos vala!
de mí e de vuestro padre,   bien avedes nuestra graçia.
Id a Carrión   do sodes heredadas,
assí commo yo tengo,   bien vos he casadas."
Al padre e a la madre   las manos les besavan;
amos las bendixieron   e diéronles su graçia.

Mio Çid e os otros   de cavalgar penssavan,
a grandes guarnimientos,   a cavallos e armas.
Ya salien los ifantes   de Valençia la clara,
espidiéndos de la dueñas   e de todas sues compañas.
Por la huerta de Valençia   teniendo salien armas;
alegre va mio Çid   con todas sues compañas.

Viólo en los avueros   el que en buena cinxo espada
que estos casamientos   non serién sin alguna tacha.
Nos puede repentir,   que casadas las ha amas.

126

El Cid envía con sus hijas a Félez Muñoz. Ultimo adiós.
El Cid torna a Valencia. Los viajeros llegan a Molina.
Abengalvón les acompaña a Medina. Los infantes piensan
matar a Abengalvón

here we are before you both,   our lady and our lord.
Now you send us   to the lands of Carrión;
we owe it to you to obey you   in whatever you demand.
And thus we beg   your blessing on us both.
Send messages to us   in the lands of Carrión."
My Cid embraced them   and kissed them both.

125

*Jimena says good-by to her daughters. The Cid mounts
to see the travelers off. Bad omens*

   Their mother embraces them   twice over:
"Now go hence, daughters,   and the Creator bless you,
and take with you   your father's blessing and mine.
Go to Carrión,   where you are heirs;
in my eyes it seems   that you were well married."
They kissed the hands   of their father and mother,
who both blessed them   and gave them their grace.
   My Cid and the others   began to ride;
there were great provisions   and horses and arms.
The Heirs have ridden out   from Valencia the Shining;
they have said good-by to the ladies   and all their
     companions.
Through the farmlands of Valencia   they ride, playing
     at arms;
My Cid goes merrily   among all his companions.
   But he who in good hour was born   looked upon the
     omens
and saw that this marriage   will not be without stain.
But now he may not repent   for both of them are wedded.

126

*The Cid sends Félix Muñoz with his daughters. The last
good-by. The Cid returns to Valencia. The travelers
arrive at Molina. Abengalbón accompanies them to
    Medinaceli.*
The Heirs consider killing Abengalbón

"¿O eres mio sobrino,   tú, Félez Muñoz,
primo eres de mis fijas amas   d' alma e de coraçón!
Mándot que vayas con ellas   fata dentro en Carrión,
verás las heredades   que a mis fijas dadas son;
con aquestas nuevas   vernás al Campeador."
Dixo Félez Muñoz: "plazme d' alma e de coraçón."

    Minaya Albar Fáñez   ante mio Çid se paró:
"Tornémosnos, Çid   a Valençia la mayor;
que si a Dios ploguiere   e al Padre Criador,
ir las hemos veder   a tierras de Carrión."
—"A Dios vos acomendamos, don Elvira e doña Sol
atales cosas fed   que en plazer caya a nos."
Respondien los yernos: "assí lo mande Dios!"
Grandes fueron los duelos   a la departiçión.
El padre con las fijas   lloran de coraçón,
assí fazían   los cavalleros del Campeador,

    "Oyas, sobrino,   tú, Félez Muñoz!
por Molina iredes,   i yazredes una noch;
saludad a mio amigo   el moro Avengalvón:
reciba a mios yernos   commo elle pudier mejor;
dil que enbío mis fijas   a tierras de Carrión,
de lo que ovieren huebos   sírvalas a so sabor,
desí encúrralas fasta Medina   por la mí amor.
De quanto él fiziere   yol daré por ello buen galardón."
Quomo la uña de la carne   ellos partidos son.

    Yas tornó pora Valençia   el que en buen ora nasció.
Piénssanse de ir   ifantes de Carrión;
por Santa María d' Alvarrazín   la posada fecha fo,
aguijan quanto pueden   ifantes de Carrión;
félos en Molina   con el moro Avengalvón.
El moro quando lo sopo,   plógol de coraçón;
saliólos recebir   con grandes avorozes;
Dios, que bien los sirvió   a todo so sabor!

"Oh, where are you, my nephew,   you, Félix Muñoz:
you are cousin to my daughters   and love them with heart
      and soul.
I command you to go with them   all the way to Carrión;
you will see the inheritances   which have been given to
      my daughters
and with news of these things   return to the Campeador."
Félix Muñoz said,   "It pleases my heart and soul."
   Minaya Alvar Fáñez   stopped before My Cid:
"Let us go back, Cid,   to Valencia, the great city,
and if it please God   and our Father the Creator,
one day we shall go to see them   in the lands of Carrión."
"To God I commend you,   Doña Elvira and Doña Sol;
behave in such manner   as shall give us cause for
      pleasure."
The sons-in-law answered,   "May God send that it be so."
Great were their sorrows   when they came to part.
The father and the daughters   wept from their hearts,
as did also the knights   of the Campeador.
   "Hear me, my nephew,   you, Félix Muñoz;
go to Molina   and spend the night there;
in my name greet my friend,   the Moor Abengalbón;
let him receive my sons-in-law   with his fairest welcome;
tell him I am sending my daughters   to the lands of
      Carrión;
let him serve their pleasure   in whatever they need
and, for love of me, bid him escort them   as far as
      Medinaceli.
For all he does for them   I shall reward him well."
They parted, one from the other,   as nail from flesh.
   He has turned back to Valencia   who in good hour
      was born.
The Heirs of Carrión   ride forward;
at Santa María of Albarracín   the camp was made;
from there the Heirs of Carrión   spur forward at all
      speed;
they have come to Molina   and the Moor Abengalbón.
When the Moor knew they were there   it pleased his
      heart;
with great rejoicing   he rode out to   receive them.
God, how well he served them   in whatever they pleased!

229

Otro día mañana   con ellos cavalgó,
con dozientos cavalleros   escurrir los mandó;
ivan troçir los montes,   los que dizen de Luzón,
troçieron Arbuxuelo   e llegaron a Salón,
o dizen el Anssarera   ellos posados son.
A las fijas del Çid   el moro sus donas dió,
buenos seños cavallos   a ifantes de Carrión;
tod esto les fizo el moro   por el amor del Çid Campeador.

  Ellos vedien la riqueza   que el moro sacó,
entramos hermanos . conssejaron traçión:
"Ya pues que a dexar avemos   fijas del Campeador,
si pudiéssemos matar   el moro Avengalvón,
quanta riquiza tiene   aver la yemos nos.
Tan en salvo lo abremos   commo lo de Carrión; •
nunqua avrié derecho   de nos el Çid Campeador."
Quando esta falssedad   dizien los de Carrión,
un moro latinado   bien gelo entendió;
non tiene poridad,   díxole Avengalvón:
"Acáyaz, cúriate destos,   ca eres mio señor:
tu muert odi conssejar   a ifantes de Carrión."

127
Abengalvón se despide amenazando a los infantes

  El moro Avengalvón,   mucho era buen barragán,
con dozientos que tiene   iva cavalgar;
armas iva teniendo,   parós ante los ifantes;
de lo que el moro dixo   a los ifantes non plaze;
"Si no lo dexás   por mío Çid el de Bivar,
tal cosa vos faría   que por el mundo sonás,
e luego levaría sus fijas   al Campeador leal;
vos nunqua en Carrión   entrariedes jamás.

The next day in the morning   he rode on with them
with two hundred knights   whom he sent to escort them;
they have passed the mountains   called the range of
       Luzón,
crossed the valley of Arbujuelo   and come to Jalón;
where it is called Ansarera   they made their camp.
The Moor gave presents   to the Cid's daughters
and fine horses for each   of the Heirs of Carrión;
all this the Moor did for love   of the Cid Campeador.
    When they saw the riches   which the Moor had brought
both brothers   began to plot to betray him:
"Now that we plan to desert   the Campeador's daughters,
if we could murder   the Moor Abengalbón
all his wealth   would be ours.
We could keep it as safely   as what is ours in Carrión,
and the Cid Campeador   could enforce no claim against
       us."
While they of Carrión   were speaking of this deceit,
a Moor who knew Castilian   heard what they said
and did not keep it secret,   but told Abengalbón:
"My lord, my master,   have a care of these,
for I have heard them plotting your death,   these Heirs
       of Carrión."

127
Abengalbón departs, threatening the Heirs

    The Moor Abengalbón   was tough and stouthearted;
with the two hundred who were with him   he came riding;
all of them were armed;   they halted before the Heirs.
What the Moor said to the Heirs   gave them no pleasure:
"If it were not for respect   for My Cid of Bivar
I would wreak such deeds on you   as the whole world
       would hear of
and I would return his daughters   to the loyal Campeador;
and as for Carrión,   you would never see it again.

El moro se torna a Molina, presintiendo la desgracia de las
hijas del Cid. Los viajeros entran en el reino de Castilla.
Duermen en el robledo de Corpes. A la mañana quédanse
solos los infantes con sus mujeres y se preparan a
maltratarlas. Ruegos inútiles de doña Sol. Crueldad de los
infantes

¿Dezidme, qué vos fiz,   ifantes de Carrión!
yo sirviéndovos sin art,   a vos conssejastes mie muort.
Aquim parto de vos   como de malos e de traydores.
Iré con vuestra graçia,   don Elvira e doña Sol;
poco preçio las nuevas   de los de Carrión.
Dios lo quiera e lo mande,   que de tod el mundo es señor,
d' aqueste casamiento   ques grade el Campeador."

Esto les ha dicho,   e el moro se tornó;
teniendo iva armas   al troçir de Salón;

quommo de buen seso   a Molina se tornó.
Ya movieron del Anssarera   ifantes de Carrión,
acójense a andar   de día e de noch;
a ssiniestro dexan Atiença,   una peña muy fuort,
la sierra de Miedes   passáronla estoz,
por los Montes Claros   aguijan a espolón;
assiniestro dexan a Griza   que Alamos pobló,
allí son caños   do a Elpha ençerró;
a diestro dexan a Sant Estevan,   mas cade aluon.
Entrados son los ifantes   al robredo de Corpes,
los montes son altos   las ramas pujan con las nuoves,
elas bestias fieras   que andan aderredor.
Fallaron un vergel   con una limpia fuont;
mandan fincar la tienda   ifantes de Carrión,
con quantos que ellos traen   i yazen essa noch,
con sus mugieres en braços   demuéstranles amor;
¡mal gelo cunplieron   quando salie el sol!
Mandaron cargar las azémilas   con averes a nombre,

The Moor returns to Molina, with premonitions of the disgrace of the Cid's daughters. The travelers enter the kingdom of Castile. They sleep in the grove of Corpes. In the morning the Heirs are alone with their wives and prepare to do them injury. Doña Sol calls out vainly. The Heirs' cruelty

"Tell me what harm have I done you,   Heirs of
    Carrión!
I serve you without malice   and you plot my death.
Here I leave you,   vile men and traitors.
By your leave I go,   Doña Elvira and Doña Sol;
I scorn the fame   of the Heirs of Carrión.
May God Who is lord of the world   will and command
that the Campeador may remain   contented with this
    marriage."
When he had said this   the Moor turned away
and they went with their arms at ready   till they had
    crossed the stream Jalón.
As a man of prudence   he went back to Molina.
  The Heirs of Carrión   have left Ansarera.
They march without rest   all day and all night;
on their left they leave Atienza,   that is a strong hill;
the mountains of Miedes   fall behind them;
upon Montes Claros   they spur forward,
and on their left leave Griza,   which Alamos peopled,
and there are the caves   where he encircled Elpha;
further on, on their right,   was San Esteban de Gormaz.
The Heirs have entered   the oak wood of Corpes;
the mountains are high,   the branches touch the clouds
and there are savage beasts   which walk about there.
They found a glade   with a clear spring.
The Heirs of Carrión   bade their men set up the tent;
there they spend the night   with as many as are with them,
with their wives in their arms,   showing them love;
yet they meant to do them evil   when the sun rose!
  They had the beasts of burden   loaded with their riches,

cogida han la tienda   do albergaron de noch,
adelant eran idos   los de criazón:
assí lo mandaron   ifantes de Carrión,
que non i fincás ninguno,   mugier nin varón,
si non amas sus mugieres   doña Elvira e doña Sol:
deportar se quieren con ellas   a todo su sabor.

   Todos eran idos,   ellos quatro solos son,
tanto mal comidieron   ifantes de Carrión:
"Bien lo creades   don Elvira e doña Sol,
aquí seredes escarnidas   en estos fieros montes.
Oy nos partiremos,   e daxadas seredes de nos;
non abredes part   en tierras de Carrión.
Irán aquestos mandados   al Çid Campeador;
nos vengaremos aquesta   por la del león."

   Allí les tuellen   los mantos e los pelliçones,
páranlas en cuerpos   y en camisas y en çiclatones.
Espuelas tienen calçadas   los malos traydores,
en mano prenden las çinchas   fuertes e duradores.
Quando esto vieron las dueñas,   fablava doña Sol:
"Por Dios vos rogamos,   don Díago e don Ferrando, nos!
dos espadas tenedes   fuertes e tajadores,
al una dizen Colada   e al otra Tizón,
cortandos las cabeças,   mártires seremos nos.
Moros e cristianos   departirán desta razón,
que por lo que nos mereçemos   no lo prendemos nos.
Atan malos enssienplos   non fagades sobre nos:
si nos fuéramos majadas,   abiltaredes a vos;
retraer vos lo an   en vistas o en cortes."

   Lo que ruegan las dueñas   non les ha ningún pro.
Essora les conpieçan a dar   ifantes de Carrión;
con las çinchas corredizas   májanlas tan sin sabor;
con las espuelas agudas,   don ellas an mal sabor,
ronpien las camisas e las carnes   a ellas amas a dos;
linpia salie la sangre   sobre los çiclatones.
Ya lo sienten ellas   en los sos coraçones.
¡Quál ventura serie esta,   si ploguiesse al Criador,

and they have taken down the tent   where they spent
     the night,
and those who waited on them   have all ridden ahead
as they were ordered to do   by the Heirs of Carrión,
so that none remained behind,   neither man nor woman,
except both their wives,   Doña Elvira and Doña Sol.
They wished to amuse themselves with these   to the
     height of their pleasure.

     All had gone ahead,   only these four remained;
the Heirs of Carrión   had conceived great villainy:
"Know this for a certainty,   Doña Elvira and Doña Sol,
you will be tormented here   in these savage mountains.
Today we shall desert you   and go on from this place;
you will have no share   in the lands of Carrión.
The news of this will go   to the Cid Campeador,
and we shall be avenged   for the story of the lion."
     Then they stripped them   of their cloaks and furs;
they left nothing on their bodies   but their shirts and silk
     undergarments.
The wicked traitors   have spurs on their boots;
they take in their hands   the strong hard saddle girths.
When the ladies saw this,   Doña Sol said:
"You have two swords,   strong and keen edged,
one that is called Colada   and the other Tizón.
For God's sake, we beg you,   Don Diego and Don
     Fernando,
cut off our heads   and we shall be martyrs.
Moors and Christians   will speak harshly of this,
for such treatment   we have not deserved.
Do not visit upon us   so vile an ensample;
if you whip us   the shame will be yours;
you will be called to account   at assemblies or courts."
     The ladies' pleadings   availed them nothing.
Then the Heirs of Carrión   began to lash them;
they beat them without mercy   with the flying cinches,
gored them with the sharp spurs,   dealing them great pain.
They tore their shirts   and the flesh of both of them,
and over the silken cloth   the clean blood ran,
and they felt the pain   in their very hearts.
Oh, it would be such good fortune   if it should please the
     Creator

que assomasse essora   el Çid Campeador!
   Tanto las majaron   que sin cosimente son;
sangrients en las camisas   e todos los çiclatones.
Canssados son de ferir   ellos amos a dos.
Ensayandos amos   quál dará mejores colpes.
Ya non pueden fablar   don Elvira e doña Sol,
por muertas las dexaron   en el robredo de Corpes.

129
Los infantes abandonan a su mujeres (Serie gemela)

   Leváronles los mantos   e las pieles armiñas,
mas déxanlas marridas   en briales y en camisas,
e a las aves del monte   e a las bestias de la fiera guisa.
Por muertas las dexaron,   sabed, que non por bivas.
¡Quál ventura serie   si assomas essora el Çid Roy Díaz!

130
Los infantes se alaban de su cobardía

Ifantes de Carrión   por muertas las dexaron,
que el una al otra   nol torna recabdo.
Por los montes do ivan,   ellos ívanse alabando:
"De nuestros casamientos   agora somos vengados.
Non las deviemos tomar por varraganas,   si non fossemos
                                              rogados,
pues nuestras parejas   non eran pora en braços
la desondra del león   assís irá vengando."

131
Félez Muñoz sospecha de los infantes. Vuelve atrás en
busca de las hijas del Cid. Las reanima y las lleva en
su caballo a San Esteban de Gormaz. Llega al Cid la
noticia de su deshonra. Minaya va a San Esteban a

that the Cid Campeador   might appear now!
   They beat them so cruelly,   they left them senseless;
the shirts and the silk skirts   were covered with blood.
They beat them   until their arms were tired,
each of them trying   to strike harder than the other.
Doña Elvira and Doña Sol could no longer speak;
they left them for dead   in the oak grove of Corpes.

129
The Heirs abandon the women (Parallel passage)

   They took away their cloaks   and their furs of ermine,
and left them fainting   in their shifts and silk tunics,
left them to the birds of the mountain   and to the wild
      beasts.
They left them for dead,   you may know, with no life left
      in them.
What good fortune it would be   if the Cid Ruy Díaz should
      appear now!

130
The Heirs congratulate themselves on their cowardice

   The Heirs of Carrión   left them there for dead,
so that neither   might give aid to the other.
Through the mountains where they went   they praised
      themselves:
"Now we have avenged ourselves   for our marriage.
We would not have them for concubines   even if they
      begged us.
As legitimate wives   they were unworthy of us;
the dishonor of the lion   thus will be avenged."

131
*Félix Muñoz is suspicious of the Heirs. He turns back
looking for the Cid's daughters. He revives them and carries
them on his horse to San Esteban de Gormaz. The Cid
hears of this dishonor. Minaya goes to San Esteban to fetch*

recoger las dueñas. Entrevista de Minaya con sus primas

Alabandos ivan   ifantes de Carrión.
Mas yo vos diré   d' aquel Félez Muñoz;
sobrino era   del Çid Campeador;
mandáronle ir adelante   mas de so grado non fo.
En la carrera do iva   doliól el coraçón,
de todos los otros   aparte se salió,
en un monte espesso   Félez Muñoz se metió,
fasta que viesse venir   sus primas amas a dos
o que an fecho   ifantes de Carrión.
Víolos venir   e odió una razón,
ellos nol vidien   ni dend sabien raçión;
sabed bien que si ellos le vidiessen   non escapara de
                                                                muort.

Vansse los ifantes,   aguijan a espolón.
Por el rastro   tornós Félez Muñoz,
falló sus primas   amorteçidas amas a dos.
Llamando: "primas, primas!," luego descavalgó,
arrendó el cavallo,   a ellas adeliñó:
"Ya primas, las mis primas,   don Elvira e doña Sol,
mal se ensayaron   ifantes de Carrión!
A Dios plega que dent prendan   ellos mal galardón!"
Valas tornando   a ellas amas a dos;
tanto son de traspuestas   que nada dezir non puoden.
Partiéronseles las telas   de dentro del coraçón,
llamando: "¡Primas, primas   don Elvira e doña Sol!
Despertedes, primas,   por amor del Criador!
mientras es el día,   ante que entre la noch,
los ganados fieros   non nos coman en aqueste mont!"
Van recordando   don Elvira e doña Sol,
abrieron los ojos   e vieron a Félez Muñoz.
"Esforçados, primas,   por amor del Criador!
De que non me fallaren   ifantes de Carrión,
a grant priessa   seré buscado yo;
si Dios non nos vale,   aquí morremos nos."
Tan a grant duelo   fablava a doña Sol:
"sí vos lo meresca, mio primo,   nuestro padre el
                                                                Canpeador,

The Heirs of Carrión   rode on, praising themselves.
But I shall tell you   of that same Félix Muñoz—
he was a nephew   of the Cid Campeador—
they had bidden him ride forward   but this was not to his
      liking.
On the road as he went   his heart was heavy;
he slipped to one side   apart from the others;
he hid himself   in a thick wood,
waiting for his cousins   to come by
or to see what they had done,   those Heirs of Carrión.
He saw them come   and heard something of their talk;
they did not see him there   nor suspect that he heard them;
he knew well what if they saw him   they would not leave
      him alive.
   The Heirs set spur   and ride on.
Félix Muñoz   turned back the way they had come;
he found his cousins   both lying senseless.
He called, "Cousins, cousins!"   Then he dismounted,
tied his horse   and went up to them.
"Cousins, my cousins,   Doña Elvira and Doña Sol,
they have vilely proved themselves,   the Heirs of Carrión!
May it please God   that their punishment find them!"
He stayed there   endeavoring to revive them.
Their senses had gone far from them;   they could not
      speak at all.
The fabrics of his heart   tear as he calls:
"Cousins, my cousins,   Doña Elvira and Doña Sol,
come awake, cousins,   for the love of the Creator!
Wake now while the day lasts   before the night comes
and the wild beasts   devour us on this mountain!"
Doña Elvira and Doña Sol   come back to themselves;
they opened their eyes   and saw Félix Muñoz.
"Quickly, cousins,   for the love of the Creator!
the Heirs of Carrión   when they miss me
will come looking for me   at full speed;
if God does not aid us   we shall die here."
Then with great pain   Doña Sol spoke:
"If our father the Campeador   deserves it of you, my
      cousin,

239

dandos del agua,   sí vos vala el Criador."
Con un sombrero   que tiene Félez Muñoz,
nuevo era e fresco,   que de Valençial sacó,
cogió del agua en elle   e a sus primas dió;
mucho son lazradas   e amas las fartó.

   Tanto las rogó   fata que las assentó.
Valas conortando   e metiendo coraçón
fata que esfuerçan,   e amas las tomó
e privado   en el cavallo las cavalgó;
con el so manto   a amas las cubrió,
el cavallo priso por la rienda   e luego dent las partió.
Todos tres señeros   por los robredos de Corpes,
entre noch e día   salieron de los montes;
a las aguas de Duero   ellos arribados son,
a la torre de don Urraca   elle las dexó.
A Sant Estevan   vino Félez Muñoz,
falló a Díag Téllez   el que de Albar Fáñez fo;
quando elle lo odió,   pesól de coraçon;
priso bestias   e vestidos de pro,
hiva reçibir   a don Elvira e a doña Sol;
en Sant Estevan   dentro las metió,
quanto él mejor puede   allí las ondró.
Los de Sant Estevan,   siempre mesurados son,
quando sabien esto,   pesóles de coraçón;
a las fijas del Çid   danles enffurçión.
Allí sovieron ellas   fata que sanas son.

   Alabándos sedían   ifantes de Carrión.
Por todas essas tierras   estas nuevas sabidas son;
de cuer pesó esto   al buen rey don Alfons.
Van aquestos mandados   a Valençia la mayor;
quando gelo dizen   a mio Çid el Campeador,
una grand ora   penssó e comidió;
alçó la su mano,   a la barba se tomó;
"Grado a Cristus,   que del mundo es señor,
quando tal ondra me an dada   ifantes de Carrión;
par aquesta barba   que nadi non messó,

give us a little water,   for the love of the Creator."
Then with his hat,   which was new, with its sheen still
      on it,
which he had brought from Valencia,   Félix Muñoz
took up water   and gave it to his cousins;
they were gravely hurt   and both had need of it.
   He urged them a long while   till they sat upright.
He gave them comfort   and made them take heart again
till they recovered somewhat,   and he took them both up
and with all haste   put them on his horse;
he covered them both   with his own mantle,
took his horse by the reins   and went off with them both.
They three alone   through the forest of Corpes
between night and day   went out from among the
      mountains;
they have arrived   at the waters of the Duero;
at the tower of Doña Urraca   he left those two.
Félix Muñoz came   to San Esteban
and found Diego Téllez,   who was Alvar Fáñez's vassal;
he was grieved in his heart   when he heard the story,
and he took beasts   and fine garments
and went to receive   Doña Elvira and Doña Sol;
he brought them   into San Esteban;
he did them honor   as well as he could.
Those of San Esteban   are always sensible folk;
when they knew of this deed   it grieved their hearts;
they brought tribute from their farms   to the Cid's
      daughters.
There the girls remained   until they were healed.
   And the Heirs of Carrión   continued to praise
      themselves.
Through all those lands   the tidings are made known;
the good King Alfonso   was grieved deeply.
Word of it goes   to Valencia, the great city;
when they tell it   to My Cid the Campeador,
for more than an hour   he thought and pondered;
he raised his hand   and grasped his beard:
"I give thanks to Christ   Who is lord of the world;
this is the honor they have done me,   these Heirs of
      Carrión;
I swear by this beard,   which no one ever has torn,

non la lograrán   ifantes de Carrión;
que a mis fijas   bien las casaré yo!"
Pesó a mio Çid   e a toda su cort,
e Albar Fáñez   d' alma e de coraçón.

    Cavalgó Minaya   con Per Vermudoz
e Martín Antolínez,   el Burgalés de pro,
con dozientos cavalleros,   quales mio Çid mandó;
dixoles fuertemientre   que andidiessen de dia e da noch,
aduxiessen a ssus fijas   a Valençia la mayor.
Non lo detardan   el mandado de so señor,
apriessa cavalgan,   andan los dias e las noches;
vinieron a Gormaz,   un castillo tan fuort,
i albergaron   por verdad una noch.
A Sant Estevan   el mandado llegó
que vinie Minaya   por sus primas amas a dos.
Varones de Sant Estevan,   a guisa de muy proes,
reçiben a Minaya   e a todos sos varones,
presentan a Minaya   essa noch grant enffurçión;
non gelo quiso tomar,   mas mucho gelo gradió:
"Graçias, varones de Sant Estevan,   que sodes
                                            coñoscedores,
por aquesta ondra que vos diestes   a esto que nos cuntió;
mucho vos lo gradeçe,   allá do está, mio Çid el Canpeador;
assí lo ffago yo   que aquí estó.
Affé Dios de los çielos   que vos de dent buen galardón!"
Todos gelo gradeçen   e sos pagados son,
adeliñan a posar   pora folgar essa noch.
Minaya va veer   sues primas do son,
en elle fincan los ojos   don Elvira e doña Sol:
"Atanto vos lo gradimos   commo si viéssemos al Criador;
e vos a él lo gradid,   quando bivas somos nos.
En los días de vagar,   en Valençia la mayor,
toda nuestra rencura   sabremos contar nos."

132
Minaya y sus primas parten de San Esteban.
El Cid sale a recibirlos

these Heirs of Carrión   shall not go free with this;
as for my daughters I shall yet marry them well!" ←
My Cid was grieved   with all his heart and soul,
as were Alvar Fáñez   and all the court.

Minaya mounted   with Pedro Bermúdez
and Martín Antolínez,   the worthy man of Burgos,
with two hundred knights   whom My Cid sent;
he commanded them strictly   to ride day and night
and bring his daughters   to Valencia, the great city.
They do not delay   to fulfill their lord's command;
they ride with all speed,   they travel day and night;
they came to Gormaz,   a strong castle,
and there in truth   they paused for one night.
The news has arrived   at San Esteban
that Minaya is coming   for his two cousins.
The men of San Esteban,   like the worthy folk that
     they are,
receive Minaya   and all his men;
that night they presented   Minaya with great tribute;
he did not wish to take it   but thanked them deeply:
"Thanks, people of San Esteban,   you conduct yourselves
     well.
For this honor you do us   in this misfortune
My Cid the Campeador   thanks you from where he is,
and here where I am   I do the same.
By God Who is in heaven   you will be well rewarded!"
All thank him for what he said   and are content;
they go each to his place   for the night's rest.
Minaya goes to see   his cousins where they are.
Doña Elvira and Doña Sol,   fix their eyes upon him:
"We are as glad to behold you   as though you were the
     Creator,
and give thanks to Him   that we are still alive.
When there is more leisure   in Valencia, the great city,
we shall be able to recount   all our grievance."

132
*Minaya and his cousins leave San Esteban. The Cid rides
out to receive them*

Lloravan de los ojos   las dueñas e Albar Fáñez,
e Per Vermudoz   otro tanto las ha;
"Don Elvira e doña Sol,   cuydado non ayades,
quando vos sodes sanas   e bivas e sin otro mal.
Buen casamiento perdiestes,   mejor podredes ganar.
Aun veamos el dia   que vos podamos vengar!"
I yazen essa noche,   e tan grand gozo que fazen.
    Otro dia mañana   pienssan de calvagar.
Los de Sant Estevan   escurriéndolos van
fata Rio d'amor,   dándoles solaz;
d' allent se espidieron dellos,   piénssanse de tornar,
e Minaya con las dueñas   iva cabadelant.
Troçieron Alcoçeva,   adiestro dexan Gormax,
o dizen Bado de Rey,   allá ivan passar,
a la casa de Berlanga   posada presa han.
Otro día mañana   métense a andar,
a qual dizen Medina   ivan albergar,
e de Medina a Molina   en otro día van;
al moro Avengalvón   de coraçón le plaz,
saliólos a reçibir   de buena voluntad,
por amor de mio Çid   rica cena les da.
Dent pora Valençia   adeliñechos van.
    Al que en buen ora nasco   llegava el menssaje,
privado cavalga,   a reçebirlos sale;
armas iva teniendo   a grant gozo que faze.
Mio Çid a sus fijas   ívalas abraçar,
besándolas a amas,   tornós, de sonrrisar:
"¿Venides, mis fijas?   Dios vos curie de mal!
Yo tomé el cassamiento,   mas non osé dezir al.
Plega al Criador,   que en çielo está,
que vos vea mejor cassadas   d'aquí en adelant.
De mios yernos de Carrión   Dios me faga vengar!"
Besaron las manos   las fijas al padre.
Teniendo ivan armas,   entráronse a la cibdad;
grand gozo fizo con ellas   doña Ximena su madre.

Alvar Fáñez and the ladies   could not keep back the tears,
and Pedro Bermúdez   spoke to them thus:
"Doña Elvira and Doña Sol,   forget your cares now,
since now you are healed   and alive, and without other harm.
You have lost a good marriage,   you may yet have a better.
And we shall yet see the day   when you will be avenged!"
They spent that night there   amid great rejoicings.
    The next day in the morning   they mounted their horses.
The people of San Esteban   went with them on their way
as far as the River Amor,   keeping them company;
there they said good-by   and turned back again,
and Minaya and the ladies   rode on ahead.
They crossed over Alcoceba,   on their right they left Gormaz;
where it is called Vadorrey   they came and went by;
in the village of Berlanga   they paused to rest.
Next day in the morning   they rode on again
as far as the place called Medinaceli   where they took shelter,
and from Medinaceli to Molina   they came in one day.
The Moor Abengalbón   was pleased in his heart;
he rode out to receive them   with good will;
he gave them a rich dinner   for the love of My Cid.
Then straightway they rode on   toward Valencia.
    The message came   to him who in good hour was born;
he mounts in haste   and rides out to receive them;
he went brandishing his weapons   and showing great joy.
My Cid rode up   to embrace his daughters;
he kissed them both   and began to smile:
"You are here, my daughters!   God heal you from harm!
I permitted your marriage   for I could not refuse it.
May it please the Creator   Who is in heaven
that I shall see you   better married hereafter.
God give me vengeance   on my sons-in-law of Carrión!"
Then the daughters   kissed their father's hands.
All rode into the city   brandishing their weapons;
Doña Jimena, their mother,   rejoiced at the sight of them.

El que en buen ora nasco   non quiso tardar,
fablós con los sos   en su poridad,
al rey Alfons de Castiella   penssó de enbiar.

El Cid envía a Muño Gustioz que pida al rey justicia.
Muño halla al rey en Sahagún, y le expone su mensaje.
El rey promete reparación

"¿O eres, Muño Gustioz,   mio vassallo de pro.
En buen ora te crié   a tí en la mi cort!
Llieves el mandado   a Castiella al rey Alfons;
por mí bésale la mano   d' alma e de coraçón,
—quomo yo so so vassallo,   e elle es mio señor,—
desta desondra que me an fecha   ifantes de Carrión
quel pese al buen rey   d' alma e de coraçón.
Elle casó mies fijas,   ca non gelas di yo;
quando las han dexadas   a grant desonor,
si desondra y cabe   alguna contra nos,
la poca e la grant   toda es de mio señor.
Mios averes se me an levado,   que sobejanos son;
esso me puede pesar   con la otra desonor.
Adúgamelos a vistas,   o a juntas o a cortes,
commo aya derecho   de ifantes de Carrión,
ca tan grant es la rencura   dentro en mi coraçón."
Muño Gustioz,   privado cavalgó,
con él dos cavalleros   quel sirvan a so sabor,
e con él escuderos   que son de criazón.
Salien de Valençia   e andan quanto puoden,
nos dan vagar   los días e las noches.
Al rey don Alfons   en Sant Fagunt lo falló.
Rey es de Castiella   e rey es de León
e de las Asturias   bien a San Çalvador,
fasta dentro de Santi Yaguo   de todo es señor,
ellos comdes gallizanos   a él tienen por señor.
Assí commo descavalga   aquel Muño Gustioz
omillós a los santos   e rogó al Criador;

He who was born in good hour   wished no delay;
he spoke in secret   with his own men.
He prepared to send a message   to King Alfonso in
    Castile.

133
*The Cid sends Muño Gustioz to beg justice of the King.
Muño finds the King in Sahagún and delivers his message.
The King promises reparation*

"Oh, stand before me, Muño Gustioz,   my loyal vassal.
In a good hour I brought you up   and placed you in my
    court!
Carry my message   to Castile, to King Alfonso;
kiss his hand for me   with all my heart and soul,
since I am his vassal   and he is my lord;
this dishonor they have done me,   these Heirs of Carrión,
I would have it grieve the King   in his heart and soul.
He married my daughters;   it was not I who gave them.
Since they have been deserted   and gravely dishonored,
whatever in this   may redound to our dishonor,
in small things or in great,   redounds to my lord's.
They have taken away wealth   beyond measure;
this should be reckoned in   with the other dishonor.
Let them be called to a meeting,   to a court or assembly,
and give me my due,   these Heirs of Carrión,
for I bear much rancor   within my heart."
Muño Gustioz   mounted quickly,
and two knights with him   to wait upon his will,
and with him squires   of the Cid's household.
    They rode out of Valencia   and with all speed go
        forward;
they take no rest   by day or night.
In Sahagún   they found King Alfonso.
He is King of Castile   and King of León
and of Asturias   and the city of Oviedo;
as far as Santiago   he is the lord,
and the Counts of Galicia   serve him as their lord.
There Muño Gustioz,   as soon as he dismounts,
knelt to the saints   and prayed to the Creator;

247

adeliñó poral palaçio   do estava la cort,
con elle dos cavalleros   quel aguardan cum a sseñor.
   Assí commo entraron   por medio de la cort
vídolos el rey   e coñosció a Muño Gustioz;
levantós el rey   tan bien los reçibió.
Delant el rey Alfons   los inojos fincó,
besábale los piedes,   aquel Muño Gustioz;
"Merçed, rey de largos reynos   a vos dizen señor!
Los piedes e las manos   vos besa el Campeador;
elle es vuestro vassallo   e vos sodes so señor.
Casastes sus fijas   con ifantes de Carrión,
alto fo el casamiento   ca lo quisiestes vos!
Ya vos sabedes la ondra   que es cuntida a nos,
quomo nos han abultados   ifantes de Carrión:
mal majaron sus fijas   del Çid Campeador;
majades e desnudas   a grande desonor,
desenparadas las dexaron   en el robredo de Corpes,
a las bestias fieras   e a las aves del mont.
Afélas sus fijas   en Valençia do son.
Por esto vos besa las manos,   commo vassallo e señor,
que gelos levedes a vistas,   o a juntas o a cortes;
tienes por desondrado,   mas la vuestra es mayor,
e que vos pese, rey,   commo sodes sabidor;
que aya mio Çid derecho   de ifantes de Carrión."
El rey una gran ora   calló e comidió;
"Verdad te digo yo,   que me pesa de coraçón
e verdad dizes en esto,   tú, Muño Gustioz,
ca yo casé sus fijas   con ifantes de Carrión;
fizlo por bien,   que ffosse a su pro.
¡Si quier el casamiento   fecho non fosse oy!
Entre yo e mio Çid   pésanos de coraçón.
Ayudor lê a derecho,   sín salve el Criador!
Lo que non cuydava fer   de toda esta sazón,
andarán mios porteros   por todo el reyno mio,
pora dentro en Toledo   pregonarán mie cort.

he went up to the palace   where the court was,
and two knights with him   who serve him as their lord.
   When they entered   into the midst of the court
the King saw them   and knew Muño Gustioz;
the King rose   and received them well.
Before King Alfonso   Muño Gustioz
went down on his knees   and kissed the King's feet.
"Grace, King of great kingdoms   that call you lord!
The Campeador   kisses your hands and feet;
he is your vassal   and you are his lord.
You married his daughters   with the Heirs of Carrión;
the match was exalted   because you wished it so.
You know already what honor   that marriage has brought
      us:
how the Heirs of Carrión   have affronted us,
how they beat and abused the daughters   of the Cid
      Campeador,
stripped them naked, lashed them with whips   and deeply
      dishonored them
and abandoned them   in the oak forest of Corpes,
left them to the wild beasts   and the birds of the mountain.
Behold, now his daughters   are once more in Valencia.
For this the Cid kisses your hands   as a vassal to his lord;
he asks you to call these Heirs   to a court or assembly;
the Cid has been dishonored   but you still more deeply;
he asks you to share his grief, King,   as you are wise,
and to help My Cid to receive reparation   from these
      Heirs of Carrión."
For more than an hour the King   thought, and said
      nothing.
"I tell you, in truth   this grieves my heart,
and in this I speak truth   to you, Muño Gustioz.
I married the daughters   to the Heirs of Carrión;
I did it for the best,   for his advantage.
Oh, that such marriage   never had been made!
As for myself and the Cid,   our hearts are heavy.
I must see he receives justice,   so may the Creator keep
      me!
I never expected   such a thing as this.
My heralds shall go   through all my kingdom
and call my court   to assemble in Toledo;

que allá me vayan   cuemdes e iffançones;
mandaré commo i vayan   ifantes de Carrión,
e commo den derecho   a mio Çid el Campeador,
e que non aya rencura   podiédolo vedar yo.

134
El rey convoca corte en Toledo

"Dizidle al Campeador,   que en buen ora nasco,
que destas siet sedmanas   adóbes con sos vassallos,
véngam a Toledo,   éstol do de plazdo.
Por amor de mio Çid   esta cort yo fago.
Saludádmelos a todos,   entrellos aya espaçio;
desto que les abino   aun bien serán ondrados."
Espidiós Muño Gustioz,   a mio Çid es tornado.
    Assi como lo dixo,   suyo era el cuydado:
non lo detiene por nada   Alfons el Castellano,
enbía sus cartas   pora León e a Santi Yaguo,
a los portogaleses   e a gallizianos,
e a los de Carrión   e a varones castellanos,
que cort fazie en Toledo   aquel rey ondrado,
a cabo de siet sedmanas   que i fossen juntados;
qui non viniesse a la cort   non se toviesse por so vassallo.
Por todas sus tierras   assí lo ivan penssando,
que non falliessen   de lo que el rey avié mandado.

135
Los de Carrión ruegan en vano al rey que desista de la
corte. Reúnese la corte. El Cid llega el postero. El
rey sale a su encuentro

Ya les va pesando   a ifantes de Carrión,

let all gather there,   counts and nobles;
and the Heirs of Carrión,   I shall bid them come there
and give just reparation   to My Cid the Campeador;
he shall not be left with a grievance   if I can prevent it.

134
The King convokes court in Toledo

"Say to the Campeador,   he who was born in good
      hour,
to be ready with his vassals   seven weeks from now
and come to Toledo;   that is the term I set for him.
Out of love for My Cid   I call this court together.
Give my greetings to all   and bid them take comfort;
this which has befallen them   shall yet redound to their
      honor."
Muño Gustioz took his leave   and returned to My Cid.
   Alfonso the Castilian,   as he had promised,
took it upon himself.   He brooks no delays,
he sends his letters   to León and Santiago,
to the Portuguese   and the Galicians
and to those of Carrión   and the nobles of Castile,
proclaiming that their honored King   called court in
      Toledo,
that they should gather there   at the end of seven weeks;
and whoever should not come to the court,   he would
      hold no longer his vassal.
Through all his lands   thus the message ran,
and none thought of refusing   what the King had
      commanded.

135
Those of Carrión beg in vain that the King should not hold court. The court convenes. The Cid arrives last. The King rides out to receive him

And the Heirs of Carrión   are gravely concerned
251

por que en Toledo   el rey fazie cort;
miedo han que i verná   mio Çid el Campeador.
Prenden so conssejo,   assí parientes commo son,
ruegan al rey   que los quite desta cort.
Dixo el rey: "No lo feré,   sín salve Dios!
ca i verná   mio Çid el Campeador;
darlêdes derecho,   ca rencura ha de vos.
Qui lo fer non quisiesse,   o no irâ mi cort,
quite mio reyno,   ca dél non he sabor."
Ya lo vidieron que es a fer   ifantes de Carrión,
prenden conssejo   parientes commo son;
el comde don Garçía   en estas nuevas fo,
enemigo de mio Çid   que mal siemprel buscó,
aqueste conssejo   los ifantes de Carrión.
Llegava el plazdo,   querien ir a la cort;
en los primeros   va el buen rey don Alfons,
el comde don Anrric   y el comde don Remond,
—aqueste fo padre   del buen enperador,—
el comde don Froilan   y el comde don Birbón.
Foron i de so reyno   otros muchos sabidores,
de toda Castiella   todos los mejores.
El comde don Garçía,   el Crespo de Grañón,
e Alvar Díaz . . . el que Oca mandó,
e Ansuor Gonçálvez   e Gonçalvo Ansuórez.
e Per Ansuórez,   sabet, allís açertó,
e Diago e Ferrando   í son amos a dos,
e con ellos grand bando   que aduxieron a la cort:
enbair le cuydan   a mio Çid el Campeador.
    De todas partes   allí juntados son.
Aun non era llegado   el que en buen ora naçió,
por que se tarda   el rey non ha sabor.
Al quinto día   venido es mio Çid el Campeador;
Alvar Fáñez   adelantel enbió,
que besasse las manos   al rey so señor:
bien lo sopiesse   que i serie essa noch.
Quando lo odió el rey,   plógol de coraçón;
con grandes yentes   el rey cavalgó

252

because the King holds court   in Toledo;
they are afraid of meeting   My Cid the Campeador.
They ask aid and advice   of their relatives;
they beg the King   to excuse them from this court.
The King replied, "In God's name,   I shall not grant you
    this!
For My Cid the Campeador   will come there
and receive reparation,   for he has a grievance against you.
Whoever does not wish to obey   and come to my court,
let him quit my kingdom,   for he has incurred my
    displeasure."
The Heirs of Carrión   see that it must be done;
they ask aid and advice   from their relatives.
The Count Don García   took part in all this;
he was an enemy of My Cid   and sought always to do him
    harm,
and he gave counsel   to the Heirs of Carrión.
The appointed time came;   they must go to the court.
The good King Don Alfonso   arrived there first,
the Count Don Enrique   and the Count Don Ramón—
he was the father   of the good emperor—
the Count Don Fruela   and the Count Don Birbón.
And many others learned in law   came from all parts of
    the kingdom,
and the best came   from all Castile.
The Count Don García,   Twisted-Mouth of Grañón,
and Alvar Díaz,   who governed Oca,
and Asur González   and Gonzalo Ansúrez
and Pedro Ansúrez,   you may know, arrived there,
and Diego and Fernando,   both of them came,
and a great crowd with them   came to the court
hoping to abuse   My Cid the Campeador.
    From all sides   they have gathered there.
He who in good hour was born   has not yet arrived,
and the King is not pleased,   for he is late.
On the fifth day   My Cid the Campeador came;
Alvar Fáñez   he sent on before him
to kiss the hands   of the King his lord
and tell him that the Cid   would arrive that evening.
When the King heard this   his heart was pleased;
with many knights   the King mounted

e iva reçebir   al que en buen ora naçió.
Bien aguisado viene   el Çid con todos los sos,
buenas conpañas   que assí an tal señor.
Quando lo ovo a ojo   el buen rey don Alfons,
firiós a tierra   mio Çid el Campeador;
biltar se quiere   e ondrar a so señor.
Quando lo vido el rey,   por nada non tardó:
"¡Par sant Esidre,   verdad non será oy!
Cavalgad, Çid; si non,   non avría dend sabor;
saludar nos hemos   d' alma e de coraçón.
De lo que a vos pesa   a mi duele el coraçón;
Dios lo mande que por vos   se ondre oy la cort!"
—"Amen," dixo mio Çid,   el buen Campeador;
besóle la mano   e después le saludó;
"Grado a Dios,   quando vos veo, señor.
Omíllom a vos   e al comde do Remond
e al comde don Arric   e a quantos que i son;
Dios salve a nuestros amigos   e a vos más, señor!
Mi mugier doña Ximena,   —dueña es de pro,—
bésavos las manos,   e mis fijas amas a dos,
desto que nos abino   que vos pese, señor."
Respondió el rey: "sí fago, sin salve Dios!"

136
El Cid no entra en Toledo. Celebra vigilia en San Servando

Pora Toledo   el rey tornada da;
essa noch mio Çid   Tajo non quiso passar:
"Merçed, ya rey,   sí el Criador vos salve!
Penssad, señor,   de entrar a la cibdad,
e yo con los mios   posaré a San Serván:
las mis compañas   esta noche llegarán.
Terné vigilia   en aqueste santo logar;
cras mañana   entraré a la çibdad,
e iré a la cort   enantes de yantar."
Dixo el rey: "plazme de veluntad."

and went to receive   him who in good hour was born.
Well prepared,   the Cid comes with his men,
an imposing company   worthy of such a lord.
When he set eyes   on the good King Alfonso
My Cid the Campeador   flung himself to the ground,
wishing to humble himself   and do honor to his lord.
When the King saw this   in all haste he went forward:
"By Saint Isidore,   this shall not be so today!
Remain mounted, Cid,   or I shall be displeased;
we must greet each other   with heart and soul.
That which has befallen you   grieves my heart;
God grant you will honor the court   today with your
        presence!"
"Amen," said My Cid,   the good Campeador;
he kissed the King's hand   and then embraced him.
"I give thanks to God   for the sight of you, my lord.
I humble myself before you   and before the Count Ramón
and the Count Don Enrique   and all who are here with
        you;
God save your friends   and above all, you, my lord!
My wife, Doña Jimena,   that worthy lady,
kisses your hands,   as do my daughters,
and beg you to partake   of our grief in this, my lord."
The King answered,   "I do so, in God's name!"

136
*The Cid does not enter Toledo. He keeps vigil in San
    Servando*

The King has turned   and started toward Toledo;
My Cid did not wish   to cross the Tagus that night:
"Grace, my King,   may the Creator bless you!
Return as you will, my lord,   into the city,
and I with my men   shall lodge in San Serván;
the rest of my vassals   will arrive tonight.
I shall hold vigil   in that holy place;
tomorrow in the morning   I shall enter the city
and come to the court   before I have broken my fast."
The King said,   "I am pleased it should be so."

El rey don Alfons   a Toledo va entrar,
mio Çid Roy Díaz   en Sant Serván posar,
Mandó fazer candelas   e poner en el altar;
sabor a de velar   en essa santidad,
al Criador rogando   e fablando en poridad.
Entre Minaya   e los buenos que i ha
acordados foron,   quando vino la man.

137

Preparación del Cid en San Servando para ir a la corte.
El Cid va a Toledo y entra en la corte. El rey le ofrece
asiento en su escaño. El Cid rehusa. El rey abre la
sesión. Proclama la paz entre los litigantes. El Cid
expone su demanda. Reclama Colada y Tizón. Los de
Carrión
entregan las espadas. El Cid las da a Pedro Vermúdez
y a Martín Antolínez. Segunda demanda del Cid. El ajuar
de sus hijas. Los infantes hallan dificultad para el pago

Matines e prima   dixieron faza los albores,
suelta fo la missa   antes que saliesse el sol,
e ssu ofrenda han fecha   muy buena e a sazón.
"Vos Minaya Albar Fáñez,   el mio braço mejor.
Vos iredes comigo   e obispo don Jerome
e Per Vermudoz   e aqueste Muño Gustioz
e Martín Antolínez   el Burgalés de pro,
e Albar Albaroz   e Albar Salvadórez
e Martín Muñoz,   que en buen punto nació,
e mio sobrino   Félez Muñoz;
comigo irá Mal Anda,   que es bien sabidor,
e Galind Garçiez,   el bueno d' Aragón;
con estos cúnplansse çiento   de los buenos que i son.
Velmezes vestidos   por sufrir las guarnizones,
de suso las lorigas   tan blancas commo el sol;
sobre las lorigas,   armiños e pelliçones,
e que no parescan las armas,   bien presos los cordones;
so los mantos las espadas   dulçes e tajadores;
d' aquesta guisa   quiero ir a la cort,

The King Don Alfonso   returns to Toledo;
My Cid Ruy Díaz   goes to stay in San Serván.
He sent for candles   to set on the altar;
he wishes to keep vigil   in this holy place,
praying to the Creator,   speaking with Him in secret.
Minaya and the other   good vassals who were there
were ready and waiting   when the morning came.

137

The Cid's preparations, in San Servando, to go to the court.
The Cid goes to Toledo and enters the court. The King
offers him a place on his bench. The Cid refuses. The King
opens the session. He proclaims peace between the litigants.
The Cid makes his demands. He reclaims Colada and
Tizón. The Heirs of Carrión give up the swords. The
Cid gives them to Pedro Bermúdez and Martín Antolínez.
The Cid's second demand: the dowry of his daughters. The
Heirs find it difficult to repay

As dawn drew near   they said matins and primes,
and Mass was finished   before the sun rose.
All My Cid's men   made precious offerings.
"You, Minaya Alvar Fáñez,   my sword arm,
come with me   and you, Bishop Don Jerome
and Pedro Burmúdez   and Muño Gustioz
and Martín Antolínez,   the worthy man of Burgos,
and Alvar Alvarez   and Alvar Salvadórez
and Martín Muñoz,   born under a good star,
and my cousin,   Félix Muñoz,
and let Mal Anda come with me,   who is learned in law,
and Galindo García,   the good warrior from Aragón;
and others to make up a hundred   from among my good
        vassals.
Put on your armor   over padded tunics;
put on your breastplates,   white as the sun,
furs and ermines   over your breastplates,
and draw the strings tight   that your weapons be not seen;
under your cloaks   gird the sweet keen swords.
In this manner   I would go to the court

257

por demandar mios derechos   e dezir mie razón.
Si desobra buscaren   ifantes de Carrión,
do tales çiento tovier,   bien seré sin pavor."
Respondieron todos: "nos esso queremos, señor."
Assí commo lo ha dicho,   todos adobados son.

Nos detiene por nada   el que en buen ora naçió:
calças de buen paño   en sus camas metió,
sobrellas unos çapatos   que a grant huebra son.
Vistió camisa de rançal   tan blanca commo el sol,
con oro e con plata   todas las presas son,
al puño bien están,   ca él se lo mandó;
sobrella un brial   primo de çiclatón,
obrado es con oro,   parecen por o son.
Sobresto una piel vermeja,   las bandas d' oro son,
siempre la viste   mio Çid el Campeador.
Una cofia sobre los pelos   d' un escarín de pro,
con oro es obrada,   fecha por razón,
que nol contalassen los pelos   al buen Çid Campeador;
la barba avie luenga   e prísola con el cordón,
por tal lo faze esto   que recabdar quiere todo lo so.
De suso cubrió un manto   que es de grant valor,
en elle abríen que veer   quantos que i son.

Con aquestos çiento   que adobar mandó,
apriessa cavalga,   de San Serván salió;
assí iva mio Çid   adobado a lla cort.

Ala puerta de fuera   descavalga a sabor;
cuerdamientra entra   mio Çid con todos los sos:
elle va en medio   elos çiento aderredor.
Quando lo vieron entrar   al que en buen ora naçió.
Levantós en pie   el buen rey don Alfons
e el comde don Anrric   e el comde don Remont
e desi adelant, sabet,   todos los otros de la cort:
a grant ondra lo reçiben   al que en buen ora naçió.
Nos quiso levantar   el Crespo de Grañón,
nin todos los del bando   de ifantes de Carrión.

El rey a mio Çid: a las manos le tomó:
"Venid acá seer   comigo, Campeador,
en aqueste escaño   quem diestes vos en don;
maguer que âlgunos pesa,   mejor sodes que nos."

258

to demand justice   and say what I must say.
If the Heirs of Carrión   come seeking a quarrel,
if such a hundred are with me   it will not concern me."
All answered,   "Let it be so, lord."
All made ready   as he had commanded.

He who in good hour was born   made no delay:
he covered his legs   in stockings of fine cloth
and over them he put shoes   of elaborate work.
He put on a woven shirt   as white as the sun,
and all the fastenings   were of silver and gold;
the cuffs fitted neatly   for he had ordered it thus.
Over this he put a tunic   of fine brocade
worked with gold   shining in every place.
Over these a crimson skin   with buckles of gold,
which My Cid the Campeador   wears on all occasions.
Over the furs he put   a hood of fine cloth
worked with gold   and set there
so that none might tear the hair   of My Cid the
      Campeador;
his beard was long   and tied with a cord,
for he wished to guard all his person   against insult.
On top of it all he wore   a cloak of great value;
all admired it,   as many as were there to see.

With that hundred   whom he had bidden make ready
he mounted in haste   and rode out of San Serván;
thus prepared,   My Cid went to the court.

At the outer door   they dismounted;
My Cid and his men   entered with due circumspection:
he goes in the middle   with his hundred around him.
When they saw enter   him who in good hour was born,
the good King Alfonso   rose to his feet,
and the Count Don Enrique   and the Count Don Ramón,
and all the others,   you may know, who were in the court.
With great honor they receive him   who in good hour
      was born.
Twisted-Mouth of Grañón   did not wish to stand,
nor all the rest of the band   of the Heirs of Carrión.

The King took   My Cid by the hands:
"Come, sit down here   with me, Campeador,
on this bench   which was a gift from you;
though it annoy some,   you are of more worth than we."

Essora dixo muchas merçedes   el que Valençia gañó:
"seed en vuestro escaño   commo rey e señor;
acá posaré   con todos aquestos mios."
Lo que dixo el Çid   al rey plogo de coraçón.
En un escaño torniño essora mio Çid posó,
los çiento quel aguardan   posan aderredor.
Catando están a mio Çid   quantos ha en la cort,
a la barba que avié luenga   e presa con el cordón;
en sos aguisamientos   bien semeja varón.
Nol pueden catar de vergüença   ifantes de Carrión.
    Essora se levó en pie   el buen rey don Alfons:
"Oíd, mesnadas,   sí vos vala el Criador!
Yo, de que fu rey,   non fiz mas de dos cortes:
la una fo en Burgos,   e la otra en Carrión,
esta terçera   a Toledo la vin fer oy,
por el amor de mio Çid   el que en buen ora naçió,
que reçiba derecho   de ifantes de Carrión.
Grande tuerto le han tenido,   sabémoslo todos nós;
alcaldes sean desto   comde don Anrric e comde don
                                                    Remond
e estos otros comdes   que del vando non sodes.
Todos meted i mientes,   ca sodes coñoscedores,
por escoger el derecho,   ca tuerto non mando yo.
"Della e della part   en paz seamos oy.
Juro par sant Esidre,   el que bolviere mi cort
quitar me a el reyno,   perderá mi amor.
Con el que toviere derecho   yo dessa parte me so.
Agora demande   mio Çid el Campeador:
sabremos qué responden   ifantes de Carrión."
    Mio Çid la mano besó al rey   e en pie se levantó:
"Mucho vos lo gradesco   commo a rey e a señor,
por quanto esta cort   fiziestes por mi amor.
Esto les demando   a ifantes de Carrión:
por mis fijas quem dexaron   yo nan he desonor,
ca vos las casastes, rey,   sabredes qué fer oy;

Then he who had taken Valencia   thanked him much:
"Sit on your bench   as King and lord;
here I shall stay   among my men."
What the Cid said   pleased the King's heart.
Then My Cid sat down   on a bench of lathwork,
and the hundred who guard him   stand around him.
All who are in the court   are watching My Cid
and his long beard   tied with a cord;
his appearance   was in every way manly.
The Heirs of Carrión   cannot look up for shame.
    Then the good King Alfonso   rose to his feet.
"Hear me, my vassals,   and the Creator bless you!
Since I have been King   I have not held more than two
        courts:
one was in Burgos   and the other in Carrión,
and this third   I open today in Toledo
for the love of My Cid,   who in good hour was born,
so that he may receive reparation   from the Heirs of
        Carrión.
They have done him great wrong,   as all of us know;
now let Counts Don Enrique and Don Ramón   be the
        judges,
and these other counts   who are not of the Heirs'
        company.
You who are learned in law,   fix well your attentions
and find out what is just,   for I would command no
        injustice.
Let us have peace today   on one side and the other.
I swear by Saint Isidore   that whoever disturbs my court
will be banished from my kingdom   and lose my favor.
I am of that side   on which justice is.
Now let My Cid the Campeador   make his demand,
and let us hear what they answer,   these Heirs of
        Carrión."
    My Cid kissed the King's hand   and rose to his feet.
"I thank you deeply,   as my King and lord,
for having held this court   for my sake.
Here is what I demand   of the Heirs of Carrión:
I am not dishonored   because they abandoned my
        daughters,
for since you, King, married them,   you will know what

mas quando sacaron mis fijas   de Valençia la mayor,
yo bien los quería   d' alma e de coraçón.
Diles dos espadas   a Colada e a Tizón
—estas yo las gané   a guisa de varón,—
ques ondrassen con ellas   e sirviessen a vos;
quando dexaron mis fijas   en el robredo de Corpes,
comigo non quisieron aver nada   e perdieron mi amor;
denme mis espadas   quando mios yernos non son."

    Atorgan los alcaldes: "tod esto es razón."
Dixo comde don Garçia: "a esto fablemos nos."
Essora salién aparte   ifantes de Carrión,
con todos sos parientes   y el bando que i son;
apriessa lo ivan trayendo   e acuerdan la razón:
"Aun grand amor nos faze   el Çid Campeador,
quando desondra de sus fijas   no nos demanda oy;
bien nos abendremos   con el rey don Alfons.
Démosle sus espadas,   quando assí finca la boz,
e quando las toviere,   partir se a la cort;
ya mas non avrá derecho   de nos el Çid Campeador."
Con aquest fabla   tornaron a la cort.
"Merçed, ya rey don Alfons,   sodes nuestro señor!
No lo podemos negar,   ca dos espadas nos dió;
quando las demanda   e dellas ha sabor,
dárgelas queremos   delant estando vos."

    Sacaron las espadas   Colada e Tizón,
pusiéronlas en mano   del rey so señor;
sacan las espadas   e relumbra toda la cort,
las maçanas e los arriazes   todos d' oro son;
maravíllanse dellas   los omnes buenos de la cort.
A mio Çid llamó el rey   las espadas le dio;
reçibió las espadas   las manos le besó,
tornos al escaño   dont se levantó.

262

to do now;
but when they took my daughters   from Valencia, the
     great city,
from my heart and soul   I showed them much love.
I gave them two swords,   Colada and Tizón —
these I had taken   fighting like a man in the field —
that with them they might do themselves honor,   and you
     service;
when they abandoned my daughters   in the oak grove of
     Corpes
they wanted nothing more of me   and they lost my love;
let them give me my swords,   since they are no longer my
     sons-in-law."
   The judges granted,   "He is right in this."
The Count Don García said,   "We must speak of this."
Then the Heirs of Carrión   walked to one side
with all their kinsmen   and the company who were with
     them;
they discuss it quickly   and decide what to say:
"The Cid Campeador   does us a great favor
in not calling to account today   the dishonor of his
     daughters;
we can easily come to an arrangement   with King Alfonso.
Let us give him the swords,   since that will end his
     demand,
and when he has them   the court will adjourn;
and the Cid Campeador   will have no more claims upon
     us."
Having decided this,   they returned to the court.
"Grace, King Alfonso,   you who are our lord!
We cannot deny   he gave us two swords;
now that he claims them   and wants them back again,
we wish to return them   here before you."
   They took out the swords,   Colada and Tizón;
they put them in the hands   of the King their lord.
The swords are drawn   and shine through all the court;
the hilts and guards   were all of gold.
All in the court   marveled to see them.
The King called My Cid   and gave him the swords;
he received the swords   and kissed the King's hands;
he returned to the bench   from which he had risen.

En las manos las tiene   e amas las cató;
non las pueden camear,   ca el Çid bien las connosçe;
alegrósle tod el cuerpo,   sorrisós de coraçon,
alçava la mano,   a la barba se tomó;
"par aquesta barba   que nadi non messó,
assís irán vengando   don Elvira e doña Sol."
A so sobrino don Pero   por nómbrel llamó,
tendió el braço,   la espada Tizón le dió:
"Prendetla, sobrino,   ca mejora en señor."
A Martín Antolínez,   el Burgalés de pro,
tendió el braço,   el espada Coláda dio;
"Martín Antolínez,   mio vassallo de pro,
prended a Colada,   ganéla de buen señor,
de Remont Verenguel   de Barçilona la mayor.
Por esso vos la do   que la bien curiedes vos.
Sé que si vos acaeçiere   o viniere sazón,
con ella ganaredes   grand prez e grand valor."
Besóle la mano,   el espada reçibió.

   Luego se levantó   mio Çid el Campeador:
"Grado al Criador   e a vos, rey señor!
ya pagado so de mis espadas,   de Colada e de Tizón.
Otra rencura he   de ifantes Je Carrión:
quando sacaron de Valençia   mis fijas amas a dos,
en oro e en plata   tres mill marcos les dio;
yo faziendo esto,   ellos acabaron lo so;
denme mios averes   quando mios yernos non son."

   Aquí veriedes quexarse   ifantes de Carrión!
Dize el comde don Remond: "dezid de ssí o de no."
Essora responden   ifantes de Carrión:
"Por essol diemos sus espadas   al Çid Campeador,
que al no nos demandasse,   que aquí fincó la boz."
Allí les respondió   el comde do Remond:
"Si ploguiere al rey,   assí dezimos nos:
a lo que demanda el Çid   quel recudades vos."
Dixo el buen rey: "assí lo otorgo yo."
Levantós en pie   el Çid Campeador:

He held them in his hands   and looked on them both;
they could not have been false ones,   for he knew them
    well.
All his body was glad   and he smiled from his heart,
he raised his hand   and stroked his beard.
"By this beard,   which none has ever torn,
thus proceeds the avenging   of Doña Elvira and Doña
    Sol."
He summoned his nephew, Don Pedro,   called him by
    name.
He stretched out his arm   and gave him the sword Tizón:
"Take it, nephew,   it has found a better master."
To Martín Antolínez,   worthy man of Burgos,
he stretched out his arm   and gave him Colada:
"Martín Antolínez,   my worthy vassal,
take Colada;   I won it from a good lord,
from Ramón Berenguer   of Barcelona, the great city.
Therefore I give it to you   that you may care for it well.
I know that if the time   or the occasion should find you,
with it you will gain   honor and glory."
Martín Antolínez kised his hand   and took the sword.
    Then My Cid the Campeador   got to his feet.
"I give thanks to the Creator   and to you, King and lord!
I am satisfied as to my   swords, Colada and Tizón.
I bear another grievance   toward the Heirs of Carrión:
When they took my daughters   from Valencia
I gave them three thousand marks   in gold and silver;
thus I did,   and they carried out their own business;
let them return my riches,   since they are not my
    sons-in-law."
    God, they groaned then,   those Heirs of Carrión!
The Count Don Ramón said,   "Answer him, yes or no."
Then the Heirs of Carrión   answered thus:
"For this reason we gave his swords   to the Cid
    Campeador,
so that he should ask us no more   and end his demands."
Then the Count Don Ramón   answered them thus:
"If it please the King,   the court speaks thus:
You must render to the Cid   what he demands."
The good King said,   "I wish it to be so."
My Cid the Campeador   rose again to his feet.

"Destos averes   que vos di yo,
si me los dades,   o dedes dello razón."
    Essora salien aparte   ifantes de Carrión;
non acuerdan en conssejo,   ca los averes grandes son:
espesos los han   ifantes de Carrión.
Tornan con el conssejo   e fablavan a sso sabor:
"Mucho nos afinca   el que Valençia gañó,
quando de nuestros averes,   assíl prende sabor;
pagar le hemos de heredades   en tierras de Carrión."
Dixieron los alcaldes   quando manfestados son:
"Si esso ploguiere al Çid,   non gelo vedamos nos;
mas en nuestro juvizio   assí lo mandamos nos;
que aquí lo enterguedes   dentro en la cort."
    A estas palabras   fabló rey don Alfons:
"Nos bien la sabemos   aquesta razón,
que derecho demanda   el Çid Campeador.
Destos tres mil marcos   los dozientos tengo yo;
entramos me los dieron   ifantes de Carrión.
Tornárgelos quiero,   ca tan desfechos son,
enterguen a mio Çid   el que en buen ora nació;
quando ellos los an a pechar,   non gelos quiero yo."
    Ferrand Gonçalvez   odredes qué fabló:
"averes monedados   non tenemos nos."
Luego respondió   el conde don Remond:
"el oro e la plata   espendiésteslo vos;
por juvizio lo damos   antel rey don Alfons:
páguenle en apreçiadura   e préndalo el Campeador."
    Ya vieron que es a fer   ifantes de Carrión.
Veriedes aduzir   tanto cavallo corredor,
tant gruessa mula,   tanto palafré de sazón,
tanta buena espada   con toda guarnizón;
recibiólo mio Çid   commo apreçiaron en la cort.
Sobre los dozientos marcos   que tenia el rey Alfons
pagaron los ifantes   al que en buen ora nació;
enpréstanles de lo ageno,   que non les cumple lo so.
Mal escapan jogados,   sabed, desta razón.

"As for all the riches   which I gave you,
either return them to me   or give me an account."
   Then the Heirs of Carrión   walked to one side
but could reach no agreement,   for the riches were great
and the Heirs of Carrión   had spent them.
They returned to the court   and spoke their wish:
"He who took Valencia   presses us close;
since he sets such store   by what is ours
we shall pay him in lands   from the country of Carrión."
When they had made this plea   the judges said:
"If such pleases the Cid   we shall not refuse,
but to our judgment   it would appear better
that the money itself be repaid   here in the court."
   At these words   the King Don Alfonso spoke:
"This affair is plain   for us all to see,
and My Cid the Campeador   has a just claim.
I have two hundred   of those three thousand marks;
they were given me   by the Heirs of Carrión.
I wish to return them,   since the Heirs are ruined,
so that they may give them to My Cid,   who in good hour
      was born;
since they must pay them   I do not wish to keep them."
Fernando González spoke,   hear what he said:
"We do not have   any wealth in coin."
Then the Count Don Ramón   answered him:
"You have spent   the gold and the silver;
here is the judgment we give   before the King Don
      Alfonso:
You must pay in kind   and the Campeador accept it."
   The Heirs of Carrión   know what they must do.
You would have seen them lead in   so many swift horses,
so many fat mules,   so many palfreys of good breed,
so many good swords   with all their trappings,
and My Cid took them   at the court's evaluation.
All but the two hundred marks   which were King
      Alfonso's
the Heirs paid   to him who was born in good hour;
they had to borrow from elsewhere,   their own goods were
      not enough.
You may know, this time   they are sorely mocked.

138
Acabada su demanda civil, el Cid propone el reto

Estas apreçiaduras   mio Çid presas las ha,
sos omnes las tienen   e dellas penssarán.
Mas quando esto ovo acabado,   penssaron luego d' al.
"Merçed, ya rey señor,   por amor de caridad!
La rencura mayor   non se me puede olbidar.
Oídme toda la cort   e pésevos de mio mal;
ifantes de Carrión,   quem desondraron tan mal,
a menos de riebtos   no los puedo dexar.

139
Inculpa de menos-valer a los infantes

"Dezid ¿qué vos mereçí,   ifantes de Carrión,
en juego o en vero   o en alguna razón?
aquí lo mejoraré   a juvizio de la cort.
¿A quém descubriestes   las telas del coraçón?
A la salida de Valençia   mis fijas vos di yo,
con muy gran ondra   e averes a nombre;
quando las non queriedes,   ya canes traidores,
¿por qué las sacávades   de Valençia sus honores?
¿A qué las firiestes—a çinchas e a espolones?
Solas las dexastes   en el robredo de Corpes,
a las bestias fieras   e a las aves del mont.
Por quanto les fiziestes   menos valedes vos.
Si non recudedes,   véalo esta cort."

140
Altercado entre García Ordóñez y el Cid

El comde don Garçia   en pie se levantava:
"Merçed, ya rey,   el mejor de toda España!
Vezós mio Çid   a llas cortes pregonadas;
dexóla creçer   e luenga trae la barba;
los unos le han miedo   e los otros espanta.

His civil claim ended, the Cid proposes a challenge

These valued goods   My Cid has taken;
his men receive them   and take them in charge.
But when this was done   there was something still to do.
    "Grace, King and lord,   for the love of charity!
The greatest grievance   I cannot forget.
Let all the court hear me   and share in my injury;
the Heirs of Carrión   have so gravely dishonored me,
I cannot leave this case   without challenging them.

139
The Heirs are accused of infamy

    "Tell me, what did I deserve of you,   Heirs of Carrión,
in jest or in truth   or in any fashion?
Here before the court's judgment   this must be repaired.
Why have you torn   the webs of my heart?
When you went from Valencia   I gave you my daughters
with much honor   and countless riches;
if you did not want them,   treacherous dogs,
why did you take them   and their honors from Valencia?
Why did you wound them   with whips and spurs?
You left them alone   in the oak grove of Corpes
to the wild beasts   and the birds of the mountain.
For all you have done   you are infamous.
Let the court judge   if you must not give satisfaction."

140
Altercation between García Ordóñez and the Cid

    The Count Don García   rose to his feet.
"Grace, King,   the best in all Spain!
My Cid has rehearsed himself   for this solemn court;
he has let his beard grow   and wears it long;
he strikes fear into some   and dread into others.

Los de Carrión   son de natura tan alta,
non gelas devién querer   sus fijas por varraganas,
¿o quien gelas diera   por parejas o por veladas?
Derecho fizieron   porque las han dexadas.
Quanto él dize   non gelo preçiamos nada."

    Essora el Campeador   prísos a la barba;
"yrado a Dios   que çielo e tierra manda!
por esso es luenga   que a deliçio fo criada.

    Qué avedes vos, comde,   por retraer la mi barba?
ca de quando nasco   a deliçio fo criada;
ca non me priso a ella,   fijo de mugier nada,
nimbla messó   fijo de moro nin de cristiana,
commo yo a vos, Comde,   en el castiello de Cabra.
Quando pris a Cabra,   e a vos por la barba,
non i ovo rapaz   que non messó su pulgada;
la que yo messé   aun non es eguada,
ca yo la trayo aquí   en mi bolsa alçada."

141
Fernando rechaza la tacha de menos-valer

    Ferrán Gonçálvez   en pie se levantó,
a altas vozes   odredes qué fabló:
"Dexássedesvos Çid   de aquesta razón;
de vuestros averes   de todos pagado ssodes.
Non creciés varaja   entre nos e vos.
De natura somos   de comdes de Carrión:
deviemos casar con fijas   de reyes o de enperadores,
ca non perteneçien   fijas de infançones.
Por que las dexamos   derecho fiziemos nos;
más nos preçiamos,   sabet, que menos no."

142
El Cid incita a Pedro Vermúdez al reto

The Heirs of Carrión   are of such high birth
they should not want his daughters   even as concubines,
and who would command them to take them   as their
    lawful wives?
They did what was just   in leaving them.
All that the Cid says   we value at nothing."
    Then the Campeador   laid his hand on his beard:
"Thanks be to God   Who rules heaven and earth,
my beard is long   because it grew at its own pleasure.
    "What have you, Count,   to throw in my beard?
It has grown at its own pleasure   since it began;
no son of woman   ever dared touch it,
no son of Moor or Christian   ever has torn it
as I tore yours, Count,   at the castle of Cabra.
When I seized Cabra   and you by your beard,
there was not a boy there   who did not tear out his wisp;
that which I tore out   has not yet grown again,
and I carry it here   in this closed pouch."

141
Fernando denies the accusation of infamy

    Fernando González   rose to his feet.
Hear what he said   in a loud voice:
"Cid, let your claim   here have an end;
all your goods   have been returned to you.
Let this suit   go no further between us.
We are by birth descended   from the Counts of Carrión:
we should marry the daughters   of kings or emperors;
we are worthy of more than the daughters   of petty
    squires.
We did what was just   when we abandoned your
    daughters;
our honor is greater than before,   you may know, and
    not less."

142
The Cid incites Pedro Bermúdez to make a challenge

Mio Çid Roy Díaz   a Per Vermudoz cata;
"Fabla, Pero Mudo,   varón que tanto callas;
Yo las he fijas,   e tú primas cormanas;
a mí lo dizen,   a ti dan las orejadas.
Si yo respondiero,   tú non entrarás en armas."

143
Pedro Vermúdez reta a Fernando

Per Vermudoz   conpeçó de fablar;
detiénesle la lengua,   non puede delibrar,
mas quando enpieça,   sabed, nol da vagar:
"Dirévos, Çid,   costunbres avedes tales,
siempre en las cortes   Pero Mudo me llamades!
Bien lo sabedes   que yo non puodo más;
por lo que yo ovier a fer   por mí non mancará.
    "Mientes, Ferrando,   de quanto dicho has.
por el Campeador   mucho valiestes más.
Las tues mañas   yo te las sabré contar:
miémbrat quando lidiamos   çerca Valencia la grand;
pedist las feridas primeras   al Campeador leal,
vist un moro,   fústel ensayar;
antes fuxiste   que a él te allegasses.
Si yo non uviás,   el moro te jugara mal;
passé por ti,   con el moro me of de ajuntar,
de los primeros colpes   ofle de arrancar;
did el cavallo,   tóveldo en poridad:
fasta este día   no lo descubrí a nadi.
Delant mio Çid e delant todos   ovístete de alabar
que mataras el moro   e que fizieras barnax;
croviérontelo todos,   mas non saben la verdad.
E eres fermoso,   mas mal varragán!
¡Lengua sin manos,   quomo osas fablar?

144
Prosigue el reto de Pedro Vermúdez

My Cid Ruy Díaz   looked at Pedro Bermúdez.
"Speak, Mute Pedro,   knight who are so much silent!
They are my daughters,   but they are your first cousins;
when they say this to me   they pull your ears also.
If I answer,   you will have no chance to fight."

143
Pedro Bermúdez challenges Fernando

   Then Pedro Bermúdez   started to speak,
but his tongue stumbles   and he cannot begin;
yet once he has begun,   know, he does not hesitate:
"I will tell you, Cid,   that is a custom of yours:
always in the courts   you call me Pedro the Mute!
But you know well   that I can do no better,
yet of what I can do   there shall be no lack.
   "You lie, Fernando,   in all you have said,
you gained great honor   through the Campeador.
Now I shall tell   of your ways:
Remember when we fought   near Valencia the great?
You begged the Campeador   to grant you the first blows.
You saw a Moor   and you went toward him,
but before he came upon you   you fled from there.
Had I not been there   the Moor would have used you
          roughly;
I passed you by   and encountered the Moor;
with the first blows   I overcame him.
I gave you his horse   and have kept all this secret
and told it to no one   until today.
Before My Cid and before all   you were heard to boast
that you killed the Moor   and had done a knightly deed,
and all believed you,   not knowing the truth.
Oh, you are pretty   and a vile coward!
Tongue without hands,   how do you dare to speak?

144
Pedro Bermúdez's challenge continues

"Di, Ferrando, otorga esta razón:
¿non te viene en miente en Valençia lo del león
quando durmie mio Çid y el león se desató?
E tú, Ferrando, ¿qué fizist co nel pavor?
¡metístet tras el escaño de mio Çid el Campeador!
metístet, Ferrando, por o menos vales oy.
Nós çercamos el escaño por curiar nuestro señor,
fasta do despertó mio Çid, el que Valençia gañó;
levantós del escaño e fos poral león;
el león premió la cabeça, a mio Çid esperó,
dexósle prender al cuello, e a la red le metió.
Quando se tornó el buen Campeador,
a sos vassallos, víolos aderredor;
demandó por sos yernos, ninguno non falló!
Riébtot el cuerpo por malo e por traidor.
Estos lidiaré aquí ante el rey don Alfons
por fijas del Çid, don Elvira e doña Sol:
por quanto las dexastes menos valedes vos;
ellas son mugieres e vos sodes varones,
en todas guisas más valen que vos.
Quando fore la lid, si ploguiere al Criador,
tú lo otorgarás a guisa de traydor;
de quanto he dicho verdadero seré yo."
D'aquestos amos aquí quedó la razón.

145
Diego desecha la inculpación de menos-valer

  *Díag Gonçalvez odrodes lo que dixo:
"De natura somos de los comdes más linpios;
¡estos casamientos non fuessen apareçidos,
por consagrar con mio Çid don Rodrigo!
Porque dexamos sus fijas aun no nos repentimos;
mientra que bivan pueden aver sospiros:
lo que les fiziemos seer les ha retraydo.
Esto lidiaré a tod el más ardido:
que por que las dexamos ondrados somos venidos."*
274

"Speak, Fernando,   admit to this:
Do you not recall   the lion in Valencia,
the time when My Cid slept   and the lion got loose?
And you, Fernando,   what did you do in your terror?
You hid behind the bench   of My Cid the Campeador!
You hid there, Fernando   and for that I now defame you.
We all stood around the bench   to shield our lord,
until My Cid woke,   who had taken Valencia;
he rose from the bench   and went toward the lion;
the lion bowed his head   and waited for My Cid,
let himself be taken by the neck   and went back into his
        cage.
And when the good Campeador   returned again
he saw his vassals   all around him;
he asked for his sons-in-law.   No one could find them!
I defy your body,   villain and traitor.
I will fight it out here   before King Alfonso
for the daughters of the Cid,   Doña Elvira and Doña Sol;
because you abandoned them   I now defame you.
They are women   and you are men;
in every way   they are worth more than you.
When the fight takes place,   if it please the Creator,
I will make you admit   that you are a traitor,
and all I have said here   I will prove true."
And between those two   the dispute thus ended.

145
Diego rejects the accusation of infamy

As for Diego González,   hear what he said:
"We are by birth   of the purest lineage of counts.
Oh, that this marriage   had never been made
that made us kin   of My Cid Don Rodrigo!
We still do not repent   that we abandoned his daughters;
let them sigh   as long as they live,
and what we have done to them   will be thrown in their
        faces always.
This I will maintain   against the bravest,
for in abandoning them   we have gained in honor."

146
Martín Antolínez reta a Diego González

Martín Antolínez   en pie se fo levantar;
"Calla, alevoso,   boca sin verdad!
Lo del león   no se te deve olbidar;
saliste por la puerta,   metístet al corral,
fústed meter   tras la viga lagar;
mas non vestist   el manto nin el brial.
Yollo lidiaré,   non passará por al:
fijas del Çid,   por que las vos dexastes,
en todas guisas,   sabed, que mas que vos valen.
Al partir de la lid   por tu boca lo dirás,
que eres traydor   e mintist de quanto dicho has."

147
Asur González entra en la corte

Destos amos   la razón ha fincado.
Ansuor Gonçálvez   entrava por el palaçio,
manto armiño   e un brial rastrando;
vermejo viene,   ca era almorzado.
En lo que fabló   avie poco recabdo:

148
Asur insulta al Cid

"¿Ya varones,   quien vido nunca tal mal?
¡Quién nos darie nuevas   de mio Çid el de Bivar!
¡Fosse a rio d'Ovirna   los molinos picar
e prender maquilas   commo lo suele far!
¿Quil darie   con los de Carrión a casar?"

276

Martín Antolínez challenges Diego González

Martín Antolínez   rose to his feet.
"Be silent, traitor,   mouth without truth!
You should not have forgotten   the episode of the lion;
you went out the door   into the courtyard
and hid yourself   behind the beam of the winepress;
since then you have not worn   that cloak and silk shirt
     again.
I shall maintain this by combat,   it shall not be otherwise,
because you abandoned   the Cid's daughters.
You may know, their honor   in every way exceeds yours.
When the fight is over,   with your own mouth you will
     admit
that you are a traitor   and have lied in all you have said."

[handwritten margin note: in his cowardice he shit in with his pants]

Asur González enters the court

The talk was ended between these two.
Asur González   entered the palace
with an ermine cloak   and his tunic trailing;
his face was red   for he had just eaten.
There was little prudence   in what he said:

Asur insults the Cid

"Ah, knights,   whoever has seen such evil?
Since when might we receive honor   from My Cid of
     Bivar!
Let him go now to the river Ubierna   and look after his
     mills

[handwritten margin note: unknown river — "where?"]

and be paid in corn   as he used to do!
Whoever suggested he marry   with those of Carrión?"

149

Muño Gustioz reta a Asur González. Mensajeros de
Navarra
y de Aragón piden al Cid sus hijas para los hijos de los
reyes.
Don Alfonso otorga el nuevo casamiento. Minaya reta a los
de Carrión. Gómez Peláez acepta el reto, pero el rey no fija
plazo sino a los que antes retaron. El rey amparará a los
tres lidiadores del Cid. El Cid ofrece dones de despedida
a todos.
(*Laguna. Prosa de la Crónica de Veinte Reyes.*)

El rey sale de Toledo con el Cid. Manda a éste correr su
caballo

> *Essora Muño Gustioz   en pie se levantó;*
> *"Calla, alevoso,   malo e traidor!*
> *Antes almuerzas   que vayas a oración,*
> *a los que das paz,   fártaslos aderredor.*
> *Non dizes verdad   âmigo ni a señor,*
> *falsso a todos   e más al Criador.*
> *En tu amiztâd   non quiero aver ración.*
> *Fazer telo he dezir   que tal eres qual digo yo."*
> *Dixo el rey Alfons: "Calle ya esta razón.*
> *Los que an reptado   lidiarán, sín salve Dios!"*
> *Assí commo acabñn   esta razón,*
> *Affé dos cavalleros   entraron por la cort;*
> *al uno dizen Ojarra   e al otro Yéñego Simenones,*
> *el uno es del infante   de Navarra rogador,*
> *e el otro es   del ifante de Aragón;*
> *besan las manos   al rey don Alfons,*
> *piden sus fijas   a mio Çid el Campeador*
> *por seer reínas   de Navarra e de Aragón,*
> *e que ge las diessen   a ondra e a bendiçión.*
> *A esto callaron   e ascuchó toda la cort.*

149

Then Muño Gustioz   rose to his feet.
"Be silent, traitor,   evil and full of deceit!
First you have your breakfast   and then you say your
prayers
and all whom you kiss   in greeting smell your belches.
You speak no truth   to friend or lord;
you are false to all   and still more false to the Creator.
I want no portion in your friendship,
and I shall make you confess   that you are all that I say."
King Alfonso said,   "Let this case rest now.
Those who have made challenges   shall fight, as God may
save me!"
    Thus they bring   this case to an end,
and behold, two knights   came into the court:
one was called Ojarra   and the other Iñigo Jiménez;
one is the herald of the Prince of Navarre
and the other the herald   of the Prince of Aragón.
They kiss the hands   of King Alfonso
and ask for the daughters   of My Cid the Campeador
to make them Queens   of Navarre and Aragón
as honored wives   blessed in marriage.
At this all the court   was hushed and listened.

Levantós en pie   mio Çid el Campeador:
"Merced, rey Alfons,   vos sodes mio señor!
Esto gradesco yo   al Criador,
quando me las demandan   de Navarra e de Aragón.
Vos las casastes antes,   ca yo non,
afé mis fijas,   en vuestras manos son:
sin vuestro mandado   nada non feré yo."
Levantós el rey,   fizo callar la cort:
"Ruégovos, Çid,   caboso Campeador,
que plega a vos,   e atorgar lo he yo,
este casamiento   oy se otorgue en esta cort,
ca créçevos i ondra   e tierra e onor."
Levantós mio Çid,   al rey las manos le besó;
"Quando a vos plaze,   otórgolo yo, señor."
Essora dixo el rey: "Dios vos dé den buen galardón!
A vos, Ojarra,   e a vos, Yéñego Ximenones,
este casamiento   otórgovosle yo
de fijas de mio Çid,   don Elvira e doña Sol,
pora los ifantes   de Navarra e de Aragón,
que vos las dé   a ondra e a bendiçión."
Levantós en pie Ojarra   e Yéñego Ximenones,
besaron las manos   del rey don Alfons,
e después   de mio Çid el Campeador;
metieron las fedes,   e los omenajes dados son,
que quomo es dicho   assí sea, o mejor.
A muchos plaze   de tod esta cort,
mas non plaze   a ifantes de Carrión.
   Minaya Albar Fáñez   en pie se levantó;
"Merçed vos pido   commo a rey e a señor,
e que non pese esto   al Çid Campeador:
bien vos di vagar   en toda esta cort,
dezir querría   yaquanto de lo mio."
Dixo el rey: "Plazme de coraçón.
Dezid, Minaya,   lo que oviéredes sabor."
—"Yo vos ruego   que me oyades toda la cort,
ca grand rencura he   de ifantes de Carrión.
Yo les di mis primas   por mano del rey Alfons,
ellos las prisieron   a ondra e a bendiçión;
grandes averes les dio   mio Çid el Campeador,
ellos las han dexadas   a pesar de nos.

My Cid the Campeador   rose to his feet.
"Grace, King Alfonso,   you are my lord!
I give thanks   to the Creator
for what Navarre and Aragón   have asked of me.
You married my daughters before   and not I;
here once again I say   my daughters are in your hands:
without your bidding   I shall do nothing."
The King rose,   and bade the court be silent.
"Cid, perfect Campeador,   I ask that it meet your pleasure
that I should consent   to this marriage.
Let it be arranged   here and now in this court,
and thus may you increase   in fiefs, in estates and honor."
My Cid rose   and kissed the King's hands:
"As it pleases you,   I grant it, lord."
Then the King said,   "God reward you well!
And you, Ojarra,   and you, Iñigo Jiménez,
I consent   to this marriage
of the daughters of My Cid,   Doña Elvira and Doña Sol,
with the Princes   of Navarre and Aragón,
that the girls may be given to them   as their honored
          wives."
Ojarra and Iñigo Jiménez   rose to their feet;
they kissed the hands of King Alfonso
and afterwards those   of My Cid the Campeador;
they gave pledges   and swore the oaths,
that all might be   as had been said, or better.
This pleases many   there in the court
but gives no pleasure   to the Heirs of Carrión.
    Minaya Alvar Fáñez   rose to his feet.
"I beg grace of you,   as my King and lord,
and hope it may not displease   the Cid Campeador:
I have heard all speak their minds   here in the court,
and now I would say   something of my own."
The King said,   "Granted gladly.
Speak, Minaya,   say what you wish."
"I beg all the court   to hear what I say,
for I have great grievance against   the Heirs of Carrión.
I gave them my cousins   by the hand of King Alfonso;
they took them in the honor   and blessing of marriage;
My Cid the Campeador   gave them much wealth,
and then they left them   to our sorrow.

Riébtoles los cuerpos   por malos e por traidores.
De natura sodes   de los de Vani-Gómez,
onde salien comdes   de prez e de valor;
mas bien sabemos   las mañas que ellos han oy.
Esto gradesco   yo al Criador,
quando piden mis primas,   don Elvira e doña Sol,
los ifantes   de Navarra e de Aragón;
antes las aviedes parejas   pora en braços las dos
agora besaredes sus manos   e llamar las hedes señores,
aver las hedes a servir,   mal que vos pese a vos.
Grado a Dios del çielo   e âquel rey don Alfons,
assí creçe la ondra   a mio Çid el Campeador!
En todas guisas   tales sodes quales digo yo;
si ay qui responda   o dize de no,
yo so Albar Fáñez   pora tod el mejor."
      Gómez Peláyet   en pie se levantó;
"Qué val, Minaya,   toda essa razón?
ca en esta cort   afartos ha pora vos,
e qui al quisiesse   serie su ocasión.
Si Dios quissiere   que desta bien salgamos nos,
después veredes   qué dixiestes o qué no."
      Dixo el rey: "Fine esta razón,
non diga ninguno   della más una entençión.
Cras sea la lid,   quando saliere el sol,
destos tres por tres   que rebtaron en la cort."
      Luego fablaron   ifantes de Carrión:
"Dandos, rey, plazo,   ca cras seer non puode.
Armas e cavallos   diémoslos al Canpeador,
nos antes abremos a ir   a tierras de Carrión."
Fabló el rey   contra Campeador:
"sea esta lid   o mandáredes vos."
En essora dixo mio Çid: "no lo faré señor;
más quiero a Valençia   que tierras de Carrión."
En essora dixo el rey: "Aosadas, Campeador.
Dadme vuestros cavalleros   con todas guarnizones,
vayan comigo,   yo seré el curiador;
yo vos lo sobrellevo,   commo a buen vasallo faze señor,
que non prendan fuerça   de comde nin de infançón.
Aquí les pongo plazo   de dentro en mi cort,
a cabo de tres sedmanas,   en begas de Carrión,

282

I challenge their bodies as villains and traitors.
You are of the family of the Beni-Gómez,
in which there have been counts of worth and courage,
but now we know well what your ways are.
I give thanks to the Creator
that the Princes of Navarre and Aragón
have asked for my cousins, Doña Elvira and Doña Sol;
before, you had them for wives, both, between your arms;
now you will kiss their hands and call them 'My Lady,'
and do them service, however it pains you.
I give thanks to God in heaven and to this King Alfonso
that thus grows the honor of My Cid the Campeador!
In every way you are as I described you;
if there is any among you to deny it and say no,
I am Alvar Fáñez, a better man than any of you."
    Gómez Peláez rose to his feet.
"To what end, Minaya, is all this talk?
There are many in this court as brave as you,
and whoever should wish to deny this, it would be to
        his harm.
If God wills that we should come well out of this
you will have cause to look to what you have said."
    The King said, "Let this talk end;
let no one add a further claim to this dispute.
Let the fight be tomorrow when the sun rises,
the three against three who challenged here in the court."
    The Heirs of Carrión answered then:
"Give us more time, King for we cannot do it tomorrow.
We have given our arms and horses to the Campeador;
first we must go to the lands of Carrión."
The King said to the Campeador:
"This battle shall take place wherever you wish."
Then My Cid said, "I will not do as they say.
I would rather return to Valencia than go to Carrión."
Then the King said, "It is well, Campeador.
Give me your knights all well armed;
let them come with me, I shall stand surety for them
and see to their safety as a lord does for his good vassal,
and they will come to no harm from count or noble.
Here in my court I set the term:
Three weeks from now in the plain of Carrión

que fagan esta lid   delant estando yo;
quien non viniere al plazo   pierda la razón,
desí sea vençido   y escape por traydor."
Prisieron el judizio   ifantes de Carrión.
Mio Çid al rey   las manos le besó:
"Estos mios tres cavalleros   en vuestra mano son,
d' aquí vos los acomiendo   commo rey e a señor.
Ellos son adobados   pora cumplir todo lo so;
ondrados me los enbiad a Valençia,   por amor del
      Criador!"
Essora respuso el rey: "assí lo mande Dios!"
   Allí se tollió el capiello   el Çid Campeador,
la cofia de rançal   que blanca era commo el sol,
e soltava la barba   e sacóla del cordón.
Nos fartan de catarle   quantos ha en la cort.
Adeliñó a comde don Anric   e comde don Remond;
abraçólos tan bien   e ruégalos de coraçón
que prendan de sos averes   quanto ovieren sabor.
A essos e a los otros   que de buena parte son,
a todos los rogava   assí commo han sabor;
tales i a que prenden,   tales i a que non.
Los dozientos marcos   al rey los soltó;
de lo al tanto priso   quant ovo sabor.
"Merçed vos pido, rey,   por amor del Criador!
Quando todas estas nuevas   assí puestas son,
beso vuestras manos   con vuestra graçia señor,
e irme quiero pora Valençia   con afán la gané yo."

Entonçes mandó dar el Çid a los mandaderos de los
infantes de Navarra e de Aragón bestias e todo lo al que
menester ovieron, e enbiólos.

El rey don Alfón cabalgó entonçes con todos los altos
omnes de su corte, para salir con el Çid que se iva fuera
de la villa. E quando llegaron a Çocodover, el Çid yendo
en su cavallo que dicen Bavieca, dixole el rey: "don Rod-
rigo, fe que devedes que arremetades agora esse cavallo
que tanto bien oí dezir." El Çid tomóse a sonrreir, e dixo:
"señor, aquí en vuestra corte a muchos altos omnes e
guisados para fazer esto, e a esos mandat que trebejen
con sus cavallos." El rey le dixo: "Çid, págome yo de lo

let this battle take place,   and I there to see;
whoever is not there   forfeits the fight
and will be declared beaten   and called traitor."
The Heirs of Carrión   accepted the decision.
My Cid kissed   the King's hands:
"My three knights   are in your hands;
here I commend them to you   as my King and lord.
They are well prepared   to fulfill what they go for;
send them with honor to Valencia,   for the love of the
    Creator!"
Then the King answered,   "May God grant it be so."
    Then the Cid Campeador   drew back his hood,
his coif of fine cloth,   white as the sun,
and freed his beard   and undid the cord.
All who are in the court   cannot keep from staring at him.
He went to the Count Don Enrique   and the Count Don
    Ramón;
he embraced them closely   and asked them from his heart
to take of what he owned   whatever they wished.
These and the others   who had sided with him,
he begged them all   to take what they wished;
and some of them take   and others not.
He bade the King keep   the two hundred marks
and to take from him besides   as much as he wished.
    "I beg grace of you, King,   for the love of the Creator!
Now that all these things   have been provided for,
I kiss your hands   and with your grace, my lord,
would return to Valencia,   for painfully I took it."

Then My Cid commanded that mounts and whatever
they needed should be given to the messengers from the
Princes of Navarre and Aragón, and he sent them on their
way.

Then King Alfonso mounted, with all the nobles of his
court, to ride out with My Cid as he left the town. And
when they came to Zocodover, the King said to My Cid,
who was riding on his horse, which was called Babieca:
"Don Rodrigo, I should like to see you urge your horse
to his full speed, for I have heard much of him." The Cid
began to smile, and said, "Lord, here in your court are
many nobles and men who would be most pleased to do
this; ask them to race their horses." The King said to him,

que vos dezides; mas quiero todavía que corrades ese
cavallo por mi amor."

150

El rey admira a Bavieca, pero no lo acepta en don. Ultimos
encargos del Cid a sus tres lidiadores. Tórnase el Cid a
Valencia. El rey en Carrión. Llega el pazo de la lid.
Los de Carrión pretenden excluir de la lid a Colada y
Tizón. Los del Cid piden al rey amparo y salen al campo
de la lid. El rey designa fieles del campo y amonesta a
los de Carrión. Los fieles preparan la lid. Primera
acometida. Pedro Vermúdez vence a Fernando

El Çid remetió entonces el cavallo, e tan de rezio lo
    corrió,
que todos se maravillaron del correr que fizo.
El rey alçó la mano, la cara se santigó:
"Yo lo juro par sant Esidre el de León
que en todas nuestras tierras non ha tan buen varón."
Mio Çid en el cavallo, adelant se llegó,
fo besar la mano a so señor Alfons:
"Mandástesme mover a Bavieca al corredor,
en moros ni en cristianos otro tal non ha oy,
yo vos le do en don, mandédesle tomar, señor."
Essora dixo el rey: "Desto non he sabor;
si a vos le tollies, et cavallo no havrie tan buen señor.
Mas atal cavallo cum ést pora tal commo vos,
pora arrancar moros del campo e seer segudador;
quien vos lo toller quisiere nol vala el Criador,

286

"Cid, I am contented with what you say, but nevertheless
I wish you to race your horse, to please me."

150

*The King admires Babieca, but will not accept him as
    a gift.*
*The Cid's final orders to his three champions. The Cid
    returns to*
*Valencia. The King in Carrión. The time for the fight
    arrives.*
*Those of Carrión try to ban Colada and Tizón from the
    fight.*
*Those on the side of My Cid ask the King's help and ride
    out onto the*
*battlefield. The King names the judges for the combat
    and admonishes*
*those of Carrión. The judges prepare for the fight. The first
encounter. Pedro Bermúdez overcomes Fernando*

Then the Cid set spur to his horse, who ran so swiftly
that all who were there marveled at his speed.
The King raised his hand   and crossed himself:.
"I swear by Saint Isidore   of León
that in all our lands   there is not such another knight."
My Cid has ridden forward   on his horse
and come to kiss the hand   of his lord Alfonso:
"You have bidden me race   Babieca, my swift horse;
neither among Moors nor among Christians   is there such
        another;
I offer him to you as a gift.   Take him, my lord."
Then the King said,   "I do not wish it so;
if I take your horse from you   he will not have so fine a
        master.
Such a horse as this   needs such a rider as you
for routing Moors in the field   and pursuing them after
        the battle.
May the Creator not bless   whoever would take your
        horse from you,

ca por vos e por el cavallo   ondrados somos nos."

Essora se espidieron,   e luégos partió la cort.
El Campeador a los que han lidiar   tan bien los castigó:
"Ya Martín Antolínez   e vos, Per Vermudoz,
e Muño Gustioz,   mio vassallo de pro,
firmes seed en campo   a guisa de varones;
buenos mandados me vayan   a Valençia de vos."
Dixo Martín Antolínez: "Por qué lo dezides, señor!
Preso avemos el debdo   e a passar es por nos;
podedes odir de muertos,   ca de vencidos no."
Alegre fo d' aquesto   el que en buen ora nació;
espidiós de todos   los que sos amigos son.
Mio Çid pora Valençia,   e el rey pora Carrión.

Mas tres sedmanas de plazo todas complidas son.
Felos al plazdo   los del Campeador,
cunplir quieren el debdo   que les mandó so señor;
ellos son en poder   de Alfons el de León;
dos días atendieron   a ifantes de Carrión.
Mucho vienen bien adobados   de cavallos e de
                                        guarnizones;
e todos sos parientes   con ellos acordados son
que si los pudiessen apartar   a los del Campeador,
que los matassen en campo   por desondra de so señor.
El cometer fue malo,   que lo al nos empeçó,
ca grand miedo ovieron   a Alfonsso el de León.

De noche belaron las armas   e rogaron al Criador.
Troçida es la noche,   ya crieban los albores;
muchos se juntaron   de buenos ricos omnes
por veer esta lid,   ca avien ende sabor;
demás sobre todos   i es el rey don Alfons,
por querer el derecho   e ningun tuerto non.
Yas metien en armas   los del buen Campeador,
todos tres se acuerdan,   ca son de un señor.
En otro logar se arman   ifantes de Carrión,

since by means of your horse and you   we have all
    received honor."
    Then they parted   and the court rode on.
The Campeador gave counsel   to those who were to fight:
"Martín Antolínez,   and you, Pedro Bermúdez
and Muño Gustioz,   my worthy vassal,
maintain the field   like brave men;
send me good news   to Valencia."
Martín Antolínez said,   "Why do you say this, lord?
We have accepted the charge,   it is for us to carry it out;
you may hear of dead men   but not of vanquished."
He who in good hour was born   was pleased at this;
he said good-by to them all   for they were his friends.
My Cid rode toward Valencia   and the King toward
    Carrión.
    The three weeks of the delay   have all run out.
Behold, the Campeador's men   have come on the
    appointed day;
they wish to accomplish   what their lord had required of
    them.
They are protected   by Alfonso of León;
two days they waited   for the Heirs of Carrión.
The Heirs come well provided   with horses and arms,
and all their kin with them   and they had plotted
that if they might draw   the Campeador's men to one
    side
they should kill them in the field   for the dishonor of their
    lord.
They were bent on evil   had they not been prevented,
for great is their fear   of Alfonso of León.
    My Cid's men held vigil by their arms   and prayed to
    the Creator.
The night has passed   and the dawn breaks;
many of the nobles   have gathered together
to see this battle,   which will give them pleasure,
and above them all   is the King Don Alfonso,
to see that justice is done   and prevent any wrong.
The Campeador's men   have armed themselves;
all are of one mind,   since they serve the same lord.
In another place   the Heirs of Carrión arm,

sediélos castigando   el comde Garçi Ordóñez.
Andidieron en pleyto   dixiéronlo al rey Alfons,
que non fossen en la batalla   Colada e Tizón,
que non lidiassen con ellas   los del Campeador;
mucho eran repentidos los ifantes   por quanto dadas son.
Dexiérongelo al rey,   mas non gelo conloyó;
"Non sacastes ninguna   quando oviemos la cort.
Si buenas las tenedes,   pro abrán a vos;
otrosí farán   a los del Campeador.
Levad e salid al campo,   ifantes de Carrión,
huebos vos es que lidiedes,   a guisa de varones,
que nada non mancará   por los del Campeador.
Si del campo bien salides,   grand ondra avredes vos;
e ssi fuéredes vençidos,   non rebtedes a nos,
ca todos lo saben   que lo buscastes vos."
Ya se van repintiendo   ifantes de Carrión,
de lo que avien fecho   mucho repisos son;
no lo querrien aver fecho   por quanto ha en Carrión.
    Todos tres son armados   los del Campeador,
ívalos veer   el rey don Alfons.
Essora le dixieron   los del Campeador:
"Besámosvos las manos   como a rey e a señor,
que fidel seades   oy dellos e de nos;
a derecho nos valed,   a ningún tuerto no.
Aquí tienen so vando   ifantes de Carrión,
non sabemos   qués comidrán ellos o qué non;
en vuestra mano   nos metió nuestro señor;
tenendos a derecho,   por amor del Criador!"
Essora dixo el rey: "d' alma e de coraçón."
    Adúzenles los cavallos   buenos e corredores,
santiguaron las siellas   e cavalgan a vigor;
los escudos a los cuellos   que bien blocados son;
e' mano prenden las astas   de los fierros tajadores,
estas tres lanças   traen seños pendones;
e derredor dellos   muchos buenos varones.
Ya salieron al campo   do eran los mojones.
Todos tres son acordados   los del Campeadore,

290

the Count García Ordóñez   giving them advice.
They raised a complaint   and begged King Alfonso
that Colada and Tizón   should be banned from the
     combat
and that the Campeador's men   should not use them in
     the fight;
the Heirs deeply regretted   having given them back.
They begged this of the King,   but he would not consent:
"There in the court   you objected to none.
If you have good swords   they will serve you,
and the Campeador's men will be served   by theirs in the
     same way.
Rise and ride out on the field,   Heirs of Carrión;
you have no choice,   you must fight like men,
for the Campeador's men   will not lack for anything.
If you win on the field   you will have great honor,
and if you are beaten   put no blame on us,
for everyone knows   you have brought this on
     yourselves."
The Heirs of Carrión   now repent
of what they had done,   they regret it deeply;
they would have given all Carrión   not to have done it.
     The Campeador's men,   all three, are armed;
they have gone to see   the King Don Alfonso.
Then the Campeador's men   said to him:
"We kiss your hands,   as our King and lord;
be a faithful judge   today, between them and us;
aid us with justice   and allow no wrong.
The Heirs of Carrión   have all their kin with them;
we cannot tell   what they may or may not have plotted.
Our Lord commended us   into your hands;
see that justice is done,   for the love of the Creator!"
Then the King said,   "With my heart and soul."
     They bring out   their fine swift horses;
they blessed the saddles   and mounted briskly;
the shields with gilded bucklers   are at their necks;
they take up the lances   tipped with sharp steel,
each of the lances   with its pennon,
and all around them   many worthy men.
They rode out on the field,   where the markers were set.
The Campeador's men   are all in agreement

291

que cada uno dellos   bien fos ferir el sove.
Fevos de la otra part   ifantes de Carrione,
muy bien acompañados,   ca muchos parientes sone.
El rey dioles fideles   por dezir el derecho e al none;
que non varagen con ellos   de sí o de none.
Do sedien en el campo   fabló rey don Alfonsse:
"Oid que vos digo   ifantes de Carrione:
esta lid en Toledo la fiziérades,   mas non quisiestes vose.
Estos tres cavalleros   de mio Çid el Campeadore
yo los adux a salvo   a tierr de Carrione.
Aved vuestro derecho,   tuerto non querades vose,
ca qui tuerto quisiere fazer,   mal gelo vedaré yove,
en todo myo reyno   non avrá buena sabore."
Ya les va pesando   a ifantes de Carrione.

   Los fideles y el rey   enseñaron los mojones,
librávanse del campo   todos a derredor.
Bien gelo demostraron   a todos seys commo son,
que por i serie vençido   qui saliesse del mojón.
Todas las yentes   esconbraron a derredor,
de seys astas de lanças   que non llegassen al mojón.
Sorteávanles el campo,   ya les partien el sol,
salien los fideles de medio,   ellos cara por cara son;
desí vinien los de mio Çid   a ifantes de Carrión,
e ifantes de Carrión   a los del Campeador;
cada uno dellos   mientes tiene al so;
Abraçan los escudos   delant los coraçones.
abaxan las lanças   abueltas con los pendones,
enclinavan las caras   sobre los arzones,
batien los cavallos   con los espolones,
tembrar querie la tierra   dond eran movedores.
Cada uno dellos   mientes tiénet al so;
todos tres por tres,   ya juntados son:

how each of them   would attack his man.
On the other side   are the Heirs of Carrión,
well accompanied,   for they have many kinsmen.
The King appointed judges   to decide what was just and
    what not,
and commanded that none should dispute   their yes or
    their no.
When they were in the field   King Alfonso spoke:
"Hear what I have to tell you,   Heirs of Carrión.
This fight should have been in Toledo   but you did not
    wish it so.
These three knights   of My Cid the Campeador
I have brought in my safekeeping   to the lands of Carrión.
Now fight justly   and try no trickery,
for if anyone attempts treachery   I am here to prevent it,   *godlike*
and he who tries it shall not be welcome   in all my   *Alfonso*
    kingdom."
The Heirs of Carrión   were much cast down at this.
  The judges and the King pointed out the markers,
then all the spectators went from the field   and stood
    around it.
They explained carefully   to all six of them
that he will be judged conquered   who leaves the field's
    borders.
All who stood about there   then drew back
the length of three lances   beyond the markers.
They drew lots for the ends of the field — the sunlight in   ←
    each half was the same —
and the judges went from the center   and they stood face
    to face,
the Cid's men facing   the Heirs of Carrión
and the Heirs of Carrión   facing the Campeador's men;
each of them   faced his own opponent;
they hugged their shields   over their hearts,
lowered the lances   wrapped in their pennons,
bent their faces   over their saddletrees,
dug their spurs   into their horses,
and the earth shook   as they leapt forward.
Each of them is bent   on his own opponent;
three against three   they have come together.

cuédanse que essora cadrán muertos   los que están
                                    aderredor.

   Per Vermudoz,   el que antes rebtó,
con Ferránt Gonçalvez   de cara se juntó;
firiensse en los escudos   sin todo pavor.
Ferrán Gonçálvez   a don Pero   el escudol passó,
prísol en vázio,   en carne nol tomó,
bien en dos logares   el astil le quebró.
Firme estido Per Vermudoz,   por esso nos encamó;
un colpe reçibiera,   mas otro firió:
crebantó la bloca del escudo,   apart gela echó,
passógelo todo,   que nada nol valió.
Metiól la lança por los pechos,   çerca del coraçón;
tres dobles de loriga tenie Fernando   aquestol prestó,
las dos le desmanchan   e la terçera fincó:
el belmez con la camisa   e con la guarnizón
de dentro en la carne   una mano gela metió:
por la boca afuera   la sángrel salió;
crebáronle las çinchas,   ninguna nol ovo pro,
por la copla del cavallo   en tierra lo echó.
Assí lo tenien las yentes   que mal ferido es de muort.
En elle dexó la lança   e mano al espada metió,
quando lo vido Ferrán Gonçálvez,   conuvo a Tizón;
antes que el colpe esperasse   dixo: "vençudo so."
Atorgaróngelo los fideles,   Per Vermudoz le dexó.

151
Martín Antolínez vence a Diego

   Don Martino e Díag Gonçálvez   firiéronse de las
     lanças,
tales foron los colpes   que les crebaron amas.
Martín Antolínez   mano metió al espada,
relumbra tod el campo,   tanto es linpia e clara;
diol un colpe,   de traviéssol tomava:

<u>All who stand about</u> fear they will fall dead.

Pedro Bermúdez, who had made the first challenge,
came face to face with Fernando González,
and fearlessly they struck each other's shields.
Fernando González pierced Don Pedro's shield
but drove through upon nothing and touched no flesh,
and in two places the shaft of his spear snapped.
Pedro Bermúdez remained firm, he was not shaken by
    this;
he received one blow, he struck another,
burst the shield's buckler and broke it apart,
cut through it all, nothing withstood him,
drove his lance through to the breast close to the heart.
Fernando was wearing three suits of chain mail and this
    saved him;
two folds were pierced and the third held firm,
but the mail and the tunic with its binding
were driven a hand's breadth into the flesh,
so that the blood ran from Fernando's mouth,
and the girth broke, nothing held it;
Fernando was flung to the ground over the horse's
    crupper.
It seemed to those who stood there that he must be dead.
With that Pedro Bermúdez left his lance and laid hand
    on his sword.
When Fernando González saw him and knew Tizón,
he said, "I am beaten" without waiting for the blow.
The judges agreed and Pedro Bermúdez left him.

151
Martín Antolínez defeats Diego

Don Martín and Diego González struck with their
    spears;
such were the blows that both were broken.
Martín Antolínez set hand on his sword;
it is so bright and clean that it shines over all the field.
It struck a blow which caught him from the side; fellow blow

el casco de somo   apart gelo echava,
las moncluras del yelmo   todas gelas cortava,
allá levó el almófar,   fata la cofia llegava,
la cofia e el almófar   todo gelo levava,
ráxol los pelos de la cabeça   bien a la carne llegava;
lo uno cayó en el campo   e lo al suso fincava.

     Quando este colpe a ferido   Colada la preçiada,
vido Díag Gonçálvez   que no escaparie con el alma;
bolvió la rienda al cavallo   por tornasse de cara,
espada tiene en mano   mas no la ensayava.
Essora Martín Antolínez   reçiból con el espada,
un cólpel dió de llano   con lo agudo nol tomava.
Essora el ifante   tan grandes vozes dava:
"valme, Dios glorioso,   señor, cúriam deste espada!"
el cavallo asorrienda,   e mesurándol del espada,
sacól del mojón;   don Martino en el campo fincava.

     Essora dixo el rey: "venid vos a mio compaña;
por quanto avedes fecho   vençida avedes esta batalla."
Otórgangelo los fideles   que dize verdadera palabra.

152

Muño Gustioz vence a Asur González. El padre de los
infantes declara vencida la lid. Los del Cid vuelven
cautelosamente a Valencia. Alegría del Cid. Segundos
matrimonios de sus hijas. El juglar acaba su poema

     Los dos han arrancado;   dirévos de Muño Gustioz,
con Anssuor Gonçalvez   cómmo se adobó.
Firiénsse en los escudos   unos tan grandes colpes.
Anssuor Gonçalvez   forçudo e de valor,
firió en el escudo   a don Muño Gustioz,
tras el escudo   falssóle la guarnizón;
en vázio fue la lança,   ca en carne nol tomó.
Este colpe fecho,   otro dio Muño Gustioz:
por medio de la bloca   el escúdol crebantó;

it split apart   the top of the helmet
and it broke all   the helmet buckles;
it sheared the head mail   and to the coif came;
head mail and coif   it cut through them,
razed the hair of the head   and came to the flesh;
part fell to the field,   the rest remained.
  When the precious Colada   had struck this blow
Diego González saw   that he should not escape with his
      soul;
he drew on the reins of the horse   to turn away;
he had a sword in his hand   but did not use it.
Then Martín Antolínez   struck him with his sword,
a blow with the flat of his sword,   not with the edge.
Then the Heir   shouted aloud:
"Bless me, glorious God,   lord, save me from this sword!"
Reining his horse,   keeping his distance from the sword,
he went beyond the marker;   Don Martín stayed on the
      field.
  Then the King said,   "Come to my side;
with what you have done   you have won the fight."
The judges agree   that what he says is true.

152

*Muño Gustioz defeats Asur González. The father of the
Heirs declares the combat won. The Cid's men return
cautiously to Valencia. The Cid's joy. The second
marriage of the daughters. The bard ends his poem*

  Two have been defeated;   I shall tell you of Muño
      Gustioz
and how his fight went   with Asur González.
They struck great blows   on each other's shields.
Asur González   was vigorous and brave;
he struck Muño Gustioz   on the shield,
drove through the shield   and to the armor,
then his lance cut through on nothing,   touching no flesh.
When this blow was struck,   Muño Gustioz returned
      another:
he split his shield   at the middle of the buckler,

nol pudo guarir,   falssóle   la guarnizón,
apart le priso,   que non cab el coraçón;
metiól por la carne adentro   la lança con el pendón,
de la otra part   una braça gela echó,
con él dió una tuerta   de la siella lo encamó,
al tirar de la lança   en tierra lo echó;
vermejo salió el astil,   e la lança y el pendón.
Todos se cuedan   que ferido es de muort.
La lança recombró   e sobrél se paró;
dixo Gonçalvo Anssuórez: "nol firgades, por Dios!
vençudo es el campo,   quando esto se acabó!"
Dixieron los fideles: "esto odimos nos."

    Mandor librar el canpo   el buen rey don Alfons,
las armas que i rastaron   elle se las tomó.
Por ondrados se parten   los del buen Campeador;
vençieron esta lid,   grado al Criador.
Grandes son los pesares   por tierras de Carrión.

    El rey a los de mio Çid   de noche los enbió,
que no les diessen salto   nin oviessen pavor.
A guisa de menbrados   andan dís e noches,
félos en Valençia   con mio Çid el Campeador.
Por malos los dexaron   a ifantes de Carrión,
complido han el debdo   que les mandó so señor;
alegre fo d' aquesto   mio Çid el Campeador.
Grant es la biltança   de ifantes de Carrión.
Qui buena dueña escarneçe   e la deza despuós,
atal le contesca   o siquier peor.

    Dexémonos de pleitos   de ifantes de Carrión,
de lo que an preso   mucho an mal sabor;
fablemos nos d' aqueste   que en buen ora naçió.
Grandes son los gozos   en Valençia la mayor,
porque tan ondrados   foron los del Canpeador.
Prísos a la barba   Roy Díaz so señor:
"Grado al rey del çielo,   mis fijas vengadas son!

nothing withstood his stroke,   he broke the armor;
he sheared it apart   and, though not close to the heart,
drove the lance and pennon   into the flesh
so it came out an arm's length   on the other side,
then he pulled on the lance   and twisted González from
     his saddle.
When he pulled out the lance   González fell to the ground,
and the spear shaft was red,   and the lance and the
     pennon.
All fear that González   is mortally wounded.
Muño Gustioz again seized his spear   and stood over him.
Gonzalo Ansúrez said,   "For the love of God, do not
     strike him!
The field is won   and the combat is finished!"
The judges said,   "We agree to this."
     The good King Don Alfonso   sent to despoil the field;
he took for himself   the arms that remained there.
The Campeador's men   departed in great honor;
with the aid of the Creator   they had won this fight.
Hearts were heavy   in the lands of Carrión.
     The King warned My Cid's men   to leave at night
so that none might attack them   and they have no cause
     for fear.
They, prudently, ride night and day.
Behold, they have come to Valencia,   to My Cid the
     Campeador.
They had left in shame   the Heirs of Carrión
and fulfilled the duty   they owed to their lord;
My Cid the Campeador,   was pleased at this.
The Heirs of Carrión   are in deep disgrace.
May whoever injures a good woman   and abandons her
     afterwards
suffer as great harm as this   and worse, besides.
     Let us leave this matter   of the Heirs of Carrión;
they take no pleasure   in what has befallen them.
Let us speak of him   who in good hour was born.
Great are the celebrations   in Valencia the great
because the Campeador's men   have won great honor.
Ruy Díaz their lord   stroked his beard:
"Praised be the King of Heaven,   my daughters are
     avenged!

Agora las ayan quitas   heredades de Carrión!
Sin vergüença las casaré   o a qui pese o a qui non."
   Andidieron en pleytos   los de Navarra e de Aragón,
ovieron su ajunta   con Alfons el de León.
Fizieron sos casamientos   don Elvira e doña Sol;
los primeros foron grandes,   mas aquestos son mijores;
a mayor ondra las casa   que lo que primero fo.
Veed qual ondra creçe   al que en buen ora naçió,
quando señoras son sues fijas   de Navarra e de Aragón.
Oy los reyes d' España   sos parientes son,
a todas alcança ondra   por el que en buena naçió.
   Passado es deste sieglo   mio Çid de Valençia señor
el día de cinquaesma;   de Cristus aya perdón!
Assí ffagamos nós todos   justos e peccadores!
   Estas son las nuevas   de mio Çid el Canpeador;
en este logar   se acaba esta razón.

Now freed of all debts   is their heritage in Carrión!
I shall marry them now without shame,   let it weigh on
   whom it will."
   The Princes of Navarre and Aragón   continued their
      suits,   .
and all met together   with Alfonso of León;
The wedding is performed   of Doña Elvira and Doña Sol;
the first marriage was noble   but this much more so;
to greater honor he weds them   than was theirs before.
See how he grows in honor   who in good hour was born;
his daughters are wives of the Kings   of Navarre and
      Aragón.
Now the Kings of Spain   are his kinsmen,
and all advance in honor   through My Cid the Campeador.
   My Cid, the lord of Valencia,   passed from this world
on the Day of Pentecost,   may Christ give him pardon!
And may He pardon us all,   both the just and the sinners!
   These were the deeds   of My Cid the Campeador,
and in this place   the song is ended.